DEEPEST FRANCE / MYSTERIOUS DAYS

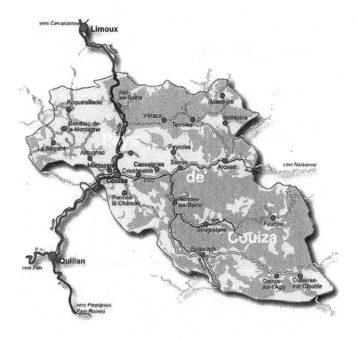

Deepest France

Also by Julius Raper

Without Shelter

From the Sunken Garden

Ellen Glasgow's Reasonable Doubts

Narcissus from Rubble

Lawrence Durrell: Comprehending the Whole

DEEPEST FRANCE:
A Novel of the French Grail

MYSTERIOUS DAYS:
Return to Deepest France

PAIRED NOVELS
BY
JULIUS RAPER

iUniverse, Inc.
Bloomington

Deepest France: A Novel of the French Grail/ Mysterious Days: Return to Deepest France Paired Novels

Deepest France Copyright © 1987, 2002, 2003, 2011 by Julius Raper
Mysterious Days Copyright © 2011 by Julius Raper

This is a work of fiction. All of the characters, names, incidents, organizations, and dialogue in this novel are either the products of the author's imagination or are used fictitiously.

iUniverse books may be ordered through booksellers or by contacting:

iUniverse
1663 Liberty Drive
Bloomington, IN 47403
www.iuniverse.com
1-800-Authors (1-800-288-4677)

Because of the dynamic nature of the Internet, any web addresses or links contained in this book may have changed since publication and may no longer be valid. The views expressed in this work are solely those of the author and do not necessarily reflect the views of the publisher, and the publisher hereby disclaims any responsibility for them.

Any people depicted in stock imagery provided by Thinkstock are models, and such images are being used for illustrative purposes only.

Certain stock imagery © Thinkstock.

ISBN: 978-1-4620-3028-6 (sc)
ISBN: 978-1-4620-3029-3 (hc)
ISBN: 978-1-4620-3030-9 (e)

Library of Congress Control Number: 2011911459

Printed in the United States of America

iUniverse rev. date: 07/18/2011

Author's Note

Readers of mysteries will likely notice a handful of elements in *Deepest France* not commonly found in such works. The novel tells *two* family stories. In one, a remarkable child is murdered. In the second, a mystery novelist, Milt Walters, uses this terrible event and a series of email exchanges to guide his daughter Anthi through the ins and outs of the art he practices professionally. The two stories fold together and may, or may not, balance one another. In a nostalgic, even playful, way, Walters refers in scattered emails to 'Pop Ups'. Although he borrows this label from the three-dimensional storybooks he read Anthi in her early years, the *Pop Ups* are, in fact, the sections in which he feels inspired to enter the troubled minds of the major French characters, thereby adding a special dimension to his bare-bones account of the murder and its aftermath.

Readers will also come across two interrelated elements of legendary history. The first, *the French Grail*, expresses the French national character as surely as the more familiar cup made of expensive metal tells us much about British character. In France, the Grail (SanGraal) sometimes is said to have contained the Royal Blood (SangReal) brought to France in the womb of Mary Magdalena. This was the argument of *Holy Blood, Holy Grail* published by Michael Baigent, Richard Leigh, and Henry Lincoln in 1982, three years before Walters and his daughter first visit the places these paired novels call Deepest France. In this region, Magdalena herself was sometimes viewed as the remarkable female figure known as the *Dark Madonna* or the Black Virgin. The Black Madonna is found in over a hundred churches in France and in several hundred more around the globe.

--JR

For

Fern Rowanne Raper

Keith Alexander

Henriette Alexander-Christensen

"None Better"

To Franca, to Aldo, still—

For Les Issambres

And the Clue.

Kung said: …

"And even I can remember

A day when the historians left blanks in their writings,

I mean for things they didn't know,

But that time seems to be passing."

Ezra Pound, Canto XIII

He moves the pieces and they come

somehow into a kind of order.

Euripides, *Helen*, trans. Lattimore

Deepest France

One

Child in Deepest France

Rennes-les-Bains—A four-year-old boy missing since last Thursday from his home in Rennes-les-Bains, Deepest France, was found this morning in the Salz River just below this charming little village of fewer than a thousand inhabitants. Local officials have identified the boy as Charles Plantard, son of Philip Plantard, the maire *(mayor) of this small resort known chiefly for its thermal baths and historical importance.*

Officials added that the body was discovered, with arms and ankles bound in rope and drawn tightly against the torso, lodged under a low footbridge over the Salz within 100 meters of the village. Preliminary indications, they continued, are that death occurred before the boy entered the river inasmuch as the body bore upward of a dozen wounds probably inflicted by a long knife or other sharp instrument.

Young Plantard was still wearing the blue trousers and shirt and purple coat he had on when his mother, Christine Plantard, 25, also of Rennes-les-Bains, sent him to the baker's for bread and, according to official reports, kissed him good-bye for the last time. Investigations are continuing.

Since you asked, dear Anthi, this is the story that gripped the heart of the French nation that spring we spent in France, the drama that millions of French men and women rushed each morning to their newsstands and televisions to follow, as layer after appalling layer revealed itself to them, like the proverbial onion of truth peeled before their eyes.

You were only fourteen, almost fifteen, too young then to notice much that mattered to news reporters. But if, as your e-mail says, you really want to become a writer—now that you have sent your young flame back home to St-Cloud and B2B companies like yours in Paris are beginning to tank—exploring the mystery of "little Charles" (the French papers affectionately christened him "petit Charles" almost from the start) may interest you again. It would illustrate the bare-bones process of creating mystery stories as concisely as any disaster I know. And I plan to keep my suggestions to the bare bones.

Are you sure you are willing, though, to give up an office along the Champs d'Elysee and your apartment near the Bois de Boulogne—both, I suppose, elegant with French mirrors and gilded furniture—for the iffy existence of a beginning writer or even the up-and-down life of one with a handful of books who spends his days knocking about a solitary house staring at rows of photos of you and Nicky as he puts off creating his next sentence out of thin air? Only if you are certain, will I continue my mélange of mystery and "sullen art." But if I digress to excess, or you decide your sacrifice would be too great, it's up to you to send an e-mail correcting the course I'm taking.

For starters, I want to confess that those of us who do this thing are not always the best teachers when it comes to explaining how we accomplish it. So much of real writing simply happens—things just pop-up, like those three-dimension books we read together when you were a three-year-old and we were all living in Salonika. You know the ones, the picture books you liked before you turned to French graphic novels about that flaming-haired Gaul warrior named Asterix or those about the balloon-faced, cotton-top little detective called Tintin—long before you became absorbed in Narnia tales. As we move along, I have to trust that parts of this story will keep popping up so that I—or the two of us—can fill gaps and answer the questions that still hang like ghost mists over the murdered boy.

The grim mystery of little Charles dropped into my lap during that brilliant spring in Les Issambres, a tiny little dot hidden along the south coast midway between the autoroute exits for Ste. Maxime and St. Raphael. Paolo (you remember Paolo?) had taken a house for the month in France, and he and Sylvana—they were still married then—had been generous enough to invite both you kids and me to stay with them. You flew in from Athens, but your mother wouldn't let little Nick out of her sight.

"Anthi would be with him," I tried explaining.

"I don't care," your mother said. "He's not even ten yet."

There's not much a man living in Virginia the way I was, and am, can do to make a wife from whom he's separated by more than an ocean act the way he believes she should. Except send more money.

"Be grateful I'm letting Anthi come!" your mother said.

"I am," I said, "but I need—"

"How do I know you'll send her back?"

My stuff wasn't selling well at the time (my experiments too erotic, I guess, for the decrepit eighties) so I had no money to spare. I was going to need every dollar for our trip. I said what I could: "I will. I always send her back"—then crossed my fingers and put your flight on a credit card. A week after I arrived in France, you were waiting, your long curls gold and blonde from the Greek sun, eager for rescue from the sweltering, sea-lit airport in Nice. That was that. Nicky, with his flashing eyes and careful smile, I would have to do without for another six months.

Mornings, while you slept, I walked down to the village to buy a fresh loaf, pastries, and the papers to carry back up the hill to

Paolo and Sylvana. It was all Sylvana would let me do—otherwise you and I were their guests. While you kids slept in, we adults enjoyed our long breakfasts with the news, huddled from the salt-laced breeze behind the bougainvillea that covered the front terrace of the house.

Between the sweets and the coffee one morning, Paolo tossed the *France-Soir* into my lap.

"You make any sense of this Plantard mess?" he asked, with a provocation in his eyes. The morning before, when he mentioned President Reagan's surprising popularity that spring in France, he'd had the same look, and we argued politics for an hour.

"Which Plantard?" I knew the name, of course, but not from the papers. Plantards figured importantly in materials I was exploring for our trip together.

As soon as I saw the picture Paolo had framed by folding the paper, I understood exactly what mess he meant. Each morning at the newsstand, the same little boy—dark curls, soft open smile, and one big ear jutting out from the hair—had stared back full face from one paper or another. Other mornings, his photograph simply caught my eye. After Paolo's question it held me mesmerized.

The face possessed a fascinating quality. It looked totally familiar—yet the dark eyes understood things no child his age could be expected to grasp. Puzzled, I began buying papers like everyone in the village. At first the tabloids, simply for the pictures. These covered each move the boy's mother made, described the roses on his small grave, her visits to the grandmother. The daily trivia. They referred also to an ongoing trial. But nothing about the earlier months of the mystery.

So, Anthi, lesson number one: It was as though Paolo and I were beginning a book in the middle. He was curious also and felt as lost as I did in the tangled references to incidents, already several months old, that had become part of every French tabloid reader's fund of memory. With a mystery, we have to become a bit lost before we find ourselves.

"Do you suppose there's a library with the old papers, like back home?" I asked.

"Naaa," Paolo said. "We would have to go to Cannes—or Nice. Don't even think of it." He was only guessing, but I enjoyed the Milanese—almost New York—certainty with which he disguised his guesses.

Sylvana, serious Sylvana, hesitating at first to give the daily revelations her attention, appeared confused: "What is this story you two are always talking about? The mother is very attractive, isn't she?" Sylvana was a beauty herself, but sometimes she liked to fish for compliments.

"Definitely," I said. "But not by Milan standards. Too wide-eyed and too innocent."

"It is why the press keeps up the story—they like her pictures," she said.

"Something deep in those eyes," Paolo said. "I like that in a woman."

"After sixteen years, you tell me—" Sylvana said, and shared her restrained laugh. "It is her eye shadow."

"The boy has the same look," I said. "It's not makeup."

Over lunch that day, Anthi, I tried telling you a few of the details I had picked up.

"Who killed him?" you asked.

"I'm not sure. They had a man in jail, but they let him go. I can't figure out why. If we could find the old papers—" I wanted to draw you into the mystery. "It may be the family I was telling you about. The same Plantards."

You said, "It's a good story, daddy. If you hear more—" With that, you bounced down the veranda stairs behind Paolo's daughter and son.

That spring, you probably have forgotten, not many things could hold your interest other than the two friends you hadn't seen for a year, your fantasy novels, and Duran Duran. When you were younger and all of us lived in Greece, I would entertain you with tales of the gods and goddesses. But after things fell to pieces between your mom and me (too many Greek delights, I guess—and probably not far different from the Paris variety) you were reading the books for yourself, over and over, and filling in all the gaps in what I had told you. I was proud of you. Did I ever tell you that?

For our time together in France, I knew I needed a new story to tie us together—since that is one thing, one big thing, stories do—and I needed a good one if I was going to keep you with me, contented, for a month. One of the reasons you had agreed to come to France was that I promised you a fresh angle on the Grail legend.

"Something new about the Grail? Really?" you had shouted, to reach across Greece, all Europe, and the Atlantic. "Remember, Dad, Mom took me to Avebury and Glastonbury."

"But this is the *French* Grail, young lady. A new cast of characters—the Plantards. It's a totally different thing," I said.

"Totally? Are you sure?"

"Absolutely!"

At the time, I confess, I didn't know much about the Grail in France, so while we were enjoying the good hospitality of Sylvana and Paolo, I was catching up on the stories, and I was pleased whenever my research held your attention. "There's this family, the Plantards, over in the mountains above Spain, and they may have, in a weird way, been connected to Mary Magdalena and the Grail," I'd said, not wanting to give too much away.

Maybe it was the way the French version emphasized Mary Magdalena that first hooked you. I also found that focus exciting—because it seemed more contemporary than the usual British legends of knights lost in the thickets of their solitary quests. But it was the power of the story to focus your attention that mattered most. And that was never when Paolo's kids were around, or Duran Duran was playing in the little arcade above the beach.

"Save me a few inches of the sand," I called after you and your friends.

"We're not going to the beach," you shouted back.

"We'll need to know where."

"To play the fussball and video games first. Maybe the beach after that."

"See you—" But you were gone.

Another lesson: When a writer's story starts sluicing along, almost anything can become grist for the mill. There in Les Issambres I realized that the mystery of Charles Plantard fit in neatly with the Grail search I had promised. The crime occurred in the region of France we would be exploring. Though the Plantard name figured in the books I was reading, I wrote that off—in my own mind—to coincidence. Even so, in order to stir up your enthusiasm, I stressed the possible link between the French Grail and young Charles, about whom I was becoming increasingly eager to know more.

In Les Issambres, on the cool veranda or barely warm-enough beach, the more I read about the murder the more I realized that there were just too many stories for me to make sense of them all. Later, back here in Virginia, when I rummaged through old French newspapers to fill the gaps the best I could, the mystery grew more complex. For a year the press came out every day with a new version. A reporter got his hands on something the father, the mother, or one of the villagers in Rennes-les-Bains said, and this new angle generated an entire new set of motives and possible murderers. Poulin, the captain of the police, or Mathieu, the investigating judge, would call in a new panel of experts. And everything would change. In court, the defense attorney, the prosecuting attorney, each had his set of witnesses. Every witness had a story that he or she insisted was vital to the investigation.

Such versions and revisions went on for over two years. Slowly the reports migrated to the middle pages, or the back sections, of the papers. Then the French appeared to have lost interest, and the story died, with the murder still unsolved. The passage of time and news of other violent acts pushed it from their minds. For me, however, it was not so easy, probably because few tragedies compare with the loss of a child.

So be it, I told myself. This is what we have to deal with, Anthi. Gaps to fill. Good. My work as a writer has been cut out for me. Yours too, if you want to take up the trade. But remember, it's not just "whodunit?" It is also "what, when, where, and why?" "Why?" most of all. Always "why?"

We can be sure that millions of French readers were drawn to the mystery of little Charles because it centers on the murder of a child. Maybe the French have an inordinate need for the child, especially for the innocent child like four-year-old Charles with his auburn hair, his large brown eyes, the wisp of a curl hanging down over his forehead, and a smile spread from the protruding ear to the hidden one. After all, it was the French who invented the nobility of the innocent—it was the French who invented Rousseau. The French have needed the simple child for centuries. Before Rousseau there was Jeanne d'Arc. So it is not only the actual little Charles or a little Jeanne or little Gregory that I refer to when I mention "the child"—but something deeper. Something elemental that every story, even those in the tabloids, should possess.

The story I would like to tell each time I begin is a simple love story about one man and an interesting woman, or a small number of such women. One way or another, each book I've created has been a story about a man looking for a simple love. A man who believes that somewhere in the world he enters every day there is a woman he can love with every particle of his being and who will love him the same. This is the story I always want to write. (I hope my confession doesn't embarrass you, Anthi—now that you are an adult and living in Paris on your own. If it does, just e-mail me back, and I won't do it again.) Instead of my familiar story of men and women, I find myself drawn, like the French, to the murder of little Charles. It, too, must contain some essential mystery.

ii

mdwaters
To: anthi_cwaters@ezrite.com
Re: explanation

Anthi,

I hope that you received the pages I sent yesterday by Overnight, that they will contribute to your progress as a writer, and that those days we shared have not been lost completely. Although, if I'm doing my work effectively, you will not need to rely on personal memories because I feel obliged to fill gaps as I go. Not all the gaps, however, if I am to produce a story that represents the limits of what we can ever know—no matter how loudly absolutists shout the contrary.

Anthi_cwaters
To: mdwaters@urtoo.com
Re: hair

Yes, I did receive them, and I am sure they'll help me learn some of the nuts and bolts of writing—writing mysteries, at least. I will get back to you as soon as I have time to read them closely.

I did glance through a few pages and want to remind you that *my* B2B (that's Business-to-Business, Dad) group is still going strong—so I plan to keep my *job de jour*, to butcher a phrase. Also, my hair is now cut pretttty damn short and is red as a Red Delicious apple.

It *has* been a while since I was in Virginia for a visit, or you in Paris. How is your current "friend"? I didn't especially like the one you were seeing last time—not that I have anything against Asian women.

So far as your confession goes—no, it doesn't embarrass me. Not as much as your books used to. At first I believed you were working out your problems with Mom, that both of you were middle-aged hippies, or had been hippies. After I read the classical Greek play about the death of Herakles, I remembered what his wife says—that "Eros rules even the gods, and no one should risk trading blows with him." Then I decided that what you write is really fiction. After that, I learned not to read your novels, and that was okay. But this one sounds different.

Do you think the mystery you speak of has anything to do with Nicky or me?

mdwaters
To: anthi_cwaters@ezrite.com
Re: changes

I will miss your hair. Lots of changes, young lady. Mine grows thinner every day. (I wish my gut would.)

I'm not seeing anyone special these days. Just writing.

Little Charles *is* a different challenge. And I'll keep your "mystery" remark in mind. But another lesson: much of our work goes on out of sight. Too much clarity is not always a blessing—especially as the starting point. Our discoveries have to slip out, as a real writer once said.

So back to the mystery at hand …

To refresh your memory of those years with research, since an immersion in detail always seems necessary for a good story, my patient daughter. Only afterward, according to Murphy's Law (Gardner Murphy, that would be), comes the incubation in memory, then the lightbulb illumination, followed by frequent tests of our inspiration. I wonder if you recall the way Rennes-les-Bains extends along the banks of the Salz River where it drops into a mile-long pan between several "horns" of the Corbieres, the lovely wooded mountains just to the east of the upper valley of the Aude River. Those peaks, I believe, explain the names of the two villages, *Rennes*-les-Bains and *Rennes*-le-Chateau, that define our story of Charles— for *renne* is not French for queen (*reine*), as I told you then, but for the horned reindeer that, along with bear and boar, once ranged those mountains—and may still do so, though you and I saw none. Even in early winter, the evergreen of all the holm oaks and the red of the deciduous oaks, among the chestnuts, would display the fire of life those shy beasts embody.

At the north boundary of Rennes-les-Bains, the river falls again and flows on into the Aude outside the small town of Couiza. Just north of this abrupt drop, wedged under the low footbridge I once pointed out to you, the bound body of little Charles appeared, newspapers agree, on an overcast wintry Saturday in late autumn.

At first local officials would not admit what seemed apparent to everyone, that the failure to discover the body under this frequently used bridge until Saturday morning implied that it had not been placed in the river before Friday night. Until they could explain the boy's whereabouts from Thursday until Saturday, they preferred to deny the obvious. To alert Frenchmen and Frenchwomen, this failure no doubt raised an intriguing question about the degree to which the truth, like history, "consists of lies agreed upon." (Those are Napoleon's words, and he should have known.) Not until they were cross-examined in court would the regional officials (who had to be called in by the little boy's father, the mayor of Rennes-les-Bains, from the police station in Couiza) admit to the reasonable supposition that the body had not been in the river before Friday night.

Where, then, in a village the size of Rennes-les-Bains, could little Charles have been hidden from Thursday, when last seen, until Saturday?

Rennes-les-Bains, remember, consists of two streets running the length of the mile-long pan between the mountains. The main road, freshly asphalted when we were there, rises from a valley road traveling between Couiza to the west and Arques to the east, to a height of 310 meters, as high as the Eiffel Tower. (In Deepest France there are very few coincidences.) This is the road that motor vehicles take and where we parked; it runs along the west bank of the Salz. Less than a block away on the east side of the river, at a level some ten meters lower, lies a track of yellow gravel traveled chiefly by pedestrians and an occasional pack of horses from the stables located on the route from Couiza to Arques, where you and I hired those heavy-hipped nags for our romp through the wheat fields and green vineyards.

The footbridge in question connects the two main roads below the village. Within the village two other footbridges serve a similar function, as does a third a short way above. Thus the footbridge is a major thoroughfare, relatively speaking. Had the body been there before Friday night, someone would certainly have seen it. Bodies under bridges do not go unobserved for two days—especially in Deepest France.

From the perspective of the Paris newspapers, Deepest France is no doubt located elsewhere than the area surrounding Rennes-les-Bains, just as, say, for someone living in the upper Middle West, the Deep South would likely include Virginia and the Carolinas. But Paris, as you know from working there, often falls back on attitudes based on class and education, positions that also become agreed-upon lies and a filter distorting reality. Rennes-les-Bains is deep in the ancient land of Razes, the country of the Visigoths, who ruled from this center for three hundred years after they invaded the Roman Empire. In 410, the Visigoths conquered Rome itself, sacking its great treasures, and then transporting their plunder to their future strongholds in the northern reaches of the Pyrenees. Their spoils, some say, included the *Sangraal* itself (*whatever* that precisely was).

This region is also the southernmost corner of the nation. At the same time, it is sufficiently distant from the capital to serve as a mirror of all we need to believe about such psychological entities as the Middle West, the Deep South, the Middle East, Darkest Africa, Outer Mongolia, the Upper Amazon, and Aboriginal Australia.

Good. It will serve as the setting our elemental mystery requires.

iii

When Monsieur Philip Plantard was informed of the conditions under which his son's mutilated body was discovered, his immediate reaction was one of considerable rage. "I will get those pig bastards! I will make them pay," a well-placed source quotes him as shouting.

Madame Christine Plantard's response to the news was more subdued. "I am glad little Charles has been found. At least his suffering has ended. I don't know what will happen now."

The same source adds that once Christine Plantard returned to the shelter of her chambers in the old hotel that she and Philip Plantard have restored and now operate in Rennes-les-Bains, she collapsed into a deep sleep in which she remained throughout Saturday and well into the middle of Sunday.

Local investigations continue.

Anthi, we have to recognize that ours is a reality that comes to us through the multiple voices and images of the papers, television, gossip, books, and other media. It is a reality composed of selected facts, insinuations, and gaps. So be it. This leaves room for the educated guesses, and intuitions, of trained writers like the one you say you wish to become. But, as a result, to seem an accurate mirror of present-day reality, our writing must encompass the multiple voices and dialects and jarring discontinuities of contemporary experience, not just the familiar dialogue and extended descriptions that older fictions pretended to pass along. Such writing may sometimes resemble a mishmash of styles. But it is a calculated one.

What, for example, did the reporter wish to imply by the two phrases "considerable rage" and "more subdued"? That one parent was guilty and the other was not? If so, which parent would have perpetrated this act of horrible violence—the rageful one or the subdued one? Faced with such ambiguities, I find it helps to speculate.

To a French reader, or an American one, Philip Plantard's reaction seems understandable. His photos in the papers picture a quiet, handsome man with soft brown hair and dark eyes filled with purpose. His son has been brutally murdered. Such violence against children always strikes us as abhorrent. Christine Plantard has apparently drowned in her shock. Her eyes as she is leaving the morgue are those of any mammal caught in a sudden bright light. To an average reader, then, the innuendos about the two appear to be a wash.

What puzzles me, as a storyteller, in Plantard's response was the way he seemed to refer to a specific "they," as though he had some clear notion who "they," the "pig bastards," might be. In a small village like Rennes-les-Bains, one assumes that there are very few strangers, very few people whose attitudes and actions the inhabitants fail to know in depth. In Rennes-les-Bains the lives of all the local people have no doubt been woven together, like strands of a single story, for generations, for centuries even. Philip Plantard no doubt thought he had a reasonably clear idea who murdered his son.

Can you see little Charles yet, my daughter? Doesn't he look very much the way you did when you were four, with his large, open eyes, his hair over his forehead, that one protruding ear, the smile? Or like Nicky when he was that age? And the father—aren't his feelings very much what yours might be if you were a father coping with similar circumstances? As a writer, such echoes are gifts you must learn to work with.

The mother's reaction too seems altogether human. After the sleepless nights of fear and futile hope in which she likely invested all her emotion, she clearly has collapsed in exhaustion. Even her hair, in the news photos, though less soft than her husband's or her son's, has lost its body and fallen to her slumping shoulders. Only a woman of uncommon energy could have done otherwise than falter.

I remain a little curious, though, about the muted quality of her response. Perhaps because I am a father, not a mother, I am puzzled by the way one could, as she seems to have done, hand the future over to the Fates. No doubt a wisdom both comforting and ancient lies behind her reaction. Perhaps my surprise at this resignation has to do with her French roots and my being American. Americans, we all have heard, are creatures of simple willful actions. What about the French? I never imagined they were so resigned to fate.

To me, Christine Plantard remains a mystery. Given the choice, I would rather read about her than about her husband, or even little Charles. For she appears to be the most impenetrable of the three.... No, I am wrong about this. Charles's inner world has vanished from us forever, disappeared into the triple black holes of the boy's singular innocence, childhood's amnesia, and death. The best we can do with his lost world is to revisit his last day using the backward vision of adults. Even this approach, flawed though it may be by distance, requires the tool of access that distinguishes novelists from historians: the gift I've already called a "pop-up."

The three—Charles, Christine, Philip—all contain that mix of enigma and familiarity that takes hold of a writer's mind the way that a river, both mirror and mystery, grips the imagination. In our immersion, it is when these two come together, as a small boy's final day, that the unexpected begins to take place—

And the pop-ups begin.

iv

Charles
Pop-Up

In the cave where he played with friends he had met in bright cartoon books his mother and father read him, Charles flowed in and out of adventures with Tintin, Tom, Arthur, Percy, and a collection of other night companions whose names he sometimes could not recall by day, including that crazy little fellow his own size with the long yellow mustache and a funny tin cap with wings. Ast'ricks was the name, Charles remembered now, still only half awake, working against time to drift back into total sleep.

And when his mother called again, he hoped it would be to send him on an errand his friends would want to join—because they refused to go to nursery school with him, or to visit his uncles and aunts. And it made them very uncomfortable when all there was to do was sit around the kitchen while his parents argued about maids who hadn't shown up for work. He would rather just keep on playing with his companions here in sleep than get up for any of those boring chores—though, best he could figure, today must be a weekday, and eventually they would take him to the babysitter's. He'd much rather keep on sleeping. This was the easiest way: to say adieu to Tintin and just fall off into the swirling dark.

"—arles!" she screamed from somewhere outside the cave of darkness. "Char— …," it came closer. "*Charles!*" It was right on top of him now. She must be in the room, and if he wasn't careful she would wiggle in between him and his friends, and they would all go away. "You get out of there right this minute.… I have something you can do for me."

"I'm sleeping, Mommy! I can't do it right now," he tried to tell her, and buried his head between his long cylindrical pillow and the soft sagging mattress, hoping that somewhere down there he would find Arthur. Arthur would know what he should do. "Let me sleep a little bit more. It's a story."

"Your father is out of croissants. He needs you this minute to run to Madame Roux's. As soon as you get your clothes on. He needs them now. Their Highnesses are waiting! You know what that means."

Oh yes he knew. It meant that when any of "their Highnesses" called he had to jump—as though *they* were his mother and father— or Arthur and Percy combined. But every guest who came seemed to be a His or Her Highness.

As he scrunched deeper into his cave, his mother went away, and he saw Arthur in all his silver armor standing with his feet planted firmly atop a small rise in the gravel path he was climbing beside the river. But Arthur had taken off his helmet, and his hair shone gold above the silver casing. Beneath the silver, Charles saw a fringe of purple trimmed with silver thread. "How are you, Charles?" his confidant asked in his warm, deep voice. "Mommy wants me to go pick up croissants," he said, pleased that someone wanted to listen. "From Madame Roux?" Arthur asked, and led him to a boulder between the path and the river so that they both could sit. "What is so bad about Madame Roux? She gives you an apple brioche, doesn't she?" "Nothing bad about her—" "What is the matter then?" "I would have to leave you—and Tom and Percy with his quest—and my friends." "Oh, I see," Arthur laughed. "If that is all, it is no problem. I will go with you." "Will you, Arthur?" "Certainly I will. And we will have adventures wherever we go!" "Can we?" "Why not? Is that not what kings are for?" "I didn't know." "Just keep one eye awake so you see where you are and the other asleep so we can see each other, and we will go on a delicious quest. You will make your father proud of you." "My right eye's for waking; my left's for dreaming! I remember what you said." "You can tell your mother you are ready now to come to her assistance."

Confident because Arthur was with him, he slipped his head from under the pillow and, without opening either eye, spoke to the impatience he felt still trying to slip into his world of friends and dreams. "I can go now, Mommy."

"I've put out your shirt and pants. You'll be blue today. And don't forget your coat. It's wet outside—bitter cold—you'll need protection. And stop by the dining room. I'll give you the list to put in your pocket."

"Will you give me francs this time?"

"Tell Madame Roux to charge them. Your father will pay next time he's in."

"Can I have a tart, Mommy?"

"Madame Roux gives you a brioche, doesn't she? That should be sufficient."

"I give the brioche to my friend."

"If Jacqueline wants Stephen to eat brioches, I'm sure she'll buy them for him," his mother said, and she turned to leave his room. But at the door she turned around and added with a smile, "And remember, whatever you do, stay away from the old Marti mansion. You mustn't go near it. It's the property across from your sitter Jeanne's house—that's too far up river. Especially today."

"Okay, Mommy."

It wasn't Stephen who ate his brioches, but he knew better than to mention Arthur. The only time his parents had any use for Arthur or Percy was when they wanted him to do something for their Highnesses: "Think how Sir Percival would like *his* towel left lying on the bidet!" his mother would say. Or his father would ask: "Would you answer *Arthur* with that look in your eyes?"

"Just say nothing, little friend," Arthur cautioned from somewhere behind him, "—though they are mighty sweet brioches that woman makes! Perhaps you will spare at least one bite?"

"You can have the whole thing if you like," Charles said, and shed the light pullover in which he slept, slipped into a clean undershirt, and pulled on the midnight blue turtleneck his mother had put out for him.

"No, no. A bite will do," Arthur sighed, staring through the walls as though he could already see the pastries in Madame Roux's little shop. "Do not forget your coat—so we will be twins." He tugged at the tail of his own shirt showing under his silver coat.

"That's why I made her buy me the purple one," the boy replied, his smile open enough to confide his deepest secret. "So I can be exactly like you."

"Let us go now," his friend said, and patted Charles encouragingly on his shoulders. "Our companions in arms may need us."

Out in the hallway, the sound of the river grew strong, the steady, gentle grind of the water sliding over the cement slip below the row of tall windows that ran along this side of the hotel. The boy glanced to his left to the dimly lit, damp-smelling, still unrestored end of the long hall of windows and doors. Alone, he would not even look in that direction. But Arthur walked behind him now. "Let's check on Tintin."

"There's no need. He is already up and about. I met him as he and his dog—"

"Snowy—"

"—yes—as he and Snowy were starting out after that villain he calls Capone."

"I would like to see him."

"It's probable we will run into them. We always do."

"If you are sure."

"Have confidence, young friend."

Knowing his hero would follow, Charles led the way along the corridor to the shadowy end where the red exit light perked feebly in the gloom. With boldness that came as much from his tall friend as his own chest, the boy descended the emergency stairs to the redecorated area of the fine old mountain hotel his father had worked so diligently to restore.

On the main floor, the second above the river, they followed the rose-carpeted corridor that ran along the high windows opening over the fast-moving water. Opposite the windows, the row of grey, ancient doors stood at attention with a royal bee carved in each corner and a svelte young angel in the middle, her feet set on a globe and her upraised hands poised to place a garland of laurel on whoever entered.

"Do not forget your mother," Arthur cautioned as they approached the public end of the hallway.

"She said the dining room, didn't she?" The boy turned in at the last door on the right, just before the exit to the terrace that connected immediately to an old plank bridge spanning the river to the street.

At the far end of the dining room, he saw two couples plus a family of four sipping coffee while they waited for their *petit dejeuner*. The room filled the boy with a rich, musical blend of odors: the sharpness of the coffee, the smoothness of the orange preserves, and the softness of fresh bread. Steering raggedly between the giant buffet to the right and the three occupied tables, his mother, her lovely dark hair fallen across her forehead, an apron over her sweater and corduroy jeans, worked to keep their guests content with butter, preserves, and bread. As soon as her busy eyes noticed him, they turned stone-cold, and she hurried to the door where he waited. He knew he hadn't done what he should.

"That took long enough," she scolded, even while a tardy smile showed she was pleased to see him at last. "You remembered your coat—good. Here's the list. Put it in your pocket, and don't take it out until you hand it to Madame Roux. Tell her that their Highnesses are starving. Even if the croissants are a little dry, have her send them on—and hold the sack tight. There shouldn't be any cars in the street this early, but one of your cousin Claud's trucks might be driving through. Keep an ear out—they make lots of noise going uphill. Be sure to stay away from the Marti property. And keep your eyes open. Hurry now!"

"Can't you say hello to Arthur, Mommy?"

Her nervousness broke for a brief moment into bewilderment before she understood. "Hello, Your Majesty," she said and laughed. "Now, get out of here with that tomfoolery!" She shooed them along the corridor to the main exit to the busy street.

v

Anthi_cwaters
To: mdwaters@urtoo.com
Re: more explanation

Dad,

I like your story of little Charles (whom I vaguely remember, I think) and his family. I even enjoy your rehearsing our "ole times on the Mediterranean." And I know I asked for advice about writing. But I do wish you didn't have to keep interrupting a good mystery with digressions *about* the story. All I or any reader wants is a simple story. So I am feeling some ambivalence about your "melange."

And I don't really know what to make of your Arthur character. I believe I understand the idea behind "imaginary friends," but they are usually roughly the same age as the child who imagines them, aren't they?
Anthi

mdwaters
to: anthi_cwaters@ezrite.com
re: Wait!

Dear Impatient Young Lady,

You have to give me time to show you that this cannot be a "simple story." To prove, in fact, that there are no longer any "simple" stories. The novel has grown old—full of conventions. Especially the mystery story. To make it novel again, one (he or she—*you*) must disappoint expectations. But explain your disruptions as you go, or your reader will turn churlish on you. And he or she may anyway.

For example: Readers want to get lost in stories. And, willy-nilly, a writer may wish to overpower readers, if only by drawing them into a romance or a thriller. As a result, every reader stands in danger of allowing this power play to take place, especially readers looking for escapes that seem real. In truth, there no longer are any "escapist" stories. Romance or thriller—or whatever—the books we choose reveal as much about ourselves as about the "world" they create. The mystery of little Charles I intend to write has to make it clear that we too often allow ourselves to become engrossed, willing prisoners of the stories we read.

To be an honest writer, dear daughter, you must recognize the dangers of your readers' eagerness to buy the tired tricks of verisimilitude, and you have to find ways to guard against their falling prey to your sleight of hand. Not all writers, you know, are as innocent as the unassuming tale-spinners like you or me. And they never have been.

As for your second quibble, the one about imaginary friends, they need not be the same age as Charles. Every child needs a father like Arthur. What grown-up wouldn't swap his profession for a companion like the King? If I had the tools to understand the boy's fantasies, they would tell me what I wish to know about his shaping years and the world in which he lived. But as a writer you have to trust your readers to figure out things like that. You can only give them the images and the words—not the child's thoughts exactly, since Charles is not yet conscious of what goes on inside him, or even that he has an inner world—just supply the words for the things he sees and touches, whether they are there or not.

A child like Charles has to invent, from the friendly figures his culture offers, an imaginary world to make up for his powerlessness in a jungle of creatures twice his height and four or five times his weight. In a struggle of forces so unequally matched, only someone like Arthur can restore the balance. Arthur, along with the boy's friends---those yet to come along. And sometimes even friends like Arthur and Tintin and the rest fail to counter the enormous forces working against a child. When that happens, we read about some tragic event like the murder of little Charles.

Anthi_cwaters
To: mdwaters@urtoo.com
Re: no more explanations—for now.
   I'm still not convinced, Dad.
   But let's see what you have up your sleeve.

mdwaters
to: anthi_cwaters@ezrite.com
re: Fine!

That's all I ask from my doubting daughter—that she obey her skeptical spirit. You didn't settle in France for nothing, did you? Was it a Frenchman who said "a reasonable doubt is the safety-valve of civilization"? No, now that I think about it, it was a Virginian. And a woman!

vi

Less than a week after the press reported the reactions of Charles's parents to his death, French readers, who by this time, Anthi, like American counterparts in such cases, had ceased to puzzle over the murder of a four-year-old in Deepest France, had their waning interest abruptly reawakened when the morning papers informed them of a critical development.

Philip Plantard had notified local police that during the past year he and his family had received several anonymous messages warning that, should they persist in their "pigheadedness, dire consequences were certain to follow." The number, according to local officials who refused to be more specific, fell somewhere between half a dozen and ten messages.

"Yes," the same officials admitted when pressed by reporters, "the messages appeared in a written form. But there also were telephone threats—we have not yet determined the exact number." The consequences referred to were not specified. Nor did officials clarify the recalcitrance of the Plantards that the notes mentioned. But "a well-placed source in the region has assured the press that the insult has to do with positions Monsieur Plantard has taken during the past two years as the mayor and business leader of Rennes-les-Bains." The notes, the papers concluded, have been turned over to handwriting experts for analysis.

From other sources, dear Anthi, I have put together a few details about Philip Plantard. Yes, this is more of that bothersome but essential background. Although such research reads like clunky pages from a history or biography (an effect I'll emphasize here, for mentoring reasons), it contains absolutely vital information. The newspapers I have collected from France, however, are slow reaching the Library of Virginia I use in Richmond. Issues run painful months behind the events they cover. Some issues never arrive. Others, when I find them, have great, ragged holes where someone—a school kid or sex-starved Virginian—has ripped out the quarter-page photos of lovely half-nude women (a newspaper practice common in France and, like other customs we take for granted, worth examining, but not in our story of little Charles). Given my own need to understand this crime, all the gaps left by the international postal service and by the raging hormones of adolescents, no matter what age, tempt me to fill holes in the record with inventions of my own. But only the cheering and popular mystery writers tell us that every crime leads to a solution without gaps or alternative explanations. Although that is not our goal here, we can't ignore the details, disjointed as they may be, that we have at hand.

At the time of his son's death, Monsieur Plantard was approaching his thirty-fourth birthday. The pictures I have collected (and there are many, for all the characters became favorites of the journalists—I'll attach a few, if you want) show a robust man of medium height with brown eyes, brown hair curled like the shells of snails, and the strong body of a former athlete or a man whose work requires physical exertion. Often in the news photos he wears what appear to be brown or charcoal corduroy jeans with a polo shirt of a muted dark color. His family has lived in the region for as long as anyone the papers talked with can recall. His father, now dead, was the greengrocer and newsdealer of Rennes-les-Bains. His uncle, a retired stone mason, still lives in the nearby town of Arques, a tiny farm village built between two remarkable chateaux, one of them a tall, square structure with a tower on each corner and a dungeon that the books I've located on Deepest France call a monument of military architecture. (Anthi, I wish you had gone with me the morning I visited Arques.)

When Philip was twenty, according to the Paris magazines, he left Rennes-les-Bains to begin his studies in the law faculty of the University of Montpellier, one of the capitals of the ancient province of Languedoc. The limited resources of his family forced Plantard, like many of his classmates, to divide his time between his studies and self-support. He found work in two or three hotels in Montpellier, and gradually the center of his interests shifted from the law, which, I imagine, had attracted him less as a discipline than as a means of attaining the social position he associated with lawyers, doctors, and other leading professionals. The sole photograph from this period shows his hair grown out about his ears and a polo shirt that must be yellow, a pale green, or another of the light colors in which such shirts are made. The law gave way to two interrelated interests: hotel management and the fertile historical mysteries of the region in which he grew up.

Considering the shabby little hotels you and I stayed in and in which Philip likely clerked while he studied, it is a wonder he did not quit the field as quickly as possible. We can only imagine that the mistakes his employers made inspired his native intelligence with a vision of possibilities they had not pursued. At any rate, after two years, he left the law faculty and Montpellier altogether and moved to Carcassonne, the grand commercial center of the Aude wine region. Here he became assistant manager and night clerk of a newly opened three-star hotel. There are several black-and-whites of him now with clipped hair and an open-collared, long-sleeved white shirt—photos which suggest to me that he took his position at the hotel with increased seriousness.

Plantard's move to Carcassonne must have also pleased him for more personal reasons. The sights the city offers are compelling, but here I have to resort to printed sources since during our visit you were sleeping off a cold, and I couldn't leave you in the car to enter its walled center. The brochures I brought back show the yellow brightness of its rough stepped walls, the grey spires of the turrets, the countless irregularities of the double battlements, the earliest of which was the work of the Visigoths themselves. Guidebooks highlight its cathedral, small houses, narrow and winding streets, and the viscounts' palace at the center protected by an immense moat and giant double towers. It is the grandest medieval fortress in Europe, a picture out of romantic history or a fairytale. Too bad you and I didn't have time to make the return visit I promised. My fault.

Prior to its fall in the thirteenth century to the northern French and the papal crusaders against the Albigensians, Carcassonne had come under Frankish rule (in the eighth century), traced its roots to Roman founders (in the first century), and, most compelling for Plantard, had sheltered the Visigoths and their stolen treasures with its ramparts, during the fifth century, as they organized their conquests of the kingdom of Toulouse. Under the Visigoths, Toulouse became the kingdom of Septimania, and (perhaps because they were believed to have the Grail) it expanded until it took in the better part of southern France. It now included the Razes region vital to our story—an area named, my Cassell's suggests, for the raiders (*razzia*) who settled it, but more likely, I believe, for the lovely, sometimes treacherous race (*raz* or *ras*) of the Aude River. This region remained the secret center of Philip's life until his son's death. I see him, full of fire, rushing from stone to stone of the city's dense past trying to put the pieces together, pursuing his own Grail. I trust that in his hurry he had the good sense to shed his white shirt and go back to the comfort of his polo favorites.

The history, Anthi, of this deep center of French culture remained a small blur, pages I failed to notice, even to mark, in my college text, until I found myself drawn into little Charles's story. By the time you were in college, I doubt the Visigoths were mentioned at all. It's disconcerting to discover that a pocket of time about which I was ignorant can suddenly prove as central to my sense of the past, especially to what went wrong in Deepest France, and to our concept of the Grail, as the Aude has become. It makes me wonder whether our history—all our systems of knowledge—may be little more than a honeycomb containing similar cells of ignorance as numberless as the undiscovered bodies of the night sky. There's so much work for novelists to do. I can only applaud Philip Plantard's own efforts to fill the gaps in his heritage—though he unfortunately never connected Mary Magdalena to the *San-graal* or the *Sang-real*.

Carcassonne lay less than fifty kilometers, not even an hour's ride south in the plodding local bus, from the shaded quiet of Rennes-les-Bains, so that whenever Philip had two days free from his hotel duties he was able to return to his home—though his father was now dead, his siblings married, and his relationship with his elderly mother generally a stormy one. On these trips, he extended his research to the local history of the area, which more and more seemed bound up with the story of his own family. He insisted that all his free days coincide with the weekly bus trips to his village.

During the third year of visits to Rennes-les-Bains, for reasons not immediately clear to the reporters who put together Philip's personal story from interviews with relatives and neighbors, he began visiting Mlle. Christine Boudet, the soft-eyed sixteen-year-old daughter of a widowed mother. For two years Philip plagued the two Boudet women, even though the mother, neighbors thought, was much too old for him and young Christine, a pretty, smiling brunette, noted especially for those deep brown eyes in which even harmless elderly neighbors got lost, was the childhood sweetheart of Claud Plantard, one of Philip's own cousins. To the village at large, his interest seemed less romantic than historical, for Christine's mother's father, they all remembered, had been the brother of the village's abbot at the turn of the century, an eccentric old gentleman who had taken an antiquarian interest in the Razes.

Whatever Philip's motives, after two years of visits, he persuaded Christine's mother to let the young woman marry him. As far as the village knew, Christine offered no objections. For, according to rumors, she had quarreled with her old sweetheart, Claud Plantard, over some matter, perhaps Philip's frequent visits to the house, and she and Claud had clearly broken off their relationship before Claud moved to Narbonne, where he worked as a stone mason like his father before him. When Philip asked for her hand, young Christine's heart appeared, to interested neighbors, completely free of the former entanglement. In short, theirs was the sort of romantic story that makes life in small towns, French or American, tenable for those too settled in practicalities to possess tumultuous passions of their own.

Enough background, Anthi, for now…. So—where *were* Charles and Arthur yesterday when I stopped for a nap? Yes, I remember: their quest for croissants was just beginning.

vii

Charles
Pop-Up

Out on the terrace, the boy leaned against the iron railing overlooking the concrete slip into the river that once had served as the *blanchisserie*, or laundry, for the whole village.

"Mommy's never nice to you, Arthur. She's too busy, I guess."

"Yes. Hers is a hard place in life. But as long as your father is on our side, my young friend, we will do well enough," Arthur replied, and leaned beside him to look down to the river. "Your eyes are better than mine. Is there any sign of Asterix down there?"

"He's not at this guardpost yet."

"Probably he has decided it is too messy out today for Roman soldiers—or Italian tourists. They were never able to take these mountains in wintry weather."

"Still, we'd better check the back road for him, don't you think?"

"As long as you do not forget your errand."

"First things first, Your Majesty."

"Be careful. No one must hear you call me that."

"Don't worry—we're safe out here."

"You know the place. You lead—I will follow."

Charles stepped out onto the narrow footbridge suspended like a gangplank over the shelf of cement and boulders. The river, spilling from a deep, dammed pool at the south end of the long hotel, ran swift, green, and clear below. Often the boy had wondered what he would feel if he jumped into the river from this high up. But at this point the water was too shallow to try, and it seemed much farther down to him than the eight or ten meters it probably was. Crossing over the planks, he peeped into each of the five wooden flower troughs hanging at equal distance along the handrail, but only black stalks remained of the small annuals his mother had planted in the spring.

"You coming?" he called to his friend, who had stopped midway the bridge to gaze into the stream.

"Be right there. I thought I saw a trout."

"They're there."

"You think we could spear a few? I do enjoy a nice trout panned in fresh butter."

"Be easier if I asked Cook to fix one for dinner."

At the end of the bridge the boy turned right through the pebble garden, as barren this time of year as his mother's flower troughs, and crossed to the steps that carried them up to street level. There they went left and walked in the street itself between the parked automobiles and the trickle of moving ones, hurrying past the still-waking houses and shops, each of which showed two or three stories above the street yet hid as many levels descending to the river. After two village blocks, the boy turned left again onto the square and kept going.

"What about Madame Roux's? Have you forgotten?" his large, elegantly tinned companion inquired, nodding to a shop they passed midway along the square but on the opposite side.

"We've got friends to check on. We'll see her later…. Besides, she's not open yet."

"The papers are out."

"They're always out. Nobody steals in Rennes-les-Bains, you know that."

"Not newspapers, I suppose."

Between the walkway and a giant oak, the boy spotted a small sardine tin someone had left out for the cats that patrolled the square. Without thinking, he gave the can a solid whack with the side of his blue leather shoe and sent it skidding like a soccer ball with a good backspin three or four meters ahead. Immediately he went charging after the can for the follow-up kick but heard a horrendous clatter behind him as though a giant had mimicked his kick but had picked a metal garbage bin in place of the tin can. He looked back to see Arthur rushing toward him like an iron glacier stumbling downhill. The boy stopped—and stepped aside to let his friend rumble past on his way to the tree he had chosen to brake his momentum. The sudden move with the can, the boy decided, had been a mistake. Slow and steady, he knew, was the only way to travel with armored friends.

At the rear of the square they turned left again on a small street that descended to an arched bridge wide enough to carry only one automobile at a time. On the other side of the bridge the boy hesitated and looked both ways, to his right along the gravel road upstream through the woods and to his left down the cement street back to the rear of the hotel.

"Who first?" he asked.

"God only knows where we will find Tom this time of day. Let us check on Percy. Would very much like to see him again—catch up on his Grail adventures. We might discover Asterix has showed up by now."

"Okay." He led his comrade in armor left, down to the first level of the village above the river. Fortunately, no one except himself had seemed to notice the great clatter back in the square or the alarming scrape, drag, and rattle of the metal boots along the white cement street. To passing villagers, Arthur simply seemed invisible. At least no one stopped them to ask what they were up to. In effect, they had the bridges, paths, and alleyways to themselves and could do what they liked. No question about it, imaginary people were the best friends of all. Outside the hotel, with Arthur or the others, the villagers hardly seemed to see the boy either, as though his companions' invisibility rubbed off on him. This made him want to try unusual things, movements he wouldn't attempt without friends—perhaps flying out over the river like a hawk. But he had to think about Arthur. If kicking a can could be so much trouble, he had to forget about flying. He would never be able to fish his friend out of the river. Even so, he preferred going about his own enterprises this way so much more than being back at the hotel, where his parents could always see him, especially at the wrong times; or worse, where he could see them—at all the worst times.

In the hollow at the rear of the hotel, where the short flight of stone steps rose to the flimsiest of the suspended bridges in the village, they descended into the well where the emergency stairs came out. From this side the water-warped old door was locked. But the boy had shown all his friends how easy it was, with the flat ice-cream stick he'd hidden in the crack under the sill, to pry between the door and the jamb and lift the lock, thus gaining access to the numerous unused and, in the basement level, unrestored chambers of the once regal, and still imposing, hotel. From frequent practice, he knew exactly where to place the stick to catch the flat metal latch with his first jab.

Inside, the basement reeked of mildew and onions, and except for light from the far end, the corridor was dark and damp, so dark that now the boy found himself clumping clumsily along at a pace similar to that of his well-fortified friend. Here and there, huge burlap bags and baskets abandoned at this unused end of the hall obstructed their already halting progress, and from time to time Arthur would pause to disentangle some corner of his armor, usually an ankle pivot, that had snagged in the loose-weave of the hemp sacks, and the boy would take advantage of these moments to shake dust and mildew from his trousers where they had rubbed against a wall or a basket.

"Where is he?" the boy asked.

"I left him in the third on the right," Arthur grumbled back, and the boy could tell his friend didn't enjoy this dark any more than he did.

"Why down here? There's nothing but potatoes and onions—and cold blackness."

"I tried to persuade him to take a room up beside Tintin somewhere."

"He should have."

"Our friend has ideas—about caves and treasures, dark holes, discomfort. He believes it helps him with his sacred quest."

"Percy's not *stupid*."

"Of course not. But sometimes I wish he could employ a little moderation—view this whole Grail idea in the larger perspective."

"What you mean?" For the boy, the Grail meant gold and horses. It meant horses and adventure and huge starbursts of golden light. But mostly it meant horses.

"Please do not get me started," Arthur said.

"Sorry."

"It is fine with me if he wants to break his neck climbing Montsegur in his Sunday suit—or work up a sweat chasing churches through Ussat and Ornolac. That is the work my men do—good knights' work. But let him keep out of the caves."

"Caves?" The boy had a personal interest in caves today. "What's wrong with caves?" He knew there was a cave beneath the Marti mansion, but his mother had told him not to go there.

"Percy has not been right since he returned from Lombrives. Lombrives is one hole that would take the best out of any of us. They claim she is the largest maw in all Europe. You go down that one, at the very least you will come up with your joints rusty." To underscore, Arthur banged his iron elbow against a stone doorpost. "And you can catch your death of cold down that one. Or worse."

"You believe that happened to him?"

"Wouldn't be surprised. These tin cans," Arthur took the skirt of his metal coat in his hands to rattle it, "aren't very effective when it comes to keeping the heat in or the damp out." He paused to run his hand over one of the doors. "This one, this is Percy's. The piece of ribbon covering the angel's bosoms, it is his. Good old Percy, crystal-pure to the core." Arthur gave the handle a good warning rattle and, with a bang of his elbow, shoved the door open.

Only the smell of mildew and the threat of absolute darkness rose to strike them in the face.

viii

Anthi_cwaters
To: mdwaters@urtoo.com
Re: critique unsolicited

Not much happened in that pop-up, Pops. Except kicking a tin can. Arthur? Get real now! He was my hero onciponatime.

Seems the old creative flame was running low there—or on kerosene.

mdwaters
to: Anthi_cwaters@ezrite.com
re: Yes, but ...

The goal, young lady, is to recapture a bit of the innocence, the *dolce far niente*, of childhood. (That's Italian, I think, for "sweetness of doing nothing." But then your Italian must be better than mine.) And a five-year-old's Arthur would differ, I imagine, from a teenager's. His Arthur would surely kick a tin can he found at his feet, wouldn't he? And make other mistakes. Even an exceptional child like little Charles, and everyone reports he seemed extremely precocious, would, I'm sure, enjoy moments of sweet mindlessness. I hope he did—even on his last morning, as his hero (and yours) led him—disastrously, I would add—where we know he went.

And, yes, Anthi, one's inspiration for a pop-up inevitably fails, but only for the moment, I hope. When it does, we have to fall back again on e-mail and on what the library files have to offer. Emerson said somewhere that books are for the scholar's idle moments. You do remember Emerson, don't you? If not, Poe then, and his response, I think, to Milton: that there *are* no long poems. (A paraphrase.) Only short ones embedded in mountains of prose. Surely you lived in Virginia long enough to come across Poe's weird stories? He had useful things to say about mysteries.

What, then, do the books—our papers and magazines in this case—tell us?

This: That a year after their engagement was announced, Christine, now almost twenty, and Philip, twenty-eight, married in the small church of Rennes-les-Bains, where her relative, Abbé Henri Boudet, had served as parish priest eighty years before. The wedding pictures in front of the church capture Christine in a knee-length fluffy dress of silk or taffeta, possibly an off-white or beige, rather bland for the color-crazed seventies, and Philip in the wide-lapel, dark corduroy suit men often preferred at the time. Both are wide-eyed and grinning. A year or so later, as neighbors recollected for reporters, little Charles was born, and Rennes-les-Bains considered the happiness of the attractive young Plantards complete. The rest of France did not yet care. Not the way I do, or the way I hope you, Anthi, have come to care.

During the year between his engagement and the marriage, Philip had the good fortune to win support from the regional branch of the National Institute for Economic Development through Tourism in restoring and managing the lovely old hotel built in the eighteenth century on the site of the Roman baths in Rennes-les-Bains. Related magazine photos have him wearing the white shirt again, often with the sleeves rolled up and an earnest dark tie: a worker but respectable, perhaps a politico of the future, but for now focused on his hotel.

Although he found the exterior walls of the long, three-story stone and stucco structure still standing, the interiors of its seventy-odd rooms were in a sorry state: the basement and lower floor had been used, when not flooded, to warehouse local grains and food commodities and, during the worst of winters, for housing cattle.

With money from the tourist institute, Philip renewed the red tile roof, scraped the floors and walls, repainted the older row of rooms over the river a warm rose red and the newer row behind them a serviceable grey; and still he found funds for refurbishing twenty-two of the rooms to a level of comfort that met national standards. His success in this venture not only began to attract a new breed of outsider, the tourist, to the quiet village—in addition to the elderly and rheumatoid who traditionally soothed themselves in the healing minerals of the baths—but also inspired such admiration in other natives of the area that, shortly after the birth of Charles in 1980, when it was time to select a new mayor for Rennes-les-Bains, Philip Plantard appeared everyone's obvious choice. He added the requisite suit jacket, but not of corduroy now, the photos reveal. For the present, it seemed that his personal affection for his region had also become the passion of his neighbors, a combination that anyone might envy.

In his new position, Philip proposed and executed (sometimes high-handedly, one neighbor reported) the policy of restoring the village's ancient baths and its poorly maintained houses. Beyond restoration, he insisted that new growth take place at a very gradual, carefully monitored pace, so as not to damage the region's natural beauty. The remodeling of his hotel stood as the prime argument for the process he proposed. The opponents of Philip's program of gradualism consisted of a small minority of the town's merchants and their families led by two or three local construction interests. Though vocal in their protests that Plantard was obstructing the potential of the area for progress, his critics failed to attract local support.

Despite his good cheer and usually easy-going demeanor, Plantard as mayor was able to exercise considerable influence, the papers learned, when the local governing council was asked to allocate land for a large tourist complex on the southern edge of the village. Philip opposed the plan with the general argument that such growth would quickly run out of control and on the specific grounds that several giant cromlechs and dolmens, unexplainable prehistoric circles of stones standing on end, remained in the area and that the basement of an older building that would have been demolished, a grey stone house that figures prominently in our mysteries, Anthi, was said to contain an entrance to one of the numerous prehistoric caves found in the area. The land became, instead, the site for a small campground, town park, and three private villas. As Plantard (tieless, sleeves rolled again) told one reporter, he was discovering to his surprise that he enjoyed using his position to further his good cause, even though the group of opponents now included his own cousin Claud Plantard (who had returned to the area to expand the construction company taken over from his father) as well as the local clan that originally owned the plot in question.

To me, Anthi, if you have persisted through the necessary details, Philip Plantard's story is a reassuring one. In his determination, which shows in his eyes, I find qualities that seem almost old-styled American, especially his driving will and his hard work to make a place for himself in the village he loves so intensely. These should appeal to our readers. At the same time, who can help admiring his wisdom in resisting the otherwise unrestrained destruction of this little Eden in the low mountains of France. His stand seems all the more admirable when we consider that, as the major hotelman in the village, he could only have profited from the wholesale development of tourism. I feel comfortable putting myself in the place of an individual with Philip's values—in order to let him come to life in my mind. Doing so brings out some of the best in me. Perhaps this is why I need to believe that places like Deepest France, and people like Philip and his family, still exist. Their stories so easily become our own. And the best of Philip surely must have passed into Little Charles, whose innocence again pulls me back to our account of his final morning.

ix

Charles
Pop-Up

"Hello, Percy. It is me and the boy," Arthur called into the musk and dark of the dungeon-like space.

"Over here," a voice piped back feebly. "Under the window."

"What is wrong?" Arthur groaned, and they both plunged through the heavy reek of mildew toward the voice.

"I'll get the window," Charles volunteered, though he knew from experience that alone he couldn't manage the stout vertical bolt that ran the height of the hotel's shutters.

"See about Percy," Arthur said. "I will open the shutters." And he had them apart before the boy could locate their friend's outstretched arm.

The wash of watery grey light that the opened shutters admitted revealed the toneless shape of Percy draped over two huge potato sacks and a lowly bag of cabbage, the latter squeezed in between the others to support his hips.

"What happened?" the boy demanded.

"When you started getting worse, you should have warned us," scolded Arthur, with authentic concern.

"It happened last night. My fever shot up. I was too weak to move. Fortunately, Madeleine came by this morning." For the first time, the intruders noticed the frightened girl, a mere child no more than eleven or twelve, huddled in the corner. "Do not be scared, my little one. This is my king, Arthur, about whom I told you. They have come to help. I sent her to the royal encampment, my liege—she could not find you."

"I had come for the boy. We were in his room," Arthur said. "What do you need—water, food? I know you would refuse strong drink, though it might revive you."

"Madeleine brought me warm milk and honey. I am feeling better. Weak still, but the fever has broken."

"You have to get out of this damp hole."

"We have dry rooms up with Tintin," the boy volunteered.

"I must send the girl to see about the room." He raised his upper body the best he could. "But I need something from the boy other than a room."

"When she goes, tell her to speak before she knocks," Charles warned. "Tintin's probably set to ambush Capone's boys. If she doesn't speak up, it could be a disaster."

"The boy is on a mission for his mother," Arthur said. "Perhaps I should take his place."

"This task requires one of *them*, Your Majesty."

"What are you up to, Percy?"

"In the ancient cave at Lombrives, I went down too far. At about two hundred meters, I reached a cavern—a hundred meters high, with a great vaulted ceiling. The walls down there are covered with inscriptions and impossible drawings. Down where the last of the sainted Cathars probably perished."

"That is why you went?"

"They were the last men known to have 'It' in their possession."

It was not the first time the boy had heard the "It" pronounced that way. His father sometimes spoke with the same emphasis.

"You have already *seen* it, Percy." For some reason, Arthur didn't use the same emphasis. "Possession may not be what matters."

"The inscriptions were sky signs," Percy, revivified by their conversation, continued, apparently ignoring Arthur's observation. "As you know, I have spent many years attempting to read the signs. And the signs on the walls in Lombrives confirmed what I have seen each place I have been."

"So?" Arthur interjected.

The boy had learned to be patient when these two talked—or

argued, as was usually the case. It was much like listening to his mother and his father. He heard their words and had no idea what they were quarreling about, only that what they said stayed with him like pictures he saw in his books. The give and take of these two became another adventure for him, and it was a good deal more exciting than Madame Roux's croissants.

"All of them point to this area—and to the boy's family."

"Please, we must not get him mixed up in your mission, Percy. His family was spared the Germans' quest in this region."

"It is not my fault. He already is. He is a Plantard—the rightful one."

"So, what do you want?"

"There are caves here too. The signs keep pointing me back to the caves here."

"The way Rennes-le-Chateau did?"

"Exactly."

"And the book by that Mad Abbé?"

"You know French is not a tongue I understand. Only sun signs. But that book is part of it."

"What do you need from the boy?"

"I'll do anything, Percy," Charles blurted out, now that he felt he again understood what they were saying. "I want to help you more than anything."

"Do not be so eager, my boy," Arthur cautioned. "Not until you hear. A knight-in-training should be ready to serve. But always reserve a *soupcon* of sound sense about your errands. Knights can come up with some damned fool notions."

"Arthur, my king, when did I ever—" the prostrated Percy began, obviously setback by His Majesty's implications.

"Not you, Perce. You have served me well, old friend."

"So you will not object?"

"I suppose I will consent."

"Charles, listen to what I am about to tell you."

"I will, Percy."

"The old Marti property, Charles. You know where it is?"

"Of course." Hadn't his mother reminded him it was up the river?

"There is someone up there disturbing things. You will recognize the parties."

"Who are they?"

"In the basement," Percy continued, "if the signs are correct, you will find an entrance to one of the caves."

"One of them?" Arthur asked.

"Perhaps *the* cave," Percy corrected.

"It is in there, you think?"

"Possibly. The chances are so good I cannot afford having the wrong ones get there first."

"The wrong ones?"

"The dark line, Your Majesty." His words sounded like those Charles heard his father mutter when he didn't know the boy was listening at the kitchen door.

"But the wrong ones cannot see it, can they?"

"It is not a matter here, Your Majesty, of visions or hallucinations. Here we are considering *physical* possession of the Sacred Cup. The visionary rules may not apply in this situation. In any case, I refuse to take a chance."

"And the boy is appropriate?"

"The best, Your Majesty. His family is the reason he has been selected. And he has a special gift in these matters."

"Of course."

"But, Charles, you must be careful." Percy gathered strength as he stared the boy firmly in the eye.

"I will—I always am."

"I mean *extra* careful, my little friend. These people are more dangerous than Asterix's Romans and Tom's Injuns combined. They are meaner even than Capone's boys that Tintin is pursuing."

"This is an adventure, isn't it!" the boy bubbled, stirred by a rich mix of fear and impatience.

"The best, Charles," Arthur assured him, placing his gentle iron hand on the small shoulder.

"The very best!" added the now recumbent Percy, and stretched his right hand out to take the boy's.

"What must I do?"

"In about twenty minutes I want you to pass by the Marti place. Observe what is happening—where the activity is. Take a look inside, locate the cave's mouth, if you can do so without getting caught."

"Should I speak to the grown-ups there?" There was something else Mama had said about the Marti mansion, but this wasn't the time to remember her words.

"No need for that. But if it happens to be a natural response, it may be better than pretending you have not seen them. Do what feels appropriate. You have excellent instincts, I am sure—far beyond your age. But do not attract attention, whatever happens."

"I will be there to help," Arthur reassured the boy.

"I have considered that, Your Majesty," Percy said, hesitantly. "If you do not object, Sir, it may be safer if you do not accompany him."

"They never see me," Arthur said, reading his old friend's mind.

"I know. I know. But the chance always exists that one of them might. It is not impossible for them. This is an unusual region, with exceptional people. Think of the boy. It is simply that the others never put their minds to it. But one of them might."

"Improbable."

"We are working with a number of unknown factors around

Rennes-les-Bains. The *dark* line exists here as well as the light. And the three of us simply do not know about the powers of the dark."

"You have a point."

"Perhaps you can find a vantage from which to watch, unseen."

"In case something unexpected occurs," Arthur added, pleased to be back in the adventure.

"Exactly. It is what I would do, if this malady had not prostrated me."

"You restore yourself. We can handle this."

"Sorry to lay it upon you. But the Quest must be protected."

"Of course." Arthur pulled the boy to his side. "We must be on our way. Will you be comfortable, Percival?"

"Have no worries, my friend. Madeleine ministers to all my needs. Isn't that so, my child?" The lovely waif, having gathered a modicum of courage during their conversation, politely nodded from her corner. "She knows the hotel like the palm of my—of her hand." Almost bodily, Percy seemed to force his mind in a different direction. "No one should be at the Marti property before eight. You may want to attend to your mother's errand beforehand."

"Excellent suggestion," Arthur said.

"No, no. If I go back, she won't let me out again. She'll make me get ready for the sitter's—and that would throw Percy's whole quest off."

"Well, suit yourself—just as long as you remember you have a mission for her too."

"Don't worry."

"On your way then," Arthur added. "But do not arrive there too early. Your lingering would attract attention."

"I have a couple of stops first," the boy said and, with Arthur scraping behind, started for the hall.

"Do not forget!" Percy, seemingly restored by their visit, called from his three sacks.

"Impossible!" the boy replied, squaring his head and shoulders with a show of confidence.

Back in the dark, they entered a section of the corridor obstructed by great barrels of pickles, local wines, and olives, in addition to a gauntlet of bags and baskets that seemed to jump out at them. But they were drawing nearer the end, where the single small pane in the door to the kitchen spilled a postage stamp of light into the darkness.

At the door the boy made Arthur wait while he climbed up on a black wine barrel and looked in. This way, without fear of being seen, he often had studied his father.

Philip Plantard was standing by the stove with a long wooden spoon in one hand and an open book in the other, his once white shirt stained back and front with steam and perspiration. His hair had fallen over his eyes like a brown shade. Before him a large pot boiling happily away contained what the boy knew would be the *plat du jour*, a spicy concoction of chicken or beef in rich wine with white onions and garlic buds that bubbled up as surface space allowed and sent their rich odor through the cracks around the door where the boy stood. It smelled like chicken. Whatever his father had selected, the difficult work now lay behind him, for he was so deeply absorbed in his book that the spoon arm dangled at his side. A few times the boy had discovered his father with his arms wrapped around the young woman who once helped in the kitchen. But his mother and the girl had argued over the amount of pepper to put in the steak-with-pepper, and the girl had quit in a huff.

Generally he found his father singing madly among his steaming pots like a musical sorcerer—or simply reading, as he was now. So often had his father tried to tell him about the Celts, the Romans, the Visigoths, the Merovingians, the Cathars, the Knights Templar, the Holy Grail, and other episodes from the history of their village and area that he supposed the book in his father's hand must be some new, or very ancient, account of the region. For his father, the books seemed to hold a deeply satisfying mystery locked inside, one that meant as much to him as the adventures with Arthur and his friends meant to the boy. When any book about the village he hadn't read fell into his hands, his father became a man reborn, high-spirited, on fire with curiosity. Between books, as he went about his duties for the hotel, he visibly sulked, his energy low, his patience thinner than the crystal in which he served their "Royal Highnesses" their aperitifs. At any rate, this morning his father obviously wasn't steaming over a few croissants to serve their "Highnesses," still waiting at the top of the iron steps that circled to the dining room, and this discovery put the boy at ease about the mission for Percy.

"He appears content," Arthur reassured, as though reading the boy's mind.

"Fine. We can see about Ast'ricks and Tom, can't we?" Charles jumped down from his perch and headed for the door that led out onto the lower patio. "Shhh, don't let him hear."

"Quiet as a chapel mouse."

Except for a pair of round cafe tables and a few metal chairs that his father left out for guests who, on sunnier days, preferred their coffee out-of-doors, the patio, formed by the cement apron before it dipped into the fast quiet flow of the river, was empty. A few meters to the right of the door the two took the half dozen stone steps that climbed the rock wall to the street back of the hotel, and the boy started downstream to where he reasoned he would find Tom.

"My friend," Arthur called from the top step, where he had paused, "where are you going?"

"Tom's waiting downstream, at the low bridge. At least, it's where we usually meet."

"But Ast'ricks will be at the campground—upstream—waiting for his scouts to report on Roman movements."

"I hate to keep Tom waiting, Sir. You know how excited he gets. If you think—"

"No, no. I am sworn to assist Ast'ricks against the Romans. And you are obviously eager to find Tom. We could separate now, take care of our obligations, and meet at the Marti property, as Percy suggested. I promise to stay out of sight."

"You must stop the Romans, Sir. I'll take care."

"Do exactly as Percy said. Act as you would normally. Keep Tom away from the door. Make certain not to attract attention. And stay out of the basement—unless you are certain you can enter and leave without danger." Then as an afterthought, Arthur said: "Better still, keep Tom away altogether."

"I know, Your Majesty. Caution's the key."

"On your way, son. Remember, my spirit will be with you, whatever comes about. You are a special young man to me. And to many others."

"I know, Sir. I'll be safe."

"Only if you are careful," Arthur called back, as he started upstream to locate his agitated companion.

x

Anthi_cwaters
To: mdwaters@urtoo.com
Re: gender

    I find it a little odd, Dad, that there are so few women in Charles's imaginary world, other than that frightened little Madeleine. And what is Percy up to with her anyhow?

mdwaters
to: anthi_cwaters@ezrite.com
re: I thought you would

    I also find it a little strange. But he's a product, Anthi, of his time and place. For a child who seldom steps outside his door without convincing his mother he must, having companions like Arthur, Tom, Tintin, and Asterix may be an absolute necessity, even in a safe village like Charles's. And the two giants to come, Jean and Beylibaste? Obviously the necessary equalizers. It might also be normal, I guess, for a boy to invent a gentle, strong woman's support to carry on such adventures.

    A pop-up, though, has a logic of its own, one we must trust, especially if this sort of inspiration is, as I believe, the greatest power we have working for us as storytellers. Perhaps Charles shares the average small boy's aversion to female playmates (remember Dennis the Menace?). Perhaps his fantasies have been limited by the largely woman-less fictions they draw upon. Perhaps he is simply reacting to what we have seen of his mother, that she intruded—or attempted to—between Charles and his dreams. It may be that, somewhere down the road, you will be able to help me with this and similar parts of the story?

About ole' Percy and the waif---

They come from another country, don't they? A child's world. And from the past—when innocence was a creature that is extinct today but was no less dangerous than varieties that exist now.

All Charles's friends are good guys, or appear to be so—until we stop to consider where they are leading him. In this they resemble other myths in our story.

Anthi_cwaters
To: mdwaters@urtoo.com
Re: oh!

I see. I think.

mdwaters
to: anthi_cwaters@ezrite.com
re: **So—**

Where was Charles when I broke in again? Yes, Arthur had just told him good-bye.

xi

Charles
Pop-Up

The boy waved once to the silver back, which failed to return the gesture; then, facing the opposite direction, he ran past the last cluster of houses on his right, the last on the left, and sprinted onto the gravel path downhill toward the bridge where he hoped to catch the youngest of his friends. Though the crossing lay only a hundred meters or so beyond these houses, the brush and small trees crowding the river blocked his view until he made his sudden descent to the sloping woods below the village. Coming around a bend in the stream, he reached a break in the trees through which he saw his associate in adventure standing in the middle of the bridge looking down into the water as though watching a large fish or an image of himself. As always, Tom had on a red plaid shirt, high-top-jeans, and, as a concession to Charles and the quartz terrain, ankle-high shoes. He held his ragged straw hat behind him in both his hands.

"Tom—I'm coming," the boy shouted over the clamor the water made against the rocks. But, with more alarm than delight in his red face, Tom looked up and, with a downward arc of his arm, gestured for silence.

Only then did the boy realize that his friend from the Mississippi was not alone. On each end of the bridge, like guardians, stood a hulking fellow dressed in a long white robe with a hood over his head and only his nose and chin visible. The sleeves were cut from the robes so that the heavy arms of the two, naked from the shoulder, hung down like pairs of tanned, muscular sausages. The boy recognized the robes from a book his father had recently read him: Tom Sawyer's guards were wearing the garb of the ancient Cathars of Languedoc. The Purest of the Pure, Keepers of the Sacred

Cup. They were the first of this persuasion ever to turn up in his adventures. When he realized who they were, his breath stopped in his throat.

"What's happening? Where'd you find these men?" Charles asked in a whisper, as the hooded figure at his end of the bridge, on a signal from Tom, allowed him to pass. Tom's gesture restored the smaller boy's breathing.

"They're willing to help. That fool yellow-headed Gaul friend of yours, Ast'ricks, sure as shooting's not much help! This is Jean de Montsegur," he added, nodding toward the bony-faced hulk the boy had passed, "and Beylibaste—" he pointed toward the round red face at the other end. "Boys, meet Charles Plantard—"

"Ah, yes, Charles Plantard—" the bony-faced one sputtered, with obvious pleasure. "My honor to meet you at last."

"Mine also—" Beylibaste grunted.

"Charles will help us," Tom began. "We've been waiting for you, little fella."

"I came as soon as I could. There's just too much going on this morning. Percy, Mommy, Ast'ricks—"

"I know, I know. When it rains, it pours alligators. Most days it's just deadly dull.... But I got an adventure today that'll make your sweet tooth ache."

"I hope I have time—"

"You have, you have—for this one!"

"Tell me—"

"Injun Joe's in town—"

"No!" the boy exclaimed, incredulous. He remembered Injun Joe's scowling, twisted face from the story in which he first met Tom, and though his father was holding the book, he had ducked his face behind his bedspread until his father turned the page.

"I'm sure—" Tom wagged his head assertively, as though to shake all possible doubt from his or his friend's mind. "These fellows here described him to me, down to the last hairy wart. Didn't you, boys?"

The two white forms nodded obediently.

"These two've been guarding a cave here in Rennes-les-Bains 'bout as long as anybody can recollect. Hid some terrific treasures in there— But we won't go into that." As he talked to the boy, Tom's brow crumpled and his eyes turned inward until he seemed to disappear into another time, another place. "Then a few days back some people started poking around their cave. Like I say, the description fits Old Joe to a tee. And they're afraid Joe'll find their loot. For sure, he's not the kind to have that stuff."

"You're right. The wrong kind can't have it."

"What's really got me upset is, it's possible he's got Becky tied up in there!"

"No—not Becky!"

"Or her older sister— I tell you, their description's the spitting image of Becky. I know she wouldn't be with that ugly old son of a gun if he hadn't tied her up with some kind of a spell or the other. We've got to stop that horse thief so we can set her free."

"Yes, we have to."

"I knew you'd be on our side, my friend." The older boy pounded the younger one's back enthusiastically. "Let's go, boys. No use putting it off."

"Right, my lord." Jean, the sharp-faced Cathar, reached into the brush at the end of the low cement bridge and pulled out four man-high sticks worn skin-smooth through handling. Three of these he distributed to his comrades.

"Heck if I know where they get this 'my lord' talk from, but it kind of grows on you," Tom confided to Charles; then, noticing the difficulty the boy was having handling a staff twice his height, he added, "You've got to balance it on your shoulder." He illustrated. "Or carry it balanced level with the ground—" He took his own rod at midpoint and allowed it to dangle by his side as they started back uphill toward the village along the road Charles had just traveled.

"Why do I need this thing?" The boy wagged his stick awkwardly.

"According to the boys, it's regular equipment for this sort of caper. Can't run off the pope's people without good, stout staves, they say.... The way they see it, the guys in the cave are working for the pope, the king in Paris, and the Inquisition. I tell you, Charles, this one has got all the markings."

"It may. But I still have trouble with this pole.... If I carry it down like this, the end keeps dipping and hitting the path. And if I carry it up, it gets caught in the trees," the boy had to stop to retrieve his rod from the low-hanging branch of a holm oak, "—like this."

"It's fershur a nuisance. But you better hold on to it, cause if we run into Joe in that cave, we're gonna need all the weapons we can lay our hands on."

"What's this cave, Tom? I know there must be a hundred around. But I'm thinking it must be the same one Percy's got his eye on. Can't be that many with people poking around in them all at once."

"Caves always draw folks, like daubers to dirt."

"Especially here around les-Rennes. Daddy says it's because of the treasures." They were on the gravel road now. With no trees overhead, their way, though still uphill, was less difficult for Charles.

"'Cept Percy's not looking for regular treasure," the older boy corrected.

"His must be worth something—it's gold, isn't it?"

"We're talking about big treasure here, Charles. Huge. Piles and piles of gold.... What Percy's after is—something different."

"I don't really understand what this Grail's all about." Believing he should, the boy hung his head.

"Likely I don't neither. But the Grail's the grandest adventure of them all—and that's dangburn good enough for me."

"Me too, I guess." Then a new thought restored the boy's enthusiasm. "Wouldn't it be royal if somehow they were the same cave—Percy's and the Cathars'. Wouldn't that be an excitement! Whoever dreamed of a challenge like that?"

"Might just be what we got in store for us. Cause these two fellas," he waved his stick at the two white shapes they were following, "tell me they're the jokers that had Percy's cup last time anybody knows anything 'bout. Jean's bunch saved it from the pope's soldiers at Montsegur—way back there sometime. The pope needed it in the worst sort of a way—to make him look good. And they've been protecting it ever since—not too long ago from that loco German who wanted it so he could boss the world."

"My gosh, I've got to warn Percy!"

"You ever hear of a place hereabouts called the Marti place?"

"It is the same!" Charles exploded. "That's the spot Percy wants me to explore."

"Ain't that something. I told you this one had all the signs."

"But the people in there can't be Injun Joe and Becky—"

"How come?"

"Cause Percy said I'd know them."

"Well, you do, don't you?"

"I've only seen them in my book—and once in a TV picture show."

"I don't know nothing about this teebee you can see. But since that's how you knew me first—you must know them too."

"You could say so—but Percy told me they are the other kind of people. You know—" the boy, not wanting to offend his friend, hesitated, "—real people."

"Real folks. Story folks—" Tom sputtered, a little irritated but with understanding. "Can't say I know the difference anymore.

Especially these days. Like you say, you already knew me—from teebee, or whatever. I never held it against you none that you're just a regular boy. Besides, you tell me, will you, what your life would be like if there weren't no kind of folks except the real ones!"

"I wouldn't have any adventures to go on. Just errands."

"Exactly."

"And I'd mostly get bossed around all the time. By big people. Real ones."

"Certainly no kind of way for an adventrus boy like you to grow up, is it." To underscore what he said, Tom kicked a pecan-shaped stone four or five meters up the road, and the boy, all at once getting the hang of how to carry his staff straight and clear of his limbs, charged after the would-be kickball.

"You're right, Tom." The boy gave the stone a solid whack the way he had the can in the square, and Tom ran ahead to follow through. Real or not, folks his own age, the boy realized, had advantages when it came to kicking.

"Or a girl either, for that matter. And that's why I've got to rescue Becky from that Injun."

"But Joe's not a real—"

"I told you, it don't really matter that much. He's a groan-up, ain't he?"

"Not all grown-ups are bad. Arthur, and Percy, Ast'ricks, … Tintin."

"Well, Arthur and Percy ain't real no more. As for the other two runts—don't nobody know what they are."

"They're my friends."

"Tintin's okay—especially for a Frenchman." Too late, Tom remembered whom he was talking to. "Sorry, Charles. I don't really know nothing about Frenchmen—except you and Tintin—and what good ole Huck told me onct about a rapscallion calls himself the long lost Dolphin. He must've been a fish outa' the water. It's only that this groan-up named Clemens been putting his words in my mouth so long now that sometimes they just pop out, and I can't seem to help it no way."

"I don't mind, Tom. Stuff like that happens to me sometimes."

They had followed their two guides up the grade of the river back into the village and were now approaching the rear of the hotel, where Charles remembered his mother was waiting. The Marti property lay another five hundred meters or so ahead, beyond the central square but on this side of the river. "I have to be careful my parents don't see me, Tom. I'm late with the brioches—or whatever it was Mommy told me to pick up."

"Let 'em slide this time, boy. This is The Big One, I tell you. Besides, when did groan-ups ever pay any mind to what kids're doing?"

"They're good enough at interfering."

"I never had that kinda family, I s'pose. If you're worried, you can walk in between Jean and Boolabaisse up there. Onct you're in between two big fellars like that, no way the other kind's gonna see you. I'll be right behind."

Charles crept forward so that he was practically wrapped by the ample folds of the white robes the two giants wore. As they continued beneath the high windows of the red stucco walls beyond which he could almost sense his parents waiting, he felt the stout bones and strong leg muscles of his guardians at work. Protected by their robes and all their force, the boy felt more security than he ever had known in his life, even with Arthur—he felt very nearly invincible. Bring on Injun Joe, he shouted quietly to himself. Bring on Capone's boys. Bring on the pope, the Romans—the whole Inquisition! He felt defended. He was among friends.

From the number of people sauntering about the square now, he realized it must be almost eight. The village was beginning to come to life. Several of the older women were out with their dogs.

Half-asleep kids were stumbling through to school. Two or three men ambled along on their way to the morning paper and a bitter, thick coffee from the cafe. Still, not one of them seemed to notice the odd brigade of the little local boy accompanied by two white-robed medieval monks and an American river rat as they crossed the arched bridge to the square side of the river and moved upstream around the village church. Here the boy had been told one of his ancestors once presided. They kept on their way to the Marti property that lay the other side of the river, where it still ran a cloudy white because the kaolin-rich Blanque joined it a few hundred meters upstream.

Beyond the church, the houses began to thin out until the village was once more only two houses wide, a row running along each bank, with trees again between the houses. The four adventurers crossed the old stone bridge to the less-developed side and followed the easy gravel road through the trees.

All at once, at the final bend before the Marti house came into view, Asterix, his yellow whiskers flapping, his two white eagle feathers laid flat atop his tin cap, popped out in front of them, as though he had materialized from one of the tree trunks, and threw his gnarled finger up before sealed lips. Taken by surprise, the boy felt an impulse to shout, but in the nick of time he checked the urge.

"They're all in there!" the red-faced Gaul whispered, almost giddy with hysteria.

"Your Romans?" Tom demanded, his own face steaming with anger. "We're after Injun Joe. No time now for Romans."

"The Romans, Capone's boys, even your old Injun! You name 'em, they're all after it. And they're in there!"

"No kidding!"

The small Gaul almost wagged his whiskers off. "I left Tintin and Arthur hiding behind the trees and came to warn you guys. Percy showed up too—but too weak, I'm afraid, to be much help. We've got to stop 'em before they find all the treasure."

"We're with you in this one, if you're right," Tom said.

The boy felt a gentle vacuum of relief replace the tightness that had squeezed his stomach at the sudden confrontation of his two friends: this was the way he felt when his mother and father made up. Now his pleasure was complete: nothing could make him happier than having all his valiant companions joined together against their combined enemies. If every day could start like this one! Never had he imagined—

"What's the plan?" Tom asked.

"Now you're here, we've got them outpowered."

"How many 're in there?"

"Nobody knows. We only see one or two at a time. But no matter how many, they can't stand up against what we're going to hit 'em with!"

He means the Assembled Forces of Good, the boy told himself. And I am going to be part of it—

Asterix motioned them off the path into the cover of the trees and steered them cautiously to the adult-high bushes, where the boy spotted Arthur's silver boots protruding from a clump of wild rosemary. As soon as Arthur and Percy heard them, they both stuck their heads out from the brush and signalled for silence. Clutching their staves, the boy and his brigade scrambled into the cover beside the others.

"Glad you made it," Arthur said, and tapped him, not very gently this time, on the shoulder. "Sorry about the brioches—"

"Croissants," the boy corrected.

"Whatever your mother said."

"I certainly wouldn't miss this for—for anything."

"If you look carefully, you can catch somebody moving about in there." Arthur motioned to the half-opened basement door of the old house, where grey stucco had weathered away to reveal the dark native rock beneath. "At the back there you can see the mouth of the cave that has everyone so stirred up."

"I can't make it out."

"Neither can I. Only the shadows."

"It is there," Jean de Montsegur assured them.

"It certainly is," Beylibaste added.

"They're all in there," Tintin's thin voice piped fiercely from a bush way the other side of Arthur.

"Just as the signs indicate," Percy concurred, also from the other side of Arthur, but nearer than Tintin.

"You save your energy, Perce," Arthur said. "The boy has come now. He will take your place. You could not help much in any case."

"I fear His Majesty is right," Percy groaned, and moved his hand feebly toward the door. "Otherwise, I would not miss this encounter." Then, as an afterthought: "Be careful, my little friend. You may be able to handle these people better than any of us."

"Why?" Charles asked. Percy's assertion had startled him.

"You will see."

"Look!" Arthur interrupted. "Did you notice that? Somebody is hiding behind the door."

"We've got to make our move!" Asterix said, seeking to take command.

"I'll count to three—" Tom said.

"No, I'll count—" Asterix countered.

"Everybody down and ready," Arthur ordered.

As he sank to his knees much like a runner at the starting blocks, the boy turned his eyes to one side and slightly to the rear. The house behind him across the river belonged, he knew, to one of his sitters. In an instant he saw her shutters were partway open. Wouldn't it be splendid if Jeanne were watching him now. Only this could have added to the joy he already felt.

"One—two—three!" Tom, Asterix, Arthur, and Tintin screamed all at once, and all of them leapt out of their hiding place like a squad of helicopters on television dropping from the clouds.

At the start Tom and Tintin led the charge, with the boy and Asterix side by side, and Arthur, the boy could tell, just behind. The boy held his staff above his head, ready to strike. Midway across the path, the boy broke past this vanguard and plunged earnestly on toward the half-open door and the shadows beyond, where now all the Romans, gangsters, wild Indians, and inquisitors had become one final familiar enemy.

At the threshold, in a moment that swept over him like wind off snow, he realized that Arthur no longer followed, Tom and Tintin ran no longer within reach—indeed, that, like the Cathars, they had vanished. His staff too was gone.

With one foot already over the sill, he turned in time to see Percy shrug his shoulders lamely and disappear.

As the heavy gloved hand came from the darkness to grasp his shoulder, he knew that his valiant friends had left him totally alone. The next second, he remembered his mother's words.

But the smile that swam down to greet him was a familiar one—and altogether real.

xii

Anthi_cwaters
To: mdwaters@urtoo.com
Re: odd again

To me, Dad, it is interesting the way all the elements in his fantasies finally come together.

mdwaters
to: Anthi_cwaters@ezrite.com
Re: my surprise too

This is what I mean by every pop-up having an internal logic. It's not as though I planned them to work like this. It's just the way the vectors of force in the episode naturally extended themselves out. Every character arrives at the mine on the Marti place, each for his own reasons.

Of course you realize, Anthi, that none of our story about little Charles's fatal morning ever appeared in *France-Soir* or any publication covering the case. It never came out at the trial of Charles's accused murderer. No one has had access to the boy's final hours except the two of us. Why not? Because this is the work of the fiction writer, to solve the myriad mysteries that surround our lives (and death, as in poor Charles's case) the only way possible. Through speculation, interpolation, extrapolation, the educated guess. In other words, through the imagination. One of my favorite poets speaks of the "keener sounds" we must create to fill the gaps that occur at the "ghostlier demarcations" of our knowledge of the world. Well, I would never claim that the mystery of this child's murder compares with those taken up by Darwin, Einstein, or any of our culture's most brilliant "poets," but the difference is one of degree not kind.

The work of the lowly novelist like myself, or yourself if you pursue your ambition, is much akin to theirs. Like them, we do the best we can with the materials we have available. Because the raw materials by themselves are never enough, we have to elaborate, using all the powers at our disposal. We have to come up with hypotheses of various stripes and shapes. In this fashion, we offer the answers we can. And they are "probably true enough," as Master William once said. For a time they will suffice. Perhaps forever, so long as a creator with greater powers of empathy and imagination does not take up our questions again.

What we cannot do nowadays is pretend to omniscience. Omniscience may be the most dangerous fiction of all. It is too nineteenth century, too Spencerian—too Social Darwinian. Or should I say too Homeric, too Mosaic? The great peril is that omniscience misleads us. It can lull readers, whole cultures, into a false sense of knowing that creates a risky sense of security in some—and worse, an inflated feeling of authority in others. From both of these excesses, great miseries flow. We have to find some way to avoid omniscience in the stories we tell, for it creeps into all we write, even presumably limited accounts coming from a personal storyteller like the ones I employ here. Readers are used to it. They long for it the way a small child craves a parent's protection—an Arthur. And too many makers of fictions—call them scientists, call them poets, mystics, or ideologues—have pretended to give us the answers we desire, only to set us up for the rude awakenings that mark a culture's collapse.

Omniscience robs the world of its mysteries, including those surrounding the death of little Charles, which we were investigating, in our fashion, when I jumped into his story with both feet the way you or Nicky once would have saluted a puddle. When the mystery feels most potent and our energies feel steady, the moment has arrived when we should step aside and let it have its way.

Anthi_cwaters
To: mdwaters@urtoo.com
Re: Yes!

You have a habit of not practicing what you preach, Dad.

mdwaters
to: anthi_cwaters@ezrite.com
Re: Yes,

I hate preachy novelists too.

Lawd, child, I'm afraid you started me up again....

Call me a raving pedant, but these are things I discovered working with Charles—with the reasons he became a victim of "benevolent forces." Stories that just flow, which "hang together," have their orderly beauty, but they also have their risks, and some of these are far from aesthetic.

Certainly the order that imagination can provide draws us back to the fantasies of childhood—as it does to myth, fiction, the arts in general. And, for that matter, to journalism, history, metaphysics, and science—though generally we forget that the latter approaches also create order through imagination. Clearly the press forgot this possibility as it pursued and convicted the major suspect in the death of little Charles.

And what are we to say about the manner in which Charles's imaginary world, this day, collided with reality, a crisis the boy could not have anticipated? Even though this dilemma in no way diminishes the energy and good humor his imagination engenders for those privy to his mental world, it does create a problem. Whoever, or whatever, greeted him in that cave came from another dimension—a world beyond his imagination. It was the element for which Charles had no preparation. But whose order ever anticipates such possibilities? You wonder, young lady, why your parents still worry about you and Nicky now that you both have your own lives, he out in Palo Alto and you abroad?

Such shocks to our dreams, though inevitable, seem always to arrive unexpected. Perhaps all systems of orderly Truth must exclude the anticipation of these shocks so that they may pretend to be complete. That could be what we require of them. If so, Anthi, I prefer the order of fictions, for they know what they are. Provided they do not forsake their birthright by aspiring to resemble reality. Only a fiction that knows its limits can entertain systems of order with an eye to exposing their gaps and fallacies. Millions of intelligent men and women have died for a Reality that a decade, or century, or millennium, later became a simple myth. Only fools would die, or kill, for a fiction.

Now, dear daughter, the launchpad is complete. Please bear with me as I see if this bird—our story—can fly.

Two

xiii

Police officials in Couiza today released preliminary reports from the handwriting experts investigating threats of retaliation that Philip Plantard of Rennes-les-Bains received in the months immediately before his son, four-and-a-half-year-old Charles Plantard, was discovered, bound, gagged, and with multiple knife wounds, in the Salz River. After examining numerous handwriting samples taken from the extensive Plantard clan and other persons living in and around Rennes-les-Bains, the experts have concluded that the threatening messages included eccentricities of penmanship with remarkable similarities to those in samples taken from Monsieur Plantard's cousin, Claud Plantard, owner of a construction company active in the region surrounding Rennes-les-Bains.

Monsieur Claud Plantard has been taken into custody for questioning in the case. Local officials refused to speculate about a possible motive for the crime. But our correspondent in Couiza has been able to learn that Claud Plantard, for many years before Philip Plantard returned to Rennes-les-Bains to live, had been a frequent guest in the home of the then Christine Boudet (now Md. Philip Plantard). Our correspondent adds that the two Monsieurs Plantard have also had business disagreements in recent months.

With this news report, readers all over France, even those who had hitherto ignored the cruel murder of little Charles, began to perk up their ears. No one can blame them. In such matters French readers do differ from American. Which of us, Anthi, given the intriguing details the papers reported, could fail immediately to see the motives for the murder? It seemed obvious that Claud Plantard had continued to resent his cousin's intrusion into his relationship with Christine Boudet, that though he had moved to Narbonne, then Perpignan, he had nursed his jealous rage in exile; that though he had returned to Rennes-les-Bains to begin his own construction business, he, in truth, was drawn back by much more personal and deeper motives than simply modernizing and vastly expanding his father's brick-mason interests.

Photos accompanying the first mention in the press of Claud Plantard show a man with some of Philip's good looks, but without the dark hair and with a somewhat flattened nose and a flat, hard glare in his eyes, though the pictures are not mug shots. As I first read the arrest reports some months later, it appeared clear as water over rocks that the cousins' conflict of visions over the rate at which the village should grow had simply provided the spark that detonated Claud Plantard's much older anger against Philip—and now against Christine as well. It took no special genius to perceive that the most vulnerable element in the young couple's life, as in other young parents' lives, must be the child who, given his irresistible looks, had undoubtedly become their pet and their pride. And that was where the vindictive Claud elected to strike. No jury could fail to convict Claud Plantard of willful, vengeful homicide in the brutal death of little Charles. Why shouldn't French readers simply sit back now and wait for the intimate details that would necessarily precede the decision of the court?

French readers, at this point in the case, were destined to be disappointed. The prosecutor, a young man not many years older than Philip Plantard and a product of the Montpellier law faculty, chose, for a variety of reasons, the most obvious of which had to do with the stolid nature of the law itself, to argue that Claud Plantard's motives arose chiefly from the cousins' conflict of economic ambitions, thus building his case upon the foundation created by the threatening notes, whose handwriting was the major piece of physical evidence tying the defendant to the boy's murder.

"And I will demonstrate beyond the shadow of a reasonable

doubt that, driven by professional resentment and personal greed, Claud Plantard did deceitfully lure little Charles Plantard, his own blood relative, into the street-level basement of an abandoned house, strike him with a large stone, and, while the helpless child still lay unconscious, bound his limbs in ropes, gagged his mouth lest when he woke he scream for help, and then did viciously and repeatedly stab the helpless boy until he was dead. I shall further offer evidence to suggest that on the second night after this brutal murder, Claud Plantard did drag little Charles from a concealed cavity in the natural rock face of one wall of the same abandoned house, place his now cold body in a large black plastic bag, and drag this hideous container, under cover of darkness, to the precipitous riverbank that waited only three meters from the door of the house, across a narrow gravel path, and push the little boy over the edge into the seemingly quiet but rapidly moving flow of the stream, which in turn carried the incriminating product of his brutal crime another nine hundred meters to the low footbridge where, because fall rains had swollen the river more than Claud Plantard imagined, it lodged until two teenagers on their way to the bakery discovered it the following morning."

And that, pure and simple, proved to be all the argument that Pierre de Batz, the blackhaired, sharp-faced prosecutor, made. He produced experts to show that small gravels from the cavity where little Charles was concealed and from the path across which his body was dragged were taken from his clothes by police scientists, and that small strands of the victim's hair and blood stains matching his blood type were found in the basement and cavity, along with fibers matching those in a wool coat frequently worn by Claud Plantard.

Neighbors of the Marti property, a prune-faced elderly woman and her twisted, wasted husband, came forward to testify that, on previous occasions, they had seen Claud Plantard entering or examining the abandoned house. "I knew Monsieur Plantard by his face. I knew his father. I know what sort of work they both do," the old woman reported. "I assumed he was planning to restore the old building—or tear it down and put up a hotel. Isn't that what they mean to do with all our houses? I had no way of knowing he had murdering his little cousin in mind," she said, before the defense attorneys objected.

Followers of the trial, who now included the great majority of French adults as well as Sylvana, Paolo, and myself on our veranda in Les Issambres, of course were disappointed, as I imagine you are, that nothing about Claud Plantard's earlier relationship with Christine Boudet Plantard came out in the testimony on either side. That emotional connection had been shelved behind someone's old law books. It was easy to see why Philip Plantard and Monsieur de Batz had elected to protect Madame Plantard, whose loss had become the nation's, from a traumatic cross-examination about her early emotional life. De Batz obviously believed he had made an irrefutable case. Even so, the large audience of the trial felt cheated.

Most readers agreed, though, that the prosecution had achieved its main end: it had made the case against Claud Plantard, and, one way or another, the threat he represented was to be removed from society. All sensible people, I believe, Anthi, would concur that men and women capable of murdering children, whether emotionally or physically, should not go free. No matter how we disagree on other ethical questions, we know that violence against the child violates our deepest values. Those who commit these crimes, one imagines, must even despise themselves, no matter how helplessly they find themselves driven by their vicious passion. So the community of readers conceded that justice had triumphed although the trial had served truth and human curiosity less well.

In such cases, readers wait for the other shoe to fall—and usually go unsatisfied. Only in fiction can they expect to be gratified. Here is one juncture at which the story of little Charles surpasses what we reasonably expect from our lives. Or from most fictions.

xiv

Defense lawyers, in cross-examining Philip Plantard, opened an area, Anthi, that intrigues me. In an apparent attempt to discredit the motive for the murder postulated by the prosecution, Claud Plantard's lawyer, Jean-Paul Arrends, sought to prove that Philip Plantard himself was an eccentric, if not a bit of a crackpot—and certainly not a practical man of affairs whose business acumen anyone could take seriously enough to commit a murder over. Arrends's purpose here shows clear in his words; Philip's, on the other hand, we have to imagine.

"I am certain, Monsieur Plantard, that you would agree with me—indeed, with most of us in this court—" the attorney said to the cautious witness, "that the historical records of our region present a rich and fascinating array of events and riddles. Is this not so?"

Philip Plantard hesitated. He felt overly warm in his pear green shirt, brown-striped wool tie, and brown cord suit jacket with wide lapels. Basically he trusted Monsieur Arrends. But something in the way the lawyer's short muscular body, bound in a silver suit, leaned against the table between them as he framed his question suggested a crouching animal, or perhaps a shark with its front fins stiff on display.

"Would the witness please answer Monsieur Arrends's question?" the judge prompted.

"Yes. I agree," he conceded, but remained wary of where the lawyer was leading him.

"Good," Monsieur Arrends replied, with a sudden affirmative jerk of his head as though the difficult part of this line of inquiry was behind both of them. "We in this part of the nation are blessed with a long and varied history: it might help the court if you told all of us what aspects of our past you find most compelling."

Although Arrends offered this new question as a simple afterthought clarifying the earlier one, Philip twisted in his chair in a manner that showed he did not care for this final word. He himself had not emerged altogether uninfluenced by his two years studying with the Montpellier law faculty. He knew how much weight even a poor lawyer could place on a single carelessly chosen word. "In general I find all our periods valuable and informative," he replied. "I suppose you might say I am an enthusiast when it comes to our region."

"In that case, Monsieur Plantard, it is my pleasure to know you— even under present circumstances. I too am enthusiastic about the Aude. But if I divide our history into three or four rough epochs— say, from the Roman occupation to Charlemagne, Charlemagne to the revolution, and the revolution to the present moment, would you be able to say that one period, for you, is more compelling—let's make that, 'more interesting,' if you prefer—than the others?"

"That seems a fair question, Monsieur Arrends. And, yes, I could very easily answer that the first period you mention attracts my interest more than the other two."

"The first period was the time from Roman domination down to Charlemagne, wasn't it? From about 400 AD until 800?"

"Yes, that would be about it."

"Good. That, I agree, is an exciting period. But could you tell the court exactly what it is about that period that you find compelling?"

Again Philip hesitated while he studied the small, solid attorney who had just posed the least expected query he had thus far encountered. Monsieur Arrends seemed a fair-minded man. Understandably, he was out to exonerate Claud Plantard—but to do so without distorting the facts or unnecessarily damaging the reputations of others involved in the whole sad episode. In his own grief and anger and vain denial, Philip appreciated the effort Claud's lawyer had made to keep Christine out of the trial so far as possible. Arrends's care reflected a fine sensitivity in the man, no matter how determined he was to obtain Claud's release. But then how would it, Philip asked himself, have furthered Arrends's client's cause to have brought up the complicated history of Claud's old relationship with Christine? It would only have added desperation to an already dismal situation. Claud deserved what he was about to receive. There was no need, Philip was sure Claud's attorney realized, to scar Christine's emotions any deeper and irreparably than Claud already had. Charles's death was about all any mother could be expected to endure. Philip could not be sure, however, that his cousin himself shared his attorney's opinions, for, after the hideous way Claud had found to express his stored-up envy, Philip had serious doubts about his kinsman's ability to reason. What exactly had Claud told his attorney that Arrends kept trying to characterize his historical interest as an uncontrolled compulsion? Unable to imagine where the defense wanted to take him, and having put off answering as long as he felt he could, he redirected his eyes, asking for aid, toward the thin, mustache-proud face of the prosecutor.

"Objection, Your Honor!" Monsieur de Batz called out, rising to his feet as soon as he caught Philip's now visible confusion.

"What is your objection?" inquired the tight lips above the dark gown decorated with a white butterfly bow at the Adam's apple.

"I object to the manner in which the defense has characterized Monsieur Plantard's interest."

"Objection sustained."

"Very well then—" Monsieur Arrends acquiesced, as though expecting the interruption. "Would Monsieur Plantard please tell the court exactly what it is about the period preceding Charlemagne that he, as a historical enthusiast, finds most 'interesting'?"

"I would be glad to."

"Well, please do."

"Very simply, from that earliest period the area around Rennes-les-Bains occupies a special position in French history. We played key roles in the very creation of what became the French people and the French nation. In French history, our region, the Razes, holds a position similar to the role played by Greece in European history: we were there at the start—we were the founders. That is something of which we can be proud, I believe. And something that we should never allow anyone to take from us. It is our national, and local, heritage."

Arrends paused for a moment and beamed, as though sharing in Philip's pride. In fact, he was allowing the full effect of Philip's passion to sink in with the jury before continuing. "Eloquently expressed, Monsieur Plantard. Your words inspire us all to think again of those simple men who laid the foundations for an independent people.... But now I would like to ask you a slightly different sort of question, if you don't mind."

Concerned by this shift, Philip turned to de Batz again. But the prosecutor simply signalled with a lift of his head that Philip had permission to respond.

"What I would like to know, Monsieur Plantard," Arrends continued, "is something of your own feeling about what we have heard from Madame Plantard's mother, Madame Boudet. Madame Boudet has testified that for two years prior to your engagement to the then Christine Boudet you paid frequent visits to Madame Boudet and her daughter. Is that not so?"

"Yes, that is true." Philip said but wished Christine's name had not come up again.

"And that, for much of the two years, your visits were basically of a historical nature—to ask questions of *Madame* Boudet regarding the researches of her male relative, the late Abbé Henri Boudet. Is that so, Monsieur Plantard?"

"That is true."

"So that initially your interest in the Boudet family arose from your historical enthusiasms as they led you to the Abbé Boudet of the Rennes-les-Bains parish?"

"That is a fair statement—though I did not yet know Christine Boudet, except as a little schoolgirl running about the village."

"Is it also fair to say that before you ever set foot in the Boudet home you had already read Abbé Boudet's books?"

"I had heard of them—I had not read them. In fact, I first visited my mother-in-law to ask if she had copies. Almost no one around Rennes-les-Bains had actually seen the books, although a number of people had mentioned them to me."

"Thank you for being so candid, Monsieur Plantard."

"You are welcome." Philip relaxed a little.

"Before you first called on Madame Boudet and her daughter, did you already know what you might find in those books?"

"I had been told that Boudet—Abbé Boudet—had argued in one of them that before the tower of Babel was built, the Celtic language was the universal language of mankind."

Arrends returned to the table, from which he roamed freely, to check something in his stack of notes. "That must be Abbé Boudet's 1886 work, *The True Celtic Tongue and the Cromlech of Rennes-les-Bains?*"

"That's correct, sir."

"And is that all you expected to discover in Abbé Boudet's books, should Madame Boudet have copies?"

"That was Boudet's thesis, sir. I certainly expected to find many pieces of detailed supporting information, if that's what you mean."

"Now, Monsieur Plantard, a historical scholar of your learning must have known there was more to the cromlech, or dolmen, the famous upright stones of Rennes-les-Bains, than an etymological or linguistic argument."

"Objection, Your Honor!" de Batz broke in, on his own prompt this time.

"Objection sustained. The counsel for the defense must not read thoughts into the witness's mind, nor lead the witness further than he is able to go on his own."

"Very well, then, Monsieur Plantard. What did you think of the good Abbé Boudet's thesis regarding the Celtic language?"

"It seemed eccentric."

"Eccentric?"

"Extreme. But I was prepared to maintain a somewhat open mind until I had looked at his evidence."

"Why was that?"

"Other than fair-mindedness, you mean?"

"Exactly."

"Because the Celts were our earliest known inhabitants in the Aude. Even before the Greeks and the Romans. It would be another feather in our cap, so to speak, to have participated in the original tongue of all mankind."

"And beyond that feather in our collective cap—had you heard anything at all about the hypothesis that the Abbé Boudet's book contains a coded message?"

"I am not sure I know what you mean, sir," Philip said, and looked down at his hands.

"There is a widely known rumor that, to those whose minds run on a track similar to the Abbé's—that is, to those informed in certain areas of knowledge—that the Abbé's discussion of the stones around Rennes-les-Bains provide a coded guide to important locations in and around Rennes-les-Bains. Had you heard nothing of that code?"

Philip turned in vain to de Batz, who nodded for him to answer. "Actually, I had heard something about the code, sir."

"So you knew that *The True Celtic Language* supposedly was

written as a secret guidebook to steer the initiated to the various treasures hidden in the caves and mines of our region?"

"Yes, I did know something about the supposed guide."

"Is it also true that an interest in those treasures—the gold of the Celts, the gold of the Romans, the gold of the Visigoths who had sacked Thrace, Delphi, and Rome before settling in our hills, even the sacred treasures of the Cathars and the Templar Knights themselves, said to include the Holy Grail itself—not an antiquarian interest in the history of the Aude region, initially compelled you to call on your future mother-in-law and your future wife?"

Philip found himself at a loss for words. All at once Monsieur Arrends's questions had become unanswerable. He felt Arrends was calling on him to make distinctions where they did not exist, to agree completely to statements that he knew were only half true. He looked to de Batz for help, but de Batz was lost somewhere in a profound study of his notes. Apparently, in this line of questioning, he too was out of his depth. Philip realized he would have to fend for himself—and do the best he could.

"Sir," he began, "I cannot accept your line of reasoning. Yes, I knew about the gold—and even the legends of *le Saint-Graal* . But that is not something different from the history of the Aude. It is part of our history. I went to Madame Boudet's because I love our village—and would like to see us reclaim our rightful place in the history of France. And our rightful treasures as well." That was all he wanted to say, and when the words were out he slumped back in his chair, too exhausted to defend himself against anything further Arrends might ask.

"Isn't it true, then," Arrends hurried on, eager to get everything in the record before either the judge or de Batz caught up with his argument and stopped him, "not only was your desire to learn the whereabouts of the various fairy-gold treasures of Rennes-les-Bains the chief reason for your cementing your relationship with the Boudets through marriage to Christine Boudet, but the fantasy underlying every action you have taken to oppose the progressive plans of my client Claud Plantard for the beautifully situated village of Rennes-les-Bains? Members of the jury, I submit that neither my client nor anyone else in his right minds could take seriously—"

"Objection, Your Honor!" yelled de Batz, who, as he charged the bench, seemed once more to find his footing in the river of words Arrends had poured over all of them.

"Objection sustained!" the judge shouted above all the voices. "The counsel for the defense is reading thoughts into the witness's mind again. The clerk will strike the final questions from the record."

"The counsel stands warned that the court will not tolerate such reckless procedures!" the judge added with great firmness, like a carpenter driving his last nail.

"No further questions, Your Honor," Arrends said, and strolled complacently back to his chair.

xv

Anthi_cwaters
To: mdwaters@urtoo.com
Re: But

I thought you wanted to avoid omniscience, Dad, and there you are inside Philip's mind, and it wasn't a pop-up.

mdwaters
To: anthi_cwaters@ezrite.com
Re: you caught me

I never said it's a pure science, what I'm trying to do. There are grey areas—times when illumination overtakes the incubation process. Maybe I can explain.

As soon as I read the news accounts of Arrends's cross-examination, I knew that his entire line of inquiry could benefit Claud Plantard's cause not at all—that ultimately it would prove of no significance to the outcome of the trial. And yet, as I worked on these mysteries, it provided the occasion when Philip, for me, first came to life, and I was able to move inside his feelings. I am not sure exactly what to infer from this. Fortunately, Anthi, we are not lawyers, for as lawyers we would find nothing in this transformation at all useful in court, unless, like Arrends, we simply wanted to vivify Plantard long enough to destroy him as a credible witness.

As readers, however, the situation seems altogether different. As readers we sense that at this point we touched the very lifeblood of Philip Plantard, that the history of the Razes *is* the mystery through which he lives, both as a man and as a character in this story. In a court, or life, we could not reasonably expect to have anything extraordinary come of this fact. In stories, however, we have been conditioned to believe that significant events grow out of the energy that animates a character. Surely this force will lead to another of the pop-ups that are the lifeblood, as opposed to explanation, of our enterprise here.

You may be asking yourself why you should trust me simply because I have set myself up as the "author" of little Charles's story. This is a reasonable question—one I ask myself. After all, I am one person, and the boundaries of my knowledge end, as you remind me in your most recent e-mail (thank you!), at the borders of my experience. As I've said, as modern storytellers we can make no claim for omniscience. But the violent death of little Charles has created a mystery that I cannot ignore: I must understand the conditions that make so heinous a crime possible, or else other breaks in the web of expectations all of us count on may occur and events that rival this horror become commonplace. None of us should have to live like men and women who walk down the unlit and littered alleyways of villages and cities in which they are strangers, afraid for their own lives and those of their children. Consequently, I must push through the walls that otherwise limit my understanding, and do so in the only way I know—by crossing into the kingdom of imagination. That is why I welcome Philip's coming to life in his examination by Monsieur Arrends. In it, I felt I stood at the door beyond which something more dynamic—and revealing—would pop up.

If I succeed in breaking through to the hidden dimensions, I will eventually become "omniscient"—but all-knowing, of course, only in the most limited sense: only in this little world in which a child was murdered. I mean this small world of facts, one on the verge of becoming the world in which I wait for more frequent pop-ups—those unpredictable, priceless gifts bringing the storyteller's uncommon knowledge.

While I wait, off and on I deplore our modern deprivation, since omniscience is no longer a gift the Daughters of Memory grant simply because novelists invoke them. Nowadays muses must be courted long and deliberately, and sought under the strange names I have mentioned, including extrapolation, interpolation, empathy, invention. For they are *less* the passive progeny of memory than the brash, assertive daughters of imagination. Something is lost—a sort of effortless ease perhaps. But much has been gained: the sort of honesty, integrity, dignity, and deniability that are the true birthright of fiction.

And, dear Anthi, if I succeed, by chance and effort, in penetrating the veil of wonder that surrounds little Charles, there is little reason why all of us who as readers respect enigma should not come to live, on appropriate occasions, in that realm of extended perception where we can round out the stories that most profoundly trouble us—those so compelling that we *must* complete them even when it requires sacrificing the special energies that attend mysteries.

While Arrends and Philip were tilting back there, I left out a number of details that did not seem particularly relevant to what I had selected to report. I said little about the reaction of Claud Plantard to the trial that would determine his fate. In fact, Claud Plantard, a great teddy bear of a man, with twinkling dark eyes and a long, grinning mustache, vacillated, I am sure, between desperate faith in his attorney's ability to find an angle that would set him free, and total hopelessness. When Claud heard Arrends say, "not only was your design to learn the whereabouts of the various gold treasures the chief reason for your marriage to Christine Boudet ... ," he collapsed in despair. His eyes grew dim and small. He knew that talk of fairy-gold would carry no weight in this court, where he was assumed guilty until proven innocent. Claud, we both know now, never recovered from this collapse.

I failed too to take note of the differences between French law and American practices. That is one of the dangers of having characters come emotionally to life. Suddenly one becomes oblivious to details. Even so, for our purposes here, does it really matter whether the judge and attorneys wore black-and-scarlet gowns or suits, wigs or crew cuts, maroon-striped ties or fluffy white scarves? Well, yes, it does. Our readers will depend upon such details as pegs for their visual imagination, so we, at some point, should supply them. But this, of course, is not that kind of story. It is not literal-minded like those nineteenth century books in which the author swaps his birthright as a novelist for the shackles of science and positivism. For what we are after, pure and simple, is the movement of fundamental human passions—not the specifics of French life.

It is better that I tell you these things, Anthi, than have you bear a grudge against my story because it differs from most that we read. Nothing good would come from your resentment. But much good, I think, could develop from your resistance—combined with the special imagination I ask of you. So I am laying my cards on the table as quickly as I can without losing the thread: it is important that the story seem at times to tell itself, but equally important that we both recognize what we are contributing—what you and I are doing to make the story live. Important that we remain wary and responsible.

As I said, I want to discover what it is in the French, and in you, and me, that needs the innocent child, that needs mystery, that needs Christine Boudet Plantard. And since much of this knowledge will come through our emotional imagination, we both recognize, don't we, that it is far more important than the usual verisimilitude of realism? It is through pop-ups, which have a dynamic all their own, that the emotions most manifest themselves.

To be perfectly explicit, my contract, as I see it, is to supply just enough material detail to create the screens upon which you and I can project the little Charles in ourselves, the Philip, the Christine—even the unfortunate Claud Plantard in all of us. Only this, and nothing more. Certainly not enough detail to swamp all our faculties in the seductive pieties of land, nation, race, and language, the excess in which too many earlier readers and writers desired to drown. Our needs—and fears—are distinct from theirs. This difference too would warrant exploration—were there world enough and time.

xvi

Claud Plantard's case was indeed desperate—for the reasons I have already mentioned, Anthi, and for another I have saved until now.

Before examining Philip Plantard, immediately after questioning the elderly couple who lived beside the abandoned house where the crime presumably took place, Monsieur de Batz called fifteen-year-old Jeanne Roux to the stand. "Little Jeanne," as the French press quickly dubbed her (though she is not at all little), is the daughter of Claud Plantard's mother's brother. Although she is Claud Plantard's cousin, she is not kin to Philip Plantard—so far as anyone who testified knows, although in the district of Rennes-les-Bains most longtime inhabitants are related if one traces the family trees back far enough.

Little Jeanne appeared in court wearing a light-grey, knee-length dress with a high tatted-lace collar. She looked bashful, her eyes turned toward the floor, her mind seemingly turned in upon her private world—until the magistrate spoke her name. In response, she looked up with bright grey eyes and from that moment appeared very much at ease with the officers of the court. Monsieur de Batz questioned Jeanne with great gentleness, as one might handle a crystal pitcher too fragile to hold the liquid it contains. Perhaps de Batz was responding to the sense that she seemed so delicately balanced. As someone said, she combined "the face of a child with the silhouette of a woman." Immediately one felt off balance with her—uncertain how to treat her, what to expect.

"Is it true, Mlle. Roux, that your house faces the abandoned Marti property across the Salz River?"

"Yes, sir," Jeanne answered with great earnestness, apparently eager to be helpful.

"Would you say you have a clear view of the Marti property?"

"Very clear, sir. There are no trees at that point along my side of the river—only some low bushes. But my window is up higher than the bushes."

"Thank you, Jeanne. The court appreciates everything you have to share with us." Monsieur de Batz said and smiled at the judge as though soliciting his concurrence, and the judge complied. "Now, Jeanne, how wide is the Salz as it flows beneath your window?"

"I'm not good with distances, sir, but I imagine that it is twenty or thirty meters at that point."

"That's a very good guess, young lady. We have had it measured, and it is exactly twenty-seven meters at that point—not very wide at all?"

"No, sir."

"And is it true that on the morning that most interests all of us here, you were dressing for school behind the half-closed shutters of your room?"

"Yes, sir. That's the way I dress every morning—with the shutters open enough to let in the morning light and let me see what's happening across the river, but not let anyone look into my room."

"Many of us here, I expect, know exactly what you mean." Monsieur de Batz faced the crowd as though cueing them to smile their agreement, then turned back to his witness. "What do you usually see out your window as you dress?"

"In the summer there are riders who come along on horses from the stables at Caussagne—or men coming down along the river to open their shops." She paused before adding, "Not much else, sir."

Jeanne, as she answered Monsieur de Batz' questions, felt she was in a splendid dream. She knew that she had not yet said anything that mattered. But she sensed that it would be better if she allowed the suspense to build. She had watched *Dynastie* and knew how to save the surprise until last. And this was just like being on *Dynastie*. Monsieur de Batz seemed almost as handsome as an American star—he knew exactly how to lead her along so that she could drop her most shocking surprise into his stream of questions at exactly the right moment. And she already knew what that surprise would be. She had talked to the police long enough to figure out what would bring the startled response from her audience that she longed to hear. And afterward, there would be newsmen outside to ask her more questions—and then dozens of cameras. Tonight she would be on television—all over France—just because she was trying to be helpful. It was more than she had imagined even in her wildest television fantasies. She would be the heroine of every home in France. It was almost as exciting as being Jeanne d'Arc and Alexis Carrington combined. When she thought of it, she could hardly breathe. But she would have to blot all of that from her mind now to focus on Monsieur de Batz's questions. There was nothing she wouldn't do to help him, especially when he laid his hands on the banister in front of her and his voice rose to emphasize his point. In that moment she wanted to reach out and touch his fingers, long smooth fingers so unlike Claud's red, calloused ones. What would their stroke feel like?

"Jeanne, I do want you to take time to think carefully. So I'll ask you once more: What exactly did you see out your window the morning that concerns all of us here?"

"Since it was a Thursday, I was putting on my tan corduroy skirt and my beige blouse. As usual, both my Mommy and Daddy had gone to their work. I was just buttoning my skirt when I happened to see little—Charles Plantard—coming from the bridge above the hotel and starting up the hill."

"Can you tell the court what Charles was wearing that morning?"

"He had on blue trousers and a purple coat, just like the television reported."

"Had you ever seen Charles there before in the morning?"

"In the morning?" Jeanne paused to prepare her answer. "Not

often. It was out of his way if he was going to the bakery for Madame Plantard. That was the reason I kept my eye on him."

"Where did you believe he was heading?"

"He seemed to know where he was going. He didn't look here and there, like children do when they are playing around outside. He headed straight for the old Marti house—like he had an errand."

"Now, Jeanne, did you see anything unusual about the Marti house?"

"Yes, I did."

"And what was this?"

"The basement door was open. Usually there's a lock on it."

"Anything else?"

"I could see someone moving about inside."

"Beyond the door. Could you see who it was?"

"No, not at first."

"Could you at least make out whether the intruder was a man or a woman?"

"In the dark of the basement all I could I make out was the shape of the coat."

"And did that tell you anything about the individual in the shadows?"

"It was definitely a man's style coat, sir."

"A man's style coat? How was that, Jeanne?"

" It was cut straight—square down below the waist—and had what looked like a fur collar, like a horse collar, but not cheap looking."

"Thank you, Jeanne. I think we know the type.... And now, as Charles came nearer—did anything happen?"

"Just as Charles reached the door, the person inside stepped into the open door area and stuck out a hand to take the boy's shoulder."

"How did Charles react? Did he appear surprised or startled?"

"I didn't think so. He seemed to know the person—even to be expecting a friend or relative."

"As though they were relatives?"

"Objection, Your Honor," the defense groaned, almost apologetically.

"Objection sustained," the judge said, as annoyed as everyone in the court by this interruption in Jeanne's story. "The witness must stick with the facts—not indulge in speculations."

"Very well, Your Honor," de Batz conceded, without once taking his eyes from Jeanne, who felt admiration and appreciation in the warmth of his eyes. "Tell us, Jeanne, when this person stepped from the shadows, could you see who it was?"

"I could, sir."

"And you could tell whether it was a man or a woman?"

"Yes," Jeanne replied, knowing that her moment was near but not wanting to rush it, any more than Monsieur de Batz, her counterpart in the excitement of it all, wanted her to hurry toward the final surprise.

"And, Jeanne, was it a woman—or a man?"

"It was a man, Monsieur de Batz," she said, and listened for the first catch in the collective throats of the court. She seemed to breathe an energy, a superfluous but welcomed power, from the excitement in the air.

"And, Jeanne, think carefully now."

"I will, sir."

"Did you recognize that man?"

"I did, sir." With the first audible gasp, she knew her moment of glory would not escape her.

"Could you tell us who he is?"

"I could, sir." In the creak of the benches, the murmurs, the rustle of legal pads, she could hear them groping for the next crumb she would feed them. Monsieur de Batz had coached her, told her to remain calm, go slow, but now she felt in control and able to set the pace she desired. It would be cruel, she knew, to make them wait any longer. "He is sitting in this room, sir. He is the man over there beside Monsieur Arrends—my cousin, Claud Plantard!"

No one, except Claud Plantard, could have been disappointed by the audible shock that filled the court. Jeanne felt satisfied beyond anything she had dreamed. She had never experienced such warmth, so much attention, such power. She expected Monsieur de Batz to take her hands in his.

Yet, here in her triumph, the rest of her life already threatened to become, she feared, a waste land of shabby moments impotent to match this one. Her admiring audience appeared dramatically fulfilled. Reporters, too agitated to remain on their assigned benches, stared daggers at competitors clustered between themselves and her. But Monsieur de Batz beamed his contentment at young Jeanne like a father or a lover she had altogether pleased.

To Jeanne, staring into his approving eyes, it was a lifetime before the judge attempted to quiet the court, and it was another ten minutes before he succeeded in giving the floor back to de Batz.

"Jeanne, if you feel you can bear the excitement of answering a few more questions today—"

"I think I can, sir." She, in truth, did not want to leave the stand. She already sensed that she would miss these minutes with Monsieur de Batz before the eyes of the court. At some level only a little deeper than full consciousness, she was beginning to dread her life outside this room, dread the moment when this rush of success would end. For the present, her future felt like a total blank. She could no longer imagine facing the world out there—at least not the world beyond the newsmen and cameras through which she knew she would have to swim. The spaces beyond already seemed a horizonless desert of vacant days.

"If so, could you tell the court what occurred—what you

witnessed after Claud Plantard laid his hand on little Charles's shoulder?"

"Claud drew little Charles, too quickly I felt, inside the basement."

"Did you find anything strange about this?"

"About Charles's letting Claud tell him what to do?"

"Yes," de Batz replied with a patience she had never experienced from her parents but wished to feel again and again.

She tried to match his calmness: "Not at all."

"Tell the court why not."

"I knew Charles and Stephen, Claud's own son, were best friends. They are—were—the same age. They played together all the time. They were cousins or something."

"So … Charles knew Claud Plantard?"

"Knew him very well. I've babysat both Charles and Stephen. At Claud's house."

"And I'm sure you did a very fine job."

Jeanne looked down at the grey of her lap as if she had difficulty accepting his compliment. "I like to babysit them—" she began, then abruptly added, "Stephen is so strong, despite his—his disadvantage—and Charles just bubbles—bubbled—with the joy of—of life." For a moment, she felt she would falter. "Monsieur Plantard, Christine—all of us carried on conversations with Charles like an adult. He was only four, almost five, but he understood everything. Children's games didn't interest him. He jumped right into our discussions. It was so unfair for him to die—he was the most grown-up, the brightest little boy, I've ever known." Jeanne buried her face in the hands she raised like a mirror in which she might judge her performance.

De Batz waited a minute or two before speaking. "Jeanne, I know it is difficult to remember these things—difficult for all of us, and especially for you since you knew Charles so well—but would you say there was anything else unusual about what you saw that morning?"

"Only the quickness with which Claud drew my little goose into the basement—and that they appeared to have *planned* to meet in that scary old house where no one goes anymore."

"Anything else?"

"Perhaps what I could see Claud doing with Charles."

"What was that?"

"Well, they were standing in the shadows now, but it looked to me as though Claud was questioning the little boy."

"Questioning? What's so unusual about that? After all I am questioning you right now. I hope you don't feel in danger?"

"No, not a bit. It's just when I think back over all that's happened since then. It's unusual, isn't it, for adults to take what a four-year-old says so seriously. When I babysit I know I pretend to ask the little things serious questions, but it's only a game. And Claud was talking with Charles like he had something important to say."

"Of course, under the circumstances, you couldn't make out what it was."

"No, sir."

"What happened then?"

"The questions lasted a few minutes—then Claud led Charles away from the door, and I went off to school."

"Thank you, Jeanne. This has been a hard day, I know, for you."

"I only want to help, sir."

"I'm sure you do. And it would help us all if you would answer one more question that must be on everyone's mind."

"If I can, Monsieur de Batz."

"Why, on Thursday and Friday, when Christine and Philip Plantard and everyone in Rennes-les-Bains was desperate to find little Charles, did you not come forward with what you had witnessed?"

Before answering, Jeanne took time to make a detailed study of the far wall of the courtroom. When she spoke, her words came as straight and even as the teeth that cut them off at her lips. "I did not hear about little Charles until after dark on Thursday when I came back from school—and what I heard was only in bits and pieces. I did not even connect Claud to the disappearance."

"And why was that?"

"Because he is my cousin. I have known him too long to think he would be tied up in the disappearance of little Charles."

"That seems natural to me. But what do you believe now?"

"Objection!" Arrends groaned.

This time the judge obeyed his heart rather than the rules. "The witness has worked too hard to stop her now," he mumbled into the billowing sleeve of his gown as his right arm shot up—then tapped his gravel lightly against its cradle. "Overruled."

Oblivious to Mathieu's faux pas, Jeanne gave her questioner a long, dramatically bewildered look, one she believed would fill the evening screens in a million homes. "I don't know what to think any more. He must be capable—of things—if he wrote those messages. I only know what I saw. I just want to help." Everyone, she sensed, could tell that she was about to cry.

"Thank you, little Jeanne. You have been—extremely helpful." With a glow of accomplishment, Monsieur de Batz faced the president of the court. "That is all, Your Honor."

The girl wanted him to face her, but he did not.

xvii

Monsieur Arrends was almost as gentle with Jeanne as de Batz had been. He realized, Anthi, that Jeanne's story had already sealed the fate of his client. He knew that the talk in the street for weeks now had condemned the author of the vengeful messages—rumors ricocheting from bar to bar had proclaimed Claud Plantard an animal that deserved to die. A seasoned attorney, Arrends realized there simply was no way he could muster sympathy for a child murderer. Claud might as well have been a collaborator from the old Vichy regime. Who was there that a defense attorney could call to the stand to express, or even feel, compassion for a criminal charged with a crime like the one Claud stood accused of committing? Claud's advocate could conceive of no angle he could use to discredit little Jeanne. Even the weak point in her testimony—that she had not come forward until after the handwriting experts implicated his client—only drew sympathy to her as a young woman who still possessed strong family loyalties.

Rather than risk what little respect he and his client could anticipate from the frightened, well-meaning jurors in the streets, Arrends decided to ask little Jeanne only one or two polite questions. Afterwards, he threw poor doomed Claud upon the mercy of the judge, a cherub-faced young man who certainly would not harden his heart now, no matter how responsive he might be to the will of the mob.

"Guilty, Your Honor," the verdict came back. Exactly as Arrends expected.

The papers immediately clamored for the maximum punishment: "How can we be certain that innocent children will not be drawn again and again into the unconscionable hatreds and jealousies of adults if criminals like this are not shown the full wrath of the *nation*!" After seeing the papers, Arrends encouraged Claud Plantard to pray that the man now called "le petit juge" would not feel intimidated.

Suddenly, the day after the verdict, the miracle occurred. Arrends was swimming through the great cloud of gloom that had filled his home when all at once he saw "little Jeanne" on his television, but this time weeping, and saying things he could not have imagined.

"I only wanted to help. But I can't let him die because of me. I believed after the handwriting experts spoke that it must be Claud. I have reasons not to like Claud, but I don't want him to die. He doesn't deserve to die—no matter what he did. I lied because I wanted to help Charles's parents. I never saw him in that house. I never saw him that day with little Charles. I never saw anything!"

While Arrends, like all of France, stared, a captive audience frozen before the icy screen, Jeanne buried her sobs in those womanlike hands. Then she peered deep into the heart of the dark circuitry: "Please forgive me! Please forgive me! You shouldn't have asked me!"

As soon as the childlike face disappeared and Arrends was able to tear himself from the surface that had absorbed him, he reached for his phone, not knowing whom to dial first—the judge, Claud's wife, or the prison—thinking only the simple, clear thought: "We will call for a mistrial, a lovely, sweet, irresistible mistrial!"

xviii

Jeanne
Pop-Up

When I came out, all of them were screaming.

"Jeanne! Jeanne! You were the star, Jeanne. What is it like? Is it what you wanted?"

If I was the star, why were they screaming? A star is someone you respect.

"I don't know—" I said.

"What'd she say?" They were growling now. They looked so hungry they scared me. When the two policemen broke through to me, I followed them out of fear. When people grab at you like they could eat you, I don't want to talk to them. Not even television people.

And at home, father was sitting at the kitchen table, scowling. The way he did the first night I stayed out late. If he'd known I was with Claud, he would have killed me.

This time I had nothing to hide. "I was with the gendarmes, Papa."

"I know where you were," he said. "Everybody knows."

"I didn't have anything to say to the television. I didn't think they would—"

"You found plenty to say to the court, didn't you? Apparently you like the police better than newspeople—"

He never lets me finish what I need to say. I tried to explain: "I wanted to—"

"—or your own family."

"What—" He's so unfair.

"You heard me, you little—"

"If he is the—"

"He is still your family—you should—"

"He's a Plantard, not a—"

"Don't you interrupt me, you turncoat!" I didn't know what he was calling me. But the way he said it told me enough. "My *sister* is his *mother*. You betrayed your own—" His face was scorched with so much anger I don't think he even saw me—his own daughter. They meant more to him.

"I wanted to—"

"Get up to your room, damn you. And don't move until I come."

My room was dark, but I couldn't open the shutters. If I hadn't seen Charles across the river, none of this would have happened. I lay across the bed and prayed it would end—that I would never see any of them again. Even if I had to go blind.

A rough edge on the curve inside my cheek began bothering me. I sucked it between my teeth and tried to bite it even. What I tasted was blood.

Below, I could hear father answer the phone. I hoped it was only the clerk at his bookstore, or mother calling from the bakery.

After a minute, though, he came up and stood in the light at the door. He had on his red hunting jacket.

"Get up. We have to meet someone."

I knew better than to ask questions. He threw me my ski jacket. I got up and followed....

At the main road he turned right, toward Arques—toward the sea. I was too scared to think. I saw the stone tomb, the old chateau with the dungeon. He kept going east, headed toward the sea: the wrong direction for winter. He wants to hide me.... He might as well drown me—

In front of the new chateau he turned left, and something bright switched on in my mind: He is taking me to Phillipe Marcel. Phillipe saw me on television. He wants me in one of his films. I remembered renting Phillipe's horses from the stables and riding with Claud into the hills. It was July, and the wheat was so golden I could hear it popping as it ripened. Even above the hooves. I told Claud, but he didn't hear. Up there, we were alone, no one to see us.

After Phillipe's chateau, father made the first short turn and drove into the alleyway dividing the rows of shops and connected houses. We are going to Uncl'Erre's, I told myself. Then it came to me: He is *Claud's* father.

Before I could get out, Uncl'Erre was standing in the basement door. I knew he wouldn't hurt me, no matter what. Uncl'Erre makes me feel good. His head comes up to my chin; his face is red, and his belly is always popping out of his workshirts, like an elf.

This time he wasn't smiling. He gave father his hand: "Etienne."

"Get in, Pierre," father barked.

Uncl'Erre nodded in my direction: "Jeanne." Still he didn't smile.

"Uncl'Erre." I crawled into the backseat.

"One minute. I have to get something," he said, and vanished into the kitchen, the one room in the house where he had lived since his wife left. When I played in there, it was the best room in the world. Because he told me stories. Or I would see Claud. Under the sideboard, with his mining tools and Claud, was my favorite spot. Until Uncl'Erre was caught at Rennes-le-Chateau, dynamiting. Then mother said it wasn't safe with the tools. I never knew why he was using dynamite near the church, unless he was looking for the treasure from his stories about the chapel.

He came back wearing a green field jacket and carrying a crumpled piece of cardboard. It looked like the inside of a roll of bathroom tissue.

As soon as he was settled beside Father, he reached the cardboard over his shoulder. "This is all he could find to write on." He shrugged his shoulders. "More than we had." I knew where he meant: in Russia—when he was a prisoner during the war. "It is for you, little one." He thrust it toward me.

I pulled away, afraid of it. Father backed from the alleyway to the square and turned the car toward Couiza, or home.

"I don't know what it says," Uncl'Erre said. "It's a message he made me promise to bring."

"I've got nothing to say to him." We both knew we were talking about Claud.

"It's what he wants to say. I promised."

"Uncl'Erre—" I begged, but took the spool.

"Read it, girl," father growled over his shoulder.

I unfolded the spiral, taking only a segment at a time: "—never meant to hurt you." Then: "Listen to the Order." And back to the first part: "Why did you do it? I never—" Without going over the rest again, I threw the message on the seat beside me.

"What did he say?" father asked.

I ignored him. "What's the Order?" I asked Uncl'Erre.

He turned to Father. I could see the questions in his eyes. Father looked at him.

"Are you going to tell her?" Father asked.

"It is between her and Monsieur Charles," Uncl'Erre said.

"Charles? What Charles?" I sobbed. But neither of them seemed to hear.

"I am just driving," Father said, his eyes on the road now as we passed the old dungeon again. "I am not sure I need to get—pulled into this Order business."

"Who will she obey?"

"I see what you mean," Father answered.

"That's it, then," Uncl'Erre said.

I tried to figure what they were talking about—at least where they were taking me. In case I had to get back by myself.

As long as they weren't heading toward the sea, we would stay on familiar ground. I thought about my other problems: Claud … and the Order, whatever it was. Claud had mentioned the Order once: "They are people who are trying to help the Plantards." "The Order?" "What Order? Forget I mentioned it."

We were standing in the den in his new house, surrounded by all that glass and those bright yellow bricks. So up-to-date it made my mouth water every time I went to babysit. Claud had come in from the patio, where Stephen and little Charles were riding tricycles. He caught me going through the mail on his desk.

"This seal—what does it mean?" I was waving a beige envelope with a gold crest in its corner. There was no return address, just Claud's number, the gold crown set on a plant, and two egg-like disks. I had pulled the envelope out of the pile because of the disks, which were raised so they seemed to leap off the beige surface. On one, three birds were standing; on the other, there was a six-pointed star I remembered from a book we read in school about a girl in the Low Countries during the war.

I heard Claud cross to where I was standing with my back to him. His arm circled my shoulder and pulled me against his stomach. I felt his brick-rough hand go in my collar and take my breast. It still felt too good for me to pull away.

For a second I let him study the letter. Then I went stiff—and nodded at the door to the kitchen. "Watch it, love. They may come in the back." All at once I fell back, safe, into the gentle pressures of his body.

"It's from some people I know in the North," I felt him whisper through my hair.

"Men, or women?" I had turned to give him my lips but stopped to ask my question.

"Men—" he said.

He added, "mostly," so gently that I decided not to hear. I

reached my free hand behind his head and brought his mouth to mine.

"God—you are a *hungry* kitten, aren't you," he bubbled, when I had had enough to let him speak.

"What'd you expect? Isn't it what you wanted?" Sometimes I did not understand him at all. It was what I wanted, what I had never gotten enough of. Not from Augustin or other boys I had gone off with—until I told them what to do. Mostly they just talked—about braces or mopeds. "If it isn't, you shouldn't have started me—"

For two weeks we had been acting like this every time we found ourselves alone. Every time I came to sit with Stephen. Every evening he drove me home after dark. Afternoons after school when he picked me up in Couiza. In another week we would become lovers, the most natural thing, I believe, I have ever done. What was unnatural was putting on a sullen schoolgirl face to match his bossy grown-up voice the second Jacqueline stepped in the house. Or having to pull away from him every time I heard Stephen coming, the way I had to do that second in his den.

"What do they do?"

"Who?" He crossed to the cabinet where Jacqueline hid the liquor.

"Your friends in the North." I went over to the chair to pick up my coat and book bag.

"They are people trying to help the Plantards." He poured a half glass of pastis and went to the kitchen for ice. I crossed behind him on my way out the backdoor. His mind seemed someplace else—probably because she was due home. I hated bumping into Jacqueline. But he seemed hungrier to have me when there was a chance she would get back before I left.

"How?" I asked.

"Who?"

"The Order."

"What Order?" He looked off in the direction of Stephen and Charles in the kitchen. They were spreading butter and preserves on bread from the basket I had left on the table. "Forget I ever mentioned it," he said.

And I let the Order slip from my mind. Never thought of it again. Until now. I tried to fold my body into the contour of the car seat, the way I had melted against Claud. But father's bullying me left me too nervous. All of it did: the trial, the questionings, the judge, and the cameras. I had too many things on my mind to melt. If I did, I was afraid I would get so small I would slip through the crack in the seat. I chewed the inside of my mouth again. When I was with Claud my mind was filled with him and me. It was like testifying—or talking to the cameras: I felt as big as both of us. I could melt all the way into his skin without falling. With Claud there hadn't been space for troubles like the Order. Now I wished I had asked him again. Maybe I would have an idea where I was going.

Father drove past the old tomb and turned almost immediately onto an unpaved road that climbed the hill into the woods.

After a kilometer or so of winter ruts, he drove into a clearing. I could look out over the countryside to—I must have looked through the Col du Paradis. I saw the lake where Claud took me sailing and then to lunch. Afterwards, in the auberge by the lake we— No, I didn't want to think about that. Or the road after the Col, where it turned south toward Perpignan, the beach at St. Cyprien.

Uncl'Erre told father to stop at a gate—wide enough for three cars. Uncl'Erre hopped out and went to talk into a phone set in one of the stone posts. A noise said something, and he swung the gate open. The road improved. It was like a road in an American movie, winding upward through the woods and pastures. There were high rail fences along the road, and they led us to an opening covered by tall oaks. A villa stood in the grove; it was white stucco, with a red roof and shutters. Beside it, I saw an old grey stable. The villa was new.

"Claud's work," my uncle said. I could tell he was proud, and angry.

It was the nicest new house I have ever seen, almost as large as the old buildings in les-Bains. It was more impressive even than Claud's house. It was French all the way through. It made Claud's look too modern, like something in too many movie. I didn't know that people around here could live in places like this—except Phillipe Marcel. But he's a movie star.

"Whose is it?" I asked.

"You'll see," father barked, and cut the motor.

"It won't be long now, little one," Uncl'Erre said. He was always nicer than father. Then, he surprised me: "Wait in the car, Jeanne, please. One of us will come back for you."

"Don't try to run away," Father snarled. Both of them were getting out. "There's no place here the dogs couldn't find you."

"Dogs?" The bully knows what scares me. When I was five I tried to feed a tourist's poodle. It nearly snapped my hand off. He just watched.

"Don't be afraid, my child," Uncl'Erre whispered to me through the crack in the window. "The dogs are always under control. It will only be a minute."

They moved across the yard to the double doors, and I fought the temptation to follow, or to get away before they came back. I looked for signs of the animals, and I decided they must stay in the stable. I wouldn't stand a chance. Either way I went, they would be on me in a second. I wished I had never met anybody connected with little Charles.... Except Claud. I did not regret a minute I had spent with him. Not a second. Not one. And they all thought I hated him—just because I had spoken up. Maybe I don't understand. It wasn't times we were together that made me want to hurt him. Not really hurt him. Just want to tell him how much I hate *some* of the things he said—about his women. And hate what I saw. At the beach.

The villa door opened. My heart went crazy: it was Father coming back.

Before he could get the car door open, I was asking questions: "Where's Uncl'Erre? Isn't he coming back with us?"

"Out of there, girl," he ordered. "They are prepared now."

"For me?" I didn't move. I couldn't.

"Out, damn you!" He took my arm and yanked me toward the driver's door. If my muscles hadn't acted on their own, from deeper than my fear, he would have pulled me out on my face.

He shoved me along like I was a heavy chair, and he was pushing me over the carpet. I listened for the dogs. Where were they?

The carved door to the house was still open a crack. He pushed me up against it and on into the marbled lobby. I saw the stone steps that curved once on their way to the second floor. They looked lovely. But he pushed me away from the steps toward the large door on the left. I waited there, thinking about the dogs still, while he turned the latch, then shoved me into a large room. It was a study, with light from outside leaking through the shutters. Before my eyes adjusted, I saw something that stopped my breath.

There were two white shapes, one of them tall and stiff.

Then I realized they were men, wearing robes and hoods made out of silk. There was a table with one candle between me and them. The only thing alive in all that white was their eyes. Through the slits I could see the eyes, wet, glowing like an animal's. I had seen robes like these before. In a movie about a town in America where men in robes frightened black people. I hated those men. And here they were, ready to hurt me.

From nowhere, a chair appeared on my side of the table, then two more on the other. The robed shapes started to sit down.

"Have a seat," a voice said. I realized it came from the smaller man. It was Uncl'Erre. I obeyed. I noticed the carving in the top of the table. It was a large crown and disks like the seal that had caught my eye in Claud's den. This is the Order, I said to myself. I looked for other signs. There were pictures on the walls but not enough light for me to make them out. I saw a cabinet in the far corner, but I couldn't make out the carving on the doors.

"We did not wish to frighten you, young woman," the tall man said. His bony hands slipped out of the large cuffs and lifted the hood. "Your father believed our requests would carry more weight—if we wore our—this attire." His face was long and bony, and it was foreign to my memory. Yet familiar, as though I had seen it in a dream. I remember his ears, which hooked like bat wings, and the thin lips, which he kept pressed tight like a sewed up wound. The pain in his eyes cut into me until I shrank in my seat.

Uncl'Erre had also raised his hood. "Jeanne, my child, this is Monsieur Plantard," he said. "Charles Plantard." He nodded with respect.

"Charles?" I stared at the stranger and searched his face for a clue. "You must be *his*—" I said, but no word seemed to fit.

"Little Charles?" the pressed lips said. "He was another branch—too distant to explain."

"But me—why?" My chest wanted to cry, to soften the edge in his eyes. I forced the need down into my arms and my legs.

"We know nothing about the boy," he said, and turned his burning eyes to something above my head. "It is Claud who concerns us."

"Claud," I echoed, feeling he had hit on something I *could* understand.

"We must save Claud from—from this shame," he said, and Uncl'Erre nodded again. In the dark between me and the door, I heard my father grunt his agreement. "You have condemned him to his death. The family can't—"

"Death? Death?" Suddenly there was so much weight on my chest that it seemed to explode. I thought there was no death penalty, but I realized what he meant. "I only told what—" I began. But for the first time what I had done broke through the floor I had built over it. All my tears rose up and swallowed the words: "I loved— him," I heard myself groan. "He shouldn't have—"

When I could see again, I realized that neither man was looking at me. They were staring at the seal in the tabletop.

The stranger did not speak; he was waiting for me to finish with my grief. "Uncl'Erre told me he built your house," I said, with no sense of what I meant.

"He does good work."

"He never mentioned a house he had built for a Plantard." I wiped the tears away with the sleeve of my jacket.

"I am usually in Ly—in Paris," he said, and his voice, if not his eyes, felt less cutting. "We must not talk about Claud's past— We care nothing about what may or may not have happened between you two. It is his future that is in danger."

"I didn't know they would—" The tears started again.

"We want you to reconsider—" I felt his eyes searching mine. There was a human warmth now. "What did you *actually* see that morning? For the good of Claud—"

"I saw—I saw Charles—at the Marti house." What did he want me to say? Why did I have to guess? All he had to do was tell me.

"And Claud?"

I didn't know what to answer. The stranger just stared and waited.

The noise his chair made pushing back from the table made me jump. "It is not only Claud whom you have placed in danger, girl—" He stood and lifted the candle from the table. He waved it toward the pictures along the wall. They were portraits. "It is the Plantard name," he added. "The entire Plantard line."

With the candle in the air I could see ten or twelve portraits. Men and women who seemed to grow into kings and queens as I looked down the wall. The pictures stretched back in time. By the time he put the candle back on the table, I had seen at least one woman dressed like a queen, two or three men in crowns, one of them with long, stringy hair. At the other end, someone with a dark beard who looked like a saint.

"Plantards were the ancient counts of the Razes," he said. "They have a *place* in the history of the nation."

"But I *saw* Claud at the house—" I said, trying to argue him down. His words carried a passion I knew I must not confuse with meaning.

"*That* morning?" His voice sounded firmer than my own.

I didn't like answering his questions any more. He wasn't treating me the way the captain, or Monsieur de Batz, had. I wasn't sure I wanted to answer him at all. He was beginning to sound like Father. And I was starting to slip through the back of the chair. With Father I always end up getting smaller, and then I give in. "I saw *some*one—" I heard my voice. I told myself I mustn't whine.

"Was it Claud?" he barked at me, exactly like Father. "It is the Plantards you are trying to ruin. We cannot allow you—"

"It is France, you little—" Father said, and checked himself in front of the stranger. "Your own flesh and blood."

"And a man's life, my girl," Uncl'Erre pleaded. I knew he could have said it was *his* son.

"What can I—" I said, before the tears made it impossible to talk. Except to myself: *He shouldn't have. He just shouldn't.* I was remembering the look in his eyes on the beach. St. Cyprien, where he owned an apartment in a building he had built. I remembered the beach. What could I do? "What—" I said out loud.

"My dear Jeanne," the stranger said. All at once he was as gentle as Monsieur de Batz. "You have decided to reconsider. I am so relieved. I know a gentleman from Paris—a reporter who is still in Couiza. He will arrange a conference tonight with the cameras. You will have an opportunity to explain the gap in your account. It will take only a minute, and then all this will be over."

He explained the arrangements—I wasn't listening. I was thinking of Claud and the beach, and of why I couldn't hold out any longer. He had invited all of us for Sunday. We took both cars from les-Bains. I squeezed in with Philip and Christine and Charles—in the back with the dear little boy. I didn't want to ride with Jacqueline. Claud tried to get me to…. On the beach when I took off my top, all of them stared at me. I saw the light in his eyes. He was proud of me, I could tell. I knew I looked good to all of them. Even the little boys—though they were too bashful to stare, and threw sand at me. I could see Christine knew…. And afterwards, he swam out to the raft with her! They lay there, too close. I think he kissed her. I saw the look in their eyes when they came back. They couldn't hide it. Neither of them could. The next day when he picked me up, I couldn't keep from saying it: "I *saw* you with that woman!" "What woman?" "Monsieur Philip's wife, you toad!" "Christine?" "I saw you." "You little fool! I loved Christine when I was ten. She's ancient history." "I don't think it's that ancient." "Don't worry about it. You make her look like an *old* woman." "She's only—" "Forget her, you little pie, and come here." I slipped into his arms. But I didn't believe him, not really…. My fear grew from that first suspicion. My mind poisoned itself until—until I was ready to do anything to pay him back. Even if I was wrong about Christine, there were others, weren't there? There were things he said, little insinuations to make me think I might lose him—to keep me on my toes. To let me know I wasn't the only— The only what? *The only sex pie in les-Rennes*, he said…. When I thought of the raft, I hated him—and loved him—hated him while I loved him. Because I loved him. I wanted him blotted out—gone forever…. But not dead. I never wanted *all* of him dead. I never meant to do that.

I let Uncl'Erre lead me back to the car. I thought of the cameras I was going to face again. They were like Claud now. I no longer wanted to feel them caressing my skin. I could already see them staring at me the way Father does.... I turned and found him glaring: *I told your mother you were a born liar!* his eyes said. His curse.

I had let them force me. Father, the stranger, even Uncl'Erre. They had me workable as Mama's dough. After facing them, cameras were almost a comfort. Not a lover anymore. But like turning to the sun of an old friend's face—a friend who is angry, but still a friend.... So I let go of all the tears I hadn't used on the stranger.

"I don't want him to die...." I wept into that tiny red light and the large eye. They drew me and everything else into the darkness inside. They rolled all of us up into one thing, a ball of dough. France loved me again. "Why does it have to fall on my shoulders," I cried. "I can't handle it."

I was too exhausted to stay up and watch. I missed all the reports. It isn't like feeling drained after making love with Claud. But making love comes closest. Something has finished, and all I can do is think about it. My emptiness is their fault, the reporters'—and Father's, for making me face his friends.

What can I do? Shuffle across these old floors in my slippers and robe, that's all. There's no place to go now—nobody I want to see. Not ever. Everybody knows now what a fool I made of myself. Everybody in France saw it "live." Everybody except me.

xix

Anthi_cwaters
To: mdwaters@urtoo.com
Re: Not exactly a pop-up

Dad,
Aspiring Minds Want to Try.
If you don't mind my popping up, I'd like to try. Would this help round out your intriguing Jeanne episode?

Set on catching the late news, Jeanne attached herself to the television. It would help, she felt, to watch rerun reports and see exactly what she did. Aside from this, she felt completely flat. She chewed at her fingers.

In time, she dozed, only half-asleep, an ear out for the news readers, her robe pulled close to her chin against the cold that seemed everywhere now. Each time the sound rose ... She woke ...

She opened her eyes: a girl who looked something like her was staring back. She leaned forward from the edge of her chair, impatient to blend into that face and become it. Tears burst from the other girl's eyes, coursed down her cheeks. Her face twisted, showed her pain, her remorse. Why does it have to fall on my shoulders? *she said.* I know what you feel, *Jeanne whispered.*

But the girl looked ugly—and old. Like an old woman. The picture went crazy, the face swollen, deathly orange, her hair bleached yellow, eyes wild and green, mouth a blackened open nought.

That's not me, she told herself. She can't be.

She gnawed her finger, searching for the quick—for a pain deep enough to be her.

xx

mdwaters
to: anthi_cwaters@ezrite.com
re: Excellent!

Well done, Daughter. Your invention hit the nail dead on the head. Of course, the girl on the screen was Jeanne! You've got the idea now. Keep 'em coming—whenever the spirit moves you, so to speak.

Anthi_cwaters
To: mdwaters@urtoo.com
Re: Thanks!

So to speak, is right, Dad. Mostly I used the things you gave me. The details. The robe. The chewing. The self-absorption. But you are right. There was a flashpoint when I realized something about her that wasn't in your *Jeanne*. But it didn't last very long. I wish it had. Is it a pop-up? It certainly isn't what you call a full-fledged pop-up, is it?

mdwaters
to: anthi_cwaters@ezrite.com
re: (No subject)

If it arrived in a flash, and was more than you knew before, it must be a pop-up. Just keep it coming, Anthi. It will get stronger— and longer—now that Jeanne is alive for you. And the others, are they breathing too?

Anthi_cwaters
To: mdwaters@urtoo.com
Re: (No subject)

You keep them coming! I'm counting on it. And, yes, the others are "kicking" more and more. Except for Monsieur Charles. He does not seem to be the same thoughtful man Jeanne's Uncl'Erre sent us to speak with in Lyon. Up there, he was at ease with the world, dressed in fresh khakis and a royal-blue ironed shirt, completely relaxed and gracious in his own walled garden.

I recognized the gold crown and plant from the gate to his garden.

mdwaters
to: anthi_cwaters@ezrite.com
re: (No subject)

Remember that when Jeanne met him she was an already frightened teenager who'd been more or less kidnapped by her father and uncle. They dragged her off to a secluded house to face a stranger, a weird man wearing an absurd costume she probably had never seen—except in some violent movie about the American Klan. He would have scared her out of her wits.

Anthi_cwaters
To: mdwaters@urtoo.com
Re: (No subject)

When you put it like that, Dad, you're probably right. Still, it's lucky you bumped into Jeanne's uncle, Uncl'Erre—so that we got another view of Charles Plantard. Where was it you'd gone? It was the morning I felt too fluey to leave the hotel in Rennes-les-Bains. I was coughing and sneezing all over the place.

mdwaters
to: anthi_cwaters@ezrite.com
re: (No subject)

That morning while you rested, I drove over to Arques to see the tomb the black book says Poussin used in his *Et in Arcadia ego* painting, the one we checked on in the Louvre. You remember it? The Order says Poussin borrowed his inscription from the Plantard family motto, and it's part of a secret code. Maybe a clue to the Plantards' buried treasures.

Anthi_cwaters
To: mdwaters@urtoo.com
Re: (question)

What did you decide?

mdwaters
to: anthi_cwaters@ezrite.com
re: (answer)

I have no idea. The tomb's just sitting there, in a pasture, circled by barbwire. The raised vault looks like Poussin's, solid, grey, and silent—but it could be a conventional design. Buried treasures don't interest me all that much.

Anthi_cwaters
To: mdwaters@urtoo.com
Re: (self-interest)

Well, they do me. To keep living in Paris, I can use all the extra money I come across.

mdwaters
to: anthi_cwaters@ezrite.com
re: life vs. fiction

We all could. But in stories, those treasures are just clichés. Did I ever tell you about Jeanne's uncle hitting on me?

Anthi_cwaters
To: mdwaters@urtoo.com
Re: what?

Not really!

mdwaters
to: anthi_cwaters@ezrite.com
re: Really!

We were driving up the hill to Monsieur Charles's villa, and he started telling me his whole story, or most of it, chiefly the part about his being a prisoner of war in a Russian jail—don't ask me why, or which side he was on.

The gravel road we'd taken came to an opening through which we could look out over the trees and hills and pink plowed fields and see halfway to the sea. We got out of the car to take it in, and I said something about how beautiful this countryside was. I don't know what Uncl'Erre *thought* I said, but the little fellow came over and wrapped his arms around my chest and laid his head against my jacket.

Anthi_cwaters
To: mdwaters@urtoo.com
Re: more explanation, please

My God, Dad, what did you do?

mdwaters
to: anthi_cwaters@ezrite.com
re: true confessions

Well, the way he laid his head there—he only came up to my chin—seemed so much like a child hugging a grown-up that I pretended it was all an innocent act, that he was overcome by the beauty and the emotion. I took him by both shoulders the way an officer would a soldier and put him at a distance. "Yes, it is an inspiring scene, Monsieur!" I said, turned, and kept on to the car.

He followed like a puppy.

Anthi_cwaters
To: mdwaters@urtoo.com
Re: congrats

Good for you, Dad! Some guys would have punched him.

mdwaters
to: anthi_cwaters@ezrite.com
re: self-interest

I needed Uncl'Erre's help, girl. He had information about the Plantards. Besides, he was too sweet and harmless to punch. Fat, round, and rosy-faced, he looked like one of Santa's elves. Now, if it had been Jeanne's father ...

Anthi_cwaters
To: mdwaters@urtoo.com
Re: don't stop now

What?

mdwaters
to: anthi_cwaters@ezrite.com
re: More confession

I'd 've beat it out of there running!

Three

Philip
Pop-Up

He pulled the long, cylindrical pillow about his ears like a collar
and pressed his body deeper into the mattress. With Christine away,
he felt no particular urge to stir. Maria, he was sure, had already
prepared *petit dejeuner* for the ten or fifteen newspeople who had
settled in for as long as it took. He could trust Maria to get the
meals—he had promoted her from cook to handling Christine's
responsibilities so he would have more time for their legal problems.
And old Louis would cover the desk. As far as he could tell, or cared,
with these two on hand, the hotel nearly ran itself. He could sleep as
late as his memories and the distress of Claud's release three weeks
before allowed.

If he could call it sleep, lying here on his stomach with the
pillow wrapped around his ears like giant muffs against the voices
that, for almost half a year now, came from every direction. Voices
filled with stories overflowing with murder, motives, rumors. Voices
from neighbors, from newsprint, voices wrapped with multi-colored
rays that bore his own likeness as they shot through the old walls.
Voices of strangers who stopped in the street across the bridge and
leaned there staring at the hotel, mumbling full volume their own
twisted suspicions of what had happened. Voices of the gendarmes
whispering solutions in his ear....

He had tried to block his ears against them all.

And Christine's ears too—against the judge. He was grateful to
have been there for the interrogations. Twice Mathieu, old swollen
eyes in an infant's face, had come to the clinic, taking advantage

of Christine, flat on her back in her delicate condition, to put his insinuations, his confusing mishmash of dates and hours and questions to her. As though she did not already have enough grief to confuse her without Mathieu going over the same ground again and again. Just implying, not really saying anything directly. As though, for some reason, she had been holding information back. She who had loved their son as much as anyone. More, if possible, than I do myself, Philip thought. As much as I love *her*. If anything happened—happens—to her, what will I do? I won't be responsible then. Any more than she is. How can she be? It cannot be right for Mathieu to interrogate her now. That shapeless grizzly hovering over my little pet. I have to be there, to keep her from worrying about what he is trying to do with all his distrust and insinuations. I have to keep him off her back. Off ours. If anything happens to her—

But there was more. For Philip had tried, among so many voices, to find his own. A voice that said, *I think, I know, I want. This is the story I will tell her about the American.* But the others came from everywhere—came so strongly they leaked through his own, like water through— No, not water. Do not think of water, whatever you do!

Like dreams, he thought, finding the word that felt safe, bringing it up in his hand out of darkness. But with it came something else less benign: part of a scene that minutes before had brought him abruptly up out of darkness, and then slipped down again, leaving him stranded with the voices: He is on the patio off the slip into the river. Sweeping dead leaves into the water. Behind him, Christine is cooking a large side of pork, American-style on an open grill someone has left close to the hotel wall. Why this dream? Because he knows builders have leaned old timbers from the roof against the outside walls, timbers tall as the building itself. They will burn; they take fire from Christine's grill. And while he scrambles across the red roof tiles drowning flames with his hose, the villagers and newsmen and the American below him eat their pork and celebrate. What they are celebrating he does not know. But every way he looks, as quickly as he damps one glowing part of the building to charred black, fire breaks out in another. As though she is trying to burn it down. Even so, he knows he will succeed, that he will never let the fire, far easier to put down than voices, get out of hand. His worry: will National Insurance pay again? As though the hotel has already burned one time but he has built it back.

Why this dream—after Christine worked as hard as he did to create a business they could call their own, and would have passed on, when the time came, to little Charles.

These nights when the window is open to the river, I dream too much, he tells himself. The way I dreamed when I worked in that old dump in Montpellier with the overhead fan throbbing all night pumping dreams into my sleep.

Finally, he just sent the dream, and its placental problems, packing. Easier than intruders to block.

And now, foreigners to deal with. Even foreigners. Not many yet, thank God. But one. This American. This crazy American who wants to help. Merde! How they all want to help. They must need to badly. Do I need help so badly? Is that why my pillow leaks? And now this American who came from St. Tropez. Walters, he called himself. Popped up one morning like any tourist. Called from somewhere out on the autoroute to make certain he would find a room. Came marching in an hour later with bags—no way to give him no for an answer—and that young thing in tow he said was his daughter. Ho, ho. Like any tourist, I thought, out for a piece of the Pyrenees, a shot at France. And brought his own young thing along. Taking no chances, this one.... Perhaps she is—his daughter. No way we will ever know, is there? Not since we stopped asking for the passports. What a world.

Had I been smart, I would have sent him back to Carcassonne—

or Narbonne. He looked harmless enough— Or maybe I really
needed to hear what he needed to tell. I imagined it would be a
change to have some tourists again, rather than the news vultures
scavenging for my grief when more and more it is anger I struggle
to feel. Some harmless tourist who had never heard of Charles and
brought none of the impossible sadness with him. Someone I could
talk to about neutral subjects: about the weather, the baths, the
region—the way I always did. How could I have known to be on
guard against— He looked innocent enough: Tropez tan, a beard,
thinning curly hair, matched nylon bags—and his young, young
thing. What a world the Americans live in.... I knew he would be
no match. I could kick his ass out in the riv—the street—any day
of the week. I am no fool. No American is going to take me for a
ride. For half a year I have been manhandling the best dirt-diggers
in France.... Had I known. Had I—

But God, I do know now. And I have to figure out what to tell
Christine—what she will say when I do.... And the problem is, I do
know—what she will say. What will be left for me to do?

"Monsieur— On this map—" The wild-haired stranger was
waving a huge accordion map in the air like a boat sail loose in
a gale. "Would you show me the road to Rennes-le-Chateau?"
What a mixture of signs— Clumsy. A tourist,... and transparently
American. But Rennes-le-Chateau should have alerted me—despite
the billowing map. If I had not been thinking about Christine
stretched out there in the clinic. Anything except my son cold in
the river.

"Rennes-le-Chateau?"

"Yes."

"A lovely village—at the top of the mountain."

"It's not on my map. How do I get there?"

"May I see it, please?" He passed me the runaway sail to fold in.

"Yes. Here. You must go back to Couiza—a dozen kilometers by the road. Turn left. And as you leave the town, you will see the road up on your left—another five, six kilometers. A pleasant drive."

"Do you go there?"

"Yes, I have been—" I found myself staring into the man's quizzical grin—only to dismiss it as another absurd trait of his kind.

"Do you go often?"

"I would not say 'often'— Why?"

"Just curious. If it's such a special place, I thought you—"

"It is historical, but—" I shrugged my shoulders. Americans never understand what history means here.

"We'll see you later, Monsieur Plantard." He grinned again and forced the folds of his map into a clumsy pile as he led his young friend from the reception out to the terrace. For a second, something about the girl's long, golden-brown hair took me back to a little girl who used to drag her doll about the square when I was thirteen. Chrissy would have been five then, pretty as a lily in June with brown wisps of hair and that faraway, serious look on her face. The first time I remember ever seeing her.

That Mr. Walters knew my name should have alerted me to the risk of having him in the hotel. But, as always, Christine, and the rumors, blocked my judgment. I had been dreaming then too. Of the early days together. What she remembered was different. I was eighteen then and playing soccer after gymnasium in the *lycee* grounds. Claud and I were on the same team. We were murdering the other guys. She came to the fence to watch. The prettiest dark eyes I had ever seen. Still are.

At dark, the two of them returned, hungry, obviously exhausted, but inflated by their little outing.

"What a place!" Walters bubbled.

Even his friend, whom I had never heard speak, had exchanged her enigmatic smile for gushes of laughter. "I'm so glad you made me, Dad. I might have missed it!"

"We'd better ask if Monsieur Plantard is still going to let us have dinner."

"The kitchen closes at eight. You have ample time—for an *aperatif.* If you would like, I will send one in to your table."

"Super. We couldn't leave the church until they ran us out," he said as they hurried to the dining room.

The next morning, I caught them leaving the dining room, as though they had spent the night in there. "So you enjoyed the church. A curiosity, is it not?"

"You have studied it?"

"There are so many rumors about the place—"

"The gold, you mean?"

"The gold, of course," I said. "And the curé who designed it—"

"Sauniere?"

"Sauniere—yes." Now it was my turn to offer a quizzical look. "You do know a bit about the place?"

"Sauniere was working for Abbé Boudet, defender of the Celtic language, wasn't he?"

"So they say." I had no desire to get caught up in the stranger's enthusiasm, which seemed now to border on mania.

"Have you studied Boudet's theories?" he asked.

"I am something of a local historian, if I do say so.... How do you know—"

"Good to hear that." You would have thought Walters had just uncorked a superior champagne.

"Actually, my wife has connections to Boudet," I volunteered.

"It's the same 'Boudet'?"

"You *have* seen the papers then?"

"Could hardly miss them, could we?" He flashed that cocky grin again.

"In America too?"

"Not there. We've been in France a month. Not a great deal to do at Les Issambres in March except read."

"So, while you are sitting at the cafes taking the sun, you amuse yourselves with the daily reversals in the story of little Charles and his village?"

"Please—" the man sputtered, clearly embarrassed. "We're not scavengers. We don't just pick the—"

"No, no. I did not mean to sound bitter. I am simply trying to state the facts. I know, it falls in your lap—all you have to do is open a newspaper."

"Must be difficult for you." His smile was gone now.

"Impossible. My hotel is taken over by journalists. They are after us day and night."

"Look, Monsieur Plantard, my daughter and I were interested in the area before we saw the papers—before we came to France."

"Boudet's gold?" I asked.

"*Better* than gold."

I looked for the light in the man's eye, but he was in dead earnest. "What is better than gold?" I asked. My major mistake.

"May I show you something?" He had begun rummaging through the blue duffel bag he carried slung over his gray jacket and came up with a thick black paperback with worn edges and thirty or forty dog-eared pages. I couldn't catch the title but assumed it was in English. "This, I guarantee, you'll find interesting," he added.

I was eager, I suppose, for anything to take my mind away from Christine, Charles, Claud—away from everything connected with grief. Another devotee of the Rennes, like myself, seemed a promising distraction, the most pleasant since October.

"Soaking up the sun in Les Issambres and reading this little book, I began, very naturally I think, to believe that our bodies are our grails. Especially with half a dozen lovely women from Brussels and Amsterdam stretched out on beach lounges taking the sun in, wearing as near to nothing as March permits. Lovely brown holy grails they were too. And bearing, no doubt about it, the *sang real* of good health itself coursing through those faint blue channels I could barely make out, without staring, you understand, under the creamy parts of their bodies.... Excuse me if I wax Irish, but the memory inspires me."

"So it is Montsegur that brings you here, where they say the Grail disappeared?"

"Montsegur, the Cathars' fortress, yes. Do you believe they had it?" He stared dead at me, as though searching for some sign in my eyes. "But something else as well—even closer than Montsegur."

"Closer?"

Then he did a strange thing. He laid the black book on the bar beside the cash register, reached into his rear pants pocket, and showed me a small wallet of travelers' checks. "I have a fifty-dollar check in here, Monsieur Plantard. I'll make a little wager with you, and the check will be yours if what I want to show you doesn't prove worth your time."

I stared back just as intensely. Did he think I was Faust or something? The man did not appear insane. "What do I have to do?"

"Simply come with us to Rennes-le-Chateau for a couple of hours. Look at what I have to show you."

"That is all?"

"Absolutely."

"And the hotel?"

"With the legal chaos you've had to deal with, am I wrong to imagine you've found good assistants?"

"If Christine or the lawyers should call?"

"Leave a message. There's got to be a phone at the church—in a shop or something."

Wary but curious, I stopped finding excuses. Even flat on her back, Christine has the presence to command nurses. They would look after her. *Everyone* wants to help the mother of little Charles. And the judge promised he will not return for at least two days. She does not need me every minute. "You have a deal: if what you show me is not worth my time, the travelers' check is mine. That is it?"

"Exactly."

I found old Louis, gave him instructions, told him my plans, and came back up here for my jacket. I stopped beside Christine's bed to daydream for a second: of times she would whisper me to come over—of how infrequent, and precious, they have become. And now she is away, and no one has a realistic guess when she will return from the clinic. But as long as the pregnancy goes better, and she stays out of reach of reporters— Nothing I can do but love her. Without her, and Charles, I do not exist.

Back downstairs, the American led me up the footbridge to the street and his little red Renault Cinq. His daughter (I finally caught the odd name: Anthi) squeezed into the back with their books and maps, and I took the front passenger's seat. Surrounded by books, she reminded me again of Christine at the *lycee* fence clutching her own little book bag....

Like this, our expedition into derangement began.

xxii

Anthi_cwaters
To: mdwaters@urtoo.com
Re: surprised

So, it's really you and me, is it? I can hardly believe it. Especially the way you picture yourself.

The portrait of me is, if anything, too flattering. I seem more mature than I was.

But why do you make yourself out to be such a clown, dad?

mdwaters
to: anthi_cwaters@ezrite.com
re: the way I figure

You *looked* mature. Remember the evening in Paris near the end of our trip when we met Paolo at a restaurant in Les Halles, the way the waiters hanging out at some of the joints to snag tourists would stare at the two of us—you had your black jeans and shirt and the beret I bought you—and they would rub their index fingers together to say I was a dirty old man to be out with a woman so young. We thought they were funny, but maybe they weren't kidding. Anyway, I'm going to use this mistaken maturity later, but for a more intelligent purpose.

About the clown: I'm doing all I can to give Philip and his "French" perspective as much authority as possible. You and I can't disappear from the events in which we played our regrettable roles. But Philip has to have his say—and have it with as much dramatic force as you and I inadvertently acquire simply by becoming storytellers. In every sense, *he* must tell his story. To which end, I will now vanish back into....

xxiii

Philip
Pop-Up

For an obsessed man, Walters handled the curves down from the village through the oaks along the river with sufficient restraint to lay my anxieties to rest. When we passed the bridge, he was considerate enough not to mention it, and I looked away.

"How's that wine?" he asked at the corner of our turn to Couiza, and motioned right, across the bare asphalt, toward Duval's Cave and its dilapidated shack.

"Blanquette?" His question seemed so normal it took me by surprise. "It is a bubbly wine, very fruity. Delicious, if you do not drink too much. Duval's price cannot be matched."

"Remind me on the way back, Anthi. I'll buy a bottle for dinner."

"If you'll remember Monsieur Plantard's warning," she said. "You don't need to go wobbling off down these streets."

She can talk! I told myself. And French too. Better than her father's.

"Can't imagine safer streets for wobbling."

"It's what France does to him, Monsieur Plantard."

"That—and the excitement of this mystery," Walters said. "It churns up the juices. Generates all kinds of energy.... You know what's up that road?" He nodded under the visor to the turn up the rugged grey rock of the mountain out our right windows.

"The stables are up— No, we have passed Caussagne. Coustaussa is up this one—only an ancient chateau. The twelfth century, as I recall. Nothing but the walls standing now. Simon de Montfort tore it down when the Inquisition marched through cleaning out the Cathars. Not much remains to see."

"Nothing about Curé Gelis?" he asked.

"Only that he was murdered in his vestry."

"All Saint's Day, 1897. Right in the middle of the Sauniere period. Gelis knew many of the secrets of the Rennes. His murderer was never found."

"What Sauniere period?" Monsieur Walters was more bewitched than I imagined.

"I mentioned him yesterday."

"Yes, the parish priest. But I have never heard of a 'Sauniere period'."

"My label," he said. "It's his church we are going to visit—he rebuilt it to Boudet's plans. You don't get the connection?"

"Afraid not."

"You have no idea what the Abbé Berenger Sauniere has to do with the Plantards?"

"Not very much," I said, not to show my ignorance. I watched fields plowed for wheat and oats going by on my left. Knowing they were growing greener by the hour promised a modicum of relief from the grief the shadows of my village held.

"Thought not.... Look, I'm going to tell you a story now that's going to spin your head around. Just sit back. I don't want you getting whiplashed."

"Whiplashed?"

"Never mind. Just listen, if you will."

Even though I followed his advice, I wasn't prepared for what this overwrought American proceeded to ask me to believe—and I would have dismissed it as total insanity, except that it made sense of so many family legends and hand-me-down tales, so many bits and pieces of gossip I had heard all my life. Even so, if I had suspected where he was leading me, I would have shut my ears like one of Odysseus's sailors, or, better still, I would have jumped immediately out of his automobile. The best I could manage was to stare at the large grey boulders out my own window and hope we came to the end of them—and the end of his story.

He did not begin by simply *announcing* he would tell me things about my son's murder that I never suspected. Had he done that I could have taken shelter in skepticism—shut my mind if not my ears. He was too cunning for a direct approach. He never gave me a chance. He began someplace in the past—and started circling, back and forth, weaving a web around Rennes-le-Chateau, drawing me piece by piece into the net of its history, the madness of his story. And once he had started, I was very nearly hypnotized.

"Boudet may have had one idea when he gave Sauniere the plans for redoing the church and the francs to start renovations, but before Sauniere finished there's every reason to believe he'd changed his plans. Or lifted them to another level. At first he was probably thinking about the local gold. But soon he had his mind on something else altogether. Because one of the first things that happened when Sauniere and his henchmen began moving things around in the rundown old church, this would have been about 1891, was that in lifting the altar stone they came across two crumbling Visigoth columns going back to the sixth or seventh century, and discovered one of the columns was hollow."

"How do you know this?"

"It's in that black book I showed you."

"You believe it?"

"Wait and see."

"If you will keep *your* eyes on the road." Although we had come into the outskirts of Couiza, he had failed to slow the car. His driving and what he had begun telling me had me so worked up that I did not think about Christine until we had passed the clinic. Now I wondered whether she had had her breakfast yet. The nurses, I hoped, had not wakened her too early. She needs her rest.

"I don't understand much about the Visigoths," Walters was saying now, "but they go pretty far back. Maybe you've studied them?"

"I have read a little."

"So has Anthi. But I'd love to hear the French side."

"Unfortunately, there is too much to say. It depends on whose point of view you take. The Romans considered them barbarians." For the next few minutes I lectured them on the swath the tribe made on their slow, steady sweep from the Baltic Sea through Russia to the Pyrenees. "They defeated the Romans at Adrianopolis—eastern Greece—just before 380."

"We're talking BC now?" he asked lamely.

"AD." After that little confession of ignorance I felt surer of myself: I could handle Monsieur Walters. I grew eloquent as I carried the Visigoths through the Balkans, the sack of Delphi, the invasions of Italy, to Rome itself. "Alaric was their chieftain. Barbarian he may have been, but he out-negotiated the Romans, and for three days his people sacked the greatest city on earth. That brings us down to 410—AD. After Alaric died, they fell over the Alps into this region, and on into Spain."

"How long'd they run things down here?" he asked.

"Oh, a hundred years or so. The domain was called Aquitaine—the center was Toulouse."

"You really know this stuff, don't you?"

"It is my hobby."

"Why?"

"My reasons are—personal."

"Family interest?"

"One might call it that."

"Thought so." He blessed me with another of his enigmatic grins. I thought of Christine taking her sedative, the look on her face afterwards. "So what came of the Visigoths?"

Before I could answer, the girl broke in from the back: "They ran into the Merovechs, and other German tribes called the Franks coming in from due North."

"That's Merovingians, sweet?"

"Exactly.… The Merovechs gave them a lot of trouble." We both listened as she recited her own studies of the way that Clovis, the great Merovingian, drove off the Allamanni and captured Burgundy, before he crushed the Visigoths between les-Rennes and Paris. "That was 507, an important year for France."

"The Merovingians—how much you know about them?" her father asked, trying, I guess, to keep me in his web. "That's the bunch I want to talk to you about."

"What is there to know? I recall that after Clovis they failed to accomplish a great deal."

"You figure why?"

"They were lazy; they did nothing but fight among themselves. Even the women would kill off rivals—sometimes their own children." His eyes seemed to open wide, but this was no longer a surprise, and I continued: "The last kings were so corrupt they left their responsibilities up to their palace mayors. And that is what enabled Charlemagne's family to come to power." I could not believe that this eccentric foreigner had brought me all this way to rehearse Merovingian history.

"The point I want to make," he turned to face me as he spoke, "is that what Sauniere found in the hollow Visigoth column has a direct bearing on those Merovingian kings—and probably on Little Charles."

"Charles? I know nothing about any of this."

"Sauniere discovered four parchments—don't ask me about details; they're in my black book, so you'll have to read it— four parchments that, taken together, prove the survival of the Merovingian's royal bloodline *after* Charlemagne's crowd assassinated the *last* Merovingian king, in 679."

"After Dagobert? Impossible." I attempted to sound more certain of myself than I wanted to be.

"Why's that?"

"I don't know everything about *Saint* Dagobert," I said, "but I remember that his son, who would have been Sigisbert IV, was killed with him, and that he was only three or four." As I finished my protest, I felt something heavy pull on a thread of memory that seemed to reach down deep into my viscera.

"No. No. That's what the histories say. According to Sauniere's parchments, Sigisbert was *rescued* by his sister, who was an abbess or something, and she hid him until it was safe to bring him down here to the Razes, where his mother was *still* a countess. Her name was Giselle, and her grandfather was a *Visi*goth king. They lived here at Rennes-le-Chateau when it was called Rhedae, after the chariots the Visigoths used."

"You tell me things I have nev—never heard." The words came hard. "What are you trying—to prove?" I wanted to know what this had to do with me and my travelers' check. And with Little Charles.

"Not even family stories?" he asked.

"Why?" He seemed to be reading my mind—I had to be careful.

"That's why I looked you up—" he said, then paused before adding: "Monsieur Plantard."

"You have my interest. But we need to turn at that corner." I pointed a block ahead. "The sign for the Chateau is hidden behind the tree." I had almost allowed him to drive through Couiza without turning, he had so tricked me with his questions.

"Got it—thanks...." Then he launched into his haunted story about three skeletons Sauniere found buried under a stone slab at the foot of his altar. Skeletons of Sigisbert, but as a man not a child, and Sigisbert's own son—and his grandson. Skeletons of royal Merovingians who had never lived. According to history. And what is there except history? All at once I wanted very much to be with Christine. I don't know what to believe if you cannot believe history. The slab had a carving on it, he said, a very ancient carving of a knight carrying a child on a horse. But the slab had been turned face down. "Sauniere's parchments explained that after Dagobert's assassination and Sigisbert's return to Giselle, the three—that's Sigisbert and his two heirs I'm talking about now—had lived here as counts of Razes.... Ever heard of them?"

"In history?" I asked.

"No—in family gossip. Stories."

"Why?" I had to be careful. What did it mean when people started throwing out history and believing family stories? I could not be certain whether my emotion was grief, anger, fear of what he was about to tell me, or an intense *desire* to have him leave me alone. Either way, I ached to be at the clinic with Chrissy— Not have this man hold me paralyzed. This stranger, I told myself, must not see my grief. I must use my anger—

"Because, according to the parchments, the name that Sigisbert took for his line was 'Plant-Ard'. You know what that means? It means the 'living shoot'—the living branch of the true Merovingian kings. It means the *true* kings of France. In place of that Carolingian bunch who killed the king, usurped the throne, and bribed Rome to validate their line."

"Plant-*Ard*, you say? I thought *that* was all family superstition."

"It's a wonder you heard anything—you've had the state *and* the church trying to stamp out the record of Charlemagne's coup."

"The church?"

"Because the Pope colluded with the Carolingian crew. Because the 'ardent' part of Plant-Ard has a hidden meaning. Before Clovis's wife made him a Christian, the Merovingian kings followed an older cult of 'Diana of the Ardennes'—Diana of the Nine Fires. The church didn't like the implication, pagan or female. And there's another reason, an important one. But we'll need Sauniere's church to explain that one."

I watched our narrow way as a small truck coming down forced us to pull off the ragged asphalt into the weeds. To the left, far below, I could see larger trucks on the valley road that winds through woods and fields, from our Rennes-les-Bains turn to Couiza. It is beautiful country, and all my life I have sensed a spiritual kinship with the hills and the divided plains. But up there, it was possible to feel that I *owned* it—that all I had to do was reach out and take hold, the way I would a painting hanging on the wall. I had never wanted to *own* the Rennes. Only to feel that I belonged—the way I belong to Christine, and she to me. The way poor Charles belonged to both of us. "So you are telling me you think I am one of *those* Plantards?"

"Somebody thinks so." He was deadly earnest again—in contrast, I realized, to the inspired comic look he had worn to recount Sauniere's story.

"You mean, don't you, that it has something—something to do with Charles?" The words came hard.

"I mean that there may be other people with an interest in whether he lived or died."

"What are you saying? Who?"

"I apologize, sir, for bringing up these possibilities. I know they must be painful. I wish I could be sure of the answer to your question. What I know is that Sauniere took his parchments to Paris to some people Boudet told him about at the Cathedral of Saint Sulpice."

"What sort of people?"

"A group of occultists, artists and architects, scholars of Freemasonry who attached themselves to Saint Sulpice."

"Occultists and Freemasons? It makes no sense."

"Don't ask me to explain. I only know that in this group, Sauniere, the beefy little priest from the provinces, a man with a glass eye, met a gentleman named Charles Plantard—another Charles—who considered himself a descendant of the royal branch of the Merovingians. You see the possible conflict, don't you?"

"If I do, it means that my—my little Charles would have been just another—little Sigisbert. Except—except he failed—to escape." He saw that—my break. I did not want him studying me. I had to shake my head to keep the time-drunkenness of this foreigner from making me dizzy. "He had no sister to save him."

"Something like that."

"But there is no Merovingian throne to fight over," I said, desperate for solid ground.

"There's something else."

"The gold?"

"That. But something potentially more earthshaking."

"What could that be?"

"When Boudet and Sauniere died, they both left secrets buried, still untold. Now, my black book ties their secrets to what one of the descendants of Sigisbert, his name was Godfroi, duke of Lower Lorraine, discovered during the Crusades. At the end of the eleventh century, this *is* in history again, Godfroi captured Jerusalem, and, during his rule as king of the Holy City, he put together evidence supporting a Merovingian family tradition that would have seemed absurd if it hadn't been so persistent. According to the legends he'd been told by his father, the Merovingian kings were descended directly from Mary Magdalena."

"That is pure *merde!*" I spat back, my anger pure now.

"Exactly what I felt."

"What, for God's sake, do the Merovingians have to do with the Magdalene?"

"Yeah, she's over there in Jerusalem, right, and the Merovingians crop up four hundred years later here in Gaul? No connection.... That's what I thought."

"No sense at all."

"But did you know that Pontius Pilate died in France?"

"What?"

"How does that make you feel? In some town on the Rhone, up near Lyon. Apparently it's in the Roman records. There'd been lots of contact between Gaul and the eastern Med back in Greek times. Along the Cote d'Azur I kept running into old Greek and Roman colonies. And Jewish too. Apparently a large Jewish community lived in the South of France."

"You could be right. I don't know. My research doesn't—"

"According to the Gospel of Peter—"

"Peter? Matthew, Mark, Luke, and—Peter?" I was beyond my anger now, into disbelief—laughter almost.

"There're these new books of the Bible that keep popping up in the deserts around Egypt. Gospels of Peter and Thomas, you know. Lots of them. Only they're not new—they're old as the regular ones, the one we're used to. But they give a slightly different story."

"It must be—" For a split second I remembered another dream I had had—last night? The night before? Christine and I were in the car. I was driving, and she was in back. We were some place on the autoroute headed toward Paris. Except it seemed more like a highway in an American film—totally empty space, like the Middle West or the desert plains. It was winter, but I had my window cracked. She leaned over the seat and pointed toward the window: "I am freezing back here." I lowered it another three inches. "Let me out. I am freezing," she screamed. But I ignored her. "If you do not let me out, I am going to *break* it." She began jabbing her elbow against her window. I smiled to myself and cranked my window *all* the way down. If she broke out, she would find nothing here except small desert towns. One or two stores with closed fronts. No planes. Not even buses. Just horrible loneliness.... The dream made no sense. But now I knew how she felt. I was trapped with this idiot who kept lowering the window. The threshold of sanity, I felt.

"They say that Joseph of Arimathea, for example, was not only a relative of Mary Magdalene but also *very* buddy-buddy with Pontius

Pilate." It was the girl this time talking from the back in a voice so soft I had to face her. She would not look at me, but stared out the window as she repeated what she and her father had seemingly gone over a hundred times. "They also say that he and Pilate worked out a scheme to get Jesus off without actually being crucified. Seems this devout fellow named St. Simon of Kyrene—that's Cyprus, I think—the one who's supposed to've helped Jesus carry the cross, ended up getting zapped by Jesus's last miracle so that in a trance he, Simon, became the man actually nailed to the cross, while Jesus rose up in the air and hung around laughing at the Roman soldiers and the people who thought he was dead."

"Jesus—laughing?" It was absurd.

"That's what they say," Walters broke in. "I know it's incredible. But these books have a lot of historical authority. They go back to the second century—as far as most of the gospels go. They simply got left out when the church fathers canonized one bunch of writings and turned down some others."

"I see *why*."

"Because they're crazy? I thought so too—at first. Then I started wondering whether stories in the regular books are any less surprising. In fact. Or only because we're used to them—because we've been taught to take a certain attitude when we think about them. Taught when we were too young to do otherwise."

I had lost track now of what the two were telling me. I remained frozen several stages back, trying to piece together the bits and pieces I had already heard. I had to do it now: we were making our last turn along the high walls just below the village. In a second we would be on the street that climbs up, past the remnants of the chateau itself, through the center to the tower. And when we stopped, too much, I feared, would begin happening for me to think clearly enough to make sense of all this suffocating information. If she were here, I told myself, she would know what to do. Christine would.

xxiv

Anthi_cwaters
To: mdwaters@urtoo.com
Re: I see

You just made me smarter to turn a two-way into a three-way conversation. Cool. I'll make a mental note.

mdwaters
to: anthi_cwaters@ezrite.com
re: good

The good old *stichomythia*, the old back and forth, worked for your ancient Greeks. Gave their plays a noble rhythm. But these times are hardly a golden age. Not even silver or bronze, I guess. The Styrofoam Age—pretending to be the Silicon Age. Or Silicone. Sillycones. Ask Hollywood.

How did I get off on those?

Don't stop me now. This is a serious part I've got to get back to … Philip is almost to the Church of Sainte-Madeleine. Don't stop me now, please.

Philip
Pop-Up

"So, if I am to believe what you are telling me," I said, sitting back to take it in, "our son was not only one of the Plantards who are heirs to the original Merovingian throne of France—but, if that fool Godfroi was up to anything more than inventing a glorified genealogy for himself, my Charles had the blood of *Marie Magdala* coursing through his veins?"

"That's right."

"And the blood of Joseph of Arimathea?"

"You're right with me, my friend—so far."

I wanted to challenge him on the idea that I was his "friend" (can't stomach pushy Americans), but too many things were falling into place: "And—and if Joseph of Arimathea in fact brought the Grail from Palestine after the crucifixion, the possibility might exist that my family either knows where it is, or—or would be the *rightful* owners? That's what you are telling me, isn't it?"

"Not 'owners,' Monsieur Plantard."

He followed the direction I indicated with my hand and drove on past the concession stand to the flagpole and the vacant lot by the edge of the cliff. Spread out below us lay kilometers and kilometers of the tranquil, ordered Razes that followed the Aude south toward Spain, a pattern of hills and plots of trees and cultivated land that never failed to lift my spirit—and yet contain it, the way a lock must contain a key. Surreptitiously, I glanced at my watch. Time for Doctor Pohere to drop in on her. I hoped she was feeling better. But not well enough to let Pohere flirt with her. He was too good-looking for a doctor: rough-looking, like Belmondo—but with hair. I never felt completely easy when she went to his office. It's worse than rape, she said. Except *you* have to pay, I said.

"What then? On my honor as a Plantard, for whatever that may be worth, we have no idea where the Grail is hidden—if it ever traveled this far."

"Not just the owners," he said again.

"You seem to be a *reasonable* man, Walters—" I gave him the benefit of the doubt. "Tell me the truth. Do you believe this—this tripe?"

"It doesn't matter what I believe. Not even perhaps what *you* believe. Somebody apparently takes it very seriously. Little Charles—your only child—is dead, isn't he? Have you come up with a motive?"

What was I to say? I wouldn't tell him why Christine was in the clinic. I refused again to show him the grief I felt, but at that moment it was difficult to keep the anger alive in my voice. "There is Claud—he and Jacqueline had reasons to envy little Charles—"

"Let's save Claud until we're inside the church. But think of it—how could killing little Charles help his Stephen? It doesn't add up that way. Anthi and I spent days at Les Issambres trying to put the pieces together. Didn't we, sweet?" She nodded from the rear. "But we didn't want to say anything to *you* until we'd checked out the church."

"And when you did?"

"The pieces all came together. In a minute I'll show you. You've got to remember that what you believe or I believe doesn't, at this point, matter. The truth probably doesn't matter that much either. We're coming up on the year 2000—there're going to be some weird stories blowing through the air."

"I do not care about the year 2000—" *with Charles gone*, I kept my tongue from saying. "I care about now—our year, 1985!"

"It's time somebody did. There're going to be a lot of desperate people out there wanting to rocket out of our century—our whole millennium. It's already started—"

So he *is* a nut, I said to myself. One more crazy crusader.

"With all they've been taught for two thousand years falling to pieces around their heads, they're ready to believe any story that seems to hang together, the more incredible the better. Anything that promises a good, strong sense of order to pump up their egos. Where I come from there's not a week the cops don't bust up one 'Order' or another that's stockpiled enough weapons to start World War III. The military are already involved, whether they know it or not. That's been—"

"That's where *you* come from. What does it have to do—"

"Because there's somebody over here who thinks that Joseph

of Arimathea transported Mary Magdalene to Marseilles after the crucifixion, and that Mary Magdalene and Joseph—probably Jesus too—joined the sizable Jewish communities already established there and, ultimately, the blood of Mary Magdalene and Jesus—" he added meekly, and paused, "bred into the Merovingian line."

"So you do accept it?" After what he had said, my fury could not match my amazement.

"I try not to—I really do. But, God knows, it gets harder."

"Who else does?"

"Whoever it is here in France who's protecting their personal interest...." He seemed to be waiting for me to tell him who that was. When he realized I had nothing to offer, he said, "But first, the church."

At the flagpole, he had turned right and driven into the grassy parking area at the foot of the grey stones of the Magdala Tower and its shapely turret. The three of us got out, and Walters came round to my side of the car.

"Be sure to lock the door, Anthi."

"Already did, Dad."

We crossed to the overarching shrubs that led into the park of Sauniere's domain. March sun bleeding through the limbs of evergreens and leafless oaks bathed the park in an underwater light. Once, when I was seeing Christine before we married, we came here for a picnic in the haunting shadows of the bower. I had thought the Boudet connection would mean something to her. We read poetry: "The Prince of Aquitaine to the ruined tower came...." We both went away disappointed. I prayed this return visit would lead to a similar anticlimax.

"You realize, don't you," Walters said, "that before Boudet and Sauniere built the tower, a cross to Saint Magdalene stood on the same spot?" We were descending the stone walk leading to the large grey house Sauniere built.

"I didn't know that. I thought it was named for our local queen."

"That too."

"Except, Daddy, Magdala *wasn't* really a queen. She was the wife of Sigisbert IV," the girl said, "and he's the one who never got to be king."

"Because, officially, he died when the pope eliminated Dagobert? It all fits, doesn't it?" What else could I say, my little Chrissy? They had worked their tale out to the letter.

"Not just the pope," the girl jumped to add. "The Carolingians. Pepin the Short ordered one of Dagobert's own servants to kill Dagobert on a hunting trip. The assassin—they say it may have been Dagobert's godson, horrible crime!—waited until he was asleep, and then ran a lance through his eye. Shakespeare must have known the story, don't you think?"

I had nothing to add. I guess he meant *Hamlet*, but the idiot and his daughter were all over the place. Nothing but horrible episodes filled the whole tale Walters and the girl had brought me. Already I had a rotten sense that nothing but added horror could come of any of the events they revealed. And yet I was allowing myself to be drawn into a vortex that already made my brain swirl as the two told me detail after detail, like children teasing an animal. And having been pulled into the first swirl, I found I could move in only one direction.

"I know nothing about the other episodes—but one thing you said is true," I heard myself mumble.

"What's that?"

"That what you had to share would interest me. Your travelers' check is safe." Not that the check had ever dazzled me the way history did, or this man's crazy energy.

"You're hooked?" A curious grin lit his round American face. The girl looked at me with a stare I took for compassion.

"Afraid so."

"Yeah, it's not a happy feeling. I know."

That, I felt, was an odd thing for him to recognize. It left me tongue-tied—I looked around for words—said the first thing that came to mind. "What have you read about this house?" We had stopped before the ornate facade of Sauniere's Villa Bethania. Directly above our heads, from the third storey, a life-sized sculpture of Jesus, with arms outstretched, looked down on us.

"It cost a fortune for a country priest to put this pile of stone together," he answered.

"Why 'Bethania'?"

"One of the Marys close to Jesus was from Bethany," the girl said. "She's associated with Magdalene."

"Everything around here's a clue," Walters said. "Boudet had it constructed that way. This is where Sauniere housed the government ministers, the statesmen, the artists, the architects, the followers of Gnostic philosophy who flocked to Rennes-le-Chateau to check out his discoveries. Even Wagner had come this way looking for Cathars—the Purest of the Pure—for his *Parsifal*."

"Gnostics?" I asked.

"Heavens, yes! We're crunching on a seedbed of heresies here, every step we take. Everything our culture has hidden for two thousand years is coming back. The repressed always returns—you know what they say."

"Back here?"

"The Cathars, the Albigensians, Gnostics, Bogomiles, Merovingians, Visigoths, Celts, the Secret Grail, the Black Madonna— you name it. All the suppressed and forgotten figures. Just names to most of us—though you, Monsieur Plantard, probably recognize some of them. Is that so?" He seemed to wait for my answer but I refused to respond before he finished. "They all passed through here. And they're probably coming back again. To haunt us—"

"Or to illumine, Monsieur Plantard," the girl broke in. "Depending on how willing we are to deal with them this time around."

"Why are you telling me these—these *unnatural* things? These heresies?" Sometimes I felt they were trying to help, other times, that, like the gendarmes and the police, they wanted only to goad me into doing something stupid. God knows, it would not take much. Twice already, Chrissy, we had hidden in wait for—him.

"In the church, things will make more sense."

We had descended to the rusted gate guarding the path to the little Church of Saint Magdalene, and before I could speak to the ticket seller, Walters had paid for all of us. This time the church seemed smaller than before, its tower squarer and more squat, its stones even older and more dismal grey.

"That's the Visigoth pillar," the girl said, and nodded toward a square granite column standing in the *petit jardin* on our left. "Sauniere found his parchments inside it. The pillar's upside down."

"Interesting," I said, already staring at the dark arch to the church. If we ever entered it, Chrissy, I had forgotten what we saw. On our picnic, I don't think we had time for the church.

"The church wasn't built until the eighth century," Walters said, "—ostensibly to protect Magdala's body. But also, it turns out, as the royal tomb of the underground Merovingians—Sigisbert and the Plant-Ards."

"This is *it* then … the family vault?" My eyes travelled up to the recessed triangle above the arched door. In the center was an agitated woman whom I took as another Madonna—distracted like you, Christine, when you have a thousand things to do. Until I noticed the name beneath the small platform on which she stood: ST. MARIA MAGDALENA, the carved letters read. To each side of Magdalena I saw two potted plants, almost man-size, each of the four bearing three rose-like blossoms arranged to form a cross. "A bit—gaudy, wouldn't you say?"

"The decorations come from Boudet and Sauniere—all end-of-the-century, pop-religious style. You take it for the symbols—otherwise it's lousy art."

"'*Terribilis est—l-o-c*—'" I tried to read the Latin under the Magdalena. "You make it out?"

"The second line is '*locus iste*'—whatever that means," Walters said.

"'It's a terrible place,'" she translated.

"You can't claim they don't warn us," he said, as though on cue.

I felt a shiver start up my back, but, realizing this was only superstition, I stopped it midway. No need to let these Americans know I had a half-meter medieval streak running up my spine.

I followed them through the arch into the church, whose stained windows admitted only a dull gloom. In the darkness, I could sense shapes and shadows waiting that seemed to have a life hidden within them. I felt more than a little unnerved: different, yet the way I felt the first night I slept in your house, Chrissy, when my father was in the clinic and Madame Boudet asked me to stay. Something waiting there in the dark seemed ready to come back to life. I tried to dismiss the feeling as nothing more than my giving in mindlessly to the theatrics of the two old priests.

"One second. I'll get the light." Walters fished in his pocket and came up with a coin that he fed into a loaf-size box fixed to the wall to the right just inside the door.

Immediately the machine clicked, and a weak underwater glow filled the room, driving the shadows for the moment back into themselves. And yet I still felt uneasy, whether because of the figures I saw or because of things Walters had said when he was preparing me. I remember a short aisle running down the center—fifteen meters, no more—to an altar with a round tower set on a square platform. Underneath I saw a scene composed of strangely lifelike color.

"Note the floor," Walters said, drawing my attention back from the far end. "The black and white squares."

It looked like a giant's game board that in its size and monotonous regularity was meant to send a player into vertigo.

"The paving stones," Walters went on, "all point dead north, south, east, west. Boudet, they say, used chessboards to encode his messages. Every letter was arranged according to the knight's move."

While I was still trying to sort out what knights' moves had to do with messages, Walters pointed to a rather harmless religious statue beneath which the girl had seated herself along the wall opposite the entrance.

"I get the sense these two were toying with the powers of light and darkness here—real end-of-the-century stuff, with the balance tipped toward the black.... Take this statue—" He crossed to the two figures, one standing, the other crouching. "—just another Jesus kneeling at the feet of John the Baptist having his hair washed, right?"

I studied the peaceful scene, an erect John bearing a flagstaff in one hand, pouring water with the other on the head of the praying Jesus, both figures almost life-size and, except for the anxiety in the face of Jesus, serene. Only the color of the robe fallen from Jesus's shoulders seemed out of place: it was a light golden red, much like fresh oxygenated blood. "Seems the usual thing to me."

"But look behind you," he ordered.

I turned to face a creature I had failed to notice as I passed it in the dark. The loathsome thing seemed now to leap out of the shadows where it crouched beneath the basin holding the waters with which one would normally cross himself as he entered the sanctuary. If you had been there, Chrissy, I would have squeezed the life out of you. It was a huge half-human form with dark earth-colored skin, gigantic white protruding eyeballs set with hideous grey irises and small penetrating pupils. Its ears were large and pointed; the nose long, cutting as a trowel; two ram-like horns erupting from the black curls that matted the wide, shallow forehead; a great gaping red mouth twisted by rage; long, black, sharp talons; and huge, leathery vampire-like wings curved like an opera cape about his shoulders. Even knowing it was only a statue, I still felt my body pull back and deep icy shivers course from my groin to my head. I have never seen a more appalling figure—not even in nightmares about Charles have I seen a face like that. And I was standing no more than half a meter from it.

"Who do you suppose this is?" Walters suddenly demanded.

"It must be the Devil—Lucifer, the Fallen One—" I sputtered, groping for a name to tame the chaos of terror I felt. *Where is this maniac taking me?* was all I could put together.

"You'd think so, wouldn't you?" The note of hysteria in Walters's voice had become a teacherly earnestness. I began to suspect that that was his true profession, that he was a crazed professor turned out to pasture twenty years early by a faculty somewhere in America that had grown impatient with his insane theories. "But here, for some reason, they call him Asmodeus," he added.

"Sounds a fitting appellation for the darkness he gives off," I said.

"Only a pesty spirit, it turns out. Perhaps they were afraid to use his other names."

"Who?"

"Boudet, ... and Sauniere. *Their* initials are there, in red, at the bottom." He pointed.

"B. S.—"

"At first I thought they might be a comment on the whole church." He looked at me and realized I didn't know what he was talking about. "In America we have an expression—" he began, then seemed to realize it was hopeless. "Never mind. They must have taken themselves seriously. You don't play with powers like these unless you think you know what you're doing. Look at old Asmo here—then look back at Jesus. What do you see?"

"They are both kneeling—"

"Anything else?"

"Not really…. Jesus is wearing red and gold. This—bastard, green and gold." I tried to be helpful—for my own peace of mind.

"Better be careful what you say about him. I don't trust the balance in here. Makes me uneasy…. What about the positions of the two?"

"Jesus has his head turned to his right, this—monster's is to his left."

"Excellent. You're catching on to the rules quicker than I did. Now what about the legs?" he asked.

I felt like a student quizzed by the teacher, and I resented the implication. I answered: "Jesus has his left knee up and his right down—" I turned back to the monster. "This creature is crouched on the opposite knee…. They are opposites, I guess."

"Exactly. But facing one another, on a diagonal, the way the knight moves. Old B. and S. were trying to tell us something about light and darkness, the mirror relationships between them. Just like the paving…. Now, let me show you something else." Without waiting he started down the aisle to the altar, leaving me to stand paralyzed beside the black demon or follow him deeper into the shadowy domain. His daughter was no help: she remained quiet in the single chair beneath the scene with Jesus and John, as though meditating—or taking shelter. I followed the American.

"As we go, check out the Stations of the Cross. Notice the black kid with the bowl, in Number One over there. There's generally no black guy in the story. And then, in Number Seven, there's Simon of Kyrene pointing to a tower. That, they say, is the Magdala Tower that we saw outside. Simon, you remember, is the fellow who got zapped by Jesus and crucified in his place. But here's what I want to show you at this end." He stopped before the altar and extended his left hand toward a porcelain-like figure set in a panel under the square platform of the altar. In the background of the panel again stood what I knew was the Magdala Tower.

I thought again of that first night I spent in your house, of the little white-lace gown you wore in the moonlight when you came to my room. How frightened I was that your mother would come in on us—with her cold chiseled face. Yet excited too that you had taken the risk. I remembered girls in the dark old hotel in Montpellier who after all their twisted experience seemed to know nothing. Yet you knew instinctively what you were doing: the way your mother slept, what would or would not wake her. Instinctively we made love in that half-light—quick, fevered, but as good as we have ever done. Christine, it is your love that keeps—

"Who is she?" I asked. She resembled a china doll, except that her hands lay piously folded on her ample lap, and her face was lifted toward the roof of the cave where she knelt. She wore a lovely creamy-gold dress decorated with flowers and trimmed at the collar, cuffs, and bottom in purer gold.

"Who would you guess?"

"Mary?" I said.

"Which?" he quizzed, with an illuminated smile spread recklessly across his face.

"Which 'Mary'?" I asked. He nodded, and, already knowing somehow I was wrong, I said, "Mother of Jesus."

"Magdalena—" he pointed to some Latin carved beneath the panel. "Kneeling in a cave."

"I understand that much."

"You notice her tears? Or the cross she's staring at?"

"It looks like two small branches, stripped, and tied together."

"But look down here, at the upright branch—"

I leaned toward the scene where Walters pointed. "There is a skull before her knees. Is that what you mean?"

"The skull—that's important. But beside the skull, the base of the cross—"

"It seems to be buried in the cave floor."

"Buried. Or—"

"Planted, perhaps."

"At any rate, growing out of the cave floor. Living in the cave—beside this Magdalene with the full stomach. Notice her stomach."

"Isn't it just her dress that is full at the waist?"

"Maybe. But I don't think so—not given everything else.... Notice the crosspiece now. Compared to the cross upright, the crosspiece is obviously dead."

"Where is this cave?"

"Lombrives? Maybe the one in Rennes-les-Bains where they say little Charles—disappeared. Who knows?"

"It cannot be Rennes-les-Bains," I said angrily.

"How can you be sure?"

"The tower in the background there, visible from the mouth of the cave. It has to be the Magdala Tower. You could not see it from les-Bains."

"Why not?"

"The mountain and the woods would block your view."

"But Boudet thought mathematically, geometrically. He would probably have seen it more from the sky looking in both directions at once.... I don't know. I'm not even sure it's Magdala Tower. Too fuzzy. But I want you to think about that cross."

"Why it is growing out of the ground, you mean."

"Exactly."

"A living religion, perhaps?" I said with genuine feeling.

"And, by her side there, the open book?"

"An open book—the unknown, … the future. Perhaps it means the future is wide open—is that possible?"

"Or a story that remains to be told? But the two branches—"

"They form a cross—"

"One shoot living, growing out of the earth—the other, dead."

"Only a—"

"Coincidence?" He looked at me like the scolding teacher he no doubt was. "In this place?" The wild certainty in his face left me no room to disagree.

"Perhaps not."

"I'll tell you what I think—"

"I am not sure I want to hear…. But go on; I won't stop you." In fact, I knew there was no way I could stop him—or stop myself from listening. His story would be the most irrational invention imaginable, and yet he had put me in a situation from which I could no longer free myself. I needed you desperately. Simply little pieces of this, and bits of that, he'd given me to hang my dreams on, or my fears, and he had drawn me into his lunacy like a child into the sea. Now there was more.

"At first I thought the two branches had to do with the two branches of the Grail story—one in England, at Glastonbury, etc., and the other here in France. That they signified one was dead, probably in England, and one living like the upright branch— probably here in the Pyrenees, because it grows out of this earth. The story is that Joseph of Arimathea carried the Grail to England as well as to Marseilles. Then I remembered the skull, right beside the *source* of the living branch, where its roots disappear in the earth. That says to me that, right from the beginning there have been two lines coming from the same source—one the line of death and the other the line of life, the living branch. And then I mixed in that odd pair there at the entrance—" He turned so that we both were facing back up the aisle toward the dark face of horror on our left and the serene tableau on the right. "Let's go back up there and take a look."

Now I followed him eagerly back to the better illumined end of the sanctuary. When we were midway between the grotesque and the Baptist, he stopped. "From here, you can take both of them in. You can understand the point. Look—both are baptismals, both offer a new life.... And over here, Jesus is on his knees to accept the waters of life from John. They're simply mirror images of the same process. They co-exist. They're balanced. It's not as though one was trying to *wipe* out the other. They're here together from the very first. Both in Magdalena's womb, maybe? If anything, this dark old fellow here is the base material—from which the gold of Jesus emerges, after it's washed clean.... Look at his right hand, the way his thumb and fingers curve to form a circle. What do you suppose that's for?"

"A sword?"

"Possibly.... Or look at John, and think of mirror images."

"Like John?" Then I understood. "A flag, perhaps."

"Good guess. What flag?"

"I pass." This man had no end of questions. If he had a point to prove, I wished he would simply go ahead and do it.

"The banner of the Carolingians? The papal colors, maybe? It's all speculation, you understand, but if Boudet wanted to reassert the Merovingian claim, he would have resented the pope's part in the assassination of King Dagobert enough to line this creature up with Rome. Besides, old Dagobert's wife, Giselle de Razes, was a Visigoth and therefore probably an Arian heretic—she separated Jesus from God and gave him an individual identity—at a time when Rome had already wrapped a circle of unity around the Trinity, or so they claimed.... But never mind all that. It's nothing but history."

"That counts for *some*thing, I would imagine." I was angry again.

"Not so much when what we're trying to do, Monsieur Plantard, is figure out what our friend Boudet was telling us here. More important than *his* message, however, is what somebody might have *believed* he was saying about the past."

"You have me completely lost now."

"I was afraid so. But it's not simple. We're talking about two thousand years. Especially two thousand years of conspiracies. Look at our American assassinations. Look at Watergate. What a mess—each of them—after the official commissions and the conspiracy hunters got their paws on them. Can you imagine what it must be like to live in countries where the governments themselves authorize the histories? God, I can't. But, in a sense, the church itself was able to do pretty much the same thing—going back to the first council at Nicea, where Constantine told the Christians to get their act together and they took old Irenaeus's list of books and set them up as the orthodox scriptures, the Bible, just like that—and everything else became heresy. That's only seventeen hundred years of suppression, but things tend to get a little blurred after they've been kept down even that long."

"I imagine they do," I said, irritated by his sudden flood of information, not wanting to sit back any longer and accept it.

"So, ... I'm going to put it as simply as I can. The way I figure it is that Boudet was trying to tell us—with the living branch and the dead, the skull at the base of the living upright, the mirror image of old Asmodeus, the font, crouching Jesus, baptizing John—that, from the very beginning and continuing down generation to generation, there have been the *two* branches, the dark and the light, the line of death and the line of life. That there are *always* two 'Plant-ards'—"

"*Assuming* for a minute they wanted to say *any*thing about the Plantards. I can try to accept the Magdalene figures.... But the Christ—" I muttered, not knowing how I meant to continue. "That goes—"

"No, listen. The way the story goes—what I decided you didn't want to hear when we were talking in the car about Magdalene and

Joseph, with me dropping a few blazing hints—is that, based on the underground Gospels, the ones Irenaeus didn't want to include, Magdalene and Joseph were not simply disciples of Jesus—"

"What?" I heard myself scream inwardly.

"They were his relatives—"

"What are you saying?"

"More than relatives. And here's the hard kernel of it all, but I have to tell you.... Magdalene was his spouse.... Do you understand what that means?" Searching for my secrets, his eyes seemed to pass through me.

"I—I'm not sure I want—"

"Magdalene bore him children—before the crucifixion, and, if Simon took his place, after as well."

"Children?" Why didn't he stop this?

"Mary Magdalene *was* the Grail— Like my lovely Belgian friends on the beach at Les Issambres, she carried the holy blood, the *Sang Real, inside* her body. That's why her stomach looks full and golden in the figure below the altar."

"Someone here is absolutely insane!" His new absurdity so stunned me I could scarcely speak. "So Charles, you are saying, sir, also carried—*that* blood?"

"Yes—in a sense, he was the Grail. And you, sir, as well. The divine line. That's it in a nutshell."

I wanted to call out for you to leave your bed in the clinic and come stand beside me as I fought off this man's deranged story. Instead, my dream came back, the last part, the picture that had woken me in cold sweat.... We were in the bedroom. You were staring at me with that cold, terrifying rage you get from your mother. Your hand was raised, with your long scissors pointed dead at my eyes. *I told you never to touch that little bitch!* Somehow I knew it was Jeanne Roux you meant. Unfair, I thought. I never— Then you sprang at my eyes with the blades. We fell, both of us, into the dark. The dream made no sense. Neither in my bed nor with this madman in Boudet's church.

I do not know how long I stood like that, wanting your help—seeing only my dream. But Walters respected my silence.

It was a while still before words came. "After two thousand years, you know, it has to be pretty damned watered down!" I mumbled. But my lame attempt to send the whole idea up on bubbles of laughter did no good. The American stared at me as though searching behind my eyes for confirmation of this madness. Even his daughter studied me.

"Not, apparently," he said, "for people who believe in blood—and hope."

"This is a hell of a lot to accept!"

"Can you blame them? It's a better story than most they'll be asked to believe between now and the year 2000. And the main parts of it have been around a *lot* longer. We've had two thousand years to get used to them. The new pieces bring it up to date, so to speak. Mary, the forbidden woman, becomes Mary the wife and mother, and moves to the center of the story. It's—it's a New Age epic. It's got about everything a believer these days could ask for—except flying saucers."

"Everything for the others, perhaps. But not for me," I protested as firmly as I could. My voice broke beneath the force of my passion.

"Probably the others are in the dark line—the dark Plantards. Remember, there must be two arteries—vessels—for the blood to flow, and the two must balance in some fashion to form a whole. You, Monsieur Plantard, and Charles are simply one half of that balanced whole."

"But Charles is dead," I very nearly wailed.

"I know, Monsieur. That isn't supposed to happen. There's supposed to be balance. But whenever one line grows greedy, it rises up to slay the other, and in doing so reveals its true color."

"The dark?"

"I would think so."

"And you figured all this out?"

"Yes."

"On your own?"

"Uhn—more or less—"

I lost my patience. "What do you mean, 'more or less'? This is important to me. Whatever craziness this may be to you, it is my son's life you are talking about. And I think I have an exceptionally sound notion of what the dark line is in this generation."

"I imagined you would. And, yes, I had help.... Let's talk out here." He led me through the entry of the sanctuary out into the churchyard and around to the ornately decorated cemetery behind the church. It was not dusk yet, as in the church I had felt it must be, but late morning, and the sun had managed to burn off some of the clouds so that from moment to moment a band of light fell through.

"Why out here?" I asked.

"I'd prefer Anthi didn't hear. Parts of it might upset her— some other things she might tell her mother. Her mother and I are separated. She's living in Greece. If we ever get a divorce, what she doesn't know can't be used against me."

"I understand." It was the first sane statement I had heard from him since we entered the chapel.

"There was a woman I met in Williamsburg—it's a small town where I work in Virginia. She had come there to live—in exile from a Latin American country where her family had ruled as dictators for a few generations. I'm not going to mention names, you understand. It wasn't so much *her* family who had been the dictators as the family that kept marrying into her family to get enough social stature to hold power. Because her line was an aristocratic one from here in the Pyrenees, but from over on the Spanish side. She's a beautiful woman, maybe ten years older than I am—that'd make her about fifty-five, fifty-seven—but she has a strange inner power that makes her seem much younger. Ageless, I'd say. She can simply touch you with one of her fingers and make you explode with sexual energy. I was attracted to her—but frightened too because of this witching power she has. I didn't get close enough to find out if the force was real or an old voodoo-type magic. I did get close enough to listen to what she had to say."

"I see." But I didn't.

"She's another branch, like yourself, but her line has married out too many times, and the name has changed. She gave me my black book, the one I showed you at the hotel, then told me about another Plantard group up in the north here who're in on the family claim. She knew that I have a personal interest in groups like this, people who feel they're on some special mission. Where I live, we see all types of individuals who feel wounded in their pride by the social changes that the past thirty years have brought. They imagine the whole world's going to hell in a handbasket. Drugs, pornography, now AIDS—you name it—all of it points to one thing: that nothing short of a New Order is going to save us. But first comes the bloodletting, the purification. It's always the bloodletting first, the sacrifices they think are justified no matter how far they go."

Why did he keep on like this? I did not understand half of what he was talking about. Now he lectured me on politics. The names, the events, meant nothing to me. The obsessed American simply droned on. No matter what I did to ignore him, he kept talking....

"—there's no doubt about it, it does a wounded ego good to feel you're on a quest to save civilization. Think about the Ayatollah. I tell you, it's getting to be the Crazy Season. We're going to see a Millennium Madness, new Crusaders, sweep through the West—and the rest of the world, for all I know—that'll make Hitler and Stalin look like Santa Claus. Unless, unless—"

"What?"

"Just a little jab, here and there—to pop the inflations when they come up. We don't want that kind of grandiose insanity happening again, after all this century has gone through—no more crusades, holy or otherwise. Especially not because some group of righteous lunatics believe they have the blood, the authority, of you-know-who in them."

Now I wondered what it would take to pop his balloon. Obviously the whole story he had worked up was doing wonderful things for his little American ego. Talk about crusades. I should have told him precisely what I thought. But I didn't.... I just listened.

"So when this woman gave me my book, I thought the group in the north, they call themselves the Order of Jerusalem, had all the markings of a sidetracked people about ready to puff themselves up to a first-rate grandiosity. I took her claims seriously. But the deeper I looked into all these connections, the more skeptical I became. There was too much to it to ask any reasonable man to believe. I felt exactly the way you must. Too many connections coming in to this center from two thousand years of underground history. I explained my skepticism to her. But when she and some mutual friends got wind I was meeting Anthi in France, they made me promise I'd drop in to investigate. She didn't know about you, Monsieur, but she had implied I'd find another line down here split off from the group in the north. Then I read your story in the papers and realized that my problem was simply that I hadn't had enough imagination to grasp the connections that make up real history. None of us do—that's why we believe the stuff they put in books."

"And you think you know where to find the other line?"

"I think so."

"Claud—and Stephen," I said, for the first time absolutely certain of my cousin's guilt. "*They* are the other line."

"I was afraid you would say that. But these people in the north,

I tell you, have taken an *active* interest. You can't ignore them—or jump to conclusions."

"Claud is right here—in les-Rennes."

"It's all speculation. Remember that."

"I will. I will," I said, not thinking what I meant—or only enough to know I must hide my new certainty from this stranger, who would never understand the excruciatingly cruel present he had brought me—or the comforting gift I would put together for you, my Chrissy. As soon as I had this merde-minded jet-set social worker out of my hair.

XXV

Anthi_cwaters
To: mdwaters@urtoo.com
Re: at last, a breather

So what do you call it, Dad, your portrait of the author as *goofy* American stranger?

By the way, thanks for the erudite lines you gave Anthi. I *wish* I had known that much history.

mdwaters
to: anthi_cwaters@ezrite.com
re: answer

I call it "leveling the playing field."
(Never tell anybody that I fudged with Anthi.)

Anthi_cwaters
To: mdwaters@urtoo.com
Re: question

Leveling what playing field?

mdwaters
to: anthi_cwaters@ezrite.com
re: answer

Given the problems of parity I e-mailed you earlier, I would call it "deauthorizing the author," if it didn't sound like a bad translation from a French theorist.

Anthi_cwaters
To: mdwaters@urtoo.com
Re: okay

Awkward, yes. But clearer—to me, at any rate.

mdwaters
to: anthi_cwaters@ezrite.com
re: (no subject)

Good. But that may mean you've been in Paris a tad too long.

Anthi_cwaters
To: mdwaters@urtoo.com
Re: caution

But aren't you afraid you've left your posterior exposed—besides making yourself look like a dunce?

mdwaters
to: anthi_cwaters@ezrite.com
re: recklessly

It's a risk I'm willing to take. And what's coming next might actually help cover my rear.

If you don't mind, back we go to …

xxvi

Philip
Pop-Up

For the stranger did not know what Philip himself would not quite remember, the dream that came to him the night after their visit to the chapel. In it he wandered through the fragments of his future, an open field that more and more became a tunnel of oaks leading in a single direction: toward an open area in the center of the woods, a clearing trampled smooth by heavy iron feet circling one another, men searching for a vulnerability against which to strike. Philip's not-remembering in no way diminished the force of his dream nor the inevitability of his action.

He is somewhere in a large store, a shopping mall. A huge department store. He is showing a book to a graceful woman in a yellow tank top, a swimming suit that flows over her lovely molded body like honey over peeled peaches. She has yellow hair, but it is cropped short like a youth's. Her mouth, nose, and eyes resemble Christine's, but she is not Christine exactly. He has seen the book in another section of the store. He remembers it.

Now he has guided her back to the shelf and pulled it down for her. It is about the Grail.

Then a second scene: He is beside her in bed—but in affection only.... Followed by a duel of broadswords, armored men. In the woods. A clearing worn smooth by iron feet circling. Men using turds from the earth to anoint their swords. And Philip dominates the field, in armor covering his chest, back, and loins. The other men fall back. He waves his sword. Is victorious.

Only the duel with the lovely woman, in armor like his own, remains. She must be the woman from the store, for beneath her plates of metal the yellow top shows through. And her hair is blond and cropped. He hoists his broadsword, holding it high. It shimmers silver and gold in reflected light, silver with swatches of gold from the lights of stores that surround the woods. He feels the power of the sword sweep down through his body until he is stiff, hard as diamond, solid muscle from his raised hands wrapped about the hilt down to the tip of his erection. His entire body erect. Never in his life has he felt this solid. His entire body one muscle-firm erection.

And when they look for the merde to anoint their swords, the turds are dried out: when the pages lift them they crumble to seeds and dust. But Philip's sword is already anointed with light and the blood of defeated men. Blood gives it the bite and force of the turds, the bitter sting. He will fight as he is. And even without anointing, his sword will buy victory. His entire body is muscle dense. He is, he knows, Lancelot, or Galahad, or Percival. His name is *Arthur*. All the men in the clearing recognize this. The woman as well. He presses his sword broadside against her side where the armor divides. They know each other, the woman and Philip. Know each other from the heart and its blood out....

Nor could the stranger yet imagine how Christine was sure to respond when Philip gathered his energy to drag himself out of his dreams, dress, collect his equipment, and drive into Couiza to share with her the long account he had prepared of his visit with the American and his daughter. For the stranger could not have heard that already, two weeks before, Christine had taken her car into Carcassonne and come back with an American-made rifle whose repeating action would fire six large shells at any target one might desire to annihilate. Not have known that Christine had paid for the weapon from her own checking account and that already on two evenings the pair of them, Philip and Christine, had waited outside his cousin's home, Christine insisting that because no one else was going to bring their son's murderer to justice, they must—

she insisting while he struggled to insinuate some of his doubt into her certainty and prayed that Claud would again spend the night wherever he thought he must sleep when he did not come home.

But now the stranger had answered Philip's own questions, settled his doubts. His resolve was as firm now as his body in the still unremembered dream. And all that counted before Charles's father acted was that he carry his gift to Christine first.

xxvii

Anthi_cwaters
To: mdwaters@urtoo.com
Re: rear unguarded

It's still showing, Dad.

mdwaters
to: anthi_cwaters@ezrite.com
re: take a chance

So be it, young woman. I never said this was a risk-free enterprise.

Anthi_cwaters
To: mdwaters@urtoo.com
Re: a plea

But Pop-ups sound like safe fun. Surely there's room to brighten them up a bit.

mdwaters
to: anthi_cwaters@ezrite.com
re: the river

Pop-up is just a kids' term for the hard truths we have to work with. And there's more to come. There's no stopping its flow now. Neither manners nor moral desires can halt the stream of events rushing toward the dark necessary sea. Sorry.

xxviii

When the grim news about Claud broke, you remember, Anthi, we were already back in Les Issambres, in the lobby of our hotel watching the news report before heading out for dinner. Philip had demanded that we leave his hotel and never again try to contact a member of his family. We acted as he asked, almost, and returned to the coast even though we knew Paolo had given our rooms to his relatives from Orleans.

These events feel now as though they happened to individuals very different from those we have become—with you in Paris and me back here. My sense is that the best way to represent them would be as another …

Father and Daughter

Pop-Up

As soon as the message flashed across the screen, Anthi turned on me that hard, nerve-dulling glare she gets from her mother, that hard-eyed stare full of disbelief, disappointment, judgment, and questions that leave no room for answers—a look she never used before her mother and I separated.

Whatever my shock from the report showed, it did not satisfy Anthi. She bolted from the wing chair and out the main entrance. I dropped my newspaper and dashed after her. But she was already out of the small courtyard and crossing the street.

At the low wall in the wooded park above the beach, I caught up and followed her along the sidewalk in the direction of St. Raphael—as though she were starting east toward Nice, the airport, Greece—her mother.

"What's wrong, sweet?" I wanted to stay calm, but our old

wounds were too deep. The wind off the sea whipped my face. I could feel myself breathing quickly, the muscles of my chest and shoulders tighten, my face and ears flood with rage—and fear.

Until we reached the end of the sidewalk she refused to answer. Halfway across the parking area for the Supermart, she spoke: "What did you say to that man—to Philip Plantard?"

I hadn't expected this accusation, and didn't handle it well: "We both talked to him. You know what we said."

"When you took him out of the church—you told him something. You made him decide to—to act. What was it, Da—Daddy?"

The way her voice cracked on the final word told me that, under her anger, she was crying. I was too afraid of her rage to appreciate her hurt. "Nothing," I said, "that you don't already know. You would have told—"

"Not about the Order and Claud, Daddy—I wouldn't ever tell him that!"

"I didn't. He already knew about Claud—"

"The rest we made up. All the connections, they were *our* invention—yours and mine." Her round cheeks burned pink with certainty.

"I tried to tell him that, sweet. But they were *his* too." Then I remembered the change that had come over Philip and added, "Some of them were—as soon as I mentioned the Order."

"You shouldn't have, Daddy. You *should*n't have done it. No matter how much you miss Nicky, you shouldn't have gotten sucked into—into *this* the way you did. Choosing Tintin, Asterix—for little Charles. You used Nick's favorite stories."

"They were yours too."

She glared at me as though I had broken some basic rule I didn't remember.

"When you were his age, I mean."

Without realizing where we were hurrying, we had cut through the park of bent and blown pines that covered the escarpment east of Les Issambres and arrived at the larger hotel where we sometimes took dinner. I had to let myself absorb her words. I knew what she said about her brother was true. Part of it. No matter how much I wanted to deny Nicky's connection to little Charles, it was the pain of missing my own son, of his mother always seeming to hold him for emotional ransom, that swamped me in the reports about Charles. For Anthi, the pull of the mystery remained more innocent. I couldn't afford to lose her too, even over this.

"It was such a deep story—" she said, "an *electrifying* one. And now—"

In silence, we crossed the coast road and went into the hotel restaurant.

As we ate, we spoke only of the food. I tried to sort out my options—the best I could, given the anger and dread between us. She still wore her glare. "*Cross me,*" it said, "*and I will explode. Just you try!*" But on Anthi with dark eyes—like mine, not her mother's icy grey ones—the look does not always convince the way her mother's does. It sends a mixed message. I imagined her rage was partly a mirror of my own. I hoped it would soften—or pass completely. Sometimes it does. At fifteen, she was an angry child one moment, an adult the next. But I was afraid to speak: the wrong word from me could spark an outburst that would drive her back to her mother. I felt helpless.

When the waiter came to take my money, Anthi turned away to look through the trees to the sea. Without facing me, she answered the questions I was afraid to ask. "I want to fly back from Nice."

"Nice?"

"Yes."

"What about Paris—the museums and the Tower?"

"I can't stand any more large cities. Athens is bad enough."

"But your mother's in the islands. With her—friend."

"I know where to reach her. I will fly to the island, whichever one it is."

Flooded with anger and disappointment, I still had the good sense to bite my tongue until it bled. It was unjust of her to blame me. We'd both invented the story. Philip Plantard was the one to blame.

But, I kept reminding myself, she's only a child. I'm the adult. I shouldn't expect her to share any of the responsibility. Not for mistakes like this one.... I had already come too near losing her—and too many times. I couldn't risk an argument. I told myself I had to let her go.

Fortunately, after a night to mull things over, she changed her mind—didn't leave. Perhaps because I didn't resist. But in a sense she's with her mother still—even in Paris. And Nicky too, in Palo Alto.... Perhaps when she reads it all—

Anthi ...

xxvix

Anthi_cwaters
To: mdwaters@urtoo.com
Re: don't

Dad, I never blamed you for Claud Plantard's death.

mdwaters
to: anthi_cwaters@ezrite.com
re: oh?

Why did you want to leave then?

Anthi_cwaters
To: mdwaters@urtoo.com
Re: explanation

It was an impulse. One that passed quickly. People have impulses, don't they? I knew you were just a messenger. People always blame the messenger. Especially when they are fourteen going on fifteen.

mdwaters
to: anthi_cwaters@ezrite.com
re: (no subject)

And especially in Greek tragedies.

Anthi_cwaters

To: mdwaters@urtoo.com

Re: (no subject)

I hadn't read any of those when I was fifteen. I was just acting like a teenager.

mdwaters

to: anthi_cwaters@ezrite.com

re: oh?

I couldn't be sure.

Anthi_cwaters

To: mdwaters@urtoo.com

Re: warning

Teenagers do try to keep grown-ups guessing.... But I have some questions too.

mdwaters

to: anthi_cwaters@ezrite.com

re: Yes

Fire away, young lady.

Anthi_cwaters

To: mdwaters@urtoo.com

Re: question

Number one is, why didn't you speak directly to me in the scene after the news about Claud? As I was reading it I noticed the difference.

mdwaters

to: anthi_cwaters@ezrite.com

re: explanation

As I put it there, we seemed different people fifteen years ago. And our fiction techniques can create order without becoming straitjackets. Basically I see all our techniques as capacitors, like those inside TVs, that enable us to do what we need to do.

To be concrete, what I had to cover in that chapter simply felt too personal. Saying it to you directly would have blocked me from ever getting it out. Saying it indirectly, fictionalizing it, helped me reach the truth I was after—all of it. I needed to push it into a distance in order to face it directly and not get mushy.

Mixing of signals is a saving grace you have. One of many.

Anthi_cwaters

To: mdwaters@urtoo.com

Re: you say

Not very many, I'm afraid.

mdwaters

to: anthi_cwaters@ezrite.com

re: *you* say

Modesty is another.

Anthi_cwaters
To: mdwaters@urtoo.com
Re: more explanation

Sure, sure. I'm about as modest sometimes as the sun rising out of the sea.

mdwaters
to: anthi_cwaters@ezrite.com
re: wrong

You'd be surprised.

Anthi_cwaters
To: mdwaters@urtoo.com
Re: another question

Yes, I would...
But moving on to my other question: Did you—do you truly believe that it was the Plantards from Paris, or the North, at any rate, who killed little Charles?

mdwaters
to: anthi_cwaters@ezrite.com
re: on with it

When you bring up the subject this way, young lady, it's time, isn't it, to dive back into our story, and pick up a thread I dropped when Philip popped up.

XXX

Yes, I did believe that the northern branch of the Plantards were the probable murderers of little Charles. But, Anthi, I had also entertained the thought, one I preferred not to share with Philip, that they had acted through local Plantards with an interest in the family claim. I have to recognize now that if their secret goal was to have the southern family eliminate one another, I could not, from their point of view, have played a more effective part.

But that was not my intention. From all I had read, deeper than my curiosity, I felt a profound sympathy for Philip. I wanted to tell him what I had learned about his family, put him in the position to act in his best interest, to react fully informed of events that lay behind his son's death. I recognized the suspicion the press had cast on Claud, and the vested interest the gendarmes still took in bringing their favorite culprit to justice. I knew the pressure Philip must have felt—given the rage under which he buried his grief—to avenge his son's murder and restore his personal honor. It wasn't a rational need, but I appreciated its depth. I was obliged, wasn't I, to offer him my information, deflect him from the vendetta against Claud, and, I hoped, spare him the grief of misdirected vengeance. For reasons such as these I stepped in.

But I simply had not imagined what Christine was thinking, what she was doing to incite her husband, the action the two of them had conspired to take during the two months since Claud was released. How could I know? Believe me.

So ... there is one story more. At least one.

Four

Jean-Paul Arrends, Claud's attorney, had arrived at the judge's chambers at ten the morning following Jeanne's emergency press conference exonerating his client—in time to meet a crestfallen Captain Poulin, head of the local gendarmes, as the tall, thin, determined young officer came out. They nodded politely, and Arrends continued in. In the small, tight room, Judge Mathieu beamed even more red-faced than usual. Like the judge, Pierre de Batz, the prosecutor, remained seated.

Mathieu spoke first: "Look, Arrends, I've learned a thing or two this morning that should please you."

"Slow down, Your Honor. Please slow down, so I can take some of it in. I'm still dancing on the roof from what little Jeanne unloaded last night," the startled Arrends said, and lowered himself into the cushionless chair next to de Batz's padded one.

"She picked prime time, I'll grant her that," the prosecutor threw in before the judge could continue.

"Oh, don't be a sore loser, Pierre," Mathieu said, without dropping his good cheer. "She's knocked some skin off all of our noses. But you've got to admit, Pierre, you've had it pretty easy—up to now."

"And so—what is this juicy new detail that's sure to make Jean-Paul's day—and mangle mine?"

Mathieu settled back into his stuffed leather office recliner and stared at the window by his desk as though what he was going to say were written there. "I've had a long talk with the gendarmes. They have been holding a number of things back—from me, as well as you two. Unless maybe they clued you in, Pierre, and you helped Poulin 'decide' what to pass on."

"Your Honor," de Batz huffed, stonefaced, "would a state prosecutor do a thing like that?"

Mathieu blinked twice as though wondering for a moment whether de Batz was attempting to be ironic, then went on. "Poulin admits, first off, that he might have leaned on Mlle. Jeanne a bit heavily. Would you call thirty-six hours 'a bit heavy,' Pierre?"

De Batz looked away. "I'm sure the captain considered it worth every minute."

"Then that's what she meant," Arrends broke in, "about being asked to do what she couldn't do."

"Perhaps," Mathieu said.

"And other things, from the look on Poulin's face," de Batz added.

"Were you jealous, Pierre?" Arrends asked.

"She only wanted to be *helpful*," Mathieu said before de Batz could respond. "Poulin took advantage of her."

"He told her *how* to help?" Arrends asked, catching the drift of the judge's revelation.

"Another thing I got out of Poulin.... I worked on him for three hours this morning. I couldn't sleep last night. I don't like being kept in the dark any more than you, Jean-Paul.... Poulin tells me there was another handwriting expert he hadn't mentioned—a woman from Paris. She disagrees with the others. I can't tell you yet whose writing she says matches the threats. It turns out none of the experts thought all the messages came from your client, Jean-Paul. But this woman from Paris fingered someone else altogether. I've ordered a second panel of experts. And I'm also calling in the national police to take over from Poulin and his crew."

"You know you have my support," Arrends said.

"Mine too," de Batz offered, with less warmth.

"I thought so. You both recognize how much interest the public has taken in the death of little Charles. We must work together to bring the right people to justice—and protect the innocent. I require that none of what I've told you be mentioned to the press until the new investigators report to me."

"I'm sure that's best for everyone," Arrends said, "not just Claud Plantard."

"If the inquiries support what I've been told this morning, I'll release your client immediately."

"And after that?" Arrends said.

"Poulin and I agree that he would not be safe in the Rennes area."

"I wonder how bitterly Philip and Christine hate him," de Batz thought half aloud.

"Poulin has heard Philip Plantard brag more than once that if the police can't bring little Charles's murderer to justice," Mathieu said, "he knows how to do it himself. He's a hothead—full of rage, that one. Can't say I blame him. Today for the first time, Poulin told me that the morning after the body turned up, Plantard got it set in his mind that the criminal was his sister's husband—God only knows why. In front of half the family he pulled down his hunting rifle and ran off to his sister's house vowing he'd take care of the bastard. Fortunately for all of us, somebody phoned Poulin, and he sent men over before Plantard got there. They convinced him that four witnesses would swear his brother-in-law had been working up on his roof that entire morning. The whole Plantard family's riddled with hatred and rage, as far as I've been able to determine. Philip, I suspect, is capable of anything. I wouldn't want to predict."

"That's why I won't fight for my man's release yet. Not until it's obvious to everyone, even Philip, that he's clean."

"That's good, because we can't keep him without Jeanne's testimony," de Batz said.

"Remember, both of you," Mathieu repeated, "nothing to the press. Nothing at all."

xxxii

Anthi_cwaters
To: mdwaters@urtoo.com
Re:

Why didn't you tag that last section as a pop-up?

mdwaters
To: anthi_cwaters@ezrite.com
Re:

You mean because no reporters were present for the conversation?

Anthi_cwaters
To: mdwaters@urtoo.com
Re:

Yeah.

mdwaters
To: anthi_cwaters@ezrite.com
Re:

It didn't take anything special to piece it together from what the papers said and what happened afterwards. Such exchanges had to have happened whether they happened or not the way I imagined them. A pop-up is not just an event. It's a gift, a gift of something like inspiration. One moment it's not there. The next it is. I don't know how else to explain it.

Anthi_cwaters
To: mdwaters@urtoo.com
Re:

The way words and pictures come together first in your unconscious, Dad, and then on your screen? Like magic?

I'm trying still to understand.

mdwaters
To: anthi_cwaters@ezrite.com
Re:

Yeah, like that. You put it better than I could.

When you create a few more pop-ups—and I hope you will—you'll catch on. I know you will.

Anthi_cwaters
To: mdwaters@urtoo.com
Re:

Thanks.

mdwaters
To: anthi_cwaters@ezrite.com
Re:

You're welcome, young lady.

Remember: it's the difference between facts and inspiration.

Trust your imagination. It is a power—and it's real.

Anthi_cwaters
To: mdwaters@urtoo.com
Re:

I'm still waiting for it to happen to me again.

mdwaters
To: anthi_cwaters@ezrite.com
Re:

Don't you worry. It will.

Anthi_cwaters
To: mdwaters@urtoo.com
Re:

So you say!

xxxiii

With regard to the reversals in the case against Claud Plantard it was easy, Anthi, for Arrends and de Batz to obey the judge's demand for silence. But it was less simple for Captain Poulin. Poulin was an ambitious young officer, not yet thirty, who had gone from his home in Lyon to the national police academy before finding himself farmed out to Deepest France, where he intended to prove himself worthy of joining the force in one of France's larger cities. Within an hour of his grilling by Mathieu, he was talking to reporters from *France-Soir*.

"You can tell the French people this: I don't aim to be made the scapegoat in this case. Not just because I did what any investigator would have done. This 'Little Judge' has no perception of real police work. He's still wet behind the ears. He doesn't understand that you can't crack eggs in kid gloves. You can't treat witnesses the way you might blessed saints. If some witness turns out to have a personality problem, it's not our fault. Our duty is simply to get them to tell their story. And if they can't tell the difference between fact and fiction, let the other side bring in the shrinks to figure it out. The defense has its methods as much as we do."

"Do you intend to stay on this case, Captain Poulin?" the reporters asked.

"Well, I don't intend to get stuck," he gave them a sardonic grin, "in Deepest—in the Pyrenees the rest of my life."

"And that means—?"

"Whatever you damn well want it to mean!" The tall, hunched officer raised his shoulders, which generally slumped like those of a man used to bending toward persons of average height, and turned away from his interrogators. "You've got your story. Now go and print it."

Poulin's angry interview forced Mathieu, tagged now as "the Little Judge," to agree to a press conference of his own—in an attempt to stop the new rumors that had begun flying here and there. To the reporters admitted to the conference room, it was clear that the cherubic qualities of Mathieu's grin had given way to something more anxious.

"Is it true, sir, that you want to make Captain Poulin the scapegoat in this case?"

"I simply want to find the criminal or criminals. I believe that is what Captain Poulin wants as well—at least when the Little Captain is not thinking primarily of his own career."

"You said 'criminals,'" one of the women, the tall blonde from *France-Soir*, began. "Is there now more than one suspect?"

"Until a case is solved, there is always a list of suspects."

"Is Monsieur Claud Plantard about to be released?"

"He is still the accused. As long as he remains so, he will be held in custody."

"Is it true that another panel of handwriting experts has been called in?" the same woman asked.

Mathieu's carefully modulated patience crumbled in sudden exasperation. "Who told you that?"

The reporter looked down at her notebook. "More than one stream flows in and out of the Salz, sir."

Mathieu composed his chubby cheeks into a smile again. "But the river is more useful if we dam up some of those streams. As a matter of fact, experts will ask for dictations from over one hundred members of the Plantard family and the Rennes community."

"Does that mean, sir," a man from Paris asked, "that the reports of the first experts have been thrown out?"

"Let's say that inconsistencies in the first reports have recently come to my attention."

"What sort of inconsistencies, please?" someone at the rear of the pack shouted.

"Who said that?" Mathieu shouted back and scanned the crowd.

When a skeletal man with long uncombed hair raised his hand, Mathieu gave his answer: "That not all of the messages came from the same hand."

"Is there more than one criminal involved, then?"

"I might just point out that most of us have more than one hand," Mathieu replied, trying to reduce the tension he felt. A few reporters snickered, but the majority failed to see any humor in his comment.

"Is it true, sir," the tall blonde, who had not laughed, said, "that a woman's hand was detected in one of the notes?"

The judge seemed irritated enough now to end the interview immediately. He turned his face to the freshly washed window of the room as though looking for an exit, paused for a moment, and then continued. "I see that there are some very large tributaries indeed flowing into the Salz these days. It is not enough to lean on young ladies—not when someone has set out to disturb the entire community. Let me say this—we are working with a large family and a small community. Many individuals may have inherited characteristics that shaped their writing along similar lines. Others were taught to write by the same teachers—the majority of whom were women. I myself cannot always tell whether a letter was written by a man or a woman. There are a number of difficulties that only the best experts can sort out."

"Are you saying, sir, that what was taken for Claud Plantard's penmanship may have been that of one of his schoolmates—or a relative?"

"For the present I am not ruling out that possibility." Mathieu's eyes shone with the light of fresh insight. "Now don't you think you have enough to fill your three columns today?"

"Thank you, sir."

"My pleasure," the judge replied.

xxxiv

Publication of Mathieu's interview brought a scrappy Arrends immediately into the judge's office.

"This changes *every*thing."

"What do you mean?" the judge asked.

"What you said about the writing sample. That blows the state's case against my client to smithereens, doesn't it? That and little Jeanne's recantation." Arrends's usually knitted brow appeared as smooth now as silk. All his hesitation had vanished.

"There are still the neighbors who saw your client around the scene. *They* at least haven't retracted what they said they saw."

"But not on the day in question."

"And the fibers, Jean."

"Fibers? You know how fibers are. We are all walking magnets for fibers." Arrends seemed determined—it showed in the light of his eyes. "I'm afraid I can't keep up my professional dignity and permit my client to languish another day in jail. We have got to get him out, until the state has a decent case to make."

"What about Poulin?" the judge asked, obviously wanting to be sure he was covering every side of the matter. "Poulin will be hot as hell. And Philip Plantard?"

"That's all one problem. It's Poulin's job to do what you say, whether he likes it or not. He has to keep Philip from getting to my client."

"I'm not sure Poulin's going to be much help. He's outraged about my calling the nationals in. As though I'd spat in his pastis."

"Get the nationals to put somebody on Philip."

"They haven't got the manpower. But I'll make the request."

"That's all we can do." Arrends appeared pleased to have had his way.

"I take it that you've already been paid?" the judge added, as though he suspected the attorney might be overconfident.

xxxv

Christine
Pop-Up

Thank God that is done, she said to herself as she watched the door close on the hunched, determined back of her husband. He will have to act now—if only to do it for me. He is a man of judgment, if a bit slow sometimes to reach his decisions. Soon it will be finished. And whatever happens cannot hurt like....

The small, catlike woman slipped back down under the clinic's stiff sheets and punched up her pillow until it concealed all except the front of her skull, the mask of suffering she had managed, she felt, so well during the months of pain, suspicion, and hate. And remorse? Yes, that too. But only for what she had refused to believe Claud had done, for the way she had allowed him to deceive her. Now that was taken care of—soon his deceptions would come to an end, his account marked paid in full. It was safe for her again to remember the good years. She had no desire now to dwell on the quarrels, the slashing separations they had inflicted on one another, the misery of their innocence. It was almost the time to think of reunions. If only all the noise, voices riding the wind like large birds, would go away. Or just quiet down so she could focus on the cries she feared least.

And the best, the happiest reunion—no question— This I know from my soul. The way I know that I have done (always done) what I had to do. The loveliest was the morning they turned him out. Never have I come so near losing him. He was gone, I thought. Forever. Had put his life in the hands of that stupid girl. I knew I had lost him. They would lock him away forever. I would never see him. But thank God, she could not even make up a story that she could stick with. Thank God she made a muddle of whatever she imagined she was trying to do.

Because of Jeanne, they knew they had to turn him loose. I had him back. Claud. Philip believes he can read my mind. *It's nerves, isn't it? Let me hold you.* His puny imagination. I lay still. Let him work. I did nothing, Claud, nothing. You were free again, Claud, and Philip gone. Finally. I phoned you. *Be careful. Where's Jacqueline?* Gone. All were gone. Except the two of us. And the mountains. Our escape. Our sacred place.

After my marriage—my revenge—he returned that time too. Had to, I told him. All we ever needed. The mountains, one or two words, our magic. No cafe, no dusty hotel bed. In this land rolling with lovers, in those days we were nameless and free.

But *now* they would know us, both of us. So it was up toward Roc-Negre we rode. After the—the footbridge, we felt our safety waited in the rock, even scrambling over such razor stones, loose from winter. I needed a second to catch my breath. And cursed myself. A second wasted. At the boulder, through the oaks and pines, I saw the rock stories higher.

He surprised me. Gliding back toward me, down the cut path. *Claud, you mustn't!* Good arms, strong rough fingers, when we fell together, to the leaves, stones. *I had lost you. This time.* Mouths together, but I heard him: *I am a Plantard! I live under the charm.* My questions were gone, all of them.

Following the dark granite wall to the mouth. Where Roman gold, Merovingians' too, he told me. The first time he brought me. Fourteen then—but here then too. The rock, the cave. Our lovely first times. Huddled under coats, then rugs, in the dark, we had all our colors. Our rainbow in the dark. Our cave. Certainly not just for sheepherders. And our luck held. *Here was our home, our only one. Always.* Always? A rug I couldn't see, the colors covering us both.

What good, strong love this time. And gentle. Our months of hurt and fear paid for. Nothing else was life. With him, under the charm again. After throwing it away, in the arrogant rush of my girlhood. Stupid revenge.

And the enigma. If only I hadn't let Philip get to me again. The same wretched questions. Living with the enigma. The torture of all those years. Waiting: Was it the light or the dark? Little Stephen, Jacqueline's flaw, so obviously lacking. And Charles all the time more radiant. With Philip's Hollywood eyes. Spaniel eyes. Axx—another second of that doting love. People without an atom of the dark in them. And Charles, with the same mindless needs. Until I wanted to— *Every*body's little Charles. Now, the same enigma again. Another one. Another five years until it manifests— I cannot go through it again. I don't care how much I'll bleed.

No, no. I have to keep this one.

But Claud deserves what he gets. After what I told Philip, he won't fail. All their glass and blond bricks. And her landscapers! What does Jacqueline know, with her factory-made tastes. And me slaving in Philip's old barn with the heat knocking. Priests run through my blood. I have a calling. Claud saw it. *Bring the Plantards back*, he said. Her flesh running with greengrocers and factory hands.

But both of us, Jacqueline, me, swelling again. *Prison does things to a man's appetites. Isn't that what they say?* We thought she would believe it. She didn't, I guess. Made her needs clear. Got her dirty claws in him again. So it's me with my little enigma, and her with that twisted bundle of darkness waiting again. But Claud won't be. One shell. Just large enough to blow out his dark Plantard heart. *It's a wonder Jeanne hasn't turned up the same way*! I could not believe what he said. *All gossip*— he said. Was it? I said. *Look, Chris, you know you are the only one I have ever loved.* And the others? *I would never do for any of them what I have done with you.* I tried to tell myself that. All the other people in my head frozen, I focused on what he did with me. No matter how lovely the others flower. How fast my arms, neck, shoulders weather.

But my mind gets flooded. Swamped by memories pulling me deeper into the drowned morning. Son now of France. No more mine or Claud's than everyone's. Sent out to fetch the croissants. *And don't go near the Marti place,* I said, knowing that—

When I saw he was gone, I left all our guests in the dining room, without their croissants, and went to my room to dress for the cold, a cave like the mountains.

I loved our cave, our mountains. And the pond. Heart-stopping summer nights we had played there. Throwing off our clothes, swimming to the moon. Invulnerable—like marble fauns. Claud and me, rifling through all the caves. *Silver nights,* I said. Simplest thing I knew, to swim our bodies together. Quicksilver. Lovers in the flesh. And nothing actual can be more sacred.

They caught us, Mother did. And his father. Showed us how judgment feels. So he had to move away, Claud did. Philip came. Slick Hollywood, like Alain Delon. No teddy bear Claud. I cut my hair, and looked just as slick as he did. He had his say, and Mother chose. Swift and crisp as that. Afterwards Claud had to come back, so I could tell him. Daytimes we had in our cave again. Nights I endured. The high, empty ceiling.

All of it was bearable. Except for two mistakes. Whose fault? Ours. Mine, since I had to decide. I grew up then. Put them away. God knows if those vultures get wind—Pray God the cook never tells. And would have done the third as well. Simple as that.

But Philip caught on. *Why do this to me? You know I need a son.* The begging in his eyes like arrows now. That gnawing hunger. Some morning I will open the paper, see him with his face between the bars screaming *Chrissy, my life.* Stupid farce! He thinks he knows love. His little hunger. Why doesn't he just—

And so you came, Charles. Bringing the torture Claud claimed as his own. I could not be sure. Not even when the boy's light showed through, binding me tighter. The stone drowning us all.

The glass to show me my loss. Love I had to break. Six years. More. Almond bitter for Plantards—who ought to live under a charm. Such things happen. Father dead, me only five. Mother forced to do it all. Without time— Without laughter in her eyes I needed desperately. Need still—to no avail. Was I the right kind of daughter. Mother already bitter. Needy. And limping, from some schoolboy prank. She should have been dancing beautifully. Not even twenty-five. With me just starting school. It does not stretch to Boudets, the charm. One plan left us, Claud and me, to outwit them all.

It was set. The seed planted weeks ago at Jeanne's, with us looking out her window: *They will all meet in the Marti's basement,* I said. His crazy knights, his heroes. I knew he would end up there, especially when I told him not to. The caves within we had explored, Claud and I. Pieces of bone, bits of pottery. No one knew what to expect there. Plantards' ancient gold perhaps. Or our dream: the Plantards' enduring claim.

What Philip finally knows. It took an American to tell him. More than the gold—kingdoms even. Claud has known for months. Branch of darkness, branch of light. All a single line. *Sang real,* regal blood, no matter the shade. Convergent in here, inside this tight drum. Rounder and rounder it swells. Titan plant inside.

So they will have to deal with me. Claud's friends from the north. The Order will. This new Plantard springing from Razes' cave. They know it.

But no more plotting. Waiting in shadows, like my dream.

No dream that morning. Ropes, stones, the knife, damn plastic that smothers. Plastic for a prince. Your voice sweet as a dove. One of *us.* Making your plans. No surprises for you. The hand least expected grasps you. *Moth*— Through my plans like steel. Panic in my womb. *We cannot*— The first stone, Claud's hands, down into the curls above your ear. *Don't you!* Did I scream it?

He slapped me. Once, twice. Sharp—full of judgment: *This is the rest of our life.* And panic vanished.

Our limp package between us, we stumbled into the first chamber. *Wait,* he said, turned on both miners' lights, and we raised the deadweight again. Two beams now thrusting at one another. Swords. Into the large chamber, the first one. A small church, the ceiling high vaulted. *Not here.* Did he speak? The narrow passage forked. Beams wrote their unintelligible script, and dull crystal glimmered. *Through here—* The cavern not much larger than a catacomb shelf, dust in the air. *For God's sake, Claud, get the masks—* I checked for the letter. I needed some of his confidence. *Don't panic. You're too intelligent for that.* I no longer felt it. Knew he had the knife but was hiding it from me. *We are under the charm—remember that.* If he said so. *Playing it smart, there is not another woman who—*

I carried the sharp, warm certainty in his eyes out into the light. To the post office. Two or three people there going and coming. No one will remember me, I kept telling myself. And they didn't.... Until they turned Claud loose. Vultures always need new meat. New experts, new results. Three or four said out loud they thought they remembered. The vultures swarmed. For fresh blood now. Mine.

But I am your mother, Charles. The French nation knows who I am. Every mother knows. I am a force in this land. Mother of France. Of innocence. The vital part.... All a hollow farce. My dream. They do not know. Not a few ignorant villagers, even a handful of experts, wrong about Dreyfus from the start.

And I have what they need under this tight skin, my drum of freedom. Your little brother. Inside me. Philip Plantard's son, for all they know, for all I know. I would simply stop eating. The press will never let them. Not your mother. And the tape the captain wants me to make. To hear the corbeaux for themselves. Those flapping noises. Me fighting them. Forcing the corbeaux cries into one voice. Not tongues. They will have to decide. See if *they* can hold it—them—all together.

When the Order speaks. The Merovingians too reborn. Royal France. Royal Farce. All of it. Claud's dear son, Philip's dead. Or vice verse, I don't know. Branch of death, branch of life. Branch of France. Corbeaux crowing through my head. In the wind. To print and picture. To France.... Farce or not, the Order needs him. Whoever believes a drop of the blood means more than a spit in the sea.

Both lines I know, the light and the dark. And what in the blood matters. The passion, fire through my veins like lightning. Claud. The passion still runs. He is dead now. Because of Jacqueline. I gave the word, the gun. Turned Philip loose, them loose. The way I let you go. Even the fire in the blood lives here. Finally here, with the voices in my head. Finally only it means a damn. Will keep me from the judge. Or bring Claud back. The silver lake. The cave—back into our cave, not that black grave. Claud's mouth feeding mine. The fire on his lips, spark in his eye. Only my mind, not the blood. Wholly mind. Unholy. Mine.

With the smile of a child, the small-boned woman pulled the covers up to her dark curls and settled down into her pillow, her mattress, prepared to sleep until her husband returned from what she told him to do.

xxxvi

Anthi_cwaters
To: mdwaters@urtoo.com
Re: At last!

Dad, I think you've been putting off Christine's pop-up, dreading it really. But I have to give it to you, I think it could be the best one yet. Surely the most lyrical.

Usually I don't care for fragments but found that, with a few exceptions, one piece led smoothly to the next. I could follow it better than I might have expected.

mdwaters
To: anthi_cwaters@ezrite.com
Re: right

Thank you, Anthi. I appreciate your response. Yes, I kept hesitating with Christine. But finally she was there—in those broken thoughts.

By this point in Charles's story, our readers ought to know the people, the place, the events well enough to jump across the rifts Christine's mind, troubled as it is, must leave in its track.

Anthi_cwaters
To: mdwaters@urtoo.com
Re: a missing part

Even though I could flow with it, I don't believe you've told all of her story. There's something, I sense, that you've left out.

mdwaters
To: anthi_cwaters@ezrite.com
Re: If so

Young woman, I have to leave it up to you to fill in those gaps. This is all I know about Christine. It's time for me to move on to the awful result of what she ordered Philip to do. And to *get lost* in my story. For both of us, I hope, to lose ourselves in it.

Anthi_cwaters
To: mdwaters@urtoo.com
Re: Really?

It's a lot you're asking of me, Dad—filling in gaps. I don't feel I'm ready yet. I will try to focus on Christine, and wiggle my way into her mind, the way it's riddled with cracks. And I'll get back to you later.

Anyway, it's been a hoot working with you on this. When I try my own, I'll count on your help. Okay?

xxxvii

Within twenty-four hours of Arrends's critical visit with Mathieu, Claud Plantard walked out of his cell in Couiza, still an accused man but free to go about his business. Mathieu and the state had to confess that they, in effect, had gone round the board, were back to start, and no one was going straight to jail. Rennes-les-Bains spun from the shock. People who had once sworn that Claud Plantard was a good man, *tres gentil*, a hard worker, very sympathetic, then had called for his death as the monster who deceived them all, now returned, to their terror, but stripped this time of confidence that they could recognize a murderer when they saw one and of the assurance that their gendarmes could protect them.

All of us, Anthi, who are parents and live in communities where small children have been abducted and brutally murdered understand exactly what the people in Deepest France were feeling. Nothing "leaves us as vulnerable," editorialists later noted, "as threats to our children." There simply is no way we can guard against this terror. It goes much deeper than all our childhood matinee fears of Frankenstein monsters, Wolfmen, revivified mummies, and other nightmares that modern medicine, Darwin, and archeology have planted in the unconscious. The Living-Dead do not lie half as deep because they are almost transparent as a metaphor for conformity and a widespread drug culture. Murdered children resonate with a more irrational force than the sexual fears of seduction and orality the airborne Count from Transylvania so effectively captures, even now that AIDS has given that phantasma a new dimension. We have no way to protect our children all the time, for each of us knows, especially if we had at least one intruding parent (and who of us did not have a mother or father who nosed about doing things for "our own good"), that constant vigilance would guarantee a fate almost as dreadful as abandonment. A child, like a tree, needs a free space in which to unfold.

It is impossible to watch a child every minute. Look at Christine Plantard as France came to know her through papers and magazines: she reported that she had taken her eye off little Charles for only fifteen minutes—and ten minutes later she was running through the door of Charles's nurse's home, throwing herself into the nurse's arms, weeping hopelessly, "Bette, I know he's not here. He's *gone*. They have taken him. If you only knew what I have gone through these five years!" to a frightened woman who told newsmen she could not help but find Christine totally incoherent. For Bette had not yet been told of the call Philip's brother had received just before he phoned Christine: a muffled voice whispering, "The child is taken. I am going to put him away. Not all your money can bring your pet, your little goose, back! I am revenged."

With Claud Plantard set free, every parent in the Razes felt he or she was sewn inside Christine's skin. Terror covered the village on the Salz like an invisible fog, and the police appeared powerless to drive it off.

The panic that an "omnipresent terror creates may compel" even an average citizen "to protect himself and his neighbors" by resorting, Anthi, to what the editorialists called "extreme measures." At times like this, actions we would not ordinarily consider take on a primitive logic of their own. Our children are in danger. Even if we have no instinct to use violence to guard our offspring, at moments like this in Rennes-les-Bains we feel we have a mandate to do whatever we must. Is it any wonder, then, that policemen, who feel this sanction more frequently than the rest of us, often wake to find they have committed an act in the name of public safety that in less driven moments they knew to be an avoidable crime? Perhaps they have killed an innocent pedestrian or motorist by violating a red light during a high-speed chase, or had their handgun misfire while holding a fidgeting petty thief until help arrived.

Is it surprising, then, that a man as personally involved as Philip Plantard—who originally could not believe that Claud Plantard would be suspected and had to be convinced of his probable guilt by the police, the press, and his own wife—would feel wrapped in such righteousness that two months after his cousin's release he would wake from his coma of mandated responsibility to find himself jailed for gunning his cousin down in broad daylight? It scares us all, I suspect, to recognize that, at a much deeper level than we care to consider, we almost understand his behavior.

Five

This time, Anthi, French readers did not have to wait for a trial to discover the details behind the crime. Everyone in the Rennes region appeared eager to tell what he or she knew—Claud's attorney, Jeanne Roux, Philip's lawyer, Christine, Captain Poulin, the judge. Everyone seemed to have a personal interest to defend. Newsmen and newswomen from all parts of France swarmed into the Razes.

"My client had a clear right to be free," Jean-Paul Arrends blustered when a woman reporter from Paris asked a question he took as an accusation. "The prosecution had no case against him. It was the duty of the gendarmes to protect Claud Plantard from the accused. Philip Plantard admits he has been pursuing my client with a hunting gun for a month, that on one occasion the accused and his wife hid outside my client's home for hours waiting for him to exit. They had the gun then. They planned to kill my client and abduct his wife and son. And if a strange car hadn't pulled up, they would have murdered him then. The police knew it. Why didn't they put a stop to that madman? No one can blame Philip Plantard for his rage. But he had no right to execute my client. The police have failed us again!"

"I didn't want Claud to die!" little Jeanne sobbed into the microphone for a handsomely groomed young announcer from Marseilles who had knocked on her door. "He was innocent—innocent! Why won't they believe me."

"Yes," barked Philip's new attorney Danton Maury, a pugnacious middle-aged man with bald forehead, when asked whether his client had visited his wife after the crime.

"And before?" inquired another anonymous reporter in the crowd outside the judge's office.

"The sequence of events we have been able to establish, and will not be inclined to deny, was as follows: My client was by his wife's bed in the clinic for three hours during the morning of the crime. Shortly after noon, he left the clinic, drove to the victim's house and waited approximately ten minutes for the victim to return from his business. Two associates and Madame Plantard, Claud's wife, were in the victim's car when it arrived. When the victim exited the vehicle, my client, wearing a hat and sunglasses, stepped from the shrubbery at the side of the house and fired once. Claud Plantard dropped immediately to the sidewalk. My client drove directly back to the clinic and told his story to his wife. She asked him to phone his brother and tell him. His brother recommended he phone the police first, and then phone me. This is the account my client, who obviously has come unglued following the tragic events that have battered his family, reported to the gendarmes. The facts, I suspect, will support his story."

"So your defense will be temporary insanity?" several chimed in from the crowd.

"What do you think?"

"What did the accused and Madame Plantard discuss that morning?" shouted a small woman immediately in front of Maury.

If he could have, he would have ignored her question, but the cameras and microphones surrounding him were now, he saw, focused on her. "Many things—" he began but hesitated before he volunteered, "including new developments in the investigation of their son's death."

"What developments?" the chorus demanded.

"Ask Judge Mathieu. He had visited them two days before."

"They talked about new reports from the experts?" asked an alert young man who had wormed in beside the small woman in the front.

"Ask the judge," a calmed Monsieur Maury answered.

"Do you expect to get your client off?" the same young man asked. Maury noticed how slicked down his mouse-brown hair was and how it differed from the wild-haired reporters around him.

"There are mitigating circumstances."

"What?" the young man with the combed hair asked as though he and the attorney were engaged in private conversation. Immediately the rest of the press became voyeurs on their way to becoming gossips.

"I would think that any man whose son died the way little Charles did would have a strong case to make— There are other circumstances."

"Yes?"

"You should talk with Captain Poulin. He also visited my client and Madame Plantard—frequently. He has a heavy investment in the guilt of the victim. He has mentioned certain things to my client."

"What things?"

"As I say, he's visited them often. I don't know all he said. But chiefly Captain Poulin has spoken of what he personally would do if his child had been murdered like little Charles."

The collective breath of the French people caught incredulously in the throat of the nation's press. "That can't be true," one reporter said, expressing the thought that appeared to freeze everyone's mind. For a long moment, no one in the always ravenous crowd knew what to ask next.

Monsieur Maury broke their silence. "Is that all?" His quizzing smile made it clear that he desired to tell them something more.

An older woman near the rear of the pack picked up his cue. "Why is Christine Plantard in the clinic?" she shouted over her colleagues' heads.

"Madame Plantard is expecting. In seven months," Maury added, and turned his back on a mob stunned into an inchoate buzz.

XXXV

"Philip was with me three hours," Christine Plantard admitted to the writer from a large Parisian magazine that had paid for the privilege of an exclusive interview from her bedside. Against the sheets and hospital gown, the drained whiteness of Christine's face reduced her appearance to two large dark eyes staring from a bank of snow.

"What did you talk about?" the reporter asked. She appeared to be about thirty-five, with green eyes and long brown hair, an auburn tint running through it. "Did you tell him about the baby?"

"What about the baby?" Christine asked, as though surprised by the question.

"That you are expecting." The reporter looked about the age to have begun worrying about having a child. Her cheeks were pressed against the supporting bones, her eyes tired and squeezed to a focus.

Christine felt she could trust this woman. "Philip already knew it. I had the test last week."

"Why are you in the clinic? Have you experienced—difficulties?"

"I am under stress. You know how that is." Yes, she knew, Christine was confident. "My doctors thought it would be safer. This way I don't *have* to talk to reporters, and police, and—and other officials, unless I'm able. So far, I have had no real problems. I keep my fingers crossed, though."

Although the reporter was dressed extremely well and wore makeup of such quality that one would have taken her for an actress, she missed no nuance. Rather than interrupt, she had made mental note of the pause in Christine's speech just before she mentioned the 'other officials'—she knew someone specific lay concealed behind the pause. Now she pursued her suspicion. "When the judge—Monsieur Mathieu—talked with you and Philip, was that one of the strains you mentioned?"

"Yes—yes it was."

"Did it affect the baby?"

The woman was very sympathetic, Christine felt, especially for a reporter from Paris. "No," Christine said. "I am a very healthy mother. I survive almost anything. Sometimes I wish I didn't." She raised her hands to her face but quickly pulled them away, as though her gesture might impugn her words.

"And was the judge's visit one of those times?" asked the writer, with a renewed show of sympathy, knowing that she probed for all her readers.

"Yes—I think it was."

"What did Judge Mathieu say?"

"It's so unbelievable. I—I can't tell you. I don't even let myself think about it. There are some things you can't even begin to comprehend—not even when people tell you as clearly as anyone can. It just makes no sense."

"I understand. You don't need to talk about it, Madame Plantard. I'll ask someone else. But what did you and Philip talk about that morning?"

"We talked—just talked," Christine answered and turned her eyes to the blank television above the woman's head.

"What did you say to Philip?"

"We just talked—"

Christine, the writer imagined, was someplace else—wherever a woman of such sadness goes to escape the curious and to seek comfort in her memory of the ones she missed.

xxxvi

"There's no way they're going to blame this on me," Captain Poulin rifled back at the pack of newspeople gathered outside the three-story building that hid his office on the second level. But his routine grin of masculine confidence crumbled.

"Monsieur Maury reports, Captain, that you went to see the Plantards frequently. Is it usual for an officer simply to drop in on victims of crime?" asked the round-faced newsman from Lyon, as though appointed by his colleagues to do so.

"There were details of the case to discuss." His wooden face was turning lobster pink. "I needed to ask questions."

"We understand, Captain…. But after Claud Plantard's release and the national police had been called in—"

"I might have been taken off the case, but I still have an interest in the family—and in justice." Poulin appeared to recover his poise, or to cover its lack with defiance.

"What would justice be in this case, as you see it, sir?" asked the appointed spokesman as he looked around himself to confirm that the others there supported his line of inquiry.

"The same as for any crime," the officer said, as though puzzled.

"And what is that, if you don't mind?"

"What do you mean? That the criminal has to be brought to account, of course," Poulin said, clearly defensive again.

"By the state?"

"Certainly."

"And if the state fails, who then?"

"No—you're not going to draw me into that." Poulin turned his head as though ready to reenter his building.

"Did you believe Claud Plantard was the criminal?" asked the reporter before the officer could depart.

"We put together a good case against him. It's still a good case—despite some frightened witnesses."

"Frightened of the police?"

"Certainly not!" Poulin, red-cheeked now, confronted the crowd. "You fellows forget this is a family crime. In cases like this, lots of pressures are working on people. You'd be surprised. My experience is that people feel free to do things to family they would never think of doing to total strangers. It's like family gives them special license."

"Perhaps," the reporter said, as Poulin's sad point appeared to sail over his head without entering his ears. "But is it true, Captain, that you told Philip Plantard that you 'knew what you would do if it had been your son'?"

"If I said something like that, I was referring to his grief." Poulin turned here and there as though trying to decide whether to look for the best way out or to stand and face the mob closing upon him. He had already waited too long—no easy escape appeared possible.

"Not to taking justice into his own hands?"

"Now that you mention it, there may have been some of that in what I said. But I knew Plantard wanted to kill his cousin—I was just trying to draw him out, uncover his plans. You guys forget that I stopped him one time. Maybe if I had drawn him out more, I could have saved Claud Plantard." Poulin's shoulders relaxed, as though he had put together a solid explanation of his conduct.

"Had you and the Plantards become friends?" the same reporter asked.

"Look, my friend, a policeman's work is complicated. I try to do my duty. I try to get close to people, draw them out. But I'm also a human being—I have normal feelings, however it appears to you fellows. The Plantards find themselves in a very sympathetic position. They are working people just like the rest of us. I may not come from this region, but I have as much compassion for them as anyone else. I would want to believe my kids, if I had kids, were safe playing in front of the house. Anybody would."

"Why," a woman interrupted, "do you believe he shot his cousin?"

"Look, lady," Poulin blurted out, "the man's son has been dead going on five months. It's been building up inside the guy. What else could he do?—with the accused running around free as an alley cat."

"Claud Plantard was free almost two months," another reporter, a man, shouted from the rear.

"Why now?" the spokesman asked, once more picking up the collective drift of the interrogation.

"Why don't you ask the Little Judge?" Poulin grumbled. "He may have an answer. He's been telling Philip and Christine *some*thing."

xxxvii

Mathieu was less eager than on earlier occasions to talk with the press, but, as he leaned on elbows over his wide mahogany desk, he realized he had little choice. Philip Plantard's new attorney and Poulin had both indicated that he held the clue to the most recent murder. Mathieu knew he possessed one clue but wasn't certain that what he had to tell the media was the ultimate answer to questions about Philip's decision to gun down Claud. The explanation just wasn't as simple as it seemed.

Events following his last interrogation of Philip and Christine appeared to form a firm chain of facts, with one action leading to another like scenes in a good story.

But Mathieu had lost his confidence in the innocence of stories. In his time, he decided, he had heard too many cases, seen too many movies, read too many novels, studied too much history. It was because of these that he generally thought of life as an iron chain of causality, composed of events that led from one to another, and so constructed that once you sniffed one or two interconnecting causes you believed you had grasped the truth of the entire story.

But with this case Mathieu realized that his confidence in such simple chains had lulled him into a dangerously innocent view of a world that laid upon his shoulders a burdensome responsibility for determining the nature of truth in his restricted—but still too wide—arena. The performance of that little cutie Jeanne Roux opened his eyes. How easily he'd been taken in by her eagerness to help. Following a chain of events to their causes the way he read books, he now knew, was like traveling around an onion with one leaf leading smoothly to the other until you returned to the place you began. You thought you knew the onion, but you had merely glided over its surface. Now he understood that there were causes hidden beneath the causes one saw, and that the so-called facts of the case meant nothing without those causes. There were hidden reasons that Jeanne Roux herself felt so compelling a need to help that she had lied to do so. He didn't understand this chaos of motives—he only recognized that they too must exist. For all he knew, at the heart of the onion one might discover a worm totally undetected during the circuit of the surface. Slicing onions for the *coq au vin* he loved to cook, he had discovered such worms more than once and hoped others had not altogether escaped his detection. Well, if they had, they certainly ended up well-cooked worms—flavoring the sauce. Everything about this case had begun to give him a sense of a hidden worm. Or of a core that itself wrapped around the onion. He wasn't certain that he desired any longer to know what that core must be.

He leaned far back and slumped down in his oversized leather chair. *What choice do I have?* he asked himself again.

Abruptly he forced himself to his feet, left his quiet chambers, and went to face the mob. *I thought this one would make my career.... Now it feels like an anchor around my neck. Christine and Philip belong to the French people now. How can I hold back what I did—what I know? All I can do is remain as truthful as I'm able—and keep peeling. God only knows what's to protect us from the worm.*

With his renewed despair he stepped out into the glare of the midday sun. It was forty-eight hours since Plantard had pulled the trigger.

Julius Raper

xxxviii

"We understand, sir, that you interviewed Philip and Christine Plantard the day before Claud Plantard was shot?" The press corps had selected a tall, slender man with dark hair and a wrinkled forehead to lead the questioning of Mathieu. The television camera with him indicated he represented a station in Marseilles.

"It was in all the papers," the judge answered. "You know it as well as I do."

"The interview took place in the clinic?"

"The papers covered all that. Look it up."

"Did you know about Madame Plantard's condition?"

"I had some indications." Mathieu tried to stare off into space. He was starting to resent the rudeness of men and women who fired insinuations of misconduct at him from all directions. Even public servants, he told himself, ought to have some defense. Sunlight leaking around his sunglasses compounded his discomfort.

"The interview must have been very urgent?"

"It was not going to keep nine—seven—months, if that's what you mean."

"Not even to the end of Madame Plantard's delicate period?"

"Under the circumstances no one could speak of an end to that period. Especially under the new circumstances." He whispered this last, knowing that he had just stepped into the machinery that could devour him.

"Then you have the new reports from the experts?"

He nodded his reluctant confirmation.

"And you discussed them with the Plantards?"

Mathieu raised and lowered his head once, twice, as though forcing his mouth to speak. "As well as other developments." His words sounded as though each of them stuck in a separate part of his throat.

"What developments?"

"Concerning the 'man' seen near the postbox in Rennes-les-Bains at the hour Charles disappeared and the final note was posted."

"You have an identity?"

"We have leads."

"You have a name?"

"Yes." His few words were starting to come more easily.

"Who is he?"

"Not a he—"

"A woman?"

"Jeanne—" someone sputtered in a fit of recognition.

"Claud's wife—Jacqueline!" another voice shouted with the same assurance.

"A woman—yes. Three witnesses place her near the post bureau at the same moment."

"Why shoot *Claud* then?"

"It must be Jacqueline!"

"The name the witnesses have mentioned is the same the new experts have given me."

"Madame Plantard!" a chorus of news ravens cried from every side.

xxxix

Jacqueline Plantard's name had appeared in the press before. During the early stages of the investigation, just after suspicion first began to center upon her husband, a bar owner in a village upstream from Rennes-les-Bains had come forward with the story of a strange man who burst into his establishment twenty minutes before little Charles disappeared, ordered a quick cup of coffee and drank it in a couple of swallows, studying the clock every second he was there. As abruptly as he came, he dashed out of the bar. Forty minutes later he returned, this time for a breakfast pastis, a choice that the bar owner found remarkable in itself, not to mention the stranger's nervousness, his readiness with six francs even before the order was given, or his continuing interest in the clock. Again he finished off his drink without tasting it—despite the anis flavor and strong alcoholic bite of pastis—and practically knocked other customers down in his hurry to leave the establishment.... The bar owner seemed eager to assist the investigation.

For several days Captain Poulin had his men out combing the riverbanks in the vicinity of the bar. After their investigations turned up the prints of a man's shoe and a woman's boot on a well-concealed bluff of the river, they worked on the hypothesis that the nervous pastis drinker with a female accomplice—perhaps Claud and Jacqueline—had brought little Charles to this point and slipped his body into the fast-moving Salz, probably with a weight tied to it by the cord that bound the child's limbs.

Immediately Poulin had a composite portrait of the clock-watcher drawn and circulated via all the French newspapers. For days the captain had his divers raking the river floor for a heavy object to fit within the empty sack the web of cord formed. For days his experts tested the speed of the river using mannikins with little Charles's size, weight, and buoyancy, but they concluded that the hypothesis was a simple impossibility. If the body had been dropped in at the bluff, it would, in the time allowed, have gone far beyond Rennes-les-Bains, provided it ever got through the sieve of the rapids half-way between the secluded cliff and the village, a feat none of the officers' mannikins accomplished. Furthermore, it made absolutely no sense, when one finally stopped to think, for the perpetrators, who otherwise seemed exceedingly cunning, to have put the victim in above Rennes-les-Bains and thus have the evidence against them ride the river into the village itself.

In the end Poulin had to admit to himself that the tracks belonged not to a pair of kidnapper-murderers but to early-morning lovers looking for a quiet place away from spouses and nosey neighbors. His men found other signs as well: a leveled area in the grass and a telltale bit of litter. Although Poulin failed to apologize to the men whose composite portrait he spread over France, he could imagine why the strange man seemed so jittery, why he took his coffee in such haste and needed the pastis afterwards. At uncharitable moments, the captain found himself wishing that the woman whose boots left the spoor would turn out to be the wife of the barman who had sent him on his expensive, time-consuming, and embarrassing snipe hunt. But such fantasies, he told himself, were simply vengeful—and none of his professional business.

Moreover, Jacqueline Plantard's fellow workers all swore that at the hour little Charles disappeared she was with them at their factory busily stitching hats together. This detail Poulin considered unfortunate. In the first place, a number of his assistants believed their composite bore a remarkable resemblance to Claud Plantard, albeit wearing a wig and a fake goatee. In addition, neither Jacqueline Plantard's neighbors nor the national press had taken a liking to her. Behind her pinched face and glasses, she appeared cold, withdrawn, cutting—overly defensive. Perhaps it had something to do with the illness of Stephen, her own son who, even though he appeared full of strength, was actually suffering from an undiagnosed nervous disease that affected his temper and his motor skills and caused his parents, especially his mother, unending stress. To Poulin it seemed callous, even cruel for the press, once the detail of the woman's boot and story of little Stephen's illness both came to light, to connect up the two in such a fashion that resentment of little Charles's good, healthy spirit and the happiness of Philip and Christine suddenly became for the press reason enough for Claud and Jacqueline to collaborate in destroying his cousin's son.

Wouldn't my work be so much simpler, Poulin sighed as he watched Mathieu's press conference alone in his small apartment above the pharmacy in Couiza, *if all I had to do was make up stories like those the newspapers put together?* Already he knew he had given in too easily to the temptation of making things hang together simply because they seemed to match. Matching evidence was the reason he had stuck with Jeanne Roux, why he'd kept after her until she came up with the story he had sensed she had in her. Trouble was it was only that—a story. He'd thought he had evidence—Claud Plantard's handwriting. And Jeanne had been in the right place at the right time. *What can you use,* he asked himself, *if you can't trust your evidence and your witnesses?*

God, he'd liked that girl. They'd worked together like beef and red wine. All she wanted was for him to put on the pressure that would tell her how she could help—for him to lead her to her story. In the end, though, it turned out to be more his story than hers. Questioning her had been like making love to a woman who likes everything you do. He should have known some of it was just noises, stuff she invented to make him happy.

The papers had done the same thing with Jacqueline Plantard, hadn't they? Her coolness and pain provided an obvious contrast to Christine's warmth. Together they made a picture—the dark and the light. There was a fancy name for that, but he couldn't remember what it was. Opposites made a good story. They sold papers.

But finally the facts just didn't add up, didn't match the known events. The distance between the two points, the bluff and the footbridge, was, Poulin now realized, too much a straight line and too much a crooked one—too short and too rocky—all at the same time.

If you ever crawl out of this sorry backwater, he told himself, *you have learned one thing that's going to help you get ahead: that not every good clue's necessarily a true one. If you ever crawl out....*

xl

"One minute! Just a minute—please!" Mathieu shouted against the overwhelming self-congratulations of the assembled press corps, who for some reason felt vindicated by the developments he had outlined. Even though no one was listening to him, he knew he had to get this new madness under control.

"You've misunderstood! Will you please calm down a minute! I don't want anyone phoning what you're thinking now into your stations! *Stop it!! Do you hear me—stop it!!*" The best he hoped for was that his command would spread from the men and women nearest him to the edges of the gang.

"Okay. Okay.... When you settle down," Mathieu said, lowering his voice, then paused before adding, "I'll tell you what is actually happening." He waited a moment longer.

"That's better. Just keep calm. As I mentioned, the three witnesses and the new panel of handwriting experts have come up with the same name based on the writing samples we gave them. It is a woman. And, in one way, you are correct. The witnesses, who know her well, now tell us that some time after *Christine* Plantard reports that she last spoke to her son alive, they saw *her* at the postbox in Rennes-les-Bains—"

"Who?" groaned someone in front.

"What are you saying?" a man farther back grumbled.

"They saw *Christine* Plantard post a letter—at approximately the time the postal service stamped on the note, the one reading 'not all your dough can save the little goose now.' The experts have substantiated this lead."

Mathieu had learned enough about showmanship to anticipate what happened next. He realized there was no use attempting to continue immediately. The news gatherers were now too busy checking what they had just been told amongst themselves to hear more from him. He settled into a relaxed position with all his weight in his right leg and listened to the voices beating around him like wings.

"Christine? The boy's mother? Little Charles's *mother*?"

"That can't be what he said!"

"He meant Jacqueline."

"Christine? Impossible."

"Not little Charles's mother! Look at the grief she's been through."

"It's all a mistake."

"Mathieu's desperate. He's lost his bearings."

"Christine, the *corbeau*?"

"That's exactly what he said. I heard him use her name, twice."

"It's not a slip."

"Christine is the crow?"

"How could we let her fool us?"

"She can't do this to little Charles!"

"She's the crow?"

"She took us *all* for a pack of fools!"

xli

Anthi_cwaters
To: mdwaters@urtoo.com
Re: Wait!

Goose? Crow? What's with the menagerie?

mdwaters
To: Anthi-cwaters@ezrite.com
Re: translation

I thought the allusions to crow and goose would likely make sense to you, Anthi, living in Paris—whereas in this somber context they will probably strike anyone from outside France as odd. The problem here is not simply one of translation from French to English but also one of translation from English to French and back to English. "Goose" is, of course, a natural metaphor for a soft, smooth, lovable child—an image implying that a parent feels excessive pride and affection for his or her child, the way a little girl grows attached to a plump, spotlessly white goose she has raised as her pet and prized possession. Some of this meaning is certainly lost on recent generations, who have never known a child who cherished a pet goose. But once reminded of those rural times, we easily comprehend what the vicious message meant to suggest, and even, if we set our imaginations free to seek out the mind of its author, sense some of the bitterness and resentment that would have motivated a gesture intended to harm a lovely, soft, white creature.

"Goose," therefore, picks up those delicate, innocent qualities that attract all of us to children—to infants we see on the streets, know among our friends and family, read about in books and the papers: the child we once knew in ourselves and now must struggle through panic to protect or even rediscover, like a man in a dream clawing his way up the collapsing ash wall of a crater into which he has fallen. But we should not forget that a goose may turn into a fierce, threatening, honking machine, especially if an outsider invades its territory. In this sense, the note may also carry a hint that the user of the "goose" reference felt he or she was a stranger to the group to which little Charles most intimately belonged. Theoretically, the word "goose" may have brought us closer to the true identity of the "corbeau," the source of the various notes and phone calls that had plagued the Plantard family—Christine, Philip, his siblings, cousins. But these associations with the 'goose' would appear to lend little support to the latest findings of the handwriting experts.

In French, as you know, Anthi, better than I do, "corbeau" may denote a crow, a raven, a corbel or bracket, a grappling iron, or a rapacious individual or priest. Although the last of these meanings might stir up memories of Christine's Boudet ties, we can be reasonably certain what the Paris press had in mind when it began referring to the author of the messages as *le corbeau*, for at the time of little Charles's death a drama by Henri Becque titled *Les Corbeaux* was playing at the Comedie-Francaise. It is the story of an "abominable businessman who ruins all the family." The press must intend to imply that someone—within or without—the Plantard family has in mind destroying the family itself for reasons that, the journalists are hinting, need discovering. From the position of the media, Jacqueline Plantard would have been the preferred suspect inasmuch as an easily understood resentment of the good health of Philip and Christine's 'little goose' compared to the nervous disorder of her little Stephen might have motivated her resentment of the competing branch of the family.

So, in a sense, "corbeau" is a much easier word to understand than "goose," for, according to one Paris newspaper, the reputation of *corbeaux* has never been good. Even Moses called them impure birds.

But translation of the word is a bit more problematic. I have chosen 'crow' rather than 'raven' because I find something extremely raucous, ugly, and boasting in the messages that preceded and accompanied the murder of little Charles, qualities I detect time and again in the large black creatures that, two or three days each year, light here in my yard to scratch for seeds, nuts, worms. But inasmuch as the French were the first to show Poe the respect he deserves, French readers might see his raven in the repeated, enigmatic, disturbing messages of the corbeau of Rennes-les-Bains. And for Mathieu to report that Christine Plantard may have authored these utterances only adds to the enigma. If she did, was it simply to throw the investigation off the trail? Or is there a clue to a deeper meaning in their terrible braggadocio?

xlii

Anthi_cwaters
To: mdwaters@urtoo.com
Re: too pedantic

Enough already, Pops, with the word associations! You call this a bare-bones mystery? It's starting to sound like a chicken-and-potatoes after-dinner academic lecture, if you don't mind my saying so.

mdwaters
To: anthi-cwaters@ezrite.com
Re: true

No, no, I don't mind. Thank you for reminding me what I set out to do. You keep me on track.

mdwaters
To: anthi_cwaters

So ... What's on your mind?

Anthi_cwaters
To: mdwaters

I was wondering—are you getting tired of your little Charles mystery?

mdwaters
To: anthi_cwaters

No. I'll get back to the story now—my word history is over.

Anthi_cwaters
To: mdwaters

Because, if you are, I've been looking into the Plantards myself. There's new material online, and I'm ready to add a few words to the tale.

mdwaters
To: anthi_cwaters

Soon, Anthi, soon.

Anthi_cwaters
To: mdwaters

Whenever you want, I'm ready to take off.

mdwaters
To: anthi_cwaters

Let me wrap up this part, and you can have it. Okay?

Anthi_cwaters
To: mdwaters

Tres bien. Entaxi.

xliii

As the astonishment of the newspeople following Judge Mathieu's revelations subsided, a new mystery dawned in their minds. The round-faced reporter from Lyon once again stood close enough to Mathieu to pose the question on the tongues of those who had ceased to reel from the blow the new evidence delivered. But despite the support he could expect from his fellow seekers of facts and the good will he trusted he shared with the Little Judge, the balding, pink-faced newsman from Lyon could not help but stumble as he struggled to phrase his query judiciously.

"Who—how—when did Christine Plantard first—learn of these new accu—developments?"

"Who, how, when— You've asked three questions there, haven't you, Monsieur Chauve?" Mathieu felt grateful for the chance to introduce a smidgen of levity into the dolorous occasion, a lightness he did not allow to continue for long. "Madame Plantard first learned of the new reports from the experts four days ago when I called her and Monsieur Philip into my chambers. Yes, that was the day before the night she was rushed to the clinic. Her doctors assure us that her hemorrhaging—which was the reason she entered the clinic—was relatively minor and ceased almost as soon as they got her comfortably on her back with her feet up. But we still waited forty-eight hours before I continued my interview, as you people in the papers so vividly put it, 'beside her pillow.' This time I took a court stenographer with me, and the Plantards decided to call in Monsieur Maury, their own attorney. Monsieur de Batz, who will continue as prosecutor, was in attendance, along with several other officials whose names you will certainly find in the stories most of you filed with your papers and channels. It was then that I passed on to the Plantards the reports of witnesses who say they saw her—Madame Christine Plantard—at the post office. Does that cover all of your questions, Monsieur Chauve?"

Monsieur Chauve was so busy scribbling that he could do little more than grunt, "Thank you—sir," before his competitors began screaming out their own speculations.

"That was the day, sir, before Philip Plantard gunned down his cousin?"

"It was the morning before Monsieur Claud Plantard was shot, yes."

"Do you believe the new developments caused Philip Plantard to take action?"

"Look here, you people, you know as well as I do that you are asking me to speculate about questions that it would be highly improper to comment on even if I was in a position to read Monsieur Plantard's mind. But ask yourself, would you want to get yourself put away for life under similar circumstances? It doesn't make sense to me. It doesn't add up."

"Even if you believed the primary suspect for murdering your child was going to go scot-free?"

"Not even then. But, remember, Claud Plantard was no longer the sole suspect."

"What do you mean, sir?"

"I mean nothing other than what I said. I am only setting the record straight. There've been altogether too many sloppy inferences in this case."

"Are you referring to the gendarmes, sir?"

"I am referring to everyone." Mathieu felt himself withdrawing into the depths of his mind, assuming the contemplative stance of a Roman senator, a pose he greatly admired. "There have been too many people making detective stories out of this case."

But Monsieur Chauve failed to honor Mathieu's need for a moment of reflection. "Did Captain Poulin indicate to the Plantards that they had the right to take matters into their own hands?"

Jerked back into the present, Mathieu grumbled, "That's a matter you should take up with the Little Captain, not me."

"Will the expectant mother be held for questioning?" one of the women in the crowd asked.

"Madame Christine Plantard, if I may remind you, is a patient in a clinic."

"And when she feels better?"

"We will take the action appropriate at that time." For a second Mathieu believed he had said all he either needed or desired to say to the press. Then a further thought occurred to him. "I can assure you this time it will be the *appropriate* action. You will recall, I know, what became of Monsieur Claud Plantard."

Before anyone could form another query, Mathieu wheeled to his right and found his path through stunned newspeople, parting before him like the biblical waves, back to his chambers.

xliv

None of us, Anthi, has the energy or the time to give to the millions of conflicting details and underlying causes that make up the biographies of people we read about in the papers. To defend our own sanity we ignore the mountains of detail and instead impose familiar patterns of cause-and-effect on the life stories that come our way.

But our own lives, dear daughter, when we examine them, do not fall into such simple patterns. The difference is that we are more willing to take time sorting out our own convoluted relationships—as long as we don't repress them—in order to arrive at a clearer understanding of reasons we act as we do. In our own life narratives we allow for improbable events that in a simple fiction would strain a reader's credulity. And we may even recognize the possibility of causes concealed within causes.

As Mathieu, Poulin, and even some of the press are discovering, if we desire to get to the bottom of the mysteries that surround the death of little Charles, it behooves us not to resort too quickly to the usual patterns of causation. I am not alone then in sensing the rashness of rushing toward conclusion, in relishing the pleasure to be found in exploring patiently (the way a gentle lover, forgive the "French" comparison, would) each dip and hollow along the way to the desired moment when everything must be revealed.

Forgive the gaps—my mistakes.

xlv

Anthi_cwaters
To: mdwaters@urtoo.com
Re: the boss lady hasn't sung!

Not so fast, Dad. Off the high horse, please, if you don't mind. I haven't had a chance yet to get my two cents in. What about the news release I'm attaching below? It appeared just days after you and I visited Charles Plantard—*le grand Charles*, we called him—outside Lyon.

Lyon—"There is no truth to any of the rumors and myths connecting the Sainte Magdeleine church in Rennes-le-Chateau with the Plantard family. The legends surrounding the royal and religious past of my family are a total contrivance created by my distant cousin Pierre Plantard," Charles Plantard of Lyon and Arques, Deepest France, announced today. Monsieur Plantard made the allegations at a special news conference held in the walled garden of his Edenic estate adorned with fruit trees and flowers and located in the countryside near this city.

"It has recently come to my attention that a connection may exist between my cousin's claims, which are too preposterous for me to reiterate here, and the notorious acts of violence lately occurring in the region around Rennes-le-Chateau, crimes too familiar to the nation and to much of the world for me to mention now. I have only one thing more to say before I end this news conference, and it is that I wish to send my personal condolences to Christine and Philip Plantard, and my apologies to young Jeanne Roux, for the distress that these absurd inventions have no doubt caused. No questions, please!"

With these few enigmatic words Monsieur Plantard dismissed the reporters and returned to the thick walls of his mansion, leaving the nation with another puzzle to add to the many already surrounding the deaths of little Charles Plantard (no known relation) and Claud Plantard. To this point no one has publicly tied the deep past of the Plantard family, that prior to the living generations, to the two murders. Nor, according to available sources, are the rumors and legends to which Monsieur Plantard alluded in his prepared statement well known outside the family.

For all your research, Dad, you must have overlooked this one. Or did it seem extraneous to your "bare-bones" mystery?

mdwaters
To: anthi_cwaters@ezrite.com
Re: doubts

Not exactly extraneous, young lady. And I did run across it. But it did not fit the portrait of Charles Plantard that the pop-up for little Jeanne presented. And *le grand Charles* was a secondary character there—chilling but relatively minor, wouldn't you say? Besides, the article calls his statement an "allegation"—a "prepared [i.e. written] statement"—and speaks of his "allusions." Doesn't sound like a guileless announcement to me.

Anthi_cwaters
To: mdwaters@urtoo.com
Re: vested interests

You know how much energy the reporters have invested in the little Charles case, Dad. They're not about to believe anything that demystifies their proven money-cow.

Aren't you invested just as heavily in the legends that take Magdalena to have been the *SanGreal* and *Sang Real*? I think you are.

mdwaters
To: anthi_cwaters@ezrite.com
Re: touché!

You may be right, girl. But I still trust my pop-ups.

Anthi_cwaters
To: mdwaters@urtoo.com
Re: my contribution

Don't despair, Dad. Not until you've eye-balled the pop-up I've been holding back. It's attached below. Do I need to walk you through the download process?

mdwaters
To: anthi_cwaters@ezrite.com
Re: trust

I believe I can handle it—like an attachment in reverse? It'll take me a few minutes. Have an Evian while you wait, why doncha'.

xlvi

Charles Plantard
Pop-Up

They were gone now, the middle-aged American and his tall, poised daughter, vanished out the wide gate of Charles's garden. No matter how addled he might imagine the American was, with his odd bookish knowledge and his wrinkled, well-traveled shirt and trousers, Charles respected the man's quirky ideas and sympathized with his having fallen into a cache of secrets that, because they were ancient, stretched far beyond his cultural reach. The daughter he trusted implicitly. She, he decided, was solid as the Eiffel—and looked it in her black jeans and her black jersey printed with the ghostly white half-mask that, Charles at the start suspected, said exactly what she thought of their visit to his garden. *Phantom of the Opera*, indeed!

Yet her father, little does she know, is nearer the truth, Charles went on to himself, than she is.

Charles was still sorting out what he felt about Uncl'Erre having dispatched the pair to him from the South. Whenever he was tucked away as now in his Lyon garden, he believed he was safe from the vortex of his family and the Order. They were the part of his life he tried to limit to the days he spent in the villa overlooking Arques, and to hours there when he was not riding or hunting with his dogs in the hills. Basically his was an orderly life these days, thanks to the speed with which Multinational Computer Company had begun to take off a year after he and Genevieve had hired on as middle managers in the French arm of the organization. Everything about computers these days was flying, and with the new desk-size machines MCC was introducing in Europe, there was no telling where one would find them next. Now that his wife had become the CFO for MCC-France, she remained in Paris at least four nights a week, leaving him here to practice his Qigong, watch the lilies bloom—as he was doing now that the Americans had left—and worry over his teenagers flirting with their friends and flying off the new fiberglass board into the still heated pool.

Uncl'Erre had phoned to say two foreigners, *tres gentils,* had come to him and asked questions that showed their knowledge and their sincere interest in the Order. When Uncl'Erre mentioned "Monsieur Charles" to the strangers, they asked him to provide them with a written introduction. But when 'Erre thought it best to check with Charles before sending them north, Charles had said he had no time for curiosity seekers. The truth was he didn't want to drag reminders of the Order into his home and quiet garden. Uncl'Erre's call came two days before Claud met his death at the hands of Philip Plantard. As soon as Charles saw the news from the South he was back on the phone to tell 'Erre he had changed his mind; the foreigners might have spotted some pertinent link he had missed. He suggested a time when he would be delighted to have the Americans for a late lunch—on the lawn, if weather permitted.

The sun today would have been too brilliant if the air were not pleasant. But the elements combined were just warm enough for his sons, still shy around young women as mature as the American's daughter, to show off their trick dives for their *copains* and, coincidentally, for the American *jeune fille.* What was her foreign-sounding name? Anthea, was it? Their luncheon went well. The cook had thrown together a lovely shrimp salad, cold slices of beef, a subtle camembert, and a fresh loaf. He himself had found a likable Macon in the cellar to cut through the beef.

But the conversation that followed dusky grapes, melon, and coffee did not settle half as well as the dark wine and coffee. His guests were still sipping reminders of the Brazilian sun when he broached the subject: "My uncle tells me that you have stumbled upon some of our family secrets?"

The American looked up from his cup, a pensive smile lighting his eyes. "Thank you, Monsieur Plantard, for mentioning that topic first. We were enjoying your excellent food and the wine too much to interrupt. And we were both afraid—weren't we, Anthi?—to bring up our reason for bothering you here." Charles noted the hesitation in the man's glance at his daughter.

"How could you possibly be apprehensive about a man like myself?" Charles sensed that his narrow face and large ears rendered his question a bit ironic.

"Not of you, sir," the young woman began as though apologizing. "Only of the topic."

"I am sorry if my family's heritage intimidates you—" Charles said, and settled back into the striped cushions of the white wrought-iron chair that matched the two in which his guests sat.

"Not that. It's what happened after we visited with Philip Plantard," the young woman quickly added. "It's not a pleasant thought, but we are afraid that what we told him may have contributed to—to what he did to Claud Plantard." She appeared relieved to have it out on the iron coffee table between them.

"So you spoke with Monsieur Philip?" Charles felt he had to measure his words carefully now. "He's a distant cousin of some sort, one I hardly know myself. Such a sad case, he and his family. His lovely wife, consumed by grief." Charles breathed deeply, one of his long chi breaths, before going on. "But I don't see what the Plantard family history could possibly have to do with their tragedy."

"I fear it has a great deal to do with their ordeal," the other man said, then sat erect as he took over the conversation with his complicated explanation.

He described the way he and his daughter had "kidnapped" Philip Plantard for their road trip to Rennes-le-Chateau and rehearsed the long story of the Plantard family, of its ties through the Merovingian and Visigoth kings to the descendants of Jesus and Marie Madeleine—

Mary Magdalena, the American called her. These were connections Charles knew well as enduring family legends, but he kept his lips sealed. Fortunate he did, he decided, for his guest began to ramble on, as though inspired—or crazed—about "the two lines of the family, the light and the dark," and the way he believed the sides existed in every generation and suspected the dark rose up against the light and tried to wrest the family claims—whether to buried treasures, unmined gold, royal powers, or spiritual ties to divinity—away from the "consecrated branch." The stranger said he was almost certain that the "anointed line" in the present generation "ran to little Charles" and that if anyone had the "divine right" to lead France it was the drowned boy. But Claud's side, he feared, had murdered Charles, and what Philip did to Claud threw the "whole logic" for a chosen line into doubt.

Having presented his case, the American fell back against his cushions, apparently in despair.

For a moment or so, during which he took another large Chinese breath, Charles wondered why they had come to him. He knew nothing about "the light and the dark" fighting each other. All this part sounded far too medieval for him to consider seriously. He did know something about "the divine right of kings," chiefly that it had not been much in favor since his compatriots had taken the blade to Marie Antoinette and Louis. But unfortunate Louis, according to the Plantard tradition, was one of the pretenders. Nowadays it was little more than family boasting to think of the Plantards as divinely descended and appointed. The claim put a little steel in the family backbone, a trace of ichor in the blood.

And all the Order ever wanted to do, Charles reminded himself, at least since I've been running things, was look after the family name. In recent memory, chiefly by defending Claud from false accusations. I never even wanted to *scare* little Jeanne—not to mention take part in some extended family fratricide. That was entirely too *Grec*!

"So *why* did you come to me, of all people?" he asked to break the heavy silence.

He didn't expect it would be the girl who answered. "You've got to do something, sir," she begged. Her eyes welled with tears, her face turned red through the deep tan one acquired in the South. "Somebody has got to stop the killing. It can't go on like this, mechanically, generation after generation!"

"Young woman, you must think I am the UN!"

"No, not that—" She appeared altogether surprised by his expression of powerlessness. "But there must be something someone can do. If not you, sir—?"

"Mademoiselle, you are a bright young woman. Surely you realize that people have been killing one another—for gold, power, land, religion—for as long as anyone remembers! I can't change the world."

"No. Not the world—" she clearly was speaking now without thinking, from a place inside her, below thought, "—but maybe change the remembering. Eliminate the 'divine' part—the sanction." What she had just said seemed to register in her mind. "Can't you change the family's *memories*, please sir?"

Her cry for help came as a slap across his face. "Our memories?" A quick, sharp slap that sent his brain spinning. "It's like asking me to change the past, isn't it? Is that what you mean?"

"Not the past, sir. Your—my Dad's—the family's memories of it. Can't you do that before someone else dies?"

"I don't know, child. I don't see how I could do that. I'm just the family's administrator—only a figurehead, really."

"Please, sir, just a new batch of memories," she said. "With no sanction tacked on."

Charles glanced at his sons lounging, complacently, safely, on the deck circling the bright jade and sapphire water. What he trembled on the edge of thinking was too horrific to keep thinking. What he knew was that these were his real treasures.

"I'll think of something, young woman. I have to try."

"You are our hope, sir. You will find a way—I know you will. You must."

"I don't know what it will be."

"Thank you, Monsieur Plantard." She appeared ready to rise from the pillows of the chaise longue on whose edge she had sat as she leaned into her passionate demand.

In an instant Charles knew he did not want her to leave—to abandon him to the charge she had pressed upon him. "Your father looks exhausted," he said. "All this has been an ordeal for him too, I am sure. Let me find him a place where he can lie down. There's a game room on the second story. Perhaps one of my sons would accept your challenge for a rack of billiards."

"It's very kind of you, Monsieur Plantard." She stood anyway. "But we've drawn upon your hospitality far too long. My father has made a reservation in Macon, near the cathedral there."

"Are you certain? We have extra rooms. He needs a rest."

"He can relax in the car while I drive. We have to press on toward Paris. There are places there he wants to check. A church, Saint Sulpice, and the Tower."

Charles knew the stories her father was chasing. False leads, he told himself.

He had tried again to persuade the girl, but she was firm. She coaxed her father from the place he had collapsed following his history lesson, and, after a few more polite expressions of appreciation, they were gone.

Now all Charles could do was stretch out on the chaise where the young stranger had lingered and decide how to respond. While his mind dealt with the appalling challenge the two left in their wake, he let his senses wander along the passages that seemed simplest. Beyond the garden wall he could hear the hum of the autoroute two kilometers to the east. From the apple tree at the far end of the lawn, where the orchard started, came the soft toe-wheet of a bird whose name he did not know but that he recognized by its black, red and white markings as a regular visitor this time of year. The honeysuckle he had smuggled in from America lent its trace of sweetness to a breeze that at the moment appeared to be increasing.

His eyes, however, ruled all his faculties, including that which must come to terms with the young woman's demand. They settled on the strong golden lily he had also smuggled in, concealed in a company carton, after he and Genevieve visited the MCC home office located in one of the southern American states. It was a rare variety developed by the company's vice president of exports, and Charles prized it as much for its name as for its stout beauty. Its creator had christened it the "Chthonic Grail," and its health showed it deserved the title. At first Charles was afraid it would not take hold in French soil, but with the early spring it displayed its slender green parts and, now, with warmer days, the plant manifest all its glory. He hoped that its rhizome would thrive in the local loam and produce generations of similar beauty. He looked forward to one day getting down on his knees and separating clusters of the roots and green shoots to transplant in every sunny corner of his garden.

That would be a chore much less grueling than the one confronting him now. In the short run he knew the part he must play. This first move would be simple. He would call in the press—or at least as many reporters and cameras as an unknown like himself could attract in Lyon. He realized it would not nearly match the mob that hung out in Couiza waiting for the most recent morsel about little Charles to drop. To bring in any newsmen at all, he knew he had to serve up his announcement alongside the little Charles story. Only after jazzing the media's appetite this way could he risk denying all connections between the murders and his family's past. In fact, he would have to reject the revered origins of the Plantards altogether. After doing that, he wasn't certain what, if anything, he would be able to salvage.

The truth was that uncertainties about the Plantard past had contended within him through at least half his forty-plus years. For as long as he could recall, he had heard rumors about Pierre Plantard, his father's cousin several times removed, a man burdened like himself with the family curse, going back to Dagobert: the elongated skull and long, thin body. When Charles was just a schoolboy or younger, Pierre *le grand* commonly served as the target for family gossip. He remembered his parents whispering after he left the dinner table about a group that Pierre began and named the Secrets of Sion or something along those lines. Through its exalted titles and its publications, some of which Charles later collected as curiosities, the Sion group tried to revive the practices and ideas of earlier organizations Pierre had sought to create. In the late 1930s he had put together a small society dedicated to anti-Semitic, anti-Masonic propaganda, but officials of the French government suppressed it. He tried again once the Germans took over, but his program must have been too absurd, or nationalistic, even for the Nazis because they refused to authorize it to exist.

Still Pierre persisted. With Petain as the puppet head of occupied Vichy France, Pierre launched his Alpha Galates, his "First Gauls" movement, a rabid clique that was esoteric, nationalistic, and feverishly anti-Semitic in a nation filled at that time with desperate associations. Politically discredited along with the Vichy government, Pierre took refuge, Charles had heard his father say, in the past by creating his own Latin Academy and planting his mother at the top as president. Again he failed. At first Charles couldn't tell whether Pierre was an eccentric, or simply a ne'er-do-well—the kind every family tried to hide somewhere.

But then he recalled the shameful parts of his parents' conversations. *Your cousin just hates the Jews—he uses them to swell himself up*, his mother would say. *He disgraces the Plantards*, Charles's father, a decent civil servant, with gold-rimmed glasses and a bald, thin brow, answered. *He pillages the past for his insane genealogies. Descended from a prostitute like the Magdalena! Who does he think he is?* When his mother said this, young Charles could feel his face on fire. *You know, dear Blanche, that Pierre didn't make* all *of that up. The family records have claimed very much the same for centuries.* His father's words had somehow calmed the boy—until his mother spoke again. *You do* believe *those legends, don't you?* she would tease with her plump smile. And his father would apologize, *If only Pierre weren't such an extremist—a crazy man. And could quit hating the poor abused Jews the way he does.* It was an argument Charles overheard many times before his father died and his mother settled into her exhausting post teaching algebra to future shopkeepers at the *ecole superieure*.

From the start, his father's confusion had become Charles's own. One thing he couldn't understand was how "Crazy Pierre" could hate Jews the way he did and in the same breath claim his family descended from Madeleine and Jesus—two Jews if there ever were any. It didn't make sense. But as an adult Charles calmed his mind by reminding himself that Pierre was not alone in his absurdity. Didn't large segments of the popular religions, he reasoned, live—and murder—under the same bad faith. Not that the thought brought great comfort to a man as earnest as Charles, who feared he himself was religious to the core.

The trouble was he found himself in recent years stretching his idea of Madeleine and what she might symbolize until he felt alone in the world. Surely Genevieve put too much of her energy into her work with numbers to understand him and the way his associations with Madeleine kept expanding. Imagining Madeleine as the true Grail led him, as he figured she might have Jesus, to other outcast women—other "dark" women. And to the dark elements, the nonspirit, physical world. And dark races, of course. All the shadowy and denied halves of our traditions. She had steered him also to the memory of the Black Madonna, much beloved by her believers scattered around the planet. And the dark Madonna carried his core ultimately to Africa and to Lucy—the one who, if the Leakeys were right, must be the real Eve, natural mother of us all.

Light of the earth, little Lucy, dear little Lucy, he muttered half aloud. First light of all of us and all our races. And *if* we all come out of Lucy, from Africa, what is there to fight about? Really, what is there? Except swollen pride, and arrogance of race, family, wealth, nation. And religion. He could not leave out religion. It was the desperate tie that bound desperate people together, he now conceded with a fathomless sigh of relief, in self-importance—in ill-founded pride.

Making so many connections all at once wearied Charles. He rose from the chaise and drew four full breaths of garden air before he crossed the few meters separating him from his lily. He stood a moment, then dropped to his knees, not in prayer but to view the plant better. Since he last checked, a dozen or so blades of grass had inched up around the strong green shoots protecting the stalk that held the golden flower aloft. His fingers began to dig and pull. His eyes, he found, were beginning to moisten.

A grown man on his knees crying, he groaned under his breath. *I hope my boys don't see this, they notice so little ...*

If they do—I can live with it. Live with my religion of one, if that's what Madeleine brings me to. Maybe the American is right: two lines every generation, one twisted, one bright. If so, I must try to avoid the twisted, mustn't I? Even when my choice leaves me alone.

All the blades were gone now. But still he dug in the loam, letting the dark French earth run in crumbs down his hands each time he raised them toward his eyes. The gold of the lily and the black of the earth glistened.

And with Lucy, he told himself all at once. *With Madeleine and Lucy. Whom I will never meet. Or maybe now and then, when I dig.*

Madeleine and Lucy, I can live with. I think I can.

But first—call in the press. Stop the blood.

Before he reached full height in his standing, he was moving toward the house and the phone.

xlvii

mdwaters
To: anthi_cwaters@ezrite.com
Re: Yes!

Yes, Anthi, first-person omniscience, that's the secret. It always is. Modest as it is, it's all we have to go on. And uses everything else. We start with what (we think) we know—and invent the rest.

Well done, my daughter. A veritable pop-up. Better than my simple bare bones. All your years of Latin show—and Nicky's Palo Alto position—the computers, I mean.

But you implied you were working on Christine—her gaps? That's what I was expecting.

Will you please plan a trip soon to Virginia—so we can polish all this up together!

Anthi_cwaters
To: mdwaters@urtoo.com
Re: Wait!

Christine again.
And home, too—maybe.

xlviii

Le Corbeau
Pop-Up

Christine. Christine. It is time.

Who is it? You—again?

Pick up the microphone. It is time.

Again?

Always. Start the tape. You will need it. All you can get. Start the tape, for the captain.

Poulin?

He will appreciate this. Start it.

I have.

He will adore you as much as he does that little bitch.

Why call her names like that? Her name is Jeanne.

She is young—you hate her because she is young and a beauty.

Why say things like that? I don't hate—

On the beach, on the beach at Perpignan, all of them were staring at her. Without clothes and money—I am sorry, but there is no way a woman keeps up with a girl her age. You know it. You saw them staring—all of them—Claud, Philip, strangers you had never met. Even little Charles couldn't keep his eyes off the health of her skin and breasts and hair, with the salt dusting them like sugar. You despised her—even before he fucked her.

Why talk to me like this? Why say these things?

I want to help you, Christine.

Help? Haven't you done enough? Killed my child, my love, made them lock Philip away? Isn't that enough? What, for God's sake, does it take?

I must crush you, Christine.

Why?

To help you—set you free.

It makes no sense. You never make sense—you confuse me.

You betrayed me, Christine.

I never betrayed you. I never knew you, until you began tormenting me.

You have always known me, Christine. When you were a girl, I came to you.

It's a lie. I never heard you.

You heard me. You called it your prayer, dreaming. But you heard me.

You're mad.

No, not me. I came to you then. In flashes—in oaks, the river, sunlight off the quartz. I spoke to you in the lake, the moonlight, in caves—the fire in his eyes.

That was different.

But you betrayed me. You sent me away. You crushed me down, Christine. When you could not *see* me, you forced me to become a voice from a distance, speaking through the phone, pinning notes to the shutters, sending warnings through the mail, stabbing holes in the tires. You would not see me; I had to come up from behind, sneak in from the night, strike where you were weakest, when you were crying in your bed—

Jacqueline, it is you! You hated Charles; I knew it.

He made you weak, Charles did. You did not know whose he was. Child of love—or acquiescence. But Claud made you weakest.

Jeanne— I didn't recognize you—with that hoarseness.

Jeanne too. And little Stephen. And even little Charles, if you listen, Christine. All the fragments, bits and pieces you have betrayed, the flashes you denied, never claimed, tried to crush down out of yourself. We came to take revenge. Come to crush you, Christine. Come to get even.... Listen. Can you hear us now?

Philip! I married you, Philip. I did what Mother told me to do.

I always did—even when we cried at night, the two of us, she and I, and what she wanted was unfair. I gave her—and you—more than I felt. Until I couldn't give any more. I had to have him back. I had to.

No, Christine—not Philip. Try again. Who is left?

Who are you?

Whom did you betray?

Not you, Claud. I never betrayed you. I loved you. *Love* you. More than my own son. My own life.

Twice, Christine. Twice.... When you married him—

I had to. Mother made me. She spoke. Not in the voice she brought at night when I cried. She spoke in that cold, vast voice of hers. With her eyes—ice, distant—the look she had from Uncle Henri. The look of death, and he from—from, I always felt, his icy God. She spoke to me with those eyes—that voice—as though *I* had killed Father, made her life what it was. We both missed him, didn't we? She spoke—what could I do? I never denied you. I obeyed her voice. I wanted her to love me. I loved you.

You made him kill me.

You told me—said there was no other way. All of it had come unraveled, our exquisite plan. There was nothing else we could do. You told me.

I did? Are you sure it was me?

The voices did. But you sounded like—more like the captain.

Me? I was your lover, Christine. And you made him kill me. I have never sounded like Poulin.

I know. I know. Claud, help me. I don't understand. I can't keep it straight, sort the pieces out. You torment me, all of you, until I obey. You drive me to pieces, until I do what you say. I have to obey.

I know, Christine. I know how impossible it feels. There are so many parts to put together. To keep straight. You are the pieces.

There's nothing you can do except obey. That's why we speak—to have you obey.

I try. I do. But you ask such horrifying things. And when the television and the gendarmes and the papers keep telling me what to do, I can't sort it out. I feel smothered—overwhelmed by what I did, might do, ought to do. By voices in the air. Sometimes I cannot tell yours from the others, and it scares me. That's why I made him kill you. I was confused.

Of course, Christine. I understand perfectly. The confusion is why you must listen carefully to me.

I am trying. I am.

You must keep these tapes a secret. You must not give them up until you have enough to show what has happened. Then you must give them directly to the judge. When he hears the voices, he will understand. He will know what to do. It is simple.

Simple? What will he do to me?

Don't worry, Christine. The French people love you too much to harm you. Philip must pay, but you are a child of France now.... There is no other way.

No other way?

Exactly.

You sound like Mother.

Where is your father, Christine?

I never knew my father.

You did, Christine. I never deserted you.

You sound like Claud.

Exactly.

No other way?

No other way.

That's what you said when I made him—

I know, Christine.

And will the voices stop?

Some of them.

Some?

The ones that drown you—the television, the papers, the gendarmes.

And you?

Where the judge sends you, you will have me always.

Always?

Always.

It seems simple.

It will be. Trust me.

Thank you. I will trust.

xlix

mdwaters
To: anthi_cwaters@ezrite.com
Re: Anthi

You amaze me!

Anthi_cwaters
To: mdwaters@urtoo.com
Re: explanation

Like you said, Pops. Take what you know—and imagine the rest.

mdwaters
To: anthi_cwaters@ezrite.com
Re: amazed still

You catch on so quickly. Hard to believe.

Anthi_cwaters
To: mdwaters@urtoo.com
Re: quick?

Since the first story you told me. That's quick?

mdwaters
To: anthi_cwaters@ezrite.com
Re: quick

And you get the final word, young woman.

Anthi_cwaters

To: mdwaters@urtoo.com

Re: one word?

Well, yes, I imagine I do.

Afterword

This fiction from Deepest France draws on several sources that picture the South of France. It could not exist without the seductive theories and myth found in the not so "little black book" Milt Walters dangles in front of Philip Plantard. The title Philip never sees, many readers will have guessed, is *Holy Blood, Holy Grail*, copyrighted in 1982 by Michael Baigent, Richard Leigh, and Henry Lincoln, and published by Dell in 1983. Other significant influences have been *Rennes le Chateau: Capitale secrete de l'histoire de France*, by Jean-Pierre and Jacques Bretigny, published by Editions Atlas (Paris, 1982), and numerous issues of *France-Soir* running from October 1984 through 1985. In these and related publications readers will discover a wealth of information about the "secrets of Rennes-le-Chateau" as well as a vastly different version of the murder of "little Charles." The fiction I have created has moved characters and events about freely, changed names where appropriate, and yoked disparate stories violently together.

As Anthi discovers, the materials related to Rennes-le-Chateau continue to grow in volume, especially online, and a search engine like Google will turn up as many theories as a reasonable reader might desire. Interest in the models for my little Charles and his family also remains alive in cyberspace.

My purpose in creating this fiction has been to dramatize the possibility that even myths of innocence have become a destructive force in the contemporary world. Could the story have been told in a simple, straightforward fashion with fewer gaps and breaks in continuity? Perhaps. But surrounded as we are by multiple sources, few of our myths of reality come to us in that innocent, coherent manner. After all, it was Ernest Hemingway who warned us to mistrust the man whose story hangs together. If that was so in 1926, how much truer it must be today.

JR
Chapel Hill, 2002

Father and Son:

Interlude between Stories

Two Letters

Milt Walters * Freelancer * Box 111 * Hurricane Pointe, VA
December 21, 2000

Nicholas Walters, MBA
234 Tower View Trail
Palo Alto, CA
Dear son,

I hear you've been curious about what has kept your sister and me so preoccupied for the past year that we have spared you our usual flood of e-mails. I appreciate Anthi's leaving it up to me to show you (though it would be harder for her to do so from Paris). Enclosed please find *Deepest France*, our maiden effort as Walters & Walters, Freelancers.

You weren't yet ten, I know, in the summer of 1985 and likely don't recall Paolo's invitation to all three of us to spend time with his family in France. At any rate, you didn't have a chance to make the trip and so didn't share the experiences (not all of them pleasurable, it turns out) Anthi and I lived through with Paolo on the coast and later in the Pyrenees with Philip Plantard and other members of his unfortunate family. These occasions would have included Philip's son, Charles, and Charles's mother, Christine, had we had an opportunity to meet them. No family should have to endure the tragedy the Plantards suffered. But then few families possess the heritage the Plantards can claim—one that goes back beyond Charlemagne, through the French Merovingians (sixth-eighth c. AD) and Visigoths (fifth c. AD), to the very origins of the French Grail with Mary Magdalena and the ancient Jewish community of southern France.

As I recall, your favorite books have usually been the famous novels by Hemingway and Fitzgerald or adventure tales of mountain climbers and explorers of geographic extremes. So our book may strike you as unusual. Think of it as unexplored territory. I call it a "composite novel"—seemingly made of bits and pieces of this and that—news articles, television news summaries, travel brochures, sentences from guide books, histories, legend, scripture, descriptions of statues, personal narratives in various voices, e-mails, instant messages, etc. It is more truthfully an effort to introduce Anthi—following her request, mind you—to the secrets I've learned about creating mystery stories, while working out some emotional business I have left over from our visit to the Plantards' forgotten part of France fifteen years ago. I hope you won't find its varied voices too baffling—especially because your sister and I have a large favor to ask when you've looked through it.

Pleasant reading,

Dad

Milt Walters * Freelancer * Box 111 * Hurricane Pointe, VA
January 1, 2001

Nicholas Walters, MBA
234 Tower View Trail
Palo Alto, CA
Dear son,

So, Nick, it is a strange, and largely hidden, family history Anthi and I have asked you to read. I trust you enjoyed its surprises well enough to do us a great service. We both have admired your string of successes using your recent degree to knock on the doors of venture capitalists and hedge-fund groups (though I have never understood exactly what they are). Would you, we wonder, be willing to use those same skills to handle a *real* challenge—one that might require you (figuratively!) to knock *down* some doors? I mean, do you think you could find Anthi and me an agent and/or a publisher for *Deepest France*? Writing is one thing; selling is another altogether! And neither of us is as extroverted as you are, young man. Not that there is anything wrong with our introversion—except that it runs against the grain of the way the world is set up. Selling books has always been a pain in the derriere for me. Usually I've known somebody who knows someone. But this story is a pet project, a special case, as you recognized, I suspect, as soon as you ran into the experimental way we felt forced to handle our materials. Anything simpler would have falsified the nature of the rich, complicated story we were telling.

So, young Door-Opener, what you say we turn this father-daughter project into a family enterprise? Make it "Walters, Walters & Walters," like a law firm? To be sure, there would be a finder's fee in it for you, since I suspect you will discover venture capitalists and hedge funds are pushovers compared to agents and publishers!

Hoping we can take you on board for this novel engagement,

Love,

Dad

Mysterious Days:

Return to Deepest France

The piper's calling you to join him.

> Robert Plant
> IV

Eliot got it wrong.
The most heinous treason
must be
To do the wrong thing
for the noblest reason.

> Milt Walters
> (overheard)

Day Seven

At least his cell was a modern one, by the standards of Hurricane Pointe back in Virginia. The bed hung from heavy chains and folded up to give Milt room to move about now that it was almost day again. The mattress, grey vinyl, was not soft but still thick enough to rest his depleted body. A metal toilet and washstand protruded from the rear wall. Aside from the sting of disinfectant, the odor seemed almost bearable. Walls on three sides were solid metal or stone, so he had a modicum of privacy despite the fourth wall of bars. Since no cell opened directly across from his, he didn't have to worry about eyes except when a jailer came along the walk between the compartments.

What worried him most was the accusation the gendarmes, who he now realized were an arm of the French military, planned to lodge against him. During the night of interrogation, they failed to explain his rights under French law and refused to detail charges. These could include kidnapping and assault—even murder if Shanti didn't make it. He hoped they wouldn't dream up some phony child abuse claim, the way Christine, psychotherapist that she was, feared they might. And there was no way, was there, that they could go back and try to pin a rap on him for colluding in the death of Claud Plantard twenty years ago. He no longer considered it possible that the cops would suspect he'd played a part in the worst of recent crimes in this part of their nation, since it was ridiculous to imagine they had even read **Deepest France**, his novel about the brutal murder nearby of little Charles.

His best defense, he told himself, would be to get his story straight and trust that it would agree with whatever statements his wife Christine, daughter Anthi, and Gloria might give. To that end he had spent his solitary hours of the night in a disturbed reverie sorting events of the past six days. He intended to do the same until the gendarmes came for him again.

Day One

Lost

As the tiny silvery-blue Citroen C.3 Milt and Christine Walters were renting wound its way inland from the south French coast toward Rennes-les-Bains, the week in Denmark already seemed an excursion into another decade. With Jutland still playing in his mind like the best music or the gentlest waves, memories erased the placid scene before him and carried him into his road trance that always made long drives not just tolerable but one of the pleasures of a too often sedentary life.

He had always meant to make his way back to the French mountain town where he had set his most ambitious book, published five years ago, but twenty years had ground by since his inspiration, and for various reasons he had failed to return. This began to change the day before Thanksgiving, 2005, when Nick, his one son, phoned to say that he and Marie had just come from the city hall in San Francisco and after living together for three years were now officially married. "But don't feel left out, Dad. We'll do it again, next summer, in Denmark." All of this seemed good news to Milt. Nothing could keep him from an occasion like that, and Jutland, where Marie's parents still lived, was, as it turned out, only two hours by Denmark's Sterling Air from Montpellier and this road to the secluded French village of Rennes-les-Bains. Even the intimations of death that Milt had been fending off for a decade would not block him from his boy's wedding and from revisiting one of the most invigorating moments of his life. Now the vital fires were running through his body again with more heat than he had felt since he met and wed Christine a dozen years before.

The itinerary he'd planned was becoming, he thought as he drove, much more than a family obligation with a voyage into nostalgia tacked on. Instead, the battle lines seemed clearly drawn— this journey seemed a clash between the fire of creativity and the pulls of age and death. How stark an encounter he did not realize because he had not taken time to read the latest papers from Deepest France and did not know what was happening to small children, some less than two years old, in the raw Pyrenees below Rennes-les-Bains.

Jutland had been bathed in the eerie northern light, the generosity of their new Danish in-laws, and the love the latter felt for Marie, their only daughter. To Milt, with Nick there, and Anthi, his own daughter, flying in from Paris, it quickly became a Danish fairytale of wild toasts and feasts replete with fresh hams, vein-clogging beef roasts and unfamiliar but tasty concoctions of marinated herring and white fish washed down by layered red wines with good legs, strong, bitter beers, and an array of liqueurs followed by all-night dancing on the hotel terrace overlooking the wide fjord at Veijle.

For Christine, whose paternal grandmother had migrated from Denmark to the American plains, the wedding trip had become a return to her roots. It thrilled her that the Danes addressed her in their own tongue before discovering she understood not a word and shifting to the English they all handled with stunning ease. The way she took to the Jutland children, many of whom shared her sinewy limbs, attractively elongated skull, and fairness of skin and hair, told both of them that she felt among her kin. Milt found her sense of belonging a great relief, since one of his goals as caring husband was to help her overcome her enduring and, he believed, destructive alienation from her own family.

For her, France, he felt, was proving less congenial. Perhaps Denmark had spoiled them both. Certainly Milt spoiled Christine by driving first from Montpellier's airport east along the south coast to Les Issambres, just beyond St-Tropez. Here they found a small family-run hotel set in a narrow strip between the shore road and the sea at the eastern edge of the modest tree-shaded beach town that held living memories for him. It was here, twenty years ago, that his quest through Deepest France for the French Grail with Anthi, only fifteen then, had begun when his friend and host Paolo tossed a copy of *France-Soir* into his lap one crisp March morning and asked, "What you make of this boy drowned in Rennes-les-Bains, the one they are calling 'Little Charles'?" This moment, unfortunately, did not belong to Christine's cache of memories—since, fragile as her sensibilities were, she had never been able to make her way through the twisted mystery he had written about the murdered French boy. She took quickly, however, to the hot sun and brisk sea, the relaxed topless beaches, and the large, strong café au lait and crisp morning pastry, with rich aromas, that became mainstays of their routine in Les Issambres.

Milt appreciated the pleasures as much as Christine did, but when he scoured through the local newsstands he could not find even a copy of *France-Soir* and wondered if the famed publication, so important to his novel research, had been forced out by the tabloids that flopped from the racks. As he rummaged, he could not avoid noticing a quarter-column piece in the thin *Var Vision* titled something like "Child's body discovered / South of Carcassonne." But his focus lay elsewhere, and the last thing he wanted was to get sucked in by any real-life echoes of his own novel. He turned away.

After their week of sun-filled bliss on the Var coast, Milt made the mistake of moving them back through Montpellier and south toward Spain, an area he knew less well. Here, in the Catalan part of France, they spent a night each in two disappointing beach towns, one much too crowded with camping families during the last week in August and the second far too rocky for sunning comfortably on the beach.

The unsatisfying beaches only compounded a discomfort that he had felt emerging since they left the spectacular wedding. He had hoped to relax by the French sea and plan his next novel, one he knew would center on a woman much like his wife, Christine. It irritated him profoundly that he had not yet found a way to write the book honestly without placing their already difficult relationship in jeopardy. Until he found a way to disguise names, places, and events sufficiently without losing the emotional truth, he felt he would be walking on eggshells rather than charging headlong into his new story. He was having to work hard to protect Christine, and their marriage, from the growing anxiety. Denial, he knew, was not his métier. He could continue to deny, but it only blocked his inspiration.

So it was with impatience that they'd headed inland to search for the remembered pleasures, real and invented, of Rennes-les-Bains, only to find themselves in late afternoon thoroughly lost but gliding up and down green, rolling hills. As though space had become time flowing backward, the unfamiliar road dropped them into the tiny shadowed square of a half-deserted village that in its tilt clearly lay at the base of a mountain already blocking the sun. None of the square's exit signs named towns on their two maps.

Just downhill from the square, however, he discovered a Bureau of Tourism. Its only staff proved to be an old gentleman sitting at a desk fingering an ancient typewriter, his back to the main door.

"Excuse me, sir," Milt said, though the man seemed not to have heard him enter. "Is there a road from here to Rennes-les-Bains?"

When the man turned, Milt saw from his dark glasses and wandering gaze that he was nearly blind. Without answering, the old man called out someone's name and led Milt across the echoing hall to a large, dusty room. It was empty aside from a narrow set of grimy shelves in dark sun-bleached wood, these bearing scattered pottery and four crusted bottles of what had to be the local wine.

Across the room stood a long table covered with orange and yellow brochures. While the blind man disappeared through another door into a storage room at the back of the antiquated building, Milt checked the leaflets. All were the same guide to the Pays Catalan and emphasized its churches and tradition of hospitality. The brochures came, he saw, in at least five languages. He found one in English and snatched it up as he turned to leave the building before the blind man returned.

To his right just before the door to the street, he glimpsed his dead uncle Madison in his sixties, his substantial loaf of steel-grey hair, hawkish beak, drained cheeks, and dagger eyes. But it was himself staring back from a hall mirror. Beneath the mirror, however, stood a scarred side table on which a single tabloid, the *Corbieres Hebdomadaire*, lay folded. He could make out several words of the headline, "*Un autre gamin … Bugarach*," which he quickly converted to "Another boy … in Bugarach." Hell, it's still going on, he thought—but quickly pushed through the heavy old door and headed toward his wife in the Citroen. He wasn't about to let any echoes of the region's past crimes keep him from returning to the Rennes.

He didn't mention the disturbing headline to usually patient, now increasingly testy Christine. Instead, they studied the map he'd fetched just long enough to agree that this village must be St. Paul-de-Fenouillet. Since they could find nothing with that name in his *Pyrenees Michelin*, they were still lost. On the new map, the shape of the region he sought startled him. It resembled images he'd seen of his own heart, broad at the top, narrow and rounded at the bottom, crisscrossed by arteries, some of which could be blocked like his own. No wonder I resonate with this place, he kidded inwardly.

Christine looked at him with bewilderment on her face. "I thought, *Milt*, you said you knew the area." The way she said his name had that critical quality he called nagging.

He had to call himself back from his reverie before answering.

"I always approached it from the north. These roads have me turned upside down." He fidgeted in his seat to straighten the legs of his shorts. "We'll get there; don't worry."

He stood again from the Citroen, sniffed the intricate dinner aromas lacing the village, and looked back toward the tourist office. Opposite it stood a woman with long hair the pure black of a raven. It spread across the shoulders of an astonishing ankle-length gown, maroon velvet trimmed down the front in gold braid. She had descended from the street, really an alleyway, opposite the bureau he'd visited. He moved several steps in her direction and said in his best French, "Pardon me, Madame. Is there a road from here to Rennes-les-Bains?"

Startled, she sized him up before asking with a non-French accent he didn't recognize, "You drivin' car for campeen?" The tightness in her dark face conveyed an anxiety he could not fathom.

"Camping?" Her answer had surprised him. "No. Not at all."

"So you make it through," she said, relaxing the muscles of her face.

"It is a rough road? Where?"

"Yes. Goes up far." She pointed back toward the square and up the mountain.

"You are very helpful. Thank you so much."

She looked toward her feet before saying, "It notheen." But she stared at him again, then added, "Be careful—you have enfant?"

"We don't," he said and, satisfied, turned toward Christine and the car.

Before he had taken two steps, her warning about the children cut through his confidence. He looked back to ask what she meant but saw only her maroon back as she vanished up the alley from which she had appeared.

"Did you see her costume?" he asked once he was beside Christine again.

"Strange," Christine conceded as once more she consulted their old map. "Algerian?"

"Gypsy maybe. Or a guide from some museum." He started the motor. For the first time it seemed to sound even looser and noisier than his long-ago Beetle.

"Probably her dressing gown she was wearing." She was comparing their older map with the new one from the tourist office.

"This late in the afternoon?" It was nearly six.

"I think I've found a road," she said. "But it's not the one you're looking for."

"Let me see."

It was not the road he sought, the one that would link their route from the south with the major road he remembered from the north. Given the smallness of the print and ambiguous position on the maps of the place names, he couldn't be sure where on this new side road Rennes-les-Bains would appear. He would have to trust his own instinct for directions since Christine made no claim for a similar sense. But as they ascended rapidly from St. Paul, the only road sign they found indicated they were heading toward *Gorges de Galamus*, a name Milt did not recognize. From the sound, he figured it must be a region with more than one daunting slit in the earth.

The twists and turns as the auto climbed did not feel especially terrifying. They were hugging the safe in-mountain side of the asphalt while hedges of laurel and rhododendron lined the sinuous ledge to their left. As the road rose they drove again into the reassuring light of the dipping sun. So he was startled when an athletic young woman wearing shorts, a tank top, and an olive-drab backpack suddenly appeared in the center of the narrow track with her hand extended to block their way.

She shouted something in French that he couldn't decode and pointed toward a stoplight on wheels he hadn't noticed. It was standing on their side of an archway over the road. He braked, and then rolled his window down to discover what they had blundered into.

As the attractive young woman came closer, she fired off another warning. He caught a few words that sounded like *"vingt-cinq"* and *"continuerez,"* meaning something, he guessed, like "you will continue in twenty-five...." In twenty-five minutes, he guessed. He pulled the handbrake and cut the motor as the young woman, almost as thin as Christine, went to direct other cars and create a queue back of them.

"Looks like we'll have to wait," he told Christine, though her ear for the language beat his own.

"Also something about an ambulance," she said, "—and a child."

"I hope not," he muttered, the horror in his own novel again threatening to inhabit his mind.

"Yeah," she said.

"You want to get out?"

"I'll keep knitting." Her needles were one device she used to hold herself together during the flights and extended drives that linked their Jutland visit to France Sud.

He crossed the asphalt track and seated himself atop the rail fence that bordered the precarious ledge. He tried to get some sense of how deep the gorge might be here, but the brush, chiefly rhododendron now, blocked his view. Even though the plants, he saw, ended a dozen yards further up the ledge, his dread of vertigo kept him near the car.

The wait became a long twenty-five, and he felt more and more awkward perched where he was, especially as other cars arrived to form a substantial queue, one that stretched at least eighty feet downhill to a bend in the road. The lithe young woman ignored him, but she chatted freely with other drivers, all of whom shared her language. He could make out scattered phrases. "A girl ... very young, yes.... Cuts? ... don't know ... a fall? ... they guess so."

So, it's not a boy this time, Milt thought with a modicum of relief. What kind of parents would drag their kids into a risky spot like this. Wilder than the Salz where Little Charles was tossed. In *Deepest France*, drafted twenty years before, Charles, a small boy, was stabbed repeatedly, bound with cords, and thrown into the river.

This time it's a girl, he reminded himself and, somewhat eased, started back to the car just as the stoplight changed and the woman with the backpack hurried toward him. "*Allons,*" she called with a great sweep of her arm in the direction in which he now had to lead a caravan of edgy drivers. "*Tout de suite!*"

"We're going?" Christine asked as he turned the switch.

"*Tout de suite,*" he grumbled and let the clutch out to start uphill. The car stalled. "Merde!"

Instantly a wail of horns sounded behind him.

"Give me a second, you bastards!" he growled.

"Don't let them get to you, dear." She patted him on the arm. "They're just being macho, and French; they can't help it."

"They should try!" He started again. This time he worked the unfamiliar clutch expertly. As the car leaped forward, he told himself, *I love the fricking French. Almost as much as Greeks. Just not when they're driving.*

"It's their problem. Don't make it yours. Remember your heart."

Helps now and then to have a retired therapist for a wife, he thought—then said, "I've got twenty flaming narcissists on my tail, the kind that bring kids to a wilderness like this. I call *that* my problem." He glanced in the rearview to confirm his count. "And now they want to start passing."

"On this road? I don't think so." She had already braced herself with one hand against the dash and was closely examining the way twisting ahead.

It narrowed now to a single asphalt lane, one hacked so deeply into the granite wall to the right that they were driving under a continuous overhang of grey stone. They seemed all at once to be moving downhill. To the left there was scarcely room for the stream of hikers, young and old, toiling toward them, some in shorts, some in what looked like lightweight wetsuits, many leaning on tall hiking staffs. They walked stiff-legged—they were going downhill, not up.

Beyond the climbers Milt could see walls of the gorge's far side, chalky white daubed with green brush, walls so vast he could find neither top nor bottom even though they were a mile or more away. He felt the two of them and their auto were being swallowed by this rupture in the mountain, into which they were still descending. Perhaps the road had peaked. As curves teetered them, up became down, and down up.

The sensation grew more disturbing but weirdly pleasant. Like being wrapped, he thought, as a baby by a blanket that had not quite begun to smother him. *Mom loved me too much?* he wondered. Where did this memory come from? He would ask Christine—but not while driving a murderous road.

Each mile they crawled, the resentment of those behind him mounted. He was sure they'd figured out he was a foreigner, a despised American even. Does the plate show it? Should have asked at the rental desk. I can't think of everything. Those bastards back there would resent any outsider guiding them through their hidden bit of deep France.

As much as he'd looked forward to returning to the region, he now knew his visit was not going to be the perfect pleasure he'd imagined. He had no business being in this obscure gorge, let along leading a pack of Frenchmen (and Frenchwomen, he didn't doubt) through their labyrinth of danger. He kept braking, slowing down for the bends, knowing this caution was a no-no. He should accelerate, take the curves at top speed, and get himself maimed. That would please the overcompensating, nouveau-voitured bastards. They watched NASCAR on the German channel; they would show an American pussy just how much speed French curves could take when a French maniac got behind the wheel of one of their *petite voitures francaise.*

He needed to check on how his rage was working now—was it violent enough to make their problem his own the way she said? He glanced at his face in the rearview.

Even as he raged, he knew his fury was unfair. Never in his visits to France had he found the people on the whole so hospitable, so willing to use a little English without forcing strangers to maul their glorious language. Still, he seethed and felt proud of it—maybe, he told himself, because way back I've got that spot of Huguenot hidden in my genes.

Washed on by anger, he approached the end of the narrow passage. Here another line of automobiles waited for a second stoplight to change so they could begin their climb along the single lane sliced into the gorge wall.

Once clear of this second queue, Milt pulled far right and slowed until all of the raging maniacs caged behind them could zoom past, some blasting their horns like ships entering port, others flipping him the bird, all turning to see what variety of *un*-Frenchman drove with such irritating caution. He hoped they saw Christine's blond hair as they sped past and took her for a German. Maybe they still hated the Germans more than Americans, but he doubted it.

Once the chest-thumpers had passed, he returned to a speed he felt appropriate for the descending curves. Soon they were cruising with ease through gentle green turns, away from a gorge where a small girl just died.

"What a lovely land," he said finally, trying to reassure his wife while calming himself down.

Then: "Lovely—and dangerous," he couldn't help adding.

Day One

Welcome Back

Their descent flattened at the edge of a plain where off to the right lay a village of old yellow houses scattered among newer pink ones, some dotted with concave, manhole-size disks. Antennae like these meant this community, lodged among wild, ancient mountains, had joined the global culture that the satellites of the new century made inevitable. Contemplating these modern artifacts, Milt was startled by a roadside sign identifying the village. *This* was Bugarach, a name he recognized at last.

As the bypass led them well left of the houses, he remembered Bugarach's cropping up in the headline he'd tried to ignore an hour ago—the one in St. Paul-de-something-or-other reporting the *gamin*'s death. Was it the same child? This one, not likely in the papers yet. His own associations were much older. The name suggested the Bogomils to him. Bogomils, Gnostic missionaries from Bulgaria, first came to his attention when he was researching *Deepest France* before and after he returned to Virginia two decades ago. Thumbing then through *Holy Blood, Holy Grail*, a quirky mix of underground history and suppressed mythology that inspired his trip and novel, he'd linked the Bogomils with the famous Cathars of this region. Sprung from Manichean roots, both sects viewed the world in Gnostic fashion, as too fallen to be endured. The faithful of each struggled to perfect themselves for the afterlife, sometimes through practices as rash as self-immolation or avoidance of sex between men and women even for creating new life. Their self-defeating idealism fascinated him.

Now, skirting Bugarach, he imagined a man and a woman,

staring into one another's eyes, trying to will another life into being immaculately—and grinned inwardly. The similarities between sects were so strong that some historians contended the Cathars had derived from the Bogomils, a name that went on to spawn words in some languages for buggery. In the early thirteenth century, both Christian heresies, he recalled, became chief targets of the brutal, nonetheless "Holy" Inquisition and the infamous Albigensian Crusade. At least his own Huguenots, Calvinists though they were, hadn't, he hoped, gone to any of these extremes.

If the Bogomils ever reached France, a village named Bugarach, he supposed as he drove on, was likely where they collected, given the way words could half conceal uncomfortable secrets. Now someone apparently had killed a child here and not, he assumed, for high-minded Gnostic reasons. He pictured the slaughter taking place on that great rock peak he saw behind the town, a mountain as incongruous in this green plain as the enigmatic rock tower from the *Close Encounters* movie. Even as these associations drew him toward the town, in his gut he was relieved that their road kept avoiding its houses and shops. And the sun, he noted, would soon pass behind the mountains to the west. They needed to step on it.

Several kilometers beyond Bugarach, after another climb, they descended to a T-junction with road signs, both of which pointed toward Rennes-les-Bains, the name it pleased him finally to see. But the signs pointed in different directions. The one straight ahead indicated four fewer kilometers than the one to the right.

"What you think, dear?" he asked.

Christine looked up from her book and studied the choices carefully. "The one straight ahead looks abandoned."

Clumps of tall grass hung over the asphalt from both shoulders and broke through the gravel-patched broken spots. "Screw Robert

Frost," he said and turned right onto the newer road. "That one must be for the horses."

For fourteen kilometers they seemed now to be heading downhill through a greener and more wooded region until their road paralleled a narrow river flowing calmly in their own direction. "This must be the Salz, where little Charles drowned," he said aloud, forgetting that despite several attempts Christine hadn't read much of his novel because it seemed "so dark." Since she didn't respond, he added for his private satisfaction, *It could be the Blanque or the Aude. Without a map, I don't know.*

His doubt didn't last long, for like the milky green river, they rounded a tree-covered bend and came upon scattered brick houses with small orchards sprawled between them and the river, then spotted a playground and an apparent bathhouse that he thought he remembered even before he saw the sign, faded black letters on stained white: CAMPING RENNES.

"It's the Salz!" he said with new energy, "and this is Rennes-les-Bains."

Christine looked up from her knitting to follow where he pointed through the windshield, "Up there on the hill behind the roses; it looks like an auditorium. I don't remember it from before. And on the left just beyond, with that yellow box out front, is the post office. Maybe you can phone Virginia from there." He swung his other arm to the right. "Over there across the river somewhere stands the Marti Mansion, where little Charles was killed."

"I know you're glad to be back, Milt," she said without much enthusiasm. Until today, knowing how she dreaded anything violent, even in movies and fiction, he had carefully tried to keep her pretty much on a need-to-know basis. But now that they were back in this village that had opened the underground passage to immense creative fire in him, he would soon have to share the story of Charles and his family with her—the complete story but preferably in bits and pieces, a Bowdlerized version she could accept without fleeing in contempt or disgust.

"Such a dreadful thing," she added, "with all those black ropes and so many wounds, I don't know how you could expect anyone to—"

"Cords. Black cords," he said. And before she could finish, he leaned toward the windshield to point out the large stone building on the same side of the road where Charles's father, part-time maire or mayor, had his office, and just beyond it he said, "This is the square that Charles in the book keeps crisscrossing his last morning, with King Arthur and the rest of his imaginary pals." The square covered by ancient trees seemed darker and much smaller to Milt, probably, he decided, because a bandstand now closed in the rear. Was that thing here back then? Dark as a gallows! Even so, he felt a warm wave of relief flow through his upper torso as the realization moved through him that he had made his way back. There had been years in between when the predictable ills of age made him fear he never would.

"The square was the center of little Charles's world," he said—as much to himself as to Christine. "This—plus the hotel."

"The square has a restaurant on each side," she said. "One's for pizza. Any others?"

He saw the two clusters of small tables and the modest signs. "There's one in the hotel. Maybe another, up a side street. There, that's new," he waved at a three-story building in pastel green, "—Esthetique something or other."

Past the square, down a walkway between rows of shops, he caught a first glimpse of the hotel once run by Charles's parents, the Plantards, Philip and Christine. The *other* Christine, he reminded himself. In the late afternoon sun the huge building glowed above the river a terracotta red and the dull yellow of sandstone, then disappeared behind more shops. "Did you see it?" he asked. "It's an ancient hotel."

"What?" She was scanning the shops.

"Charles's hotel, the other side of the river." He hoped to convey to her at least an ounce of his enthusiasm: "The Romans came for its waters." Otherwise their visit would prove a short one, not long enough for him to retrace his steps and confirm for his own satisfaction the places his novel pictured.

"There it is again!" This time between buildings he could see almost the entire hotel, and the sign, l'Hostellerie Rennes-les-Bains, in bright red-and-black letters. Apparently the building had recently been scrubbed and repainted: no longer the dank, stained building he remembered.

"The other side of the river?" she asked. "I was looking in the wrong spot. It is ancient. I'm impressed."

The ring in her voice vanquished some of his anxiety, but it would take more of her energy to lift it all.

He reached between the seat and the rear of his shorts, then into his right hip pocket, and felt for the two folded pages from his home printer. "Here, check the name on these. I just saw a sign for Hotel de France pointing straight ahead."

She took the pages and unfolded them. "What's the problem?" The way she squinted at them seemed to say this was one of his made-up worries.

"I hope I reserved with the right hotel." He nodded across the river. "Over there it says L'Hostellerie—not Hotel de France—and the one we want is over there."

"Well, this confirmation says Hotel de France." She refolded the sheets, which she dropped with a satisfied look between his legs.

The car was fast approaching the end of the main commercial street, where he'd had to park twenty years earlier. After this, it curved, descended quickly, and left the town. "Maybe they changed its name." Ahead he spotted empty spaces for parking. Or maybe, he admitted to himself, I forgot its name.

As the Citroen cleared the front of a square grey building with ornate wooden doors opening onto the narrow sidewalk, he glanced up to read the words carved in the pediment above the doors: de France.

He didn't understand. There must be a mistake. Perhaps this was the new reception office for the Hostellerie and someone would lead them over the main bridge to their room in the larger building across the river.

He'd slowed the car enough to glance just beyond the Hotel de France doors a low wood bench on which two women sat, each almost as old as or older than himself, one of them small and dressed head to foot in grey and brown, the other a bit younger covered all except her face in lacy white garments, an elegance in her dress and a mute expectation in her face. All white, not a stitch of black or color. Perhaps some sheikh's wife or mother, he thought, on pilgrimage. But the way they waited, each leaning her weight on hands clasped atop a carved walking stick, suggested something else. That they were mountain hikers perhaps. Or simply "waiters," like those who watch and hope for the distraction of disasters in *The Day of the Locust*.

Apparently it was only a ride the two on the bench were expecting, for when Milt and Christine located a parking area—things being much more organized now in a civic way than before—and walked a block back to Hotel de France, the women had gone. This Milt did not regret since their stillness seemed a tad spooky.

With the luggage still in the car, he had no problem shoving open the hotel's doors, heavy with black iron grills molded to look like small shields, and holding them wide for Christine. The glassed-in reception desk to their left stood unmanned, but it didn't surprise him in a village this small.

"Maybe there's someone in here," Christine said and crossed

right to a cracked door decorated with carved opaque glass. He followed.

As she widened the gap, they were looking into the dining room. The tables were empty, the room silent. It was so quiet that when he slipped into the empty silence, it startled him to see a woman behind the dark wooden bar to their right. She was polishing wine glasses. Milt supposed her to be one of the service staff and checked his rusty French vocabulary before speaking. "Hello, Madame. Is the reception open now. I wrote for a room."

"Oh, yes, you must be Mr. Walters," she said with faultless English. "Come with me." As she stepped from back of the bar, he noticed that she had been standing on a six-inch platform and was no more than five feet tall, perhaps shorter. She wore plastic pearl-rimmed glasses and a loose pearl-colored blouse above a dull spring green skirt. Her grayish blond hair was cropped short at right angles that shouted Nazi to Milt, but the gentleness of her voice mollified his judgment. He figured she might be an Alsatian who'd migrated west and south to avoid German neighbors. "You requested two nights, did you not?"

"Yes, but we may want to stay longer, if things work out." He handed her the final e-mail he'd received from the hotel.

"Of course." She disappeared behind the reception desk and reappeared behind its glass. Must be another platform back there, he thought. "That should not be a problem," she added.

"Good. Good. We would like to see our room, please, if it is not a bother." He still hoped the room would lie across the river and had not decided what to do if it didn't. He had no wish to offend this frail, gentle woman—she could be seventy, he wasn't sure—by rejecting her room. Despite catching a whiff now of something like an oil lamp, he figured he could spend one night in her hotel but also check out the Hostellerie and move over there for the rest of their stay.

"That will be fine." She reached her right hand up to an oak board with a dozen long-barrel keys dangling from hooks and brought down one attached to an eight-inch bronze placard with the hotel name and room number raised in the metal. No driving off, he thought, with that weight in your pants pocket.

She led them up wide dark stairs with a single turn to the first story above the ground, where she pushed a button that lit the corridor. At the second of the large double doors on the left she inserted the jangling key and let them step past her into an unlit room with a double bed and a few other items in dark but solid wood. Milt went immediately across the room and looked out the double window.

"This is the street. Do you have anything over the river?"

The small woman, whom he now considered the manager or at least the one in charge, looked disappointed but still eager to please. "I believe you wrote for a double room?"

Puzzled, Milt hesitated for a moment, but then understood. "Two beds are fine, if they are comfortable." Both Christine and he remained agile enough to meet occasionally in a single bed for an hour or so. Such visits, to his regret, were growing less and less frequent. He saw no reason to assume she was returning to the other pole of her proud bisexuality, but he feared her confusion of instincts, caused by unimaginably widespread abuse in her family when she was very young, might finally be settling into a dreary lack of sexual interest altogether. It left her fragile, a condition he regretted but felt he must respect, even protect. At any rate, twin beds were no big problem.

Without locking the first room, their guide crossed the hall and opened an unlocked double door. The twin beds before him, chiefly the mahogany boards at foot and head, reminded him of his parents' double bed as he was growing up. This time when he crossed the room it was toward a lightly curtained set of glass doors. He turned the brass handle then pushed open tall grey shutters and stepped out on a metal balcony protected by a waist-high railing of iron wrought with the same spear design as the hotel's entrance. When he leaned to look down he saw the river coursing through the shadows of the buildings—green, blue, black now. It was four stories down on this side of the building, and the vertigo so shocked him that he instantly turned back into the room and stared into Christine's eyes. "Will this do, babe?"

Her smile and the light in her eyes both said yes. Without asking whether the price was the same as the first room, he signaled approval to the small woman with the calm demeanor. She led them downstairs, gave them the correct key from the rack, and pointed out a parking space in front of the hotel next door. Apparently the motor bike leaning precariously there against the iron railing at the curb did not matter: this was not Paris, where people were so touchy about their things.

After Milt fetched the Citroen, they unloaded and crammed into the small elevator with dark wood paneling. As the lift moved slowly, he took time to notice the building's scents: a dankness that he assumed rose from the river but mixed with a petroleum odor that, when he tried to place it, brought back the kerosene lamps burning in his grandmother's house before Rural Free Electricity finally arrived and lamps disappeared. Since he hadn't noticed any oil lamps in the hotel, he decided the establishment used kerosene for another purpose, perhaps to power the elevator. Or to heat the building—though certainly it was too warm now for heat.

When he opened their door to the balcony again, a dazzling vision of the Hostellerie half a football field upstream on the opposite shore pleased him. It seemed the only sunlit building in the coolly shaded valley. The view was wonderful, they would stay here one night, he decided, then move to his old hotel and refresh pleasant memories of the place.

Behind him Christine asked, "What do we do now?"

He turned to check her mood and what the question implied. Her face showed neither impatience nor great enthusiasm. "What would you like to do, sweet?" He needed her to like "his" village.

She moved her backpack from the bed nearer the windows to the table on which she had placed her suitcase. "Move around some. We had a long ride today, too much sitting. My legs are stiff."

"Good idea," he said and for the first time allowed himself to notice how tight his back felt. Clearly the headlines he'd seen, on top of the long, troublesome drive, had penetrated his excitement and denial of them.

He closed the high glass doors. "Let's explore the town—find out if there's a room for us tomorrow night across the river." They emptied their small backpacks of everything except thin jackets they might need as the sun disappeared.

Outside the hotel, Milt selected the first left turn, and they crossed the narrow bridge, suited chiefly for pedestrians and an occasional vehicle as small as the Citroen. Here they swerved right and took the alternative road through the village, this one poorly paved, winding, and much narrower than that on which they entered town. They continued downhill in the shadow of houses several stories high on their left, a few restored, others in decay. On their right towered the back wall of the Hostellerie, a dark rose red. From his book, he recalled a small entrance at this end of the Hostellerie as well as a narrow set of stairs descending to the cement slip, the *blanchisserie*, which dipped into the river. In his novel he had let little Charles use them on his fatal morning as the boy led King Arthur about the town searching for Charles's other imaginary pals, Tom, Asterix, and Tintin. If either stairs or entrance had ever existed, neither did any longer. Milt wondered why. *I didn't just invent them, did I?*

Working uphill near the huge building's other end, he kept an eye out for the dark stairwell down to the door he was certain Charles and Arthur had used to exit the basement. If it still existed, he missed it. Much about the Hostellerie had altered. But not too much, he hoped.

After the quick climb they came to the building's south patio, a garden area bounded by a low cement wall composed of columns and a running cement banister. Already he could see through the dark windows that the room inside was deserted and that it must be a large bar, perhaps part of a dining room. His spirits dipped. He could not understand a bar standing empty so near the dinner hour. He was certain that the low iron gate to the patio would be locked, but when Christine tried the handle it opened, and they crossed the patio to the bar's glass door.

Head high in the glass someone had pasted a yellow sign the size of a legal pad, two words, one above the other: Hotel Fermeture.

"Closed. No explanation," he mumbled. "What I dreaded."

"I know you were looking forward," Christine said. "But don't get obsessive, dear. We have a lovely room. We'll have breakfast on our balcony."

She wanted to cheer him, he could tell. He would have to make do. "It's just going to be different. Not what I planned." Less chance of bumping into little Charles now.

"Let's explore the rest of the town," she said. He could see she was forcing a smile for both of them. "There'll be things to see."

They continued along the path to the next of the town's three bridges and crossed to the old church where Henri Boudet, Charles's mother's famous ancestor, the local antiquarian, had served as Abbé. It was locked.

They skirted the town square, and he followed her upstream past a *salon de thé* until they reached the deserted campground at the town's southern edge. On their way back they walked up the paved drive leading up past the rose garden to the auditorium building with a sign out front: *Cinema.*

"Want to smell the roses?"

"Why not," he said. "Didn't know there was a movie house in town. Must be new."

They walked through damp grass to the flowers, pink, a bit past full bloom, still wearing the small crystal remnants of a shower that must have passed while they were choosing their room. They sniffed the chest-high stems, but the blossoms had no odor. They still added a daub of color to all the dark greens of the village.

"You hear the music from the theater?" she said and smiled.

As she mentioned it, he noticed a dramatic theme flowing from above them, perhaps an organ announcing the climactic moment of a thriller's plot. "Let's check it out."

"Okay. But I'm hungry. Let's not stay."

They went up the steep bank of cement steps and entered the sand-colored stucco of the rectangular building. They found themselves standing in a vestibule attached to a large auditorium from which a carnation-like perfume seemed to drift. A single round table with several boxed disks—CDs or DVDs—almost filled the vestibule. To the left he stared into an auditorium lit only by a dim screen at the far end. Here a magnified woman, Nordic blonde, in a gold and sequined gown cut low over healthy freckled breasts, poured her passions into an aria whose language Milt could not identify. He supposed it was East European, but the power of the music was Wagnerian. He could not tell whether it was a concert film or a movie, but to her left on the screen he saw a baby or small child wrapped in a purple blanket lying on a table of carved dark wood. It appeared to be an altar in a chapel or church whose walls and supporting columns rose behind the soprano and the child. Her posture and voice filled instantly with ominous Wagnerian anticipation. The hand at her side clasped a knife with a long serpentine blade.

"Damn it!" he groaned. The woman with the knife rubbed up against some scene in his memory, one he had invented for his novel and did not want to revisit.

As he stumbled away from the auditorium door, he glimpsed the back of a woman dressed in white sitting just inside the door. This must be the woman he'd seen waiting on the bench by their hotel door. Her erect posture made her seem younger now: middle forties, fifty at the most.

"What is it, Milt?" Christine grabbed his elbow.

"What's this music?"

"It has to be a scene from this." She handed him a disk from the table, but he was too disturbed to read it. "Apparently it's a concert by some woman in the chapel at Rennes-le-Chateau."

"The church in my book?" It made no sense. "Who is she? What's her name?" He was still trying to focus on the cover, but his glasses were in his pocket.

"Blanche—it says Blanche de Saint-Clair," she read for him.

He gave the name time to register. "It would be some Blanche, wouldn't it?" he mumbled. "And 'Saint-Clair' figures." He was running down a list in his mind, names having to do with the roots of the menacing Order, in his novel, that preserved the Plantard family's past, its claim to the throne of France. "Has to be the singer's stage name."

"You want to go in?"

Before he could decide, an attractive Asian woman in a long black skirt and white blouse appeared from the auditorium. "Shhh!" she whispered loud enough to elicit a rustling and groans from beyond her.

The seats, he noted, were scarcely half filled. But a solid crowd for a filmed concert. Plenty of room for the two of them.

"No, no," he whispered so low only Christine could hear. He didn't care to upset her and wasn't sure he wanted to witness the scene that would follow the aria. The little he had already glimpsed seemed much too close to the headlines he'd been careful to avoid throughout their return to Rennes-les-Bains. Thank goodness, it's only a video, he told himself.

As the scolding woman shut the door behind them, he took Christine's arm and guided her silently from the building toward the street below. They did not stop for the roses.

Day One

The Children

By the time Christine and Milt reached the village square again, his agitation had subsided but not disappeared. What he needed now was a good French dinner to solidify his return to the Rennes, and he hoped Christine would be willing to eat more than a salad—to sully her "imperfect" body, as she often seemed to imply about meals, with 'impure' food. She would be the first to admit that food perfectionism and exercise bulimia were her malady and that for thirty years she had fought to stave off its usually fatal result. In their foreign adventures she generally found herself stumped by lists of ingredients, but French she knew well enough to decode. In restaurants, to be "safe", she stuck with salads, and Nicoise quickly became her staple.

Lively popular tunes rearranged as Muzak streamed from speakers attached to trees on both sides of the square, but neither restaurant appeared open yet. They were early for dinner, though the staff was stirring about in the pizza palace and a few bearded, long-haired men were sipping beer in front of the other one. This, Milt suspected, must be the real restaurant. Nonetheless, they detoured a few steps to study a menu board propped against a giant tree opposite the pizza shop door. To his surprise, in addition to a variety of pizzas, the list included Magret canard, an entrecote, a Bifteck. Perhaps he was narrow-minded, but he could not imagine that a pizza restaurant was the right place to invest in duck or beef. "Pizza tomorrow night, maybe," he said. She nodded, and they crossed the square.

The beer drinkers, two or three at a table, occupied four picnic-style boards, each long enough for eight people. The long tables seemed to belong to a bar next door to the restaurant. Immediately in front of a dimly lit entry stood half a dozen smaller metal tables scattered in no discernible order. Christine and he agreed on a metal table a comfortable distance from the open restaurant door.

They dropped their packs on one of the chairs and chose seats that gave each an unblocked view of both the empty square and the covered bandstand or stage at the rear. As they settled into their chairs, they were ready to celebrate reaching their destination after a long day of misdirection. Once more he wanted to avoid bringing up the headlines that irritated him. Then something dawned on him: "You know what? I don't think they are going to wait on us."

"Maybe they haven't opened yet."

"God, I was just getting comfortable."

"I'll go in and ask."

"No, no, I'll do it," he said and leaned on the table to push himself back to his feet. The table tilted under his weight as though it would fall over, but he and Christine caught it. "Not very well built, is it?" he muttered.

"Take it easy, babes," she cautioned. "Don't take it out on the waiter."

"I'm okay." He steered his road-weary legs up the steps and through the wide, opened door into the area of the restaurant lit from the bar to his right. Before he had a chance to speak to the woman with coffee-brown, shoulder-length hair who was tidying the bar, a man with wild black hair came from the back pushing a large cart covered with a transparent lid.

"Bon soir, monsieur," the man said. He seemed in a hurry.

"Bon soir. Are you open now?" Milt said as quickly as possible.

"In a moment please. Inside or out?"

"Out. And the carte, please." He hoped the man would know which he meant.

"If you wish, monsieur." He turned to the bar to fetch a menu bound in faux leather.

While Milt opened it and quickly scanned the bill of fare and prices, his host rolled the cart onto the wide stoop beyond the door. By the time Milt was satisfied that the list would do for Christine, the restaurateur had uncovered most of his cart, and Milt could see it was a buffet that included cheeses and pates as well as various raw and cooked vegetables.

"I think you're going to like the buffet," he said as he folded himself again into his place beside Christine. He offered her a conspiratorial smile, which she returned.

After he had negotiated with the cart-wielder, now in his guise as waiter, and surrendered the menu, he believed he could relax and chat with Christine while they took in the square. Long-haired companions had materialized from somewhere to join the beer-drinkers at the long tables. Two of these were young women. A few in the group were sipping white wine. A large white van, the type plumbers might use but obviously refurbished as a camper, had also appeared at the curb midway between the pizza place and the restaurant.

During a lull in his conversation with Christine, they noticed a tall blonde woman coming from the van's other side, leading by the hand a girl with shoulder-length ringlets and frilly white dress. The girl seemed scarcely old enough to walk about on her own and was as blond as the woman, whom Milt took to be her mother. The woman was also all in white, a bulky white sweater, probably cotton, over white trousers of the painters' pants type Milt had found so comfortable back in the seventies. She seemed vaguely familiar. With a wig and makeup she could have been the singer with snakelike blade, but the thought was so absurd he dismissed it.

Barely within the street boundary of the asphalt square, midway between the two restaurants, the woman, long-limbed and full-bodied, squatted on her haunches like men he'd seen in Egypt, and watched with a grand smile while the child twirled and danced to an exotic tune trickling from the open doors of the pizza restaurant.

He whispered a caption, "Return of the Hippies."

"Or 'The New Hippies Arrive,'" Christine, ever the optimist, whispered back.

"Retro. Tres nostalgic."

"Or they yearn for something better. Like the seventies."

"Hey, you were barely out of high school back then, young'un," he said, as their waiter, his hair now slicked down and severely parted, arrived with Milt's dish and Christine's empty plate.

"Was not," she said. "I was in college."

"Three or four colleges," he teased.

"In a daze, I admit." She stood, plate in hand.

From starvation, he added—silently, though she would have been the first to bring up her ailments. As she left the table to pick vegetables carefully from the buffet, wanting to block memories of the scene in the auditorium, he studied the square green and purple dish before him. This was, he decided, the most startling presentation of a meal he had faced in France. A smallish square of chalk-white fish lay under a bright pink sauce that he hoped would be raspberry but that looked more like a mix of beet juice and yogurt. Startling, he repeated to himself, but not appealing. Surrounding the pale fish stood four small mounds of what he supposed were vegetables disguised with visually unappealing sauces. The dinner reminded him of a palette piled with dollops of paint. He hoped it would taste better than it looked.

Christine came back with beans, peas, tomatoes, tabouli, a mere spoonful each of things that resembled his vegetables—no lettuce—and a small rectangle of pate that he doubted she would touch.

As she split off a forkful of her pate for his plate, a tall male, no more than thirty, appeared from beyond the van and squatted like the woman but on the opposite side of the tiny whirling child. Like them he wore only white—wrinkled white corduroy pants and a white sweater of a synthetic yarn. His long hair hung blond and oily well down his shoulders.

In some shadowy corner of Milt's mind, the two-year-old looked very much like his curly haired Anthi when she was that age, and the two of them plus her mother were bumming around Europe in their own camper, circling from Germany and Scandinavia to Greece and Turkey. The way they crouched appeared to set a boundary for the child's dance, protecting her from the diners. Or was this their stage, he wondered, since they made no show of visiting either restaurant, only of performing. He could easily imagine his Anthi tilting and turning the way the diva on the square now moved, though the radio music for Anthi would have come from the islands or Turkey and have ridden a flowing, more haunting rhythm.

The child was still cavorting when Christine and Milt concluded their meal, and he signed the cash-card slip for the restaurant. "How about another walk?" she said.

"It's not too dark?" He folded the slip under the tray the waiter provided.

She shook her head.

"No ice cream?"

"Later," she said.

They strolled in the direction they had taken before, stopped briefly at the town hall to read notices posted there, but found no impending entertainments among them. They pressed on until they were opposite the cinema with its rose garden, but now the building was dark and the double doors were closed tight. They turned to migrate back and found the tea salon was also dark, though the movable sign for ice cream remained, with the two wooden tables, under its portico.

An alleyway to the right led them past the dark church and to a street that rose again to the square from its river side. As they ascended they could hear the squeal of children coming from above them, and when they were shoulder-high with the previously silent bandstand they saw the bare legs and bare torsos of half a dozen young ones, some scarcely toddlers still in plastic diapers, gyrating or running wildly about the black boards of the raised platform. As many or more had poured into the square itself to do their dance, joining the petite curly-haired blonde who had begun this rite of late summer, all her white frills stripped from her now, naked as she entered the world, her pale little biscuit free for the village to see. Milt half expected to hear Stravinsky whirling above their heads driving them on. Instead the strains that ran through their small flashing limbs sounded like some pop tune with a Caribbean rhythm sung by the French version of Britney or Christina or Paris.

"Where are their parents?" Christine asked, bewilderment in her voice, as the two of them carefully skirted the improvised dance floor.

"Eating, I suppose." But when he looked around, the number of diners hardly seemed to account for all the infants.

"It's a reverse mirror of Banyuls—if you remember."

"I guess." The night in rocky Banyuls-sur-le-mer they had submitted to the nostalgia enveloping the water front by joining fifty or so couples, well past middle age, sailing across the beach town's tiled square on a long stream of golden memory tunes played by a small band on the stage. "But not the same sort of order."

"No order at all!" she said.

"I don't know whether to applaud their freedom—" The small ones brought to his mind a dozen little Pearls dancing out of control across the square of Hawthorne's Salem; then he recalled the newspapers he'd spotted. "—or to run in horror."

"Where's the horror?"

"Never mind." He didn't want to be an old killjoy. "Are you ready for a bedtime treat?"

"Why not."

They crossed to the restaurant where they'd eaten, selected two chocolate-covered vanillas on sticks from the freezer box out front, paid at the restaurant bar, and returned to the table where they'd enjoyed dinner. "These are different!" she said.

"Not the fat free back home."

"Oh." Obviously the thought of calories crushed her enthusiasm, but she continued with substantial bites.

She finished first, and he could see her staring with naked covetousness at his remaining crust of chocolate just as the music and the dancing stopped. The woman in white rose from her crouch and, the child's dress now in her hand, moved quickly to lead her bold little Pearl to the restaurant opposite Christine and Milt where the young man in white commandeered a table at the edge of the square. As she did, as though on cue, adults materialized from both sides to grasp small hands and clear the bandstand and the center of the square.

A moment followed in which nothing occurred. Then Milt detected a commotion in the street, a ringing of small bells and the scrape of feet on asphalt. A half-dozen men, all in their twenties, entered the square, arriving from up the river and from the woods that covered the severe slope behind the houses opposite.

Leading them marched a creature from another millennium, a self-created Pied Piper, Pan perhaps, costumed in a Tyrolean black velvet hat, a vest of black goat's fur, lavender lederhosen, black tights, and high-topped, fur-lined mountain boots. Each step he took produced a pronounced tap and loud jangling of bells from the seven-foot staff he carried, a lean strip of black wood with a reptilian head carved at its peak. His hair hung oily, long, shaggy, to join the great mutton chops descending from his ears to each side of his mouth, where lips and chin were shaved clean. The lips themselves curled up in a way that suggested a simultaneous smile and sneer, as though to signal what he thought of both his entourage and the audience that obviously awaited his arrival on the square.

He slipped across the asphalt, tinkling as he went, to the long tables, where the carousers cleared a seat for him. Laying his staff across the width of the table, he accepted the place provided by two young men, one with long red curls, the other with equally wild brown hair. Immediately all of them sank into conversation, at first very loud, then subdued.

Milt could hear only enough to recognize that much but not all of the talk must be in French. He supposed this weird arrival, whom Milt instantly dubbed Mutton Chops, was detailing his day's jaunt, the mountains he climbed, and the streams he followed and forded. But the subject could be anything, he told himself and turned his attention back to his dessert, now in danger of running down his fingers.

"These things are good!" Christine mumbled as she sucked juices from the bare stick.

"They are." He nibbled his final crumb of chocolate from the vanilla. "But I'm going to need to wash my hands." He feigned rubbing the stickiness against the metal tabletop.

"My melting Milt," she kidded, "always looking for any excuse to use the restroom."

"Better safe than sorry." Aging had reinforced the wisdom his father shared with him: "Never pass a restroom or water fountain, son, without taking advantage." He rose and made his way toward an uncertain destination, expecting a primitive hole in the basement floor.

It was neither primitive nor in the basement. As soon as he entered the lit part of the restaurant, a query written in his raised eyebrows, the attractive woman still perched on her stool behind the bar pointed up and to the back. Surprised, he tried to think of the French for "upstairs" and muttered, "En haut?" which he instantly feared might be German instead. But she nodded and let him continue. At least it's not Greek, he chided himself, that being the foreign language that came most easily to his tongue. The stairs were narrow and winding, the facilities bright. In the mirror over the washstand, he studied his tired face, then wet his hands and slicked down his hair.

On exiting the compartment, he nearly bumped against a small tri-legged table at the top of the stairs. On it lay a folded newspaper whose name he did not notice, so taken was he by the partially visible headline. This time he could not avoid it: "Enfant Mort" and under that: "Bugarach."

"Mort?" He still wasn't prepared to read about another dead boy in the Aude—another anywhere in this region where twenty years ago his little Charles had been stabbed a dozen times, bound in ropes, and thrown in the Salz River. But glancing quickly around to make certain no one was watching him, he grabbed the paper, folded it again, and thrust it inside his jacket.

He would have to find the courage to face it—perhaps when they were back in the hotel, or by morning at the latest.

Day Two

Morning

It didn't seem smart to pick up the paper to read at bedtime. Nor before breakfast. Instead, Christine and he headed out about 8:00 AM to find large coffees, fancy pastry, fresh yogurt, and milk, a quest that led them to the *salon de thé* that had been dark the night before. The coffee and pastry, a baton-like twist with sugar glaze that she favored, they consumed at one of the long wooden tables on the shop's small portico. The rest they would take to the hotel and eat on the balcony of their room.

At the salon's other table sat the thin fellow with long red hair they had seen with the beer drinkers last night. One of his dinner-hour companions had joined him, a smaller man with his hair equally long but brown. Milt wondered whether Mutton Chops would appear and felt both regret and relief because he did not.

Just as Christine and he were clearing their table to leave, a woman with long dark locks came across the street to sit by the first man. She had brushed her hair back in a way that left her forehead broad and pale. Her mouth seemed to grin and grimace at once, and this he took to mean that she suffered her disappointments with a smile. Milt had known women this ambivalent before and had come to love several of them.

"Cathy was sleeping. I left her in the camper. I have to work." She spoke a quiet English. "You need to get back there. We can't leave her for long."

"You locked the door?" the man with red hair asked.

As she sat, she lowered her eyes as though to show the question irritated her.

"This is a safe village, babe," her partner said. "I'm not worried."

"Are you coming?" Christine, already in the street, called back. He turned to catch up.

Back at the hotel, as she spread out their new supplies on their balcony's iron table, Milt used the room receiver and his French calling card to phone Anthi at her office just off the Champs d'Elysee. He assumed that she had returned by now from the Denmark events and was about her business. Her secretary answered and, recognizing his voice, put him through.

"Dad! What a relief to hear from you. I was worried," she gushed from her office, one so large he could hear echoes through the line. "Have you reached the village?"

"Worried why? I can still manage an automobile, thank you."

"Not the car," she scolded.

"We're in les-Bains, and the old hotel is kaput."

"Rennes-les-Bains does not ease my mind. What's going on down there?" Her voice boiled with more urgency than before.

"It's quiet, aside from *enfants* cavorting all over the place."

"Haven't you read the papers?"

From the headlines he'd tried to blink away, he had a looming sense of what she might mean. "No, no. We've been too busy just getting here." Now she was forcing the newspapers, against his will, to the center of his consciousness.

"It's started again, Dad."

"What—what's started?" he asked, dreading the answer he knew was coming.

"Like twenty years ago—when we were down there. Copycats. What we—you—wrote about in the novel."

"You mean—" he started, trying to delay her explanation.

"Little Charles. Murdered children. Only more than one this time."

"Horrible. I didn't imagine," he said, wishing his denial were true.

"You *have* been seeing the papers."

"A few headlines. And no TV." He didn't want her to realize he had the unread paper from the restaurant somewhere in the room. *Where is it?* he asked himself. Yeah—under my clothes piled on the television.

"So, get your hands on a paper. Television hasn't caught up yet, but their massive trucks will lumber in soon. And no one I've read has made the connection."

"To?"

"Little Charles, of course, in the newspapers."

"God, don't tell me."

"Listen, I've already made a plan. As quick as I can I'm flying down. What's the closest city?"

"Carcassonne—still." He knew she would be more eager to reenter their story here than he was. Or maybe he was, now that she had opened the door for him.

"There's a small airport there our company uses." He recalled how much the French pharmaceutical concern that employed her had grown over the years. "One of our jets heading south, to Spain maybe, can drop me off. Warn Christine for me please."

"She'll be fine, having another woman around." In his head he began anticipating how this would reorder his day. "Should we pick you up?"

"You two have plans, I'm sure. I'd rather rent a small car."

"It'll be good to have you with us." It always was; he already missed her and Nick—even though he'd had the good fortune to see both of his wandering offspring ten or twelve days ago at Nick's wedding. He just hoped Christine wouldn't object to her stepdaughter's intrusion. Usually they were surprisingly polite with one another.

"Don't look for me until you see me. Which hotel did you say?" She paused for a second, then said, "And check out Bugarach, why don't you."

After they had discussed the logistics of his daughter's visit and hung up, he rushed to join Christine on the balcony. Rounding the foot of her bed, his eyes involuntarily fell upon the half-hidden newspaper. Caught now between his own reluctance and Anthi's plan to involve him, he felt obliged to carry the paper with him through the curtained doors.

"She must have had a lot to talk about," Christine joked, as soon as he stepped out on the balcony. His kids, she knew, ordinarily required an inquisitors' examination to draw conversation from them.

"She's coming down to join us," he said, as low-keyed as possible, since he had not yet decided how much of his daughter's anxiety he was prepared to share with Christine.

"That will be nice," Christine said and smiled warmly. Having no children of her own, she often seemed to enjoy time spent with his. Her response appeared genuine, and over time Anthi and Nick had realized that visits with Christine did not betray their mother. "She's nostalgic for that trip you two took through here twenty years ago?"

"Something like that, I suppose."

As he spoke he arranged his heavy metal chair behind the table so that it was no strain for his gaze to follow the river, wine-bottle green in morning light, upstream to the massive Hostellerie. With the green mountain side beyond and the straight bridge plus a few solid houses in front of the ancient hotel, it became a scene from a romantic painting done by French artists a generation before impressionists blasted form and light into a million daubs and dots. The stability and comfort of the view almost overwhelmed Milt, and he sank with supreme satisfaction into his chair. Only the necessity of explaining Anthi's real motive for flying down gnawed at his ease. He would have to explain Anthi's determination sooner or later.

"So, what do you think?" he asked. "Does it get any better?" Certainly Christine must be content with this world around them.

"Positively beautiful." She poured a cup of Mueslix for each of them. "I just wish I knew what that smell was last night."

Like his daughter's purpose, Christine's anxiety could disturb his contentment. "That? It was nothing. The river maybe and coal oil—from the elevator or furnace or an oil lamp." He didn't know what he was talking about, just making comforting noises. "You'll get used to it if you let yourself."

"As long as it doesn't make one of us sick—"

Like her nerves, her stomach was more sensitive than his, so he took deeper breaths to allow her worry, her perfectionism, to slip past like the river, a skill he was trying to learn from Chinese martial arts. He added fresh milk and yogurt to his cereal. Better to put the newspaper, and Anthi's motives, off until after breakfast.

Besides, a daub of color had just popped up in the picture before him. A bare-chested man with white towels, perhaps one of the young beer drinkers from last evening, had materialized from somewhere and was moving about the cement slip that formerly had served as the blanchisserie, the laundry, of the Hostellerie. With him stood two children, both without clothes, a small boy and a slightly older girl, both very blond and tanned, whom he appeared to be bathing, though at the moment the three of them were only splashing water. The river was deemed to have healing properties, kaolin or something from the Blanque running into the Salz, the best Milt could remember, but he worried about its purity as it passed through the village.

The children carried his mind, before he could prevent it, back to the newspaper, and he felt he could no longer avoid reading it. He slipped it from the table and sat back within the metal arms of his chair, hoping to open it without the headline alarming Christine.

With the first words he seemed to be scanning lines he himself had read and written twenty years ago. The names and other particulars, to be sure, had metamorphosed in two decades. But the story was the same:

Bugarach—A three-year-old boy missing three days from his home in Bugarach, Deepest France, was found this morning in a mountain pool formed by summer rains below the ragged 1,200-meter peak just outside this charming village of fewer than a thousand inhabitants. Local officials have identified the boy as Rene Pidoye, son of Francois Pidoye, the leading hostelier of this small resort known chiefly for its historical ties to the Cathars.

The similarities to his prose were so close that he could not keep from wriggling in his chair even though his discomfort risked attracting Christine's attention. But he caught himself and continued:

Officials added that the body was discovered, with arms and ankles bound in rope drawn tightly against the torso, lodged behind a boulder in the pool within 500 meters of Pidoye's hotel located at the edge of the village. Preliminary indications are that death occurred before the boy entered the river inasmuch as the body bore upward of a dozen wounds probably inflicted by a long knife or other sharp instrument. Investigations are continuing.

Lodged behind a boulder this time, not under a bridge. But bound exactly the same. Some lazy reporter, it occurred to Milt, was using the opening paragraph of *Deepest France,* in print five years now, as the template into which he had carefully placed details of this new murder. Or the paper's editor had found the old issue of *France-Soir* that Milt himself borrowed from in his fiction. The village was not that of little Charles, the pool was not the Salz River, the family's name was no longer Plantard, but the father's profession and all the horrible events remained the same.

Obviously Anthi knew what she was talking about: something was happening in their Deepest France, and the events bore a dark resemblance to what the two of them had experienced two decades before. The shock of repetition so connected distant threads of his consciousness that a half jigger of nausea rose from the pit of his stomach. He could not finish his breakfast. His heart had accelerated so rapidly that he feared he might be at risk of another attack. All I can do, he told himself, is sit here quietly, take deep breaths, and let the serenity of the river calm me.

Ten minutes passed before Christine noticed he was not eating with the gusto that sometimes inspired her, not enjoying the cereals and fat-free yogurt that she ranked high on her slim list of tolerated foods. Along with ice cream and pastries, these furnished the carbs she would convert to fuel her daily endorphin rush. "Aren't you going to finish this?" she said as she reached for his untouched cup of Mueslix.

"Afraid our coffee and pastry killed my appetite," he said, still unable to look at the cup.

"I'll take care of these for you, dear," she said. "Mountain air makes me a little pig."

Even though she enjoyed his telling her that a pig was one thing she would never become, he was too shaken to play her game. She apparently did not notice his avoiding her cue.

When she had cleaned his cup of the final yogurty grain, she said, "If there are no big plans this morning, I think I'll go for a swim at the pool we saw glimmering down the hill."

"Despite the 97 degrees C sign?" Someone had scrawled the Celsius notation on a green board outside the pool fence. "That's next to boiling, isn't it?"

"Just some kid's joke."

"Maybe he didn't know Fahrenheit from Celsius," he said, trying to be supportive. "Either way, it's still damn hot."

"But it's a pool. I have to check it out. Why don't you join me?"

"I'm tired from all the driving." No need yet to mention what he'd just discovered in the newspaper. "I'll hang out here, I think."

"Enjoy your reading then."

"I saw a building called Health Esthetique, something like that, between here and the square. Maybe I need a haircut."

"You know I like it longer."

They both were clearing the remnants of breakfast from the table.

"It's getting shaggy I think, from the sun and sea salt." He turned to check on the bathers up the river, but they were gone. To safety, he hoped.

"You might run into some shady operators," she kidded, "in a place with a hybrid name like that. Watch your Euros."

"I should be so lucky."

After Christine headed out with her backpack, Milt spent fifteen minutes doing his customary meditative breathing exercise, Qigong's ancient Eight Brocades, beginning with "Push Heaven with Two Hands" and ending with "Stork Takes Flight." His favorite of the eight was the second Chinese posture, "Shoot Bow and Arrow from Horseback," in which the fingers of one fully extended hand formed a palm-out V and the other hand pulled back in a string-grasping fist poised at the shoulder for release. Each time he crouched to practice the stretch, he struggled to imagine where the arrow would fit in the stance. But he had no trouble imagining the claw-like fingers ripping some mugger's eyes out and the fist following through in a flash to crush the nose. Even the gentle "Brocade" euphemism couldn't hide the bloody martial origin of the exercise. He hoped he would never have to find out whether he knew the moves well enough to put them to their original use. *At my age?* Even the possibility amused him.

In that second, with the thought the posture triggered, an image from a dream, one that had wakened him at four, flashed volcanic underground flames through his memory. He and Anthi's mother were digging their hands through the sandy loam floor of a cave in Greece. Everywhere they looked they found clay objects—cups, horses, straw-like clay baskets, and a clay tray to hold the collection. The material was still damp and malleable, easy to break if they weren't careful. Somehow the cave was now in Israel; the found objects had become a set of bright pink artifacts and another of bright blue. As the tourists with them began scurrying away for their plane or boat, he reached both his hands into the floor and pulled up a huge block of hardened clay. The clay had come away as though peeling off a section of egg shell. Under the shell waited a marble-white skull, and beneath it lay a stack of other human skulls and skeletal limbs as in a charnel house. Farther down than the glittering skeletons cavorted flames of dull red and gold, part of a buried volcano and prehistoric crematorium. The fire, he told himself, was the reason humans occupied the cave in the distant beginning. He ought to tell the Israelis about the ancient site, but since his fellow tourists appeared in a panic to leave, he let the clay block fall back to the cave floor, sealing the skulls, the crematorium, and the volcano.

While the dream memory flowed through his meditation, he finished his postures, locked the windows and doors and, with a sense of solitary freedom, strolled toward his haircut. Even though Anthi had ignited the fire of a new story, one he would not resist, he could still bank the mightiest flames of the chase until he got his hair trimmed, and she arrived.

The main street through the village seemed unusually quiet, the only vehicle moving a small yellow van that belonged to the postal service. Picking up packages, he supposed. And that bookshop with magazines on the local mysteries, still closed. He wondered if it was ever open. *Good to see* Deepest France *in the window. I won't let anyone here know I'm that Milton. This is a vacation; interviewers need not apply. As though! A closed store sells a load of copies, I'm sure.*

He didn't bother crossing the street to tap on the shop's door but saw no harm in hoping he'd find it open one day. With his mind lingering on the bookstore, he almost passed the building he was seeking. Christine was wrong—it's not a hybrid; it's Santé Esthetique.

He pondered the list of establishments that used the pale green building with the pink trim. *Acupuncturist. Psychic. What's this? Trouver un Parti. Matchmakers? Must be. Dance instructor. Pilates and TaiChi. Impressive, up to date. Yoga. Uh-oh, chiropractor. Deep massage. No barber? No barber. Well—don't I deserve a massage, after the car all day yesterday. If not too Thai. Deep in the body? Or the muscle? Not too shady, I hope. It might help. Get the old bean off those butchered kids.*

He pushed the glass door open and studied a wooden directory where slotted frames with removable slivers of paper designated the locations of available services. Deep massage was ground floor rear. *Does that sound sleazy or not? To the dark end of the corridor then—here I come.* He pressed the light button and the hallway brightened.

At the end he found a door freshly painted in muted lime and a small sign instructing him to enter *s'il vous plait.* No need to knock. Just go gently. Leave all rage on the road behind.

There was no one behind the chest-high reception desk, but his entrance must have alerted a tall woman with dark hair, sharp features, and slender curved body, who came into the room from his left. Too similar to Celine Dion for his taste.

"Bonjour, monsieur. I am Aimee," she said with a smile that seemed forced. Her accent sounded more British than French.

"I am Milton." *And I could use a friend, Aimee.* The pun was so bad he was glad he hadn't spoken it aloud.

"Milton?" The name seemed to amuse her. "How can we help you?"

He'd been wrong to give his formal name; it sounded so pretentious. Quickly he described the recurring tightness in his right leg that too much sitting or walking, even one or two of the Brocades, jump-started into a pain that spread from his knee down to his calf and up to his hip.

Her face brightened. "It must be a tight IT band. And you are in luck. Gloria has just finished her nine o'clock and hasn't left. She is our specialist in IT problems."

"Wonderful," he said, with enthusiasm despite doubts about her snap diagnosis since it confirmed what he'd been told back home. "Does Gloria understand English?"

"Almost." Aimee smiled. "She's an American too." She handed him a clipboard plus a ballpoint attached with a string soiled by use. "Fill this form out, please, and she will be out for you."

Obediently he took one of three wooden chairs opposite the reception desk and began scribbling his vital stats and medical history. Just the major surgeries and the attack. *No need to go into too much detail. Don't want to scare them off.*

He had not quite finished when someone appeared in the doorway Aimee had used. It was the woman from the tea salon, the one with the ambivalent smile. *She's Gloria? But no sign she recognizes—*

"Milton?" Her greeting seemed hesitant even though he was the only client in the room.

He rose and took a polite step toward her. "Milt will do," he said. "You must be Gloria?"

She offered him a wide smile that appeared genuine. "Good guess—how can I help you?"

"You are the IT specialist?" He meant his own smile to suggest confidence that she would know ways to relieve his pain.

"You mean the area that runs from here—" she placed her fingers on the outside of her own left calf and ran them up her well-fitted jeans "—to here." Her fingers stopped where her knit shirt, mauve and almost sleeveless with a scooped top, covered the outside tip of her hip. He noticed how well the mauve complemented her dark hair, pale skin, and dusky green eyes. *Fine taste for one so young. She can't be more than twenty-five, can she?*

"My pain kicks in here, outside the right knee or behind the right hip, and runs into the right calf. The masseuse I saw in Virginia called it the IT band. Probably short for something else. I had a few sessions with her—before she left my gym."

"She meant the iliotibial band." She promptly added: "The calf, you say?"

"That's where I noticed it first."

"I see." She bent, took firm hold of his calf, and dug her fingers deep. "Myofascial release can help with this."

"Great." Clearly she knew her stuff, he decided—or knew how to talk the talk. "I've been driving more than usual."

"We'll go to my room. You'll have to finish the paperwork first."

She led him down the hall to a space scarcely big enough for her table but with a large window opening to the light above the river. A corner screen added an indirect glow from a lamp back of it. In the opposite corner a tower of triangular shelves held an ivy plant in a small terracotta vase, a jar of thick cream, and a candle. Soft New Age music came from somewhere—the cracked closet door to his left, he decided. The gentlest scent—was it lavender?—laced the room. She pointed him toward one of two wooden chairs by the door.

He wondered about his privacy with the window there, but no

building on the opposite bank rose high enough to stare in, only the mountain slope. On the table he could look out into the light. Nice!

When he handed the clipboard and completed form to her, she told him he could hang his clothes in the closet or leave them on the chairs.

"Underwear—or nothing?" he asked.

"Either," she said as she exited. "I'll be back in a few minutes."

"Nothing then, like in—" But she had closed the door. "Virginia," he added for no one's benefit but his own.

Removing each layer of his scanty summer wear felt as though he was shedding another layer of road weariness and his anxieties about Christine, the closed hotel, and Anthi's arrival, if not the mission she would have for him. He placed his multicolored shirt and beige shorts on one of the chairs. His underwear he hid inside the shorts. The clunky, dusty sandals went under the same chair, his watch and shades on a small round table between the chairs. He pulled the sheet on the padded table back and climbed up to stretch out his legs. In this light, his limbs and stomach appeared remarkably tanned and fit after the days of climbing, swimming, and sunning along the coast. Face up, he pulled the sheet to his lower chest and lay waiting.

Someone tapped lightly on the door. When she closed it behind her, he asked, "Where are you from, Gloria? You sound American."

"I am. Santa Barbara. It's above Los Angeles."

"Lovely place," he said. "One of the best."

"It was," she said.

"Will you go back?"

"Not if I can help it." She raised the upper third of the sheet. "Let's start with your back," she said.

As he elevated on his elbows and twisted over awkwardly, he grunted, "Why—ever—not?"

"I don't know—" Even face down, he sensed the hesitancy in her voice. "It's just that LA is spreading. It's like oil—spilling up the coast. I don't want my little girl growing up in that slick." She raised his right leg in the air.

"That's little Cathy?" he asked.

Her grip on his leg froze. "How do you know her name?"

"I saw you at the tea shop this morning. Sorry for listening."

She placed his leg back on the table and bunched the sheet between his thighs so that the right leg remained uncovered. "No wonder you looked a little familiar." She seemed at ease again.

"Some say," he mumbled into the soft doughnut that framed his face, "that LA is spreading everywhere, through the infamous industry it runs."

"I hate to believe it. I know that LA money is taking over Santa Barbara. Up on the ridge they call the Riviera—and over in Montecito."

"And David Crosby's got a spread out in the north, hasn't he?"

"Well, he's okay. He respects the spirit in nature. It's the crime that follows the money that drove Ted and me out." Her fingers were driving into his calf now, dividing muscles down its back.

"Ted's your—husband?" He caught his breath to keep from groaning as she hit a knot of some sort in the outside part of the muscle.

"Cathy's father is a guitarist. We're not married."

Her candidness startled him, but her ease encouraged him to ask with equal calm, "Why not?"

"I was married before—a sweet guy, but after the wedding he wanted to take control. He couldn't help it; his father was like that. I'm not sure I'm ready to try again." Whatever she was feeling appeared to feed the vigor with which she handled his leg now that she was moving up to the back of his thigh.

"I see," he grunted despite himself.

"Did I hurt you?" She eased the pressure.

"Not really. I'm sure it's doing good."

She leaned to work with renewed fervor. "We believe we can still find a better life for Cathy without getting married. We want to protect her against road rage and drive-bys and the drugs. That's why we've brought her to Ran-lay-Bands." The way she pronounced the words seemed to carry a clear California ring, one he liked. "Ted has a new band here—with local musicians."

"I see." Her strong sentiments brought to mind an odd fact a friend had passed on to him once, that Freud got the idea for his talking cure while massaging a complicated patient who liked to talk and whose chatter kept circling the problems that bothered her. Gloria's process was returning the technique to its source, wasn't it—but with the therapist doing all the talking, and her client trying to keep up. "So that's how you got here?"

"Ted and I heard about Ran in Santa Barbara. From a guy you'll see around if you stay a while."

"Which one's that?"

"He dresses sort of weird and carries a big stick." She was kneading lots of kinks now, and each one she hit made him flinch.

He recalled the fellow who parted the crowd last night in the square. "Maybe a hiking pole?"

"Carved at the top—"

"I believe I've seen him."

"He calls himself Guru Shanti, Shanti now. But when we knew him back home he was plain Freaky Claude. Always on stage."

"He is that," Milt muttered.

"He's a performer, pure and simple. He acts the clown, but Ted thinks he's brilliant. And he knows the ins and outs of this place. He was born here. He told us about the ancient Cathars, which is why we named our daughter Cathy."

"Not Catherine?"

"For us, the names are the same."

"I guess." Her explanation worked for him.

"Claude—Shanti, Shanti—says they are."

"So it was his idea—your coming here?"

"Ted met Shanti in SB—Santa Barbara—before he, Shanti, decided to return to Ran-Lay-Bands. SS sold Ted on the Cathar ideal that if we want spiritual peace we have to wash everything, ourselves, the world, clean."

While working on *Deepest France*, Milt had run across the basic facts about the Cathars, the way Rome in the thirteenth century had made this gentle group a target of the Inquisition. There was no need, he felt, to tell her just now—not as her hands working through the sheet approached the ticklish area just below his glutes—that he far preferred inclusive Taoists to the purifying sect for which she, or Ted, named their little girl. "Clear away everything?"

"You know—clean away all the drugs, the pornography, peculiar sex unions, school kids killing school kids, religions murdering other religions, destroyers of ice caps and rain forests, suicide bombers. I can keep on going, but you know what I mean, don't you? The whole modern, monster world." Her fingers, to his partial relief, veered away from the sensitive region in order to manipulate the outer edge of his right hip.

"Surely the killing and destruction have to stop, no doubt about it." He had reservations about one or two of her other fears and had a handful he'd like to add to her list, chiefly the petro-auto mafia, all purveyors of credit card quicksand, and those who expected to profit from spreading the could-be self-fulfilling prophecy of the End Times. "You can avoid the—violence here?" he wondered aloud.

"Not just avoid it—Ted claims SS has the solution. A plan to send a message, make a statement, show the world what it's doing—put an end to the insanity for all time."

"That would be something—a lot—wouldn't it." He felt her fold the sheet down from his shoulders and apply an initial pressure to his lower back. "Are you going to tell me?" he said, with no hint, he hoped, of applying pressure himself.

"Tell what?" His question appeared to have taken her by surprise. Either that, he thought, or she's just teasing me. One of the wonders of massage, I guess, the tease.

"How SS plans to end half the miseries of humankind."

"I don't know. We just arrived a month ago. If Ted's been instructed, he hasn't shared with me."

Milt pondered the implications of her answer for a moment while she moved her attention to his shoulder. "Good," he mumbled into the doughnut cushion. "That's another spot right there that I have trouble. An old injury to my rotator cup—or cusp. Or cuff. Whatever it's called."

"Cuff," she said with more gentleness than pedagogical righteousness. "Football?"

"Afraid not. Fell on some rocks on a beach. Trying to keep up with my boy." His attempt to scramble over a tunnel of boulders on Virgin Gorda flicked in his memory like the light at the end of the tunnel in which the boulders lay.

"Lots of people carry tension in their shoulders." She did not continue for a moment, then: "Time to flip over so I can work on your front."

He did as directed and waited for her next move. This way he could study the calmness in her face and eyes, admire the round strength and smoothness of her arms, and the modest crevice where her breasts began as she bent to adjust a cylindrical pillow under his heels.

"Do you have other kids, Gloria?" He grasped his hands back of his head so he could both appreciate her youthful beauty and catch any sudden changes of expression in her eyes or around her mouth.

"Just the three of us. Ted and me, and little Cathy. Plus our camper, of course." She adjusted the sheet again, pushing the right side of it quickly up into the responsive area below the join of his thighs. *Hope it doesn't respond*, he told himself. *Too much testosterone in this room. Got to neutralize it. Would be embarrassing, wouldn't it. Unless it happens all the time. Maybe it does.*

"Do you live in the camper?" The possibility brought back his own days in a camper.

"We park it along the river, back of the campground. It's good enough. And safe. We'll stay there—until the end—until Shanti, Shanti works his plan."

"You leave Cathy in the van during the day?"

"Only when she's napping and I have to work and Ted's with his friends." She started her work again, this time with the large muscle just above his right knee.

"You believe she's safe?" He didn't want his concern to alarm her. "Here—or anywhere, these days."

For a second she glanced at him, a question in her eyes. "The camper's sitting under lovely shade trees. Ran-lay-Bands is like small Kentucky towns my mom used to talk about, where people never lock their doors."

Milt couldn't hold back a short laugh. "In Virginia I have a good friend who never locks up. But every time she comes home, she opens the storm door from her carport and hollers out, 'Now, if there's anybody in there who doesn't belong, it's time to run out the front door fast as you can.' I tell her her luck's bound to run out one day."

Without laughing or even smiling, Gloria refocused on his thigh. "Now that's the type of town I'm talking about." Again she seemed to find a way to divide the muscle under her fingers in two.

As she pushed deeper into this crevice and moved upward, he savored the strange sensation and waited warily for the pleasure to change to pain. It never did. He fished for another topic: "So—what about your friend, Aimee? Does she have any children?"

"Aimee?" She didn't look up from her work. "Well, I just met her, and no, she doesn't have any."

"I see."

"Aimee was born in Indonesia. Her mother is from there; her father's an internist somewhere in Holland."

"What brings Aimee to this secret—safe—safe haven?" He half hoped her hands would continue their ascent, but realized that movement would inevitably distract both of them from his gathering of secrets. Her talkativeness reminded him of his barber in Richmond growing up. He wasn't sure he could find a more candid source for secrets.

"When her folks lived in Indonesia, tidal waves and religious fanatics pushed her family out of the islands—she mostly grew up in Holland. She was passing through on vacation with a girlfriend when she met SS. They hit it off, and she decided to come back and rent this space for massage work. We get along. I'm glad she took me in."

"Does the guru—Shanti—tell her his plan?"

"Maybe. But she doesn't reveal his secrets to me." As he was wondering whether the woman into whose hands he had delivered his limbs, etc., was a professional therapist or a happy-ending health provider, her fingers followed connective tissue from his thigh muscle to the outer edge of his pelvis and kneaded the sore area where he supposed the IT band began. *Drats, a therapist.* As before, he almost felt relieved, though he knew that he was exhausting his store of pertinent questions and that the warmth of her touch was spreading. *If I run out, rerouting my impulses is going to become a problem.*

Before the crisis occurred, an image popped into his mind, and a distracting question followed. "What do you know about the tall, very blond couple who dress all in white?"

"That white's popular here. Lots of folks wear white." She pulled the sheet down to cover his entire leg.

"They do?" He recalled the woman waiting on the bench outside Hotel de France.

"Oh, yes." She folded the sheet back just beneath his chest muscles. "Those who come here as pilgrims and devotees."

"Of—?"

"The Cathars. Seekers of purity and perfection. Willing to sacrifice the things of this world." She dug into a space two inches left of and down from his shoulder's tip, and his arm jerked sharply.

"Even massage?" he snapped, to cover his reaction.

"I'm sorry." She drew her hands away. "Did I hurt you?"

"There must be a knot there. Don't stop."

She continued, but further up his shoulder. "I haven't decided about massage," she said. "Massage, I feel, helps free the spirit from the body."

"I see." He didn't want to explain that it had the opposite effect for him and that it was everything he could do to keep his spirit and mind from sinking totally into his body and that, in fact, if the circumstances were different, merging spirit and flesh would be exactly what he wanted from this massage. "But you don't dress all in white," he said.

"That's because we are newcomers—and I don't have money for a new wardrobe, if you know what I mean."

"It makes sense." He hesitated before saying, "And your mauve blouse is very—tasteful on you."

"Thank you." She took the compliment with greater calmness than he had hoped—and began working down his pectorals. His boyish impulse was to flex the muscles but instead he said, "The couple I have in mind have a little girl about two with lots of blonde curls."

"That would be Peer and Gerta—and little Una. They drive a monster van—a truck, don't they? They're Norwegians."

"What do you know about them?" He kept sensing she would continue downward, but she retreated to his troubled right arm.

"Not very much. They just arrived. She's a singer." She focused on the muscles of his forearm and seemed to want to flatten them out.

"What sort of singer?"

"A very good one, I hear. Serious music. Opera—that fancy stuff."

Opera roused a memory in Milt.

"There's a film at the movie house, of her singing," Gloria added before he could ask.

"I believe I saw it. Part of it." It required a stretch for him to imagine the woman in the elegant gown by the sacrificial altar as the woman crouched in the village square. "She—they must be Cathar too."

"Yes, very much so. Peer tells Ted they're here because of SS—Claude."

While he contemplated the news, his soft involuntary "hummh" exhausted his ability to respond as, yanking on his forearm, she stretched his arm from shoulder to wrist straight into the air.

Obviously SS, a.k.a. Claude, was no ordinary Mutton Chop, he told himself, but a fancy leg of lamb, and people were streaming in from scattered points of the globe to hear his Big Plan and help carry it out.

Then a tiny plan of Milt's own trickled from the rear of his mind. "My daughter is joining us here from Paris," he said, "—maybe today or tomorrow. She's not too much older than you are. She'd enjoy meeting some people closer to her age than I am." Gloria was probing the sinus at the base of his skull with pressure that triggered a warm fullness in his lower abdomen, forcing a low, soft groan from him before he could ask, "Do you think—you might—introduce her to your acquaintances?"

She stood now directly at the base of his head, so close that he wished his surviving locks were fingers and he could reach out and touch the base of her stomach. "What acquaintances?" she asked.

"At the restaurants on the square. Gerta, Peer, even SS." Some part of him was trying to will his scalp into giving life to his hair, but the wild curls had a libido of their own when he failed to flatten them with water or a little lotion.

"I usually cook supper at the camper for me and Cathy. I don't spend my time on the square." With that she leaned forward above his head so that she could arrange both his arms snuggly along his sides. She bent further over him and ran her hands down the full length of his arms until he was staring up into the bountiful mauve fullness that must, he suddenly realized, still nourish little Cathy. "But I know how your daughter must feel." She pressed his arms firmly against the table and whispered, "I could meet both of you there briefly tomorrow evening."

"Wonderful!" he groaned.

"At six thirty maybe," she said and moved much too quickly, despite his out flung hand, to the door.

"Take your time getting up," she added as the door closed behind her.

Day Two

Afternoon

Dressed, standing at the reception desk with Aimee, Milt did not hesitate before scheduling his return visit with Gloria for Thursday, two days hence. When he exited the Santé Esthetique building, the weather had changed. Soft drizzle. *Christine will hate this. But it's warm. Hope a little rain doesn't get her down.*

Pulling up the collar of his black nylon windbreaker, he sauntered through the soft rain back to the hotel. He would read and wait for his wife, whose swims and shower usually took a good ninety minutes.

When he reached the room, he was surprised to find the door already unlocked and Christine sitting on the side of her bed with the television tuned to a noisy French talk show while she crocheted away.

"You cut your swim short?" he asked.

"Did you get your haircut?" She didn't look up from her work.

"No barber. Had a nice massage instead. Needed it, after all the driving," he explained.

"That sounds good."

"Your swim wasn't?" He crossed to open the glass doors and let some warm air in.

She looked up and grinned. "Well, the water must have been 98 degrees, at least. No one else was swimming."

"No kidding." He joined her quiet laughter. "You just came back?"

"Everyone was hanging on the edges or around the fountain."

"They were heat-exhausted, I guess." He turned off the television and stood by the doors for the rest of her story, which she was doling out slowly, according to some pattern she seemed to have planned.

"I was too—after I did my usual." Her grin transformed into the set lips of a boast.

"I don't believe it." The swim part of her "usual" was forty minutes or an hour. "It must be a thermal bath." Not exactly the underground crematorium from his dream, but close enough.

"I had to get my laps in." She kept her needles going.

He wished she didn't. "You're probably too enervated to do much else today."

"I don't know." She lay down the maroon piece she was making. "What you have in mind?"

"A ride into Carcassonne." His choice would have been to obey Anthi's command on the phone, to explore Bugarach, especially the mountain he'd spotted behind it where the infanticide had occurred. But that climb would seem unbearably brutal to his wife. He would have to postpone it another day. In the meantime, Carcassonne ought to provide a happy distraction, one to keep his mind off the horrors of the region.

"More driving?" She stood, took a cup, and crossed to the bathroom, where they kept their bottled water.

She's dehydrated, he told himself. "It's only an hour."

"What's there?" she asked as she reappeared with clear plastic liter bottle in hand.

"A genuine walled city straight out of a medieval fairy tale. And, according to Michelin, there's an art museum."

"You've been?" She sat again on the bed.

"Anthi and I stopped outside the walls on our way to Paris, but her cold was too lousy for her to get out. I decided not to leave her." With Anthi, persuasion was never easy.

"And the weather?" She seemed to be softening.

"It's bound to clear up."

The weather didn't, and Carcassonne provided no happy distractions.

His umbrella proved too small for both of them. Reconnoitering the narrow streets, they took turns under its protection and both quickly became soaked. They had hoped that the medieval sector of the city would be roofed, but their visit found them hopping from tower to tower along the partially enclosed walkway that topped the high walls of the main courtyard. The wind that whipped rain through the open sides of the walk turned increasingly strong and cold. Soaked to the bone, they found it difficult to focus on the recorded details fed them by the headphones they carried. What Milt chiefly noticed were the many dark corners the towers afforded for shameful deeds, under their cone-shaped, slate roofs, and the way the towers' names—Visigoth, Inquisition, Bishop's, Justice— telescoped the region's grim history. *No fairy tale, this place,* he muttered. Soon the two of them had absorbed all the wet, cold, and dismal details they could bear and plunged out into the full force of the rain to find food and, they hoped, to dry out.

After crossing the bridge from the walled part of the city to the lower commercial sector in a downpour, they looked into the first bistro they passed, but it seemed dark, empty, and cold. Trying the other side of the cobble-stone street, they found a storefront sandwich shop that was bright, warm, and not too busy. After her Fanta and his jambon avec fromage toast, they were back in the rain, only a sprinkle now, and on their way to the Musee des Beaux-Arts.

As they strolled from warm room to warm room, they hardly spoke to one another. The mix of Dutch, Flemish, Italian, and Spanish works, mingled with local painters, surprised Milt with its grace and taste. The collection seemed the model for what a modest regional museum might become.

What galvanized his attention, however, were two nineteenth century oils capturing early horrors in the history of the Aude. In one, two tonsured monks in dark robes restrained the rope-bound arms of a young man who wore slate-blue leggings and a creamy white jersey. A third monk used large shears to hack away his long, fiery red locks. Stepping nearer the wall to read the plaque, Milt was startled by the description: Evariste-Vital Luminais was the artist and *Le dernier des Merovingiens, Childeric III*, the title. Milt did not know the artist, but the "last of the Merovingians" had figured as background in his *Deepest France*. Like the later Cathars, they were considered a serious threat to Rome. Cutting Childeric's long hair this way clearly was meant to strip him of his royal powers and to transfer it to Rome's allies, the Pepins, Charlemagne's line. The Plantard family claimed the Merovingian kings, like the Visigoths— and even Mary Magdalena with all she implied—as their noble progenitors. So little Charles was their direct descendent as well. In his family's view, the divine right of kingship became a literal and blood claim. This much of French legend and history Milt had made it a point to learn.

He almost missed the second of the oils but caught a glimpse of it as he was returning through its room on his way to the exit. The slate turrets of Carcassonne seen in bright sunlight from a much darker room first caught his eye. Then he noticed a monk in a dark robe with both hands raised toward the light. Savonarola, the purifier, was his first thought, but he believed that stubborn fellow had preached his fury in Italy, in Florence, best he could remember.

He had to move closer to make out the drama in the far-right half of the painting where two gentlemen, one a bit inquisitional, he thought, calmly watched two other men perform a sinister act on a third almost obscured by one of the second pair. The blocking figure, dressed in an executioner's black hood, held a black four-foot rod in a way that suggested he was turning a screw, perhaps tightening a rope on the half visible victim in the chair. His colleague qua torturer appeared to provide another form of pain from above, although Milt couldn't make out exactly what sort of device he was employing to do so.

He strained to read the plaque. The artist was Jean-Paul Laurens, the title *Les Emmures de Carcassonne*. The monk's name, the plaque read, was not Savonarola but Bernard Delicieux. His hands are raised to defend the local Albigenses, more Cathars, Milt told himself, against the terror brought down on them by the church's crusade. More do-gooders doing bad. And if "Emmures" has to do with "mur," with wall, his mind went on, and you put it with what's happening in the picture, it must mean something like "wall-up ones," the imprisoned. Albigensian prisoners.

So they were Cathars, like the two monks he'd created to protect Charles. Not that they protected him very well. No more than any of the boy's imaginary friends. Not much help, any of them, when he plunged headlong into his fatal cave. Delicieux, though, looks like one of the good guys, standing there between his people and the exterminating angels of the church. No wonder Cathars turned their backs on the world, if they felt it belonged to the inquisitors' Rome. Like Gloria's friends think it belongs now to callous governments, mindless media, greedy smut dealers. Why aren't the prisoners wearing white? And Gloria doesn't either. Maybe only the Perfect Ones wore it. Gotta read up on these guys. Someday.

Despite their soaking by rain, the discovery of the two paintings left Milt believing their day in the city was worthwhile. He now had a better visual sense of the region's violent history, its mix of otherworldly fanatics and sacrificed innocents.

On their way home to Rennes-les-Bains, they found a warm, well-patronized restaurant in Couiza and, despite their still wet wrinkled shorts, enjoyed their best meal since Denmark: dorade for Christine, duck in orange sauce for him, plus three excellent cheeses and a small bottle of the region's red.

"I enjoyed the museum," she said between the entrees and the cheeses. "Can't say the fortress was much pleasure."

"Sorry about that, dear," he said and daubed at a spot of orange on the white linen tablecloth.

"It didn't help that you spent your time studying the most gruesome paintings in the collection. Why? I mean ..."

"Because they were relevant to *Deepest France*."

"That again," she groaned.

"Little Charles's family believed—believe—they are descended from the Visigoth and Merovingian kings."

"Like I am descended from Black Elk—" she scoffed, "—or the royals of Denmark."

"Except there's a whole body of local legend here to support their genealogy. Enough at least to make it a workable premise for my novel."

"Not that it persuaded a trainload of readers and critics." She sounded unusually angry at him. But he couldn't help the rain.

Usually when she was like this, he would tiptoe on eggshells away from her delicate sensibilities. He didn't want another break in the shell, the crystal really, of her mental health here in the boonies of France. But since she hadn't read his novel, he felt compelled to make the case for the book—and charged on.

"It was probably the holy blood dimension that turned critics off. The divine right of kings isn't really the subject most loved by today's tribe of critics," he began.

"What holy blood?" All at once she seemed interested, recovering Catholic that she deemed herself.

"Part of the tradition alive down here is that Mary Magdalena's family arranged a substitute to carry the cross for Jesus, and then whisked him away in a boat with her. They took Jesus, French legend says, to Marseilles, where he and Mary Magdalena and their child or children—became part of a large Jewish community there."

"Children—" Christine almost choked on her first nibble of soft white cheese. "What children?"

"That got your attention, I see." He allowed his inward smile to become visible.

"My mother would have dropped her beads." Christine wasn't smiling.

"For the people down here, these amorous French, Magdalena married him, bore his children, and became the living, breathing Grail since her body literally carried the holy blood into the future. Their children or child, probably Sara, called Black Sara because she may have been born during a voyage stopover in Alexandria, produced a bloodline that married with the Visigoth kings and later the Merovingian royalty. These became the 'true' kings of France—until Charlemagne usurped the title."

"That asks a lot of a reader, Milt," Christine said, shaking her head.

"It wasn't my idea, dear. I got it from a book I was reading in the early '80s—and as I was writing *Deepest France* after I came back home."

"I can't help what went into the novel now." He scraped the traces of the three cheeses from the board and applied them to his last crumb of bread. "Any more than I can help what happened after I told all this to Philip Plantard, Charles's father. I suggested that since little Charles was the chief Plantard descendant, the bloodline from Magdalena might explain the boy's murder. I asked Philip were there any competitors who might have wanted his son out of the way."

"Were there?" she asked.

"It was after this that Philip killed his first cousin, Claud Plantard."

"And you blamed yourself for that murder?"

"I do in *Deepest France*."

"To round out your plot?"

"In part, yes. It was also a kind of confession, I guess." He hadn't thought of his self-blame this way before.

"And it helped?" Her concern seemed sincere.

"But I have a new anxiety." It was then he tried to explain why early the next morning they would need to take a trip to the mountain back of Bugarach.

"You—we—have to go to Bugarach just because your daughter said so?" she asked when he described the news headlines he had avoided, the article he had finally read, and its parallels to his own prose. "Anthi's a bit of a thrill seeker, you know," she said, an edge in her voice.

"Maybe," he muttered, not wanting to get trapped in a conflict of temperaments between the two women. "I just feel a responsibility here."

Tired, irritated with one another, but content with their enjoyable dinner, they returned to the Hotel de France, where a scribbled phone message from Anthi waited at the desk. "Get ready," it said. "I arrive tomorrow—about four!"

Day Three

Morning

Over coffee on the tea salon porch, while he tried to respond with eyes and lips to Christine's account of the calories she'd consumed the previous day, Milt was straining to make out what red-haired Ted and his auburn buddy were saying at the next table. To catch their drift, he had to wait for silent troughs in the waves of Christine's recitation.

Ted's friend seemed the more worked up of the two. "What about Gloria?" he asked. "Is she down with this?"

"I don't know, Gerhardt," Ted said. He stared sheepishly across the street.

"You have to be certain," Gerhardt insisted. "Shanti's plan is too big to wait for butt-draggers."

"I—I don't—I'm not." Ted still would not look at his friend.

Milt checked to see why Christine had suddenly turned silent and found her carefully adjusting the amount of sweetener in her paper cup.

"Why not?" Gerhardt's patience seemed exhausted.

"I just—I can't—just haven't told her."

"Not yet? There's not much time left, homey."

The trendy way he said "homey" told Milt that Gerhardt was not an American but apparently had lived there and that likely he had migrated at some point from Germany.

"You don't have to remind me," Ted replied.

"Gerta and Peer are in big time," Ted's friend leaned close to say.

Milt realized Christine was standing now. She had debriefed, or made her confession, he wasn't sure which, and apparently was ready to leave.

"I guess I love our Cathy too much," Ted added. "And Gloria—"

"Peer's little Una is not exactly a devil doll," Gerhardt said, a sting of anger in his voice now.

"I know."

"We're not exactly asking you to tape explosives to your stomach, are we?"

"No, but—"

"We have to fight fire with fire. All of us have to make sacrifices, like SS says."

"I'm just not there yet," Ted apologized as he rose from his chair.

"Why the hell did you come all this way if you weren't ready to get with the program. We gotta help stop the damn insanity running this world."

"I know, I know," Ted grumbled and took a few steps in the direction of the camping site. "I'll get there."

"And Gloria too!" his friend shouted after him.

In the Citroen, half an hour later as the mountain peak back of Bugarach came into view, he turned toward Christine to say, "Thanks for coming along."

"I still don't understand why we need to visit such a tiny village. Especially when we just rode past it two days ago." The trip from Rennes-les-Bains hadn't given her enough time to settle into the needlework that lay on her lap. Instead, the drive was allowing her to sink into lethargy.

"It's certainly picturesque enough for a second look." His answer didn't sound persuasive, even to him, so he said, "And there's lots of local lore, legends we *might* dig up." Would he have to go over again the sense of personal responsibility that drove him to the site? If she didn't take what he'd said at dinner in Couiza seriously enough to remember it, that was her problem, not his. He wasn't going to bring it up again.

"Reminds me of Roquebrune—" she said. "But grey instead of brown."

Now that she mentioned it, from this distance the mountain ahead did resemble the brown massif they had spotted along the road connecting Les Issambres with the autoroute to Montpellier. As they circumvented the cluster of houses that made up Bugarach, however, what seemed a huge chimney-like peak spread out to become a giant's limestone spine.

"And—remember—" he fumbled for words, "it's here—on this mountain that the last one, the boy—died."

"Oh—" she groaned. "I guess we must."

At its foot they located a single track, overgrown with weeds recently pressed down by tires, and followed its quick turns up the mountain's side until it ended at the clime divide where green plots and trees gave way to brush. Here they parked, and their foot climb began. Near the base of one of the last of the large trees stood a wooden sign with a clear plastic box attached. Its lid half protected a handful of handouts made of folded slick paper.

Christine, invigorated now by the climb, flipped back the lid and pulled out one of the rain-stained sheets. It was covered with small print. "Listen to this," she said and ran her eyes quickly down the streaked page as she translated: "According to novelist Jules Verne, the Pech de Thauze or Bugarach provides an entrance to the caverns of the Hollow Earth rumored to be home to an alien race.... It was during his decades-long quest for this underground world, believed to be where the untouchable Ark of the Covenant was hidden, that explorer Daniel Bettex died under mysterious conditions in 1988. You are standing on unfamiliar ground, where extraordinary events have occurred and will, in all probability, occur again."

She slapped the handout against her leg and asked, "What do

you make of this poppycock, Milt? You didn't bring me here for this, I hope."

He took the sheet from her. "Tourist office baloney. I didn't know about it. Life copies art. Always has." He paused for a second as though he'd heard a bell ring, but it was a bell he would ignore as he went on: "Jules Verne, Hollow Earth, the Ark—why not Trader Vic as well?"

"You mean Indiana Jones, don't you?"

"Yeah, him too!" Milt turned away from the tourist sign and folded the handout to thrust into his pocket as he continued up the ever steeper path marked by recent use. "Ark of the Covenant, my third nut! Come on. Let me show you something. There's the other reason we're here."

"Better be good," she growled.

"I don't know about good—just important."

Soon they were pulling themselves up the limestone and granite track, using both fingers and shoes to find crevices large enough to furnish toeholds. A moldy smell almost as thick as clay filled his nostrils. His back and shoulders broke out in sweat, and his cotton shirt began to cling. Whenever he turned to check how Christine was doing, he noticed the solid line of emerald, the hardwoods and evergreens, that followed the river back into Rennes-les-Bains.

"It reminds me of Zion Park," she called when she caught him staring back.

"Yeah? But where are the sandy spots?" he complained. "How much more can your fingers take?"

"Not much. Shoes either." They wore sneakers they had updated for the trip. "Even red rock would be easier."

The torture continued for what felt like a mile but that he knew was no more than fifty yards. To his relief Christine, in front now, announced she'd spotted a yellow plastic tape strung from a ragged circle of low bushes. It defined an area to their right maybe a dozen yards across. As they drew nearer, Milt found himself staring into lemon and lime water where a colossal boulder, likely broken off the peak above, blocked the run-off. The transparent pond was roughly the size of a large backyard pool but had the shape of some malformed pear. "So, what are you really looking for, Milt?"

"This is it," he said and raised the police ribbon to crawl under it.

"You shouldn't do that," she said as she followed him.

"We're crossing the line," he said. "But it's what we came to see." His feet stirred up layers of brush and pellets of chipped limestone, releasing a heavy odor of decay.

"What 'you' came to see, babe," she chided. "What do I really know? Only that this pond looks like the one at Zion where we skinny-dipped. Maybe we should—"

Milt stopped by the pool's edge, reluctant to step into water that could wash away his sweat but that likely would feel more alkaline than Zion's. Besides, this pool contained remnants of death.

"You never finished *Deepest France*." He tried not to sound scolding.

"Well—the first sections were violent and depressing—"

"And you don't like depressing stories. Not even thoughts. Well, guess what."

"This is where one of the scenes is set?"

"Nope." He hesitated before adding, "But as I said last night, it is happening again. You read enough to know what that means."

"Are you nuts?"

"No. Afraid not." He paused to consider the implication of her question, but felt certain he was not losing his grip. "Someone's killing small children here and doing it the way they did to little Charles. This pool is one of the spots where it happened this time round. The most recent, I hope." He went on to tell her once more about the newspapers that had taunted him since Les Issambres, about Anthi's alarm and the true reason for his daughter's visit this afternoon. "You ought to read the novel, Christine."

"What's your book got to do with this—murder?" Her hand waved toward the pool.

"I hope nothing." Milt dropped his eyes. "I don't know for sure, but whoever's doing this might be using the novel as a guide."

"Oh—" she groaned, and he half-expected her to add, You are nuts, aren't you?

"I'm sorry I dragged you into this. It could get depressing. I'd hoped it was all ancient history."

"In for a penny, in for a buck," she mumbled sarcastically. "You think there's a copy around?" she said for him to hear.

"Could be." He remembered the volume he'd seen in the local-lore bookshop window across from their hotel. "In a nutshell, the case was never solved. Not in reality. But in *Deepest France,* Charles's mother, Christine, and her lover Claud kill Charles. They intend to free her from her husband Philip—there're several other motives too complicated to explain right now. Christine and Philip ran the Hostellerie I wanted us to stay in in les-Bains. Philip and Claud were cousins. Claud was killed. Little Charles and Christine become the pets of the French press. It was a feeding frenzy."

"Is that why you married me? Because my name is Christine?" she asked, her eyes dark, recessed.

"What?" It was the strangest idea he had heard recently. "No, of course not. But I did fall under her spell. Like everyone else who saw her pictures and read her story in the papers. Those dark eyes and the sad smile."

"Because she murdered her little boy?" Her voice and narrowed eyes made her discomfort plain.

"Nobody knew that. As I said, it was never solved. She persuaded everyone else she was a woman drowning in profound grief, the suffering mother of France who'd lost her only son. A modern Pieta, I suppose."

"Then why did you claim she was the murderer?" She led him to two grey knee-high stones and brushed away twigs and rotting seedlings so they could sit facing the quiet water.

"Anthi and I figured it out. We invented it—in the novel. Pure invention, I admit. But we were the outsiders. We could look at the facts without all the mother-and-child blindness. Our interpolations were probably true enough, as later events show."

"Then don't beat yourself up about it. You seem down today."

"Because of what's happening now—and what I told you last night. Because of what I did when I was here before. What I told Philip, the boy's father."

"Yes?"

"That's complicated too. You'll have to read the book to get the details. But the strange thing is that I feel more exhilarated being here again than depressed. I'm ashamed to admit it, though."

"You should be," she said, but he could see she found his ambivalence human and amusing. Finally.

"If you feel that way," he slapped his knee and stood, "you won't want to help me find out what else is hidden around here. The local Keystone Kops must have missed a detail or two."

"Of course I won't help." She rose also and looked about. "So where do I start?"

"Why don't you go uphill about twenty yards and cover that quadrant. I'll head straight out into the brush and sweep back toward the track we came up."

She agreed, and they crawled back out under the yellow tape to comb through the two sectors. It pleased Milt that the ground cover at this altitude was not the tangled briars and impenetrable vines he knew in Virginia but clusters of grass, fragrant herbs, thyme and rosemary he guessed, and shoulder-high, rock-breaking plants he could navigate by steering toes and knees judiciously around them. Aside from dried skeletons of birds and small mammals, foul reminders of goats, crushed cups, bottle shards and other signs of partying, the terrain proved sparsely inhabited.

They scoured for twenty minutes or so before a shout from Christine shattered the mountain's eerie silence. Her words weren't clear, but her excitement was.

He scrambled uphill toward the sound. Off in the distance loomed the walls of the immense grey canyon that a line of angry drivers had shoved them through two days earlier. "What is it, the blessed Ark?" he mumbled to himself.

When he was closer, she called again, "I think I found something," and as soon as he was within a few yards, she added with an outburst of panic, "What the hell is this?" She was standing erect, staring down at a spot obscured for Milt by shrubs.

"What?" he asked.

"Just some stones—I hope."

He heard the nervous edge of denial in her voice. When he stood beside her they looked down on large jagged stones, probably limestone, arranged like bricks stacked without mortar to form a sort of table maybe a foot wide by two-and-a-half long, and raised roughly two feet above the ground. Certainly it was neither as large nor as ornate as the altar table in the operatic film glimpsed in the village's cinema, but it might have served recently for an offering. Despite his effort at self-restraint, the terrible exhilaration of horror stirred in his blood

"What you make of the stains?" he asked, watching Christine carefully for her response.

Disgust twisting her face, she said, "I know what you are thinking, Milt, but these could be almost any dark fluid, even animal blood." She was too insistent.

"Yeah," he said, struggling to avoid what seemed obvious. "There're bound to be lapins in these grasses."

"Just don't go jumping to conclusions. Please, dear."

328 | Julius Raper

"Of course not," he said. In his mind's eye he saw an old man in a Bible illustration standing obedient over a rough-hewn table on which the submissive elder's son lay. Almost immediately the addled old man became a warrior equally ancient staring down at Iphigenia, his daughter, whose blood might appease another deity. Child sacrifice, he groaned inwardly. Cornerstones of it all.

"And if you do, you ought to take your fantasies to the gendarmes."

"And make them look bad? There's no yellow tape here." No matter what she said, he could not turn from his visions of child sacrifice—mirrored myths of our warrior cultures.

"For missing this?"

"And all they missed twenty years ago." More than thirty centuries we missed it, he added, trying out the new connection in the dark underground of his psyche. Little Charles just one more boy sacrificed.

"Oh," she grunted.

"Many thousands ago," he mumbled to no one but himself. Still goes on. Iraq now. All the children—and the old men. It's time it's stopped. Maybe Shanti's right.

Off in the distance, as though on cue, he spotted a small older-model sedan with a blue light on top heading from the main road north toward the worn track they'd taken up to the spot they'd been forced to park the Citroen.

"It's time to go," he called to his wife, "unless we want real trouble."

They scrambled down rapidly enough to meet the police just before they turned onto the narrow trail. As the cars passed one another, Milt smiled and waved at them the way any tourist might show appreciation for the good work they were doing protecting a treasured preserve of nature.

Milt reminded himself as he drove back that the sense of responsibility he explained to Christine above Bugarach had no relevance unless someone around les-Bains and Couiza had, in fact, read his book. And this he thought unlikely, despite the dusty copy in the store window. An antiquarian shop, of all places.

Still he made it a point, back in Rennes-les-Bains, to ask the tiny woman who ran their hotel when the shop across the street would be open. She looked at the two of them quizzically before replying, "Just a minute," then stepped once more behind the reception desk and rummaged somewhere in a drawer there.

"Voila," she said as with a grin she raised a single key on a ribbon for him to see. Without explaining, she led the two of them out the door and up the quiet street across to the bookshop.

As she unlocked the door, Milt glanced through the window to make certain his novel was still there. "You run this too?" he asked.

"Someone has to care for our local heritage," she said, a sad glow in her eyes. "Even a transplant like myself."

"I kept wondering why the shop was never open," he said and wandered through the maze of small tables and revolving racks packed with dusty French paperbacks and ragged old newsletters. Quickly he selected two of the latter, one researching legends of treasures buried nearby, the other describing local crimes of note and featuring the death of little Charles. The lead article was headlined: "Bizarre Murder Still Unsolved After Fifteen Years."

He drifted back toward the front window and attempted to snatch up his own book without attracting attention. Through the coating of dust he could make out the dust-jacket drawing in red and flesh tones of the boy, his father, and his mother set in miniature against a looming figure covered from head to foot by a silky white robe, the latter decorated only with a red cross set within a small blue circle over the heart. But as soon as he turned to pay their hostess, he saw she was beaming with a satisfied recognition.

"You sell many of these?" he asked as he handed the stack, novel on top, with a large Euro bill to her.

"A number, chiefly to foreigners, and the occasional policeman," she said. "I'll have to get change at the hotel."

"What did you select?" Christine asked as she joined them from her own rummaging. "Oh, you found it. Time to read it, I guess."

As the hotel-keeper locked the door behind them, she whispered over her shoulder, "When I received your e-mail, I was almost certain you were Milton Walters."

"Too big a coincidence, I guess," he said. For the first time since his return, a sense of genuine dread entered his bones. "Please—don't tell anyone."

"Don't worry, I wouldn't do that." She led the way back. "Local people don't like what you said. Probably the gendarmes don't either."

"I'm not surprised," he said.

"But you simply used your imagination to draw valid conclusions from the facts," she said as they reached the hotel door.

"Thank you." He followed her into the dimly lit lobby.

"I agree with where you ultimately arrived," she said and threw the bookshop key back into the drawer.

"That's good to hear." At least another outsider, relatively speaking, could connect the dots the locals had refused to put together.

"I can't wait to get started on this," Christine pealed loudly.

Day Three

Afternoon

In the hotel that afternoon Christine turned the pages of *Deepest France* while Milt fiddled about waiting for his daughter. Two uncertainties plagued him. Was the gloomy story the sole reason Christine had never taken time to finish the novel? Or were there others? The novel wasn't very long, and though experimental, most of the chapters were accessible. Perhaps it all seemed too eccentric and—and too *French* for someone with her middle-America mind-set and selective attention span, but he wasn't sure.

Whether he could trust their hostess's promise not to tell any of the villagers who he was, worried him even more. He could understand her agreeing with his conclusions simply because the Plantards, little Charles's troubled parents, were once her major competitors as innkeepers. He hoped, however, that his inferences rang true for other reasons, chiefly that, as he'd told himself, they were tied to the known facts. And if she did reveal his identity, what could happen? Surely no one remained in the area with enough personal interest in the murder to take a shot at him the way Philip, much to Milt's regret, gunned down his cousin. The Plantards had all died, been jailed, or— He paused before admitting, *I actually don't know what became of Charles's mother, Christine. She just dropped out of the newspapers. For certain, she's not running the Hostellerie. Even the head cop, Poulin, I think his name was, got transferred.*

Later, Milt heard his wife calling his name and looked up to discover he had fallen asleep in his chair out on the balcony over the river. She was still sitting across the table from him. She held *Deepest France* pressed by both arms against her breasts. "Well, I've just read this chapter on Christine through, and I still don't know what she did. All the broken sentences and memory flashes. It's too intense. So—tell me."

"It's the darkest secret in the book. It's supposed to be hard to reach ... difficult for her even to face."

"I get that. But why make it hard for your reader?"

"It's not just about knowing. It's about feeling—feeling what she felt in the broken way she did. You'll have to read it again. Maybe more than once."

"What I'm feeling now is anger." She threw the dust-jacketed book on the metal table.

"At Christine?"

"At the author—you."

"That's okay." As Milt pondered this, he stared out over the river. "With fiction," he improvised, "there's always a struggle between the reader and the author. The reader is greedy to know it *all* from the first page. The novelist needs to lift the veil one corner at the time." He paused, wondering whether his words made any sense. "But if you didn't know the author, what then?"

"I'd still be angry," she said and picked up her knitting from where it lay beside her chair.

Milt sat back hoping to slide again into his interrupted sleep. Maybe it's like spouses doing surgery on each other, he dream-thought. They shouldn't.

He knew nothing else until a pounding on the door to their room woke him.

"I can get it," Christine said, already up and squeezing through the glass balcony doors.

The book, he saw, was lying open and face down on the table. She's trying it again. "That's Anthi," he called after her. "She made it."

Tall, full-bodied Anthi was giving thin Christine a warm bear hug by the time Milt made it through the glass doors, her arms and legs bare in a flowery maroon blouse above a khaki skirt. "You two do find some out of the way places to hang out," she said, her smile spreading a generous pink glow up to the roots of dark red curls. The smile pushed her soft cheeks into the two dimples he loved, the ones he'd captured in a photo of her playing the violin at eight or nine and that still hung in his hallway back home.

"You don't remember being here?" her father said as he rushed to offer a huge hug of his own. "Shame!"

"Only what I read in our book, dad." Her embrace seemed warm and genuine. "It's been twenty years, you know."

"Catch your breath; enjoy the balcony. Then we will show you the place and refresh your memory."

Anthi's flight on the company jet had been an easy one, she said. She obviously appreciated their view of the river, and, while Christine continued her reading, she listened eagerly as he filled her in on the extraordinary scene in the square two nights before, their trip to Bugarach, and what he'd learned from his session with Gloria. "This Shanti, Shanti guy must be an authentic character," she kidded.

Her father agreed.

"Someone I ought to meet."

"I hope you will. Meet Gloria too, if things work out. And Shanti has a whole entourage he leads around. One is a woman from Norway who sings opera about sacrificing children with a snake-like dagger. Weird stuff like that. Shanti seems to have his fingers in all the local pies. I can't find out what his gang is up to, but I have this sense he knows stuff about all this—all the déjà vu murders. You should be roughly the right age to mingle in. That is, if you still want to write a mystery someday."

"Listen, my room is just down the hall," she said as she stood. "I'll go freshen and come back about four thirty, d'accord?"

He took her response as a yes. "Sounds like a plan."

When she returned, Anthi was wearing a teal peasant dress that reached to midcalf, and her hair was pulled back over her ears and fixed there by dark blue barrettes. Like Christine, Milt had cleaned up and put on different shorts, but he felt a tad tourist-shabby beside his daughter. In their group Anthi would be the center of attention, and that would clearly serve his plan.

Together the three of them revisited the streets he and Christine had explored their first night. Strolling the road behind the Hostellerie, Milt asked, "Do you remember staying here twenty years ago?"

"Here?" she asked, surprise spreading over her face.

"You wouldn't, I guess," he said. "You were down with a cold, weren't you?"

"And she was only about fifteen," Christine reminded. "After reading what's in the novel, I can understand why she's forgotten it. Ugh!"

"It *was* decades ago," Anthi said in self-defense.

"You were so helpful in figuring out what was really going on, connecting the bits of the story; I supposed you would remember," he said.

"Dad," she scolded, "don't you think the book gives me a bit more credit than I deserve?"

"Once I write it, young woman, whether it's in print or not, don't expect me to remember that it was ever any other way. So take some credit, why don't you?"

"Well," Anthi grinned, "—if you insist."

As before, the church was closed, but the sun remained high enough for them to enter the cemetery and linger among the monuments. They paused briefly to note the vault of Charles's mother's family, the scholarly Boudets, before gravitating to the back and bottom of the burial lot, where the Plantards' formidable tomb stood nearest the river. Its size and stolidity, Milt felt, imitated the enigmatic cromlechs of the region about which Christine Plantard's relative, the local cure Henri Boudet, wrote enthusiastically in the late nineteenth century. One of the smallest and newest of the plots bore a marker assigning it to "Charles, son of Philip and Christine Plantard, 1980 to 1984." Only it lay covered by a variety of flowers, some fresh, some withered, including roses that could have come from the cinema garden up the hill. Among them stood a cheap vase of clear glass holding a single plastic rose tinted black with thick paint of some sort.

Milt had noticed the vase and its contents before Anthi called out, "This looks like fingernail polish!"

"I was thinking that," he said. "Does polish come in black?"

"Goths use it all the time," Christine answered. "I used to see a couple of them for therapy." She was leading them back toward the gate they had entered.

"Among the depressives?" he asked.

"Not necessarily. Sometimes they are bipolars. Or simply acting out against parents."

"Why use it for little Charles though?"

"Well, from your novel I'd say he worked up lots of strong emotions in people." She pushed the heavy gate open and held it while they stepped through into the small yard by the chapel entrance. "Those who loved him could be using a black rose to comment on the horror of his death. Even his mother felt ambivalence. Maybe someone loved and hated—or hates—him."

"Hated him? We never met anyone like that, did we, Anthi?"

"Not in '85," she said.

"Were there any siblings?" Christine asked.

"No," he said, not giving the question much thought.

"But your—*our*—our book says Christine was pregnant at the time of the trial," Anthi said. "Did *we* make that up?"

336 | <i>Julius Raper</i>

The three of them were retracing the walk Christine and he had taken before, following the southern edge of the square past the pizza restaurant to the giant tree that stood by the main street. "To be honest, I don't remember," he said, thought a second and added, "I don't think we did. I seem to recall a photo in *France-Soir* a year later with an infant, a boy, in her arms."

"He had a name—the baby?" Anthi asked.

They stood in the street and looked both ways before Christine turned them left and marched on farther south toward the campground and the edge of town.

"Not one I recall, though I seem to remember there's one in our book. Was it Henri—or Philip. Julien even. Something along those lines. The family shows its poverty of imagination when it comes to names. They keep repeating the past."

"It happens," Anthi said. "Even in the city."

They moved along upriver until the narrow sidewalk petered out, and they had little choice but to cross the street and return. This time they heard no music trickling from the movie house, and the doors were shut. Even the roses out front had lost their moisture and appeared to be withering. "Here's where we saw the Norwegian woman's opera film with the grotesque knife."

Christine glared at him as though she wished he wouldn't keep bringing it up.

"The village is smaller than I remember," Anthi laughed.

"Aren't they all," Milt said and laughed too.

"Not much for a tourist, I'm afraid," Christine said.

"Locals all inside now," Milt said. "Wait until dinner. You'll see."

Back on the square, they claimed a metal table closer this time than the first night to the long tables, at one of which he hoped Gloria's Ted would soon be drinking. Maybe, if they were lucky, Shanti, Shanti as well. To pass the time, they would need drinks, so he went into the open bar of the restaurant to place their order: bubbly water for Christine, white wine for Anthi and himself.

By quarter to six, Ted showed up, his red hair apparently freshly washed and wild, along with his friend Gerhardt from breakfast. Soon blond Peer came from the direction of the campground and sat with the others. They appeared so animated that Milt felt a need to hear what they were saying. He wondered whether Gloria would keep her promise—without her he had no excuse to introduce himself or Anthi. He pointed Ted out to Anthi and explained his disappointment that Gloria remained a no-show. Had she said six— or six thirty?

"Who is this Gloria?" Christine, though absorbed in *One Calorie at a Time*, one of her small self-affirming books, suddenly wanted to know.

"From the massage I mentioned. She promised to introduce Anthi to a few of her group."

"Oh," Christine replied calmly. She stared for a moment at his daughter as though evaluating her for an athletic event. "Watch yourself, young woman," she cautioned and turned back to her reading.

"I'll be okay. Dad wants me to mingle with these guys and figure them out." She stared at her father. "Don't you, Dad?"

Rather than look at her or acknowledge their plan in front of Christine, he said, "I think we should go ahead and order food." He turned to his wife. "Christine, you enjoyed the salad bar, didn't you?"

"It was good enough," she said. "I'll try it again."

Anthi and he joined her, and they were well into their salads when he spotted Gloria beyond the huge hardwood tree across the square maneuvering a lightweight fold-up stroller, made of chrome and blue nylon, from the street onto the curb. In it squirmed a small, grimacing bundle that he knew must be Cathy. The baby was all in pink, but Gloria wore jeans again and her mauve top. Her eyes were scanning the square as though she was not quite certain where she should direct the stroller.

He stood to make sure she didn't miss them, and when she saw him she headed his way. "That's Gloria coming now," he informed his wife and daughter.

With friendly introductions out of the way, he pulled a chair up for the newcomer between Anthi and himself, and Anthi asked if she might hold the infant. The young mother seemed pleased to have hands freed to enjoy the wine Milt poured her. Seeing Gloria with tiny Cathy altered his perception of her. Certainly she was no longer the seductive masseuse who'd filled his fantasies lying on her table. He didn't regret those moments. When he shut his eyes he could still remember the warmth and pressure of her touch and believed that affection as well as therapy flowed from her fingers. But now she had become a young mother as well as an object of dreams. And she was sitting side by side with Anthi. The conjunction was all too confusing.

"How old is she?" Anthi asked as she pressed the child, whose hair was as red as her father's, against her chest. It pleased Milt to witness this affection in his daughter, about whose personal life he knew so little, only that though she started new relationships every year or so, none seemed to lead to anything permanent. The whole realm of commitment, he sensed, remained a troublesome territory for her generation.

"She's nine months," Gloria said, "almost ten. Her name is Cathy."

"Walking yet?" Christine asked.

"Not yet," Gloria said. "Probably too much time in the stroller— it's so convenient to push her everywhere. But any day now—a few steps. Then, no more minutes in the camper without a babysitter."

"Wish I could sit her," Anthi chimed in. "At least while I'm down here."

"Be careful, I'll remember those words," Gloria said with a large grin.

"Have you had dinner?" Christine asked.

"Yes, I heated some soup and vegetables in the camper."

"In that case, the least we can do, Milt, is order more wine for the young woman," Christine suggested.

"Of course," he replied. "How about you, Anthi?"

She seemed willing enough. Since he planned soon to have the old folks abandon the younger ones for the evening, it seemed wise to order a pichet of white rather than another bottle.

Gloria, he warned himself as he watched her sip, still existed, as she had when he was sprawled on her table, chiefly in his imagination. She must then in part be his invention. She must mirror some hidden piece of himself. But which, he didn't know. In a sense, Christine also mirrored something in him, probably his stubbornness, his will to look after himself despite the gradual erosions brought on by time. And Anthi too. Certainly she shared his drive to know what was going on around them, to find out, no matter what the risk. And his determination to warn and protect. So with these two working to reinforce his assertive sides, there was plenty of room for Gloria to coax out his longing for a warm sensuality and the healing that accepted all of him in the easy way she did. Christine, even in the years when they were sexual more often than now, had stirred a competitive mood in him. Surely he was old enough now to deserve a simple intimacy again, even if it appeared only on the table, no longer in the bed the way it did in his adventurous middle years.

Almost as soon as the new wine was poured, Gloria made his project of separation by ages simpler. She spoke to Anthi, "Your father told me you might enjoy spending part of your time here with the 'wild crowd.' What you think?"

"Sounds cool to me!" Anthi said and grinned at her dad.

"Then you are in luck. Ted, Cathy's dad, and the band are

playing tonight for a private party. It's set for the patio at the old Roman hotel across the river. The place is closed, but Shanti, their leader, has his ways."

"The Roman Hotel?" This was better than Milt had imagined. Anthi would not only meet the gang, but she might make her way back inside the magnificent old Hostellerie and revive her lost memories of twenty years ago. "You be careful, young lady. These southern guys might be a step ahead of a tamed place like Paris. You'd be surprised."

"I certainly would, Dad. You *should* know I'm old enough to take care of myself."

Instantly he felt Christine nudge his arm with her elbow. She was cuing him to say something appropriate. The best he could muster under pressure was, "Of course, dear, I know that. Otherwise I wouldn't be turning you over to Gloria and her 'wild bunch.'"

Gloria laughed, and the other women followed suit, though he didn't think his joke deserved their response.

"Appears the gang's all here," Gloria said, as all at the table turned to take in the crowd at the longer tables. Gerta but not little Una had joined Ted, Peer, and the rest, and even Shanti, Shanti had materialized unobserved, apparently via some path back of the stage. SS had doffed his mountain gear in favor of a dressier outfit, a beige, almost white, safari shirt with large lapels and buttoned-down pockets at chest and waist. In place of lederhosen, he wore slender white trousers and had shampooed his mutton chops and long curls until they stood about his face and head like a wild, dark halo. Apparently he hoped to inspire awe, but to Milt with his memories from the seventies the mane created the effect of a faux Afro. He just couldn't take a fellow who looked like that as seriously as he wanted to be taken. Obviously, though, friends his own age, Ted, Gerhardt, Peer, looked up to him. He was their leader.

"What are we waiting for?" Anthi asked as she passed Cathy back for Gloria to return to the stroller.

"Have a good evening," Christine said.

"Yes, a great time," Milton added, signaling for the check. As he waited, he watched his daughter follow Gloria and Cathy toward the pack of rowdy youths.

Day Four

Morning

As soon as he woke, he slipped on his shorts and walked down the dark hall to tap on Anthi's door. No response. He knocked, but again no reply.

When he banged hard enough to rattle both halves of the old lock, he heard a weak voice groaning, "Yes, what is it?"

Relieved, he replied in as near a whisper as possible, "Just checking. To see how your evening went."

"It went *late*. I need sleep," she half growled in a voice familiar from her teen years.

"Check with you later," he muttered.

Again no answer, so he stumbled back to his room to don the rest of his clothes for breakfast.

After coffee and yogurt fetched from their tea and grocery shop, he turned down Christine's invitation to join her morning walk. "I've got some things to take care of," he explained to his well-rested wife.

After she went out, he checked through the morning paper he'd picked up at the tea shop and was relieved to discover no new reports of murdered children, only "no progress" follow-ups on the previous cases. Soon he was out the door to keep his appointment with Gloria.

This time no Aimee welcomed him, but Gloria herself was waiting behind the desk, the first of the younger crowd he'd encountered today. Apparently Ted and Gerhardt, whom he'd looked for at the tea shop, and all the others were sleeping in this morning. But Gloria seemed refreshed. This he assumed was a sign she'd enjoyed her night's sleep. She had swapped her mauve jersey for a similar one, equally becoming, of deep forest green. The jeans she had on appeared to be those she'd worn each time he'd met her.

After her friendly welcome, she led him to her therapy room and pulled back the sheet. "How are you feeling today?"

Although it was not what he wanted to discuss, he said, "Now that you mention it, for some reason my right calf has tightened up since last night. I noticed it just walking up from the hotel. And my hip is stiff too, I guess." Talking about himself left him uncomfortable, so he added, "How are you?"

"Just fine, thank you." She began bustling about the room arranging her lotion and the face cradle before heading toward the door. "You get ready. We can talk when I come back."

When he was stretched out on his stomach under the sheet, she knocked and reentered. Before he could bring Anthi up, she had his leg up on her Styrofoam cylinder and had begun to knead, producing stabs of fiery pain each time her fingers found a new knot in the muscles there. "Do you remember when this trouble began?"

"The tightness?" he asked.

"And the pain."

He ran his mind over the previous months and came to a memory. "I would say it was last November."

"What were you doing?" she asked calmly.

"I was visiting my son in California."

"Yes? What else do you remember about the moment?"

"I guess I had returned to his apartment before anyone else. Nick and his fiancée and Christine were in the city shopping. I hate shopping, so I asked to be excused—but forgot to ask for a key to the building. So I was locked out. It was a damp, chilly day, even for the Bay area. I began walking, just to kill time. I circled the block once, but when I came back they still hadn't returned. They were late."

"You must have felt angry," she said in a way that seemed a question.

"You could say that." He wasn't sure he liked his massage accompanied by such questions.

"And discounted."

He knew she was right but said nothing.

"So what did you do next?"

"I took another walk. Two blocks this time. By now my leg was throbbing with pain. Each step it seemed to grow worse. I had to stop on a canal bridge and stare at the water and the boats for the pounding to let up. But when I began moving again, the throbbing returned."

He hoped he had rehashed enough old news for her to let him ask a few questions too, but before he could put his thoughts into words, she said, "Don't stop there. What happened?"

"I reached Nick's building and was relieved to see they were back because my calf still hurt."

"Did you tell anyone how you felt?"

"I don't think so. As soon as I sat down, the ache vanished. It always does." He checked his store of memories to confirm that this was true. "But listen, Gloria, I need to know about last—"

"Just one second, sir—" She was already working on his back and shoulder area, though he had failed to notice the part where she did his upper leg and glutes. "Are you sure this was the first time you felt that pain? Absolutely sure?"

"I couldn't say 'absolutely.' I guess you could say I felt it the day I had my heart attack, if that counts."

"That, I imagine, would count," she said without judgment in her voice.

He wasn't about to tell her that he had also felt discounted that day. By Christine this time. They were circling their block at home, and she had walked ahead to talk with a stranger, a Realtor surveying the neighborhood, and he couldn't, didn't want to, keep up. His breath grew difficult, his legs hurt, his arms became weak, his torso was heavy with sweat, and by the time they reached the house, the elephant was standing on his chest. Nor was he going to mention that was but the worst of many times he'd felt discounted, abandoned, his shrink called it, by women he loved, going all the way back to the morning when he was three and fell out of the apple tree—and the maid, not his absent mother, was the only one there to pick him up and paint him red, despite his wails for mom, with Mercurochrome. No wonder he still had a deep place in his heart for the dark-hued women who'd raised him. Instead of reciting his history, he said, "So, Gloria, who issued you a license to do psychology?"

"You think so?" she said and gave his nape a gentle pinch that felt like teasing play.

"You're damn good. Took my shrink in the States years to connect it all up." Was he giving this young woman credit for too much? So be it.

"It's an instinct, I guess," she said. "And I practice without a license over here. So don't tell anyone." She tapped him on the other shoulder. "Time to turn over now, Milton."

"It will be—our little—secret," he grunted as he obeyed.

"I like secrets," she said as she rearranged the sheet. There was a sparkle in her smile.

As much as he was tempted to pursue whatever her remark might conceal, he instead returned to the focus of his visit. "You have to tell me what happened last night. Did Anthi and SS hit it off?"

"She didn't tell you?"

"She's still sleeping," he chuckled.

"She must have stayed a lot longer than I did." She had given his calf a perfunctory probe or two and moved industriously to his upper thigh

"Yeah," he said, to both her comment and new focal point.

"I had to roll Cathy back to the camper. I was checking on Una for Gerta during the party. They'd parked their van about fifteen yards away."

"Kind of you." Obviously neither Gloria nor Gerta had seen the papers he'd read about murdered kids, not if Gerta felt comfortable leaving curly-haired little Una alone at night.

"We do stuff for one another," Gloria said with an equanimity, in her tone and face, that he admired.

"The way you introduced Anthi to your friends," he said.

"She's such a likable person, I was glad to. And so lovely. Shanti, Shanti and she—she caught his eye immediately."

"Good," he said, recalled the reason Anthi wanted to meet him, and added, "I guess."

"Oh, yes. He turned on his charm immediately. Began demonstrating the controls for the light show he's put together. Last time I saw the two of them, he was taking her on a guided tour around the place. Aimee, I noticed, looked a little envious. It's a big old barn, you know. Lots of rooms."

"I—I thought the Hostellerie was closed." Now he was concerned.

"Like I may have told you, Shanti has connections. Apparently the group that owns it lets him use it when he wants. I don't know why." She was probing deep into the cavity where his neck joined the skull, sending the warm radiation he desired from his previous visit through his arms and torso. The pleasure of her probes left him silent.

When he could find words again, he managed a hesitant whisper, "Too bad you— couldn't have stayed—longer—stayed at least until they—came back."

She worked on before answering, "It's a good thing I didn't. I think I saw someone rummaging around Gerta's van when I came back."

"With little Una in there alone?"

"In the shadows I couldn't see who it was. And whoever it was slipped away before I could climb down from the main road."

"Good thing you showed up when you did."

Rather than reply, she slipped quietly from the room.

Day Four

Later

By the time Milt had settled with Gloria and made his way back to the hotel, Anthi was up, dressed, and brushing her hair. He told her he would wait for her on his balcony. When she joined him, she was wearing a dark blue pair of long-legged shorts in the style Christine had started wearing, plus a blue and gold halter held up by large bows back of her neck and below the shoulder blades. The humidity had wound her red curls a bit tighter. Her brown eyes looked rested. She appeared to have slept well and was sporting that dimpled smile he liked.

"I hear you had a good evening," he said and stood to pull out one of the heavy metal chairs for her.

The smile vanished. "Oh? Where'd you hear that?" she said without much passion. She took the seat offered.

"I met with Gloria while you were sleeping."

"Gloria was helpful. I adore that little Cathy." Her face lit up as she said this. "And Gloria, you know, is older than you guessed. Almost as old as I am. Thirty-one, she said."

"Well, that makes sense. A few years more explained how she's figured out all the stuff she knows. Her psychological insight, at least. But not much imagination for malevolence." He paused for a moment, then said, "So, what do you make of SS—Shanti, the guru."

Amusement lit her face. "That he's about as much a guru as I am." She laughed.

"Yeah?" He didn't join the laughter.

"I'd say he's more the class clown, though he does throw out some bizarre ideas that make you wonder. A clown," she repeated and grinned before adding, "or a monster."

"A clown and a monster—with ideas that have people coming here from all corners of the planet?"

"He makes wild promises—to cure the planet of everything that ails it. No wonder the gullibles flock to him." She was grinning but seemed puzzled by the thought.

"Does Gloria strike you as especially gullible?"

The question seemed to sober her up as she searched for a possible answer. "No, not so much naive as serious and hopeful. He pulls out all the stops to suck his crowd in."

Now she was talking about issues that concerned him, how SS was able to parade about the village like the Pied Piper with the young in tow and to what end, other than self-gratification, he gathered them around him. "How so?"

"First, there's one other important detail I picked up, Dad. I asked why he was allowed to use the Hostellerie for his party and the band—since officially it's closed."

"I was curious too."

"Turns out he knows the owners. Family ties."

"So?" He didn't see where she was going.

"It's the rest of the Plantards, Dad. And the Order we uncovered back then who were pushing the family's extreme political and religious claims. Don't ask me how he's connected."

"The Order—in their masks and white silk robes and Klan symbols? That can't be!" For Milt this was totally unexpected. "The two murders twenty years ago—Claud, little Charles—must have left it in shambles. Claud's bunch were all entangled with, motivated by, the Order."

She shook her head, eyes filled with distress. "Apparently they are still around. In one form or another."

"Damn bad," he groaned. "So he's not just a clown." Milt had to know.

"Oh, he may be a Plantard, but he's still a clown. A clever

charlatan, at any rate. There has to be a third family line." Milt had divided the family, he recalled, into the dark line and the line of light, Charles's. "There's a charlatan line too, it turns out."

"I don't know what you mean," her father said. For him the Shanti he'd seen the first night back in the village, marching through the square with his animal hat, the vest, and leather trousers, seemed dark enough.

"It takes brains to be a successful charlatan. I'm thinking of the medieval claptrap he threw together for his party. If it was a party."

"Yeah?"

"Definitely." As she began recounting highlights of the event, she settled back in her iron chair and stared far down the river to gather her thoughts, a habit he recognized because she had inherited it, he liked to think, from her father, his way of going wherever he went to find his stories. Except she wasn't making it up this time, only working from memory. Sinking into a storyteller voice of her own, she went immediately to the music Shanti used, and the videos.

When Ted and Gerhardt and Peer weren't playing the grunge that passed for music, Shanti was deejaying trance groups Milt had never heard of, though he had tried to keep up with the changing tastes in music of his daughter and son. Among others, she ticked off Nitrous Oxide, Aria, 3rd Moon—bands that cranked up a throbbing heavy bass line and overlaid it with a thin, whining upper register. Like a desperate idealism, he imagined, warring against base matter. Shanti's music, he quipped, for modern Cathars.

"In fact," she said, "I figured out where he got his fancy-schmanzy Shanti, Shanti name." Pride in this discovery painted her face, especially the eyes, with a pleasure he recalled from his own early years snooping for stories.

They were dancing crazy, she went on, and a trance cut came on by Madonna, one she remembered from six or seven years ago that had nothing but foreign words in it, Sanskrit, she guessed, and the refrain kept running on, 'Om Shanti, Om Shanti, Shanti, Shanti.'

"I thought he got it from 'The Waste Land,'" her father said.

Anthi laughed again. "I doubt he's ever heard of Eliot. No, it's just good old Madonna. And I bet he has those overgrown kids believing she wrote it for him. He wouldn't have been but thirteen or fourteen though when it came out."

Still trying to extract the meaning from her half-serious comic meandering, he said, "So you figure he's only twenty then?"

"At the most." She kept on grinning. "I was beginning to feel like some West Coast Cougar-woman last night. Like I was robbing the cradle, hanging out with a kid not much more than half my age."

"You reckoned you could control that situation?"

"Absolutely. Even when he took me on his grand tour of the building."

She described the amused pity she felt for Shanti as they were wandering down the corridor she recognized from the novel. The hallway ran the length of the building with windows opening over the river, flowing smooth as the finest alto voice, on one side and pale sky-blue doors on the other, doors with white angels in raised relief holding out laurel wreaths to whoever entered. "You remember, dad?"

"Those were the rooms we slept in. Sure I do."

"That was where he put his moves on me. He tried to get me into one of them. Like I was a high school girl on a class trip."

"But you still felt safe?" This was one of those fatherly conversations he'd never had with her when she was a teenager. Maybe he'd trusted her too much then. Still, she had turned out as well as he could wish. And what was happening around them now constituted a different order of danger.

"I laughed and put him off."

"That was all?"

"He didn't take it well, my laughing." She turned inward as

though to think this through. "To tell the truth, I wonder what he'd really be capable of if he got wounded deep in his pride."

"He's carrying serious baggage around?"

"We all do when we're twenty."

"No dangerous twists?"

"It turns out he never knew his father. And his mother lived through some ordeal that left her a nervous wreck who moves from place to place. Which is why he spent his teens in California."

"That could do it to a kid," he said with a smile.

"California-bashing, are we, Dad?"

They bantered about California for a moment. Maybe he wished Nicky lived closer to home, but he kept it to himself. After he'd defended himself against her charge, he said: "You mentioned his videos."

"Oh, yes. That part of his program was impressive. He'd set up several huge screens in the dining hall—not where we had our breakfast, as I recall, but a larger room at the patio end of the building. And he had another surround screen out on the patio. His projectors kept flashing incredibly dramatic videos, the same ones over and over."

She went on to describe details of the light show Shanti staged. Most of the videos must have been slides he'd pulled together from NASA's Hubble Telescope site. She recognized some of them because Julian, the astrophysicist Milt knew she'd dated in Arizona, had made her view them. It was her duty as an informed human, Julian said, and he'd stood over her shoulder so she couldn't take her eyes off his computer screen. Shanti had re-recorded the shots in some program that allowed the projector to zoom the images in and out, in and out to the wild trance rhythms, so it seemed that she and the others who were dancing were forcibly sucked into the vortices of exploding stars, and then hurled out of them through space. "There are thousands of these mind-blowing—vast!—maws out there that spew out great cohering, or dying, blue, red, white clouds of gas and energy. He surrounded us with them," she rambled on as though straining for words to explain a realm of sensations ineffably odd.

She eventually spotted a couple of the slides she'd seen on Julian's computer. Their familiarity gave her a stable point in the irrational flood of images. One of these captured the violent supernova death of Cassiopeia A. The way Shanti showed it, crossed with scenes from Hollywood horror movies, he was propelling the whole party into the colossal jaws of some cosmic beast from the *Alien* series, with its purple fangs, green snout, and cold, reptilian, starry eyes. It terrified her when a second monster's head rushed toward her from the throat of the mother monster. But when the images and music discharged the partiers again, they continued dancing about the patio. "They howled out laughter—like the 'saved' at some jam-packed, hysterical revivalist meeting," she said.

"What a cynical production—" Milt growled as he rose nervously from his seat and went to the flower box suspended from the iron balcony and began tearing dead heads from petunia-like blossoms.

"But the most horrific, I tell you, Dad, was his Pismis 24 shot. He tossed us over and over into that superstar system, into a massive ball of fiery yellow, orange, red gases. Stars being born." When the zoom took them into it, the effect, she said, bewilderment still on her face, was like entering a vast womb-like cave with a single blue star set in the center. And when they zoomed out she could see an immense phallus above the roundness, a veritable flame-cloaked-and-hooded Lucifer presiding from his pinnacle over his burning galaxy. "There was even this like—like minor fallen angel, a dark Beelzebub, I guess, who was trying to crawl up the slope behind Lucifer and join his fiery master."

"Damn!" Milt seethed.

"Damnation's right, Dad. Might just as well have been a frieze of hell in some medieval church."

"Maybe old blind Milton did have the cosmic eyeball after all—and saw regions that only the Hubble can reveal at last."

"Wouldn't go that far, Pops," she said. "What you doing to those flowers?"

"Nothing." He looked down to find that mindlessly he was attacking the living blooms now. He stopped. "Why not?"

"Because I asked Shanti why he assembled a slide program with such horrors." With one hand she brushed dead petals from the table where Milt had tossed the ones he hadn't hurled into the river below. Most fell through the metal grating that formed the floor of the balcony to join the dead ones in the river.

"Good thinking, young woman." He came back to the table and took his seat. "What'd he say?"

"Pretty much what the medieval priests and Milton could have said, had they been frank. That he needed to impress his friends and followers with his techno-hocus-pocus to show just how alien and violent the world, the whole universe, even its farthest reaches, turns out to be. They're not really kids—except when befuddled by special effects like their video games. It's the extreme videos, I'm talking about."

"But why pull a vicious stunt like that?" Milt asked, pretty certain he knew the answer.

"So when he calls for extreme measures they will keep following where he leads—and be prepared for some great sacrifice. Like you said, he's an up-to-the-minute Gnostic trying to rocket out of a world he's convinced himself is absolutely corrupt."

"But the religious Gnostic, like the Cathars—not the intellectual Greek variety."

"What religion doesn't do the same?" she said.

"Paris— its skepticism—has really gotten to you, hasn't it, young lady? The religious fanatics do."

"Don't blame it on Paris, Dad."

"I can remember when you were a smiling pagan, dear." He wanted to reach out and hug her. And would have, had she still been fifteen.

"The world has changed," she said. She gave him a grin.

"It has," he said. "But—" He left his final word hanging in the air, unsure what to add that might salvage some of her old broad religious impulse.

"One other thing will interest you." Suddenly she was serious again, and her eyes showed her hesitating to go on.

"What's that?" he said to encourage her.

"When I asked him about the hotel—"

"Why he was allowed to use it for the band and the party?"

"He just gave me a mocking smile and said, 'That's for me to know, Miss Walters, and you to find out.'"

"So he's figured out you are *that* Walters, hasn't he?" This news was worse than he had expected.

"Probably so." Confused, she dropped her head.

"Oh, sh—merde—" The last thing he needed was any of the Plantards to know Anthi and he were back in Deepest France. "He's going to be on his guard. Whatever he's up to."

They were late getting started in the afternoon, but the three of them calmly toured the area north and east of Rennes-les-Bains to the medieval village of Arques and its Cathar museum. Before they left the hotel, Milt had asked Anthi if she wanted to revisit Rennes-le-Chateau, which lay to the west.

"I'm not sure," she said. "I had a long night. And it must be a mess now."

"What you mean?" Christine asked.

"Mobbed—is more like it," Anthi said. "Since the *Da Vinci Code* hysteria."

"Oh," Christine said. "I hadn't thought of that."

"Since the movie is out, French papers have picked up on its being the spot where the book's basic assumptions sprung up," Anthi explained.

"We'll have to catch it later," her father said. "One way or another."

So on their way out of town, after passing the Armchair of the Devil, the stone mound with a seat cut into it—another altar, Milt thought—they bore right toward Arques. There they climbed the elegant tower of the thirteenth-century *donjon*, with its spy windows and arrow slits, its fireplaces on the middle levels, and raucous birds flapping in the ceiling on the top floor. After a late lunch in Arques they continued east to the crumbling grey chateau at Auriac, whose gold mines from the eighth century once made rich the monks in Albieres to the south and the lords of the Rennes region.

By the time they returned to les-Bains, their bodies were demanding a late afternoon nap or a French roast, and they headed straight from the car to the square and the coffee. As they waited for a fresh brew, though it remained much too early for dinner Milt noticed three new faces at one of the bar's long tables: a man, a woman, and a child about four. They had the golden skin and fine features of people he'd met from North Africa. The woman, who was about thirty-five, wore her dark hair under a silky brown scarf. The boy seemed a reversed-color version of little Una the first night, with his raven curls and clean white kaftan decorated with elaborate embroidery much like pastel robes Milt had bought Nicky and Anthi in Cairo souks. The woman no doubt had waves or curls like the boy's—since the man's dark hair lay flat on his skull, and his wide mustache grew equally straight. Milt supposed this handsome trio might be the latest family to join Shanti, Shanti's elaborate campaign to make the flawed world better.

He was hoping the three were not as he spotted Gloria, dressed still in the forest green blouse, steering her stroller furiously their way from the direction of the campground. She appeared enormously agitated, a state he found odd in a young woman whose usual composure he so much respected.

As soon as she entered the far side of the square she called out to them, "Anthi, Christine, Milt— Have any of you seen Gerta or Peer? I can't find them!"

"Afraid not," Milt said, speaking for the three of them.

"I've looked everywhere I can think of," Gloria said as she collapsed breathlessly in the chair Milt pulled up beside Anthi. "Their van is gone."

"They're probably driving around," Anthi said, "seeing the sights."

Gloria obviously took little comfort from Anthi's words. "It's very strange," she replied. "I spoke to Gerta after my morning session."

"Yes?" Milt said. He appreciated her confidentiality in not mentioning his own hour with her in the morning. If Anthi and Christine decided they also wanted massages, he knew the three of them would never find time to do the things they needed to do.

"I went over to their van. I was thinking Gerta and I could talk a bit while the children entertained one another. Una adores Cathy. But Gerta acted all discombobulated. She said Una was still sleeping. That seemed unusual—at noon. She promised she'd see me this afternoon."

"Perhaps Una was worn out from the party last night," Milt said.

"No," Gloria answered. "I was keeping an eye out for Una last night. She didn't even make it to dinner."

"That's right, Milt," Christine said.

"I'm really worried now about whoever it was last night that I scared away from their van."

"Oh, yes," Milt said, not wanting to let on that he had already heard about the intrusion.

"If anything happens to their beautiful little girl, I will feel horrible," Gloria groaned and visibly sank into more self-recrimination. "The van is gone," she muttered again.

"Don't beat up on yourself," Christine, always the good therapist, cautioned. "I am sure they'll turn up soon. And be okay."

Gloria appeared to accept the comfort of the older woman, even with an added grain of salt.

Milt and Anthi, however, looked at one another with the unsteadiness of two swimmers over whom a seven-foot wave of the salty Atlantic had just crashed.

Day Five

Early Morning

Before eight, Milt made his way alone into the hotel dining room, where the breakfast staff had prepared a handful of tables at the end overlooking the river. He had decided he needed to check out the petit dejeuner, but Anthi again was not awake when he knocked, and Christine said she preferred to breakfast on the fruit, cereal, and milk left from the day before, and then take her morning walk. All the tables in the hall had thick white cloths and turned down crystal glasses for water, but by the windows, on the sunrise end, the tables also stood ready with substantial creamy white plates and equally weighty silverware that he took for stainless steel until he raised his knife and recognized it was real.

Since extremely polite guests already occupied three of the other tables, he broke his hard-crusted *baton* and sipped the splendid dark roast coffee as quietly as possible. A youthful member of the small female staff speedily refreshed his cup and added a juicy brioche plus a selection of, she said, locally produced honey, jellies, and butter. Although it resembled the fare he had sampled at other French hotels, the tastes seemed richer and more satisfying. Food, however, was not what he came for, and now, on his third cup, he feared his true purpose would remain frustrated.

For much of the night Milt had lain awake, the sheet up to his shoulders, struggling to disentangle the uncertainties plaguing him. How ominous was it that Gloria, the evening before, could not find the Norwegians—Gerta, Una, and Peer? In the early morning he'd remembered Gerhardt's remark the day before that Gerta and Peer were firmly "down with" the program Shanti, Shanti was devising to cure the contemporary age of its ills. By now, he hoped as he raised his cup again, Gloria had, or soon would, find her three friends and their van safely back under a giant shade oak in the camping grounds.

The anxiety centered on SS's use of the Hostellerie had also disturbed his sleep. Exactly what degree of kinship to the Plantards and their secretive Order qualified the odd young man for unrestricted use of the sealed building? The longer he'd floundered in bed, the more this mystery disturbed him. Now, with his morning wits finally about him, Milt thought he knew one person who might be able to answer the question. And this was the reason he was taking his breakfast alone. As the minutes went by, he felt a growing awareness that his purpose would be thwarted.

Then a soft voice from behind him dispelled his anxiety. "Monsieur Walters, how good to see you at one of our tables."

He began to rise to welcome the manager of the hotel, but she commanded, "Don't stand, please. You must enjoy your coffee."

He paused midair to honor her suggestion. "Only if you will sit and join me, Madame—Madame—" He didn't know where to go from there in addressing her. Aside from a soft green blouse replacing the pearl-grey one she'd had on the first day, she looked much the same, although the smile seemed a few degrees warmer.

"Madame Strauss," she said helpfully.

"Madame Strauss," he had probably been correct, he told himself, about her Alsatian origins, "I have something I'd like to ask you."

"Me?" She seemed truly surprised. "I hope I can help." She took the seat across from him and motioned the young server for coffee.

As she did so, a blue light flashed insistently above the white curtains that covered the lower half of the salon's front windows. It paused for an instant and then sped along northward. He assumed there'd been an accident on one of curves that made up the torturous road through the Gorges de Galamus, and someone was on the way to a hospital. At least they didn't turn on a siren, he told himself.

"It has to do with some of your competition—the Hostellerie. I hope you don't mind." He was trying to introduce the topic as gently as possible.

"I don't know. What is it?" Apparently his lead-in had pricked her curiosity.

"My daughter, Anthi, attended a dance party over there two nights ago."

"Yes, I heard the racket—the music, I mean," she said, grinning through the pearl-rimmed glasses as though bad taste in the competition, even out-of-business competitors, pleased her.

"What puzzles me is that the young man who threw the party seemed to have the run of the place. He showed Anthi all around— even the guest rooms."

"I bet he did," she said suppressing an obvious smirk that Milt felt safer ignoring.

"Didn't you say a corporation of some sort had taken it over?"

"Yes," she grew serious, "but the family controls the group. You must be talking about Jean, or whatever he's calling himself now."

Something clicked for Milt when she said Jean, but he couldn't quite recall the reason. "Shanti, Shanti, I think."

"Shanti, Shanti then," she said, obviously bored by the exoticism of the name.

"When he lived in California, he went by 'Claude.'" Milt wanted to be helpful.

"Claud?" A quizzical smile crossed her face. "Now *that's* interesting. Another Claud Plantard."

"Is that the real name?" He was again thinking of the man originally accused of murdering little Charles, the Plantard cousin for whose own death responsibility continued to nag at Milt despite the efforts of several therapists and his daughter—there when it happened—to free him of self-blame. He knew he had been abysmally wrong to stir Charles's father up by pointing out to him, in their one true conversation, that his cousin Claud apparently took the family's legend of their bloodline deadly serious. The French story claimed that their heritage went back twenty centuries to Mary Magdalena. If that was true, it was a divine bloodline—and one with considerable importance in the political history of what was now France. Milt's revelation could only have contributed to the father's animus against Claud.

"I don't think so. I think his real name is Jean—Jean-Baptist Plantard, Charles's little brother. And if you were right in the novel, he could have had either of two fathers."

"You mean the baby in Christine's stomach when Claud was killed?" It was helpful to have her reminding him of some details in his novel that had slipped his mind.

"Your story ended before he was born, but you claimed she wasn't sure which of the cousins, whether Claud or her husband Philip, was the father. She named him Jean-Baptist and carried him everywhere she went. Their pictures filled the French papers."

"I saw a few of the photos," Milt said. "It struck me that she was behaving as though he was the new Charles."

"Do you suppose his mother has filled his mind with the family myths?"

"I hope not—" he said and paused to ponder the implications of all this before adding, "At some point the kid obviously decided Claud was his father. When he took the name."

"Then, in the language you used, he would be carrying the dark bloodline, in contrast to Charles's line of light?" Her mind seemed to be linked to his now.

"Maybe not," he said, hoping he was right. "From what I hear, he's promising to lead his followers to world peace. At least that's his plan, and it sounds like the line of light to me—a direct echo of Magdalena's holy husband."

"Let's hope." It was her turn to pause and ponder. "But Christine may have simply told him what she believed, and he obviously made the decision—about the name." As she spoke, Madame Strauss turned her attention from Milt and her coffee to stare out the large dining room windows over the river as though she could see the Hostellerie somewhere across the river. "If he has read your story, you know what that could mean."

"That he thinks I played a part, maybe a major one, in his father's murder." The sudden connection ran through his chest and arms like the jolt he once felt when he'd attempted to plug Anthi's lamp into the wall of their first Greek apartment, the limb-numbing shock of a 220 socket. "I—I exaggerated all that for the effect," he said. "He has to know it was a fiction." Milt's protest sounded lame—even to him.

"I'm not sure." She turned back to stare at him with her slightly ironic twist of the lips and a flash of bemusement in her eyes. Then the glint vanished. "What I'm suggesting is that the boy at some point must have identified with the *Claud* Plantard line. In your novel it is Christine who divides the family into the two lines, remember. Charles and Philip were the true Plantards, the line of light, running back through Merovingian and Visigoth kings, to Magdalena's daughter Sarah, then to Jesus and the holy blood. Your Christine claims Claud's family were the dark Plantards—the balance in every generation to the light. Isn't that right?"

As much as he preferred not to remember, Milt had to acknowledge the things he had written, knew many were his inventions (though he hadn't known about dark Sarah then). But his mind remained stuck somewhere else. His hands grasped the tablecloth and the edge of the table the way a landlubber would seize the gunwales in a rough sea. "You don't think he's planning to come after me—" he coughed out the words, "or Anthi?"

"That show-off? With those ridiculous sideburns—and the costumes he wears. Whatever for? He's just a comedian—with a plan for world peace. The town jester. Most of the time he's so high on pot he can't think straight." She was stirring her coffee again furiously and grinning at him with an expression he could not decode.

"Because when you think about it," Milt began, half realizing that he was mixing inventions from his book with rhythms from southern writers preceding him, "about his twisted life I mean, he could be capable of anything. Conceived when his mother was, the world thought, grieving the ugly murder of her only child Charles, fathered by we don't know whom, either by Philip, burning with anger and the desire for revenge, or by Claud, newly acquitted of murdering the unborn boy's older brother, then paraded here and there with that grandiose prophetic name by his mother, reeling from her own anger and guilt for helping kill the much worshiped Charles, a woman increasingly under suspicion but still maintaining her 'grieving mother of France' facade. What would all that do to a kid? And I haven't even begun to imagine what went on afterwards."

"Not so loud, Monsieur Walters. I have guests, and a hotel to run." She reached out to calm his agitated hands. "We can guess, can't we? Christine obviously grew weary of all her notoriety here and, fearful of possible charges, dragged him off to your country. You say he was in Los Angeles recently?"

"Santa Barbara, I hear." He looked up to see that more guests were filling the breakfast area. He lowered his voice. "Imagine what she had to do to get out of France one step ahead of an indictment should the police connect the dots the way Anthi and I did, and that, before Santa Barbara, she probably spent a few years in Los Angeles, where her little mother's boy from Deepest France grew up having to compete with Mexican gangbangers and angry blacks. I don't know whether he got into college in Santa Barbara, but he was a visionary, a natural 'miracle boy,' who began gathering up followers there to save the world from itself." This memory from his first talk with Gloria caused Milt to shift mental gears. "Which doesn't make real sense, when you think of it, Madame Strauss."

"What do you mean?" She seemed pleased that he finally remembered who was sitting across from him.

"His goals seem spiritual—idealistic, noble even—" He was still fighting to fend off the more ominous view of the boy that kept calling to both of them.

"If we can take them seriously. What's so terrible about that?"

"Because, as you say, he chose his name from the dark line." They both paused, seeming to puzzle their way through this enigma that they kept circling.

"Why 'Claud'?" Milt asked. "'Shanti, Shanti' makes lots more sense to me."

"Perhaps he's never read your book, Monsieur Walters."

Milt found the possibility oddly comforting.

"Or he doesn't agree with your take on his ancestors," she added with a sardonic grin.

Now, with her final words, all his new comfort vanished like seagulls from the roar of a crashing wave in which he did not wish to drown.

His ears were still ringing as he wandered, stunned, out of the dining hall and up the stairs. His intent was to wake Anthi and warn her of what he had just learned. In his bewilderment, he pounded her door with more passion than necessary. And to no avail. *Where could she have gone this early, without telling me?*

Her destination would likely be someplace that provided coffee and breakfast. This meant the tea salon. That was where he had to head—and he must find her before she ran into SS—or Gerhardt or another of Shanti's followers. *Maybe I'll meet up with Christine. No. I'd better leave a message in the room; let her know where I'm going.*

Once outside, the air felt thick with approaching rain, the pollen slowed by the humidity but still not washed away. This made his panicked, high-chest breathing more difficult. When he tried to force his breaths into his lower abdomen, it felt he was pumping congestion down his bronchial pipes, and he began coughing to bring up what clogged the air passages. A few people heading to work turned to stare at him. *They must think I'm another lung victim here for the cure.*

For the first time since he returned to the village, he had to dodge one of the absurdly small police cars speeding north along the main street, its signal lights silently flashing. He stepped up on the curb and let it by. "Guess the town got fed up with blaring sirens twenty years ago," he muttered. Cops keep out!

At the square he stopped to clear his chest once more and found himself staring at morning papers stacked in front of the pizza restaurant.

There it was again, the headline shouting, "Un Autre Enfant!" loud as the roar he had heard in the dining room.

Without pausing to pay, he grabbed up the early Rennes paper and sped through the French he could translate without thinking:

Not long after midnight today, a curly-headed blonde girl not yet three years old became the latest infant found viciously murdered in the Rennes region of Deepest France. Like previous victims, she had been bound tightly by plastic ropes, and her body bore multiple stab wounds.

Unlike others, the body was not discovered in or near a remote natural body of water. It was found carefully placed in the seat of the artificial rock formation just below Rennes-les-Bains that local inhabitants call "the Armchair of the Devil." Her small body clearly visible to anyone who passed on the main road into the village, the angelic child was one of the few known victims in the group who were female.

Local residents, who admit they are reminded of the infamous "little Charles" case two decades ago, report they knew the tiny girl as Una and her parents, alleged to be from Norway, only as Gerta and Peer, all names with a familiar literary ring. The local authorities report that her parents have not been seen since the day before the body turned up. The investigation continues.

Not precious little Una! Milt howled inwardly. Something rose from his throat to his eyes, where he could feel sudden tears forming. *How could anyone do that to her?*

Gloria was right. I should have paid attention to her panic. She was trying to do the right thing before this monstrosity occurred. And in the seat this time. Like an altar—exactly. Even the paper made it sound like a ritual. They couldn't just come out and say it was. They don't want to frighten people.

Gloria must be scared to death. Little Cathy must be high on the list. Next even. I have to find them.

He threw the paper back on the stack and plunged into the street again, heading for the tea salon. *I need to find Anthi first. We'll figure out where Gloria might be hiding with Cathy.*

As soon as the salon came into view, however, he spotted Gloria sitting at the outdoor table where he had formerly seen Ted and Gerhardt. She was bouncing little Cathy playfully on her knee and laughing with someone across the table from her whom the wall of the neighboring shop still blocked from his view. *She hasn't read the papers yet. I don't know if I can tell her—or how to tell her.*

When he was close enough to smell the roasted coffee and the toasted sugar of the pastries, he discovered that it was not Ted or Gerhardt or Shanti, Shanti with whom she was sharing her good humor but Anthi. What a relief! Double relief, he told himself as he sensed the muscles around his heart relaxing.

Day Five

The Search Begins

Milt's responsibilities weren't over. He approached the young women with a forced grin, trying to convince himself they could have been sisters joking there in their similar jeans and pullover blouses, Anthi's red, Gloria's green again. He hoped neither of them would face any danger or experience any heartbreak during the coming twenty-four hours.

"Dad!" Anthi had noticed him heading their way. She stood and pulled out the free chair on her side of the table. "I wondered when you were going to show."

"Good morning—" Gloria added, searching, it appeared, for a way to address him and deciding to avoid all versions of his name that she knew.

"Morning, ladies. How are you this humid morning? And the little one too, of course." It was difficult not to add special meaning to the final part of his greeting.

"At least I knew you weren't sneaking off for another massage this time," Anthi joked.

"Don't laugh until you've tried one, girl," he replied, careful to match her tone. "Gloria's the best." He remained behind the chair his daughter offered.

"Yes, woman. When you going to work me in?" Anthi said, passing the tease on to Gloria.

"Anytime, my friend," Gloria said, obviously pleased by her growing clientele.

He decided to halt the useless banter. "Anthi, there's a bit of business we need to discuss—if Gloria will excuse both of us a moment." He turned and led the way inside the salon's glass front.

Anthi gave her friend an apologetic look. "Don't let that little darling go anywhere," she commanded Gloria and bent to tap Cathy's chin with her index finger. "We'll be back."

"What's up, Dad?" Anthi asked, with anxious eyes, as soon as glass sealed their voices from Gloria.

"It's happened again, Anthi. At the Devil's Armchair, just out of town."

"Jeezus!" The shock showed in her face.

"Worse still, the child belonged to Gloria's friends. You met Gerta and Peer, didn't you?"

"Briefly."

"They camped side by side with Gloria and Cathy. Their little Una looked just as cute as Cathy. Cuter, if possible."

"How's Gloria possibly going to take this?" Anthi instantly engaged her problem-solving gear. "Somebody has to tell her."

"Cathy, I'm afraid, could be the next target," he said.

The thought brought the rictus of shock to Anthi's soft face.

They both turned to stare at the young mother as she bent to spoon her pet, now back in the stroller, some of the cherry yogurt left in her carton.

"I think I should do it, Dad," Anthi said, face stretched tight by apprehension for her friend.

"I won't argue with you," he said as she turned back to Gloria. "Find out where Ted is," he added but as an afterthought realized he wasn't sure which side Cathy's father was on.

Encircled by the confusing aromas of the coffee, produce, and pastries, he peered through the glass as Anthi explained why he had called her aside. Even though he could not hear what either was saying, he saw Gloria's lovely fluid face pass within seconds from interest to boundless horror and tears. The personal fear, it was clear, had not yet worked its way through what she was feeling about all Una and Gerta had suffered—Una's pain from the blade's biting edge, and Gerta's infinite loss. Milt could imagine none worse were it Anthi or his Nick. He wanted to be with Gloria before the terror hit her.

Before he could reach her, Anthi had moved to her side and wrapped an arm across her shoulders to offer comfort as Gloria clasped Cathy firmly against her chest. He applied his support over her right shoulder, letting the gentle pressure of his fingers sink into the flesh of her arm that he so admired during their first session together, half aware that he was answering the need he'd felt since then to reciprocate her healing touch. What he most sought at the moment, however, was to arouse her absolutely essential alarm as gently as possible.

"Gloria, do you know where Ted might be right now?" He recalled Ted's reluctance, in his overheard talk with Gerhardt, to get onboard with Shanti's scheme, a decision that every moment appeared more crucial, and pernicious, should he commit himself to the project. The fates of Cathy and Gloria could reside with Ted and his divided loyalties. As far as little Cathy is concerned, Ted's the swing man, Milt thought, and the danger is that, like Peer, he might go the wrong way. Difficult as it is to imagine, these guys are ready to buy Shanti's peace promise even if they have to put it above the lives of their own kids. It was worse than sending one's son off to fight in another worthless war.

To Milt, Shanti's promise was absolutely golden while his way of going about it seemed patently absurd. When he searched his own memories for the reasons anyone might arrive at the idea Shanti and his faithful were pursuing, he finally recalled how his own generation had felt about bringing new kids into the world to live under the Bomb. The image of Ginsberg's poem shaped like the monstrous Bomb popped into his mind. Now other groups of very devout kids were strapping girdles of C-4 on and blowing themselves into worms of raw hamburger. Was it for six dozen virgins? Or for a better world, one without stockpiled nuclear missiles? One man's absurdity could be another man's panacea. And too damn often.

Before he could turn his fantasies utterly loose, however, Gloria, who seemed to have had trouble focusing on his question, probably because her deepest fear was about to burst on her like a blazing desert sunrise, said, "He told me he would be with the band going over new material."

"When did he say this?" Milt asked.

"Just before midnight last night," she said, her eyes frozen open as though waiting for him to tell her what new horror her response might suggest.

"Okay, okay," he muttered, attempting to calm himself. "Do you know where?"

Her eyes want blank, then lit again. "Usually— There's a house up the mountainside. Above the store that sells books about this region."

"You're talking about the bookshop across from our hotel?" Milt asked. The part of what she said about the house remained unclear to him.

"Come on." She rose as she spoke. "I'll show you." She plopped her daughter back in the stroller. "But I'll need some help with Cathy."

"Sure," he said, as the four of them exploded into the street and rushed toward the bookstore. "We'll do our best."

Aside from a scattering of older folks browsing the handmade jewelry and homemade preserves displayed on makeshift counters under the giant trees of the square, the village appeared largely empty. Although the sun was finally penetrating the morning fog, everyone under forty, aside from Gloria and Anthi, seemed to be sleeping in. But just as they passed the booths, the first of the media trucks pulled up to the curb and parked where the poor Norwegians' van had stood their first night. France 3, he read. The first snowball. Now the avalanche begins.

Just this side of the bookshop, they spotted Christine, narrow face beaded with perspiration, coming from the small street that led to the bridge. Apparently she had taken her walk on the path running along the other bank of the river.

"What's your hurry?" she asked as she fell in with them.

"Come with us," Anthi answered. "We have to find Ted."

"Gloria's husband?" Christine asked.

"Cathy's dad," Gloria corrected as she stopped the stroller by the dark well-worn steps squeezed between the bookstore and the neighboring shop. "I have to leave this thing here." With a deft toe, she applied the brakes to the stroller.

"If you like, I'll carry Cathy first," Milt volunteered just as Anthi reached for the child. He knew the steps by themselves would eventually take a toll on his limited oxygen supply—it was best to make his contribution early. "Okay?"

"Whatever works, Dad," she said and placed Cathy in his arms.

For a bundle so small, the infant felt unexpectedly solid and heavy. "Lord, what does this little one weigh?" he groaned.

"Almost thirty pounds," Gloria said proudly. "All mother's milk."

"Must be," he said. "Strong as Super Girl, I bet."

"I hope," Gloria laughed.

"Like her mother," Christine volunteered with an ambiguous note in her voice.

"Let's go," Anthi said and led the way up the time-stained stone walk, with Christine, Gloria, and Milt trailing.

The steps, to his relief, proved both winding and shallow enough to reduce the energy he had to exert, and they climbed little more than a dozen yards before his daughter halted them and turned to reach for the squirming packet he carried.

"Thanks, Anthi," he said as he shook out his arms and legs.

"Where are we going?" Christine asked.

"Gloria will have to tell us," Anthi said as she opened the cotton blanket just enough to see the baby's eyes and scrunched-up mouth. Cathy seemed ready to cry until she saw Anthi peering in on her and broke into a grinning coo.

"We are about halfway there," their guide replied.

They trudged up another twenty yards in the shadows of joined houses several stories tall, from which the aromas of breakfast coffee and midday frying floated to mingle in the stairway with acrid odors from invisible WCs. They emerged in a small but sunlit opening where three walkways met and where they could draw in air that seemed fresh except for the odd scent that hung over them. In a second the whiff clicked in Milt's memory. Pot, he told himself. But the bouquet seemed so thick in his lungs he had to correct himself: Hashish!

"That's it," Gloria said, "that's where the smell's coming from." She was pointing toward a house in the still dark sector of the small square, the most peculiar structure he'd ever seen in the village. It appeared to have neither doors nor windows, only shutters swung wide from huge gaping openings that may once have been plate glass displays and an entry for a shop of some sort whose glass long ago had crashed under the stones of vandals or angry neighbors. Or Vichy stones, he thought.

"That's where they practice," Gloria said.

"It looks empty," Anthi said.

"Jeez, they'll never air this place out," Christine grumbled. "Dumb addicts."

"Where's Ted?" Anthi asked.

"Doesn't look like he's here," Milt said, fearing the worst, that he was with Shanti and the gang. Perhaps with them all night—and even for the sacrifice of Una.

"He has to be," Gloria protested. "There's an upstairs."

"We have to look," Anthi added.

"Now," Milt said and followed the two young women through the crumbling doorway into the dark mildew and suffocating hash of the building.

"Just don't inhale!" Christine quipped behind him.

She didn't know the purpose of their frantic search yet, so he would have to forgive her stab at humor. He cautioned: "No jokes, please."

"Is Ted lost—or just stoned?" she asked.

"Worse," Anthi said as they followed Gloria through the room weakly lit by outside light and strewn with beer and wine bottles, closed instrument cases, overturned chairs, odd lengths of plastic cord, cigarette butts, and several small telltale pipes scattered across a beat-up wooden table in the shadows that Milt nearly slammed into just before stumbling on the stairs to the next floor.

"Careful," Gloria warned as she began her ascent. "There's no light up here, and every step could be loose or broken."

Obeying her, Milt went second, leaning against the slimy wall and testing each plank with his toe before putting his full weight on it.

"Ted! Are you up there?" Gloria shouted into the blackness above them.

No answer came from above.

"Careful," Milt whispered and placed a steadying hand where he could reach Gloria, on the hip nearer him.

"Thanks," she said but didn't move away until he nudged her on.

When the two of them were on the landing of the second floor, she called out again. "Ted, we've got Cathy. She's looking for you. All of us are. Are you here?"

"Uhn?" a groggy voice groaned in the room dead ahead. Just enough light from outdoors leaked from one room for them to see that someone had not quite closed its door.

"Is that you, Ted?" Gloria shouted with renewed energy and pushed her way through the door.

"Watch it!" Milt called out as he barged after her.

"Who— Who's with you?" the dark heap in the far corner mumbled, obviously struggling for breath.

"It's me, Ted." Without hesitating she crossed to his side and propped him against her as she dropped to her haunches and his arm rose to rest on her knee.

"It's just Anthi with me. And her father. You met her the other night."

"Anthi? SS's—friend?" He seemed to cower back into his corner, desperately pulling Gloria after him.

"It's okay, Ted. It's okay. They're here to help."

"No one can help, sweet. No one. It's all—all insane." He seemed unable to squirm as far as he wanted into the grimy strips of molding that met in his corner. "Where's *Cathy*?" he called with the swollen power of panic.

"I've got her right here," Anthi offered and stepped from behind her father to hold the child out to Ted.

"She's fine, Ted," Gloria said. She took Cathy from Anthi but did not give her to the drained father. Instead she passed the girl quickly to Christine.

"Thank God!" Ted groaned as Gloria and Milt helped him to his unsteady feet, one under each arm. "I can't—tell you," he sputtered, "what—what I was afraid—" He seemed to lose his train of thought, almost consciousness itself.

"We'll get you outside," Milt said. "Fresh air'll do you good."

"And coffee," Gloria said as the two of them steered their burden on stumbling feet through the door to the unseen stairs.

Ten minutes later the six of them were sitting in wooden chairs around a metal table that had appeared on the sunlit side of the small square since they entered the house, Shanti's den as Milt now thought of it. Apparently, the square's closed doors had concealed a small neighborhood green grocer and café, and the owner, her doors now open, had brewed a pot of strong coffee for them. Its aromas were driving out the acrid odors of their climb up to the square and covering over the sweet smell from the house across from them. The tall oaks and dark walls around the square seemed to shield them from too much glare from the sun. Milt considered them fortunate to find the shop since he thought it unlikely they would have made it back to the main street with Ted in his stoned condition. While she held Cathy to nurse in her left arm, Gloria was using her right to force down Ted the dark drink unadulterated with sugar or milk.

"Here—take this," she whispered, although he tried clumsily to brush away the cup and her hand.

"Nah, I—I'm—jus fine," he mumbled.

She persisted, and under her guidance, although still confused, he seemed to be making his way slowly back to a degree of coherence.

"I have—to tell you," he said, groping for words, "wha happen."

"Just wait until you're all here, Ted," Gloria said. "We're safe now—the three of us."

"No, no," he mumbled. "Bad—bad shit com'n—"

"What did Shanti do?" Anthi broke in. "Where is he now?"

What Ted was able to explain after that, in his stumbling and broken warning, would have made little sense to Milt, did he not already possess a slightly larger understanding of Shanti's personal and spiritual history and of his grandiose project for setting things right in the modern world. Possibly Gloria and Anthi were using the same or a similar template to order the patches of his account, but Milt could not be certain despite the occasional nods of confirmation that passed between him and his daughter.

"A rehears-al, I—I th—thought."

"That's right," Gloria coached. "Then?"

"Peer—Una came," Ted managed to say. "Lacy dress—too."

From what Milt was able to stitch together, Ted came to the midnight "rehearsal" reluctantly, but Peer had showed up with little Una. She was wearing her fancy white dress, a detail that stirred Milt deeply as he remembered the petite doll dancing their first night on the square. Gloria was clearly absorbed in each fragment she could pull from Ted about his own wild night.

"Peer—cool—too cool."

To Ted, Peer had seemed much too eager to make his personal sacrifice for the lofty spiritual goal Shanti had put before him when they first met. As Ted mumbled on, Christine appeared more and more bewildered. Milt wanted to clarify things for her, but he was afraid to interrupt the already barely coherent Ted.

It was frustrating for Milt to keep from speaking and painful to watch Gloria's anxiety as she tried to remain patient yet keep Ted talking. Every fragment of his recollection required a prompt from her: the simplest question, the repetition of his most recent few words, another question, a firm shake of his shoulder or knee.

"Did the band rehearse?" Gloria probed as though hoping for a positive answer.

"No—a litt—maybe."

"So what happened then?" Gloria must have had a great deal of practice prodding information out of her stoned and sullen mate, trying to meld the bits into a coherent story—certainly since he had made her pregnant. Milt didn't understand women like Gloria, who took on obvious losers thinking they could save these guys from themselves, but he had seen many like her in his high school years. Was it some mother hen or caregiver impulse that compelled them to do it? Well, caregiver was a part he understood, since it was the role he was having to play with Christine. But not the mother hen bit. That was beyond him. Gloria deserved better, he told himself.

"Gerhardt—with me," Ted finally began again. "He want— me—to—"

"To what?" Milt demanded. It was all he could do to keep from shaking Ted too and jumping in to slap him awake. He felt his own anger and impatience building to some such action he knew he would regret.

"To—com—commit—like Peer—"

For Milt, Peer's astonishing eagerness had only one credible explanation. It had to have been the way the young Norwegian overcompensated in order to suppress his misgivings about what he was ready to do.

"I—I—like Gerta—" Ted stumbled on, trying now to be helpful. "She wanted—"

Somehow Milt managed to stitch together enough patches of Ted's night to explain Gerta's ultimate decision. As Peer told Shanti and the band, she submitted to the belief that another dramatic act was essential. But she had also begged Peer for enough hash to block her maternal feelings and chill her out. She wanted to stay behind in the van, and she felt the herb might keep her from screaming, pounding the camper's walls, or possibly killing herself.

At this point Ted seemed to fall asleep in his chair, and Anthi leaned in to prod him back to consciousness and speech. When he finally startled himself awake, Gloria resumed her interrogation techniques, while Christine glared at Milt with mounting frustration and obvious irritation. He still felt helpless to explain the situation to his wife without distracting their single source from his already frayed and knotted thread of thought.

"Gerhardt—pushing me—pushing—"

The determination of Shanti's group had continued to terrify Ted, but Gerhardt kept finding beer and hash to ease Ted's resistance.

Gerhardt worked with growing desperation to persuade his fellow rocker, his always laid-back buddy, that he must bring Gloria around and that Cathy ought to be the next necessary offering. "Cathy— little Cathy—our— I didn't know—"

If not Cathy, Ahmet, his wife Kemala, and their daughter would leap in front of them in the order of those martyred for this extraordinary cause that Ted had formerly been eager to join.

"Then Shanti—he pushed—me too—" Shanti had made it clear to the band that he was resolved to go public soon with his project, no matter what its cost to himself. Millions, when they realized the logic of his plan, would follow his example. He was confident the movement would instantly gain momentum and persuade the world that wars were a similar senseless murder of the young, a crime far worse than his few symbolic sacrifices.

Shanti's words stirred Ted. "I wanted—but I couldn't—"

Through these ploys, Gerhardt had reduced Ted, already stoned and outwitted, to a totally befuddled state. He had no arguments left to use against Gerhardt's double assault on his always timid resistance. "I couldn't—just couldn't—"

"Where is he?" Anthi demanded again. "Where is that monster with his head up his derriere?"

But Ted was obviously inspired now and couldn't stop until he was finished—or exhausted. "More babies—he needed. The Internet would—"

To make his few remaining sacrifices known to the world, Shanti would post them on all the popular online sites. Having Ahmet's little girl move ahead of Cathy, Gerhardt taunted, might not be a bad outcome. That family had just arrived from Turkey to join the crusade, and they came from a line of well-known Turkish diplomats. They would be the first Muslims to make their contribution to the cause. "Better a Muslim than another Westerner," Gerhardt had told him, "especially one from goofy California. If from LA, where's the credibility?"

All the while Gerhardt was plying Ted, Shanti, Peer and the others were downstairs making final arrangements. When Ted sputtered that he remained unsure of his willingness to take the next step, Gerhardt turned his stash and remaining crate of beer over to him along with a church key and a couple of small pipes, then disappeared. "All of it—mine—all—" By then Ted knew he was too far gone to do anything except enjoy the brew and carry on with his smoking until he passed out. Problem solved.

The longer Ted talked to Gloria the more his words cohered into phrases, his phrases into something resembling sentences. And the more sense Milt made of these sentences, the more his own thoughts spun away from what Ted was trying to say into a presence that stood behind Ted's account like a shadow, one that must define what Ted's words finally meant. But this shadow, whether Shanti or Shanti's scheme, remained too ill formed for him yet to make out its full meaning and grasp the reason it had such power over people like Ted and Ahmet. It wasn't enough, was it, to realize that Ted was a slacker, a dweeb, and a lifelong joiner. Anthi was right. It would help to know more about Shanti, to figure out when and where he planned his next sacrifice. Before that happened, Milt needed to see Shanti in action as he swayed his disciples and prepared them for their final submission to his program. Milt knew he must also keep a protective eye on Gloria and not allow Ted, when he sobered up, to get control of her mind again. That was his utmost duty in the hours immediately ahead.

"What are we going to do?" Gloria cried, her eyes still on Ted.

"I don't—" Ted began. "Nothing—" he finally mumbled. "Shanti has—"

"Break the ring in Shanti's hand," Milt thought half aloud, still contemplating the amorphous shadow.

"What?" Anthi and Gloria asked almost in unison, with Gloria's eyes turning up to him.

"Something about Shanti's ring," Christine said.

"Shanti is leading people around like animals with a ring in their nose," Milt said. "We have to get our hands on that ring and shatter it before another Una dies."

"What ring are you talking about?" Christine challenged.

"Yes, what ring?" Gloria asked, seemingly ready to spring from her chair.

Even Anthi's face looked crumpled in bewilderment.

"You should know, Gloria," he replied.

"This is too damn important, Milt," Christine barked. "Don't play coy."

"What brought you and Ted here, Gloria?"

"We came because—" she said, and hesitated as though the reason lay somewhere far back in time, "because we were fed up—afraid more and more people were ready to destroy other people and devastate the best parts of the earth, the oceans, the rain forests. That's why."

"And he promised he could bring all that to an end?"

"He promised." She seemed close to tears, her dark hair falling into her face. "That's why we came."

"And what he promised seemed so magnificent it would justify whatever methods he used?" Milt asked, coaxing her, he hoped, toward a clarifying answer.

"It seemed—marvelous," she said, great bewilderment in her face. "Like paradise. I couldn't have dreamed it would include—my baby." Her voice broke as she crushed Cathy tighter against her naked breast.

"Of course not. The idealists are always the most treacherous, aren't they?"

"Dad!" Anthi warned, but he wouldn't stop.

"Puffed up by loftiness—blinded by their noble promises. Plato, Paul. They are everywhere: Castro, Bush."

"Dad!" Anthi repeated. "You accused me of becoming a Paris cynic. Shame on you."

He hoped she was kidding. "No cynic, young woman. It's about ends and means— Ends implicit in means."

"Gerta and Peer and people I never met," Gloria broke in, "are willing to put Shanti's ideals into action." She seemed desperate to protect the cause to which she'd let Ted lead her as though that idealism was part of his initial appeal. "Even Ted had his moments. We both did." Now she was struggling against the quagmire the morning's crises found her sinking into. She pulled Cathy tighter against her breasts.

"But—" Milt began.

"But you both said *no*! You *and* Ted—" Christine said. "No. Before you went too far."

"Before you crossed that critical—lethal—line," Milt said.

"When someone has been killed. After that there's no return," Christine added.

"Killed for their ideal," Milt explained.

"If only those self-murdering martyrs for the seventy-two virgins could figure it out," Anthi jumped in, confirming family values her father had stressed with her.

"Blinded by Paradise," he said. But he knew he had been blinded himself the first day as he lay down on Gloria's paradisiacal table. And he had no regrets, he had to recognize.

"We have to stop Shanti," Anthi said. "Stop theorizing, dad."

"How?" Christine wanted to know. "Where is he?" Clearly she had figured out the mounting disaster that drove Milt and Gloria. Now she felt the need to do her part too.

"Ted, Ted—" Gloria shook her partner before he could fall back into his hypnagogic fugue or fall out of his chair.

"Wha—wha—" he stuttered

"What did you hear?"

His features, Milt realized, were as disorganized as his slurred thoughts had been; his eyebrows and lips were creeping across his face like drunken caterpillars, and his eyes were green agates on a collision course in the oval of his head.

Gloria rattled him harder. "You can't pass out again!"

"What? What, woman?" he muttered. "Let me sleep. I told—you—everything."

"Where? Where is he?" She nearly wept with urgency.

"Where's who?"

"Shanti, Shanti. Gerhardt, Ahmet, the rest of the band ..."

"How'm I 'pose to know?"

"You have to know, Ted. She's your baby too. You have to know."

As the afternoon sun suddenly broke through on the little square, her partner stared up at her with his pupils cruelly exposed to the glare.

"Shit—try Cultu—Cent'r," he said in obvious pain.

"What?" Milt interrupted.

Gloria looked up at him with terror and hope in her face. "He has to mean the Cultural Centre International."

"Where's it?" Christine asked.

"In Rennes-le-Chateau. The new building there."

"Let's get going—" Anthi said.

They stood up, all of a will—all but Gloria and Ted and little Cathy. "I can't just leave him here," she objected, her quandary obvious in her tone.

"We can't take him with us," Anthi said. "Not in his shape."

"We *need* you, Gloria," Milt said, voicing what was obvious to the others.

"Can we get him down the steps to my studio?" she asked. "If we stretch him out on the table, he can sleep it off."

Day Five

Late Morning

With a mix of care and clumsiness, Milt, Christine, and Anthi, the latter two taking turns, lugged and steered Ted down the stone steps to the street. Gloria carried little Cathy back to the stroller and then rolled her ahead of the other four as they crossed to her office. All of them working together found it difficult to weave both stroller and Ted through the line of media vans that now stretched bumper to bumper, like circus elephants, from the square past the door of her building.

With Anthi and Christine each hauling Ted along by his upper arms, Milt felt he needed to reconsider his hypotheses about Shanti's scheme and the power it possessed. Was it possible that a single, even absolutely desirable, goal could be sufficient to lure bright people like the Turkish family into his deadly scheme? He couldn't get his mind around the way such people would have to see things. If he and his companions were going to act effectively, he needed more time, and a quieter place, to consider the charlatan's method. Likely he used some form of group hysteria or mass hypnosis. Or a confluence of the two. And Milt knew a little about them both, now that he put his mind to it. One hot night under a suffocating circus tent in eastern Virginia, a fourteen-year-old boy had found himself jumping up from a metal folding chair and raising both his voice and his arms to shout praises in union with the famous visiting revivalist from Oklahoma, whose name he couldn't remember. For ten minutes as he ran overjoyed back to his aunt's home, he felt cured of his yearlong crippling leg pains. Then, as quickly as they had vanished, the sciatic stabs returned, and he nearly fell to his knees on the dusty road. Yes, he knew that group hypnosis was powerful stuff and could work. But could a rock band use a rave to create the same effect? Shanti must be employing other mind-altering schemes.

They had barely hauled Ted up on the massage table before Aimee, obviously startled, came into the reception area outside the therapy room's door. When Aimee asked what was happening, Gloria explained that Ted had gotten himself messed up during the night and that she herself needed to take care of some important business.

Aimee didn't seem surprised about Ted. "I'll keep an eye on this little darling," she volunteered as she bent to pat Cathy's curls. "Gloria, dear, you go ahead and do whatever you gotta do."

The offer perked up Milt's antennae for a second, but figuring Gloria knew what was what with Aimee, he acquiesced to her judgment.

Within minutes the remaining four had tumbled into his little Citroen, Gloria and Anthi in the back, and were winding down the road that eventually would lead to the precarious hill with the chateau and fabled small church at its peak. First, however, they had, he knew, to work their way through the police and media frenzy blocking the taped-off area around the Devil's Armchair. Fortunately, the highway gendarmes were out in force and passed them quickly through the jam so they could speed on their way against the stream of professional newspeople rushing to fill the vacuum created by the night's violence. What, Milt wondered, is our guru planning to do with so much attention?

Beyond the grey stone chateau, he found a parking place in the new lot created, since he last visited, between the church garden and a pair of red brick buildings about forty yards down the moderately steep slope. The buildings appeared new also. If they were here before, he did not remember them. He stepped from the car and pulled his seat forward so that Anthi and Gloria could exit the backseat. As he drew in a long breath of clean air, he stared out over the low rampart against which his car had stopped to take in the wide cultivated fields below and the evergreen forest beyond them. Unlike the wild regions south of Rennes-les-Bains, the fields and forest here possessed a tamed quality that approached the order of significant art. Their embodied beauty seldom failed to lift his spirits—but rough, ancient mountains lay west of them.

"This way," Gloria called out, and started toward the brick buildings behind them. "The Centre is on the second floor, I believe."

As they entered a vestibule door between two spacious shops, one featuring flamboyant local pottery, the other offering incense, oils, and honeys of the region, Milt noticed a placard set on an easel cautioning those using the stairs to be very quiet because meditation classes were in progress under the instruction of Guru Shanti-Shanti. The stairs Gloria led them up were steep, but fortunately it turned out that an American-style second story awaited them. They entered the rear of an auditorium that might accommodate roughly one hundred people in comfortably padded theater seats. A rich aroma, like that of patchouli, flavored the air. A few people sat in the rows nearest the floor-level stage, but twenty or so others stood in a large circle enacting hierarchal postures that Milt recognized as forms taken from Chinese martial practices he knew as Qigong and tai chi. These appeared to be the former and were led by a young man, in loose white linen trousers and matching martial blouse. It took a moment, but he recognized Shanti, Shanti.

Before the latter noticed their presence, Gloria motioned them to take the seats beside their knees at the dark back of the auditorium. They obeyed, and Anthi led the way into the row. From the shadows here, they were able to follow the self-styled guru as the martial class broke up and the next one began. All the participants remained despite this transition. Most selected blue and green yoga and exercise mats from a stack against the back wall of the stage and spread them in meticulous rows from wall to wall. A few older individuals, including the woman all in white whom Milt had seen on the bench in front of his hotel his first day back, took places in the front row of seats. Now that he could focus on her, her face seemed oddly familiar. With her was her companion from the bench. Those sitting assumed formal postures that reminded him of seated sandstone pharaohs. Among those on the floor, he thought he spotted Gerhardt, though his long brown hair was pulled back now to form a wild horsetail. Beside him lay a dark-haired man he thought was Ahmet and beyond him a lovely woman with golden skin he took to be Kemala, Ahmet's wife. Once the others settled on their mats, all became as still and similar as the bodies in some *CSI* episode.

As Shanti, Shanti took his place at the point where the two groups came together, Milt and his small band sank more deeply into their dark seats. Shanti, Shanti pulled his body as erect and imperial as a koros statue from the pre-Homeric dark ages. In a high-pitched singsong voice, he began instructing his followers.

"As the poet has said, the spirit is able to float above the physical world, but it sometimes prefers to plunge into living things. Then it takes up residence in the natural world that surrounds us and in the body that too often seems to imprison us as pure spirit."

With his elbow, Milt nudged Gloria, seated on his right, and whispered, "Is this what you were explaining during my first massage?"

He saw her nod once, but she didn't answer.

He nudged Christine with his other elbow. "Is this what your programs teach?"

She seemed startled by the interruption. "Higher power, yes," she whispered, clearly irritated.

"Today," Shanti resumed, "I will guide you on a little journey, a passage of images that will enable your spirit to liberate itself from the bondage of the flesh."

"New-fangled Gnosticism," he heard his daughter grumble under her breath on the other side of Gloria.

"Shh!" Christine quietly cautioned.

Shanti, Shanti did not hear as he chanted, "But you must relax those limbs and all the muscles of your torso and mind. You must breathe with me, in—and out, in—and out, as we make our ascent. When your mind begins to wander to cares of your daily life, bring it back to my voice and the sensation of your breath, your bodily spirit, as it passes in and out of your body. Relax, relax. And come with me."

Even from his distance Milt noticed Shanti's followers, their closed eyes and especially the tension that showed in their faces. He wondered about the way their bodies squirmed on the mats. It was as though they were desperate to locate the spirit said to be within them.

Shanti began describing a series of scenes that opened in a small town much like Couiza just below Rennes-le-Chateau with its bars, shops, and splendid restaurants. His vignettes followed a river like the Salz or Aude out of the town into a dark woods of oaks and evergreens. Here in the forest his pilgrims encountered an army of horrific shadows, one after the other, that Shanti claimed were the traps of the physical world: towers of finance, costly weapons of war, specters of hunger and disease, irresistible incarnations of gluttony, drink, lust.

The boy has learned a lot in twenty years, Milt said to himself. By-product of LA too—the dream factory metamorphosed for him into the greed factory.

Then Shanti led them all out of the woods into cultivated flatlands similar to those Milt had seen from the ramparts. As they passed from dark to light, Milt was surprised to feel his own spirit immediately soar within, his tense arms, shoulders, and thighs grow slack. He gave in to the sensation, even though he resented the way the guru had tricked him.

While their feet and legs plowed easily through the fields of young grasses that their guide conjured up, the latter warned, "Now we must begin our difficult ascent toward the light behind the light of these tempting green fields. We must climb the spiritual mountain until our bodies become so exhausted they let go of the soul, and we as pure spirit struggle to push the body away, destroy it if necessary and all that holds us to the flesh, even our dearest ones."

"Before we can go further, from wherever you are, on your mats or in your chairs, we must now send words of kindness to our dear ones. In silence, speaking inwardly, address them with these calming words: *May you be happy. May you be oblivious to the pain. May you dwell in peace. May you be forgiving.*"

Milt sat stunned by what he had just heard, wondering whether he had heard correctly. Had Shanti not just, in so many words, confessed to his past crimes and those he was prepared to commit soon? To confirm what he believed he'd heard, he tried to replay the chant in his brain, but astonishment blocked his recall.

Fortunately, Shanti came to Milt's aid. "Now repeat those calming words to your loved ones—and to yourself," he ordered before reciting the chant just as Milt thought he first heard it.

"Now we must begin our journey," Shanti added.

What came next seemed an arduous climb on foot, first through a canyon resembling the Galamus Gorges that Milt and Christine had taken into Bugarach. Next they made the easier stroll through Rennes-les-Bains, followed by an arduous clamber up the hairpin curves of the drive from Couiza to where they now sat, except the asphalt no longer existed, and each step of their ascent brought the pain of their scramble with hand and foot up the Bugarach peak to the murder scene. From weariness and misery, they were now prepared to will the body away. Bodies on the mats twisted more fiercely than before. Those in chairs shifted their feet about nervously. Ultimately, Shanti brought their no longer encumbered souls to the spot where the small church of Mary Magdalena outside would have stood had it not been replaced by the overwhelming ball of burning gases that Milt took for the sun itself, until he recognized that was impossible.

Shanti raised his arms toward the ceiling and shouted, "Now greet your lord and master, pure spirits. Fall on your knees and praise him."

All his followers obeyed, their eyes still closed, their faces wide open. Two or three in the front seats, taking his words literally, dropped to their knees. Those on the mats appeared totally removed from their bodies and lay as though frozen in coma.

"Praise him," Shanti cried out. "Praise the Universal Spirit. And like the wise men of old—like father Abraham himself—raise your firstborn to him as loving sacrifice!"

"Bullshit!" Anthi grumbled again and darted from her seat, stumbled over the feet of Gloria, her father, and stepmother, and then charged up the steps toward the door. Instantly Christine and Milt followed.

"*Silence!*" Shanti, Shanti commanded to their backs. "*Who dares—*" he screamed.

Only when they stood clear of the closed auditorium doors did Milt, looking back, call to the others, "Where's Gloria?" His voice broke in panic.

"I don't think she came," Christine said, anxiety obvious in the faltering of her voice.

"Damn," he growled. "Shanti must have sucked her back in."

"I hope the hell not," Anthi muttered. "You know what that means."

"We've got to go back. We can't let her do what he said."

"Little Cathy—" Anthi began, but she choked back her words with sobs.

"Look, you two," Christine said, "he knows who you are. I'm anonymous to him, so far as any of us know. I'm going back in there—to give Gloria any support I can."

Anthi and Milt stared at one another, bewildered and paralyzed.

Anthi spoke first. "She's right, Dad. Christine hasn't done anything to draw his attention. She hasn't riled him up the way you did."

"Okay, Chrissy." Milt took her hand in both of his. "But be careful, sweet." He kissed her on the cheek.

"You know I will be. I'll meet you two back at the car."

"Usually, you are," he said.

"And knock on wood I'll have Gloria with me."

She turned and reentered the heavy double doors.

Anthi and her father descended the stairs to the building's vestibule and out into the courtyard serving the various tourist shops. The noon sun had cut through the low-hanging clouds, and suddenly the humidity of the mountaintop lay upon them like a wet silk sheet. One look inside the little Citroen, and they knew waiting in it was out of the question.

"We can watch from the old garden," he said and motioned up the hill to the gray stone tower and gallery that crowned the parapet there.

They climbed the gentle slope of the parking lot only to discover that the arched metal gate at this end of the garden no longer admitted visitors as it had during their previous visits together. A sign said, "Admittance at l'Eglise Gate Only."

"Everything in this country takes a ticket now," Anthi bristled.

"I see a bench there under the trees," her father answered.

"If the birds haven't dumped all over it," Anthi joked as she followed her father along the wrought-iron fence.

With Anthi seated, Milt stood in front of her, studying the layout of the garden. Both were silent, she not allowing her eyes to wander from the building's door, while his eyes registered distances inside the fence, chiefly from the church mansion to the squat Magdalena Tower, whose rampart appeared to have been used recently as a stage. At the same time, his mind focused again on the horrific shadow that had risen up inside of him as Ted rambled through his account of the previous night. Now that he integrated the shadow with his glimpse of Shanti in action, he feared Shanti was another madman like Jim Jones, David Koresh, Pol Pot, or the leader of the Heaven's Gate gang; Rancho Absurdo, he liked to call them. Shanti belonged in the same locked ward, didn't he? They were all glib-tongued fanatics who had gotten their big trick down pat. They just came up with a "larger cause," some high spiritual goal they could use to attract masses of the faithful and trap them into carrying out deadly, stupid actions for noble reasons.

As he groped through the muck of colliding connections he glanced at his beautiful daughter and dropped beside her on the bench, hoping that by example more than words he had taught her to be wary of crazies like Jones and Shanti. Because it's never been any different, he muddled on silently. Folks have been sacrificing the life they love, their children, their family, sanity, for the impossible dreams as long as humankind has possessed a brain, at least one capable of inventing a higher reality and believing that the promise of this other world made any sacrifice worthwhile—their whole life, even.

His eyes were on the same door as Anthi's now, but his brain was making multiple fresh connections the way an old man's brain does— if it's still all there. And they've prettied up their imagined state by calling it a divinity, their paradise of virgins, of freedom, democracy, whatever. All of us acting like dumb oxen, and the madmen leading us around by the ring in our noses. It's the ring I envisioned back in Rennes-les-Bains, the one called higher truth—or higher something. It's a damn simple mechanism, isn't it? Look at what Hitler did— that's all they need to do. An impossible realm swells the superego until it eclipses our sense of the real and allows our darkest drives to join forces with conscience and ideals. After which everything is permitted. Since Freud, it should be obvious. It isn't just that God is dead, and all is permitted. It's that madmen create gods in their own image, then claim that whatever they long for is permitted—war murders, collateral damage be damned, self-sacrifice, even child-sacrifice for Shanti. Since Abraham and Agamemnon, it should have been obvious, he told himself. But even Freud refused to see it.

He looked again at Anthi, who seemed lost still in mysteries of her own invention. After what seemed a very long time, Milt checked the watch his son had given him on his birthday years ago. Only fifteen minutes had passed.

Then the door to the stairwell opened, and a dozen or so persons dressed for yoga streamed out of the building. Christine and Gloria were not among them. Their absence set all his worries free to fill his mind.

"Maybe I should go back for her," he said.

"No, no. Shanti hasn't come out yet. She's up to something, I'm sure."

Another five minutes and they saw Christine exit and head straight for their car.

When she noticed they weren't there, she looked frantically around until she found where they were. They motioned her to come to the bench, and she hurried their way.

"We were starting to worry," he said.

"Where's Gloria?" Anthi demanded.

Christine didn't speak until she reached the bench, her face tight with anxiety. "She's talking with Shanti."

"He's sucked her back in," Milt groaned as he and Anthi stood.

"I don't think so," his wife said. "When I went back in, she seemed to be in a sort of trance. I sat down beside her, but I couldn't get her attention. I put my arm around her and pulled her to me. She just laid her head on my shoulder and sat there. I shook her, shook her again, until she came out of it. She looked up in my face and smiled. She recognized me."

"Good for you, Christine," Anthi said and took her arm to squeeze it appreciatively.

"We sat there while most of Shanti's meditators left. Then Gloria took my hand and led me down to the stage where Shanti and two of his band were straightening the mat pile. She introduced me as one of her aunts from Kentucky. Shanti shook my hand and stared at me. I thought he recognized me from the square. Apparently not. He seemed happy to see Gloria and asked about Cathy. Gloria said she'd left her with Ted. Shanti asked if Ted was still stoned, and Gloria had to say Aimee was keeping an eye on both."

"Damn," Milt replied. "Wish she hadn't done that."

His response appeared to puzzle his wife. "Shanti seemed satisfied and said Ted must have some crazy stories to tell after the way he was tripping. I reminded Gloria we needed to get going. She told me to head out; she'd join me in a second."

"I think I see her," Anthi said, face bright with relief.

Gloria instantly spotted the three of them and headed their way. She was halfway to them when she called out, "He told me to join them tonight! In Limoux."

Anthi immediately placed her forefinger across her lips. Without a word more, they moved toward the car. Milt hoped to get it out of the lot before Shanti, Shanti emerged from the meditation hall and saw all of them together.

Fortunately, few cars were moving in the lot, and with no obstacles they were soon on their way down the winding road.

"I'm still shaking," Anthi announced and thrust her hand between the front seats for her father and stepmother to see.

"Me too," Christine said and turned to the two in the back. "What about you, Gloria?"

Milt caught Gloria's face in the rearview mirror. Rather than reply at once, she looked timidly out the window by her side, then said, "I guess so. But Shanti seemed pretty much the same as usual."

The response unsettled Milt even more. Had the faux guru gulled her again? To some degree she still seemed bewitched by him. They would have to be careful with her and make certain she didn't do anything dumb.

"So, are we going to inform the police?" Christine wondered.

"They might as well be from Missouri," Anthi said. "You have to show them everything. Totally lacking intuition."

"What can we show them?" her father answered in a flat, serious tone.

Gloria spoke out of her fugue: "There's nothing to take to them, is there?" She seemed too eager to make her point.

"A handful of dead children—that's something," Christine insisted.

"But how do we tie them to Shanti, Shanti?" Milt asked. "Without imagination to fill in the gaps, there's only the similarity in method."

"Ted was totally stoned. They won't believe him. Claim he was hallucinating," Milt's daughter said.

"Shanti speaks in metaphors—biblical metaphors at that. Which won't prove anything to the cops."

"The gendarmes will put it off on copycats. Copying what happened to little Charles even," Anthi added.

"I don't want to go there," her father whispered.

"They won't blame you, Dad. That would take imagination. Misguided imagination," Anthi was quick to add.

"So all we can do is—" Christine queried.

"Is keep an eye on him—on Shanti," Milt answered. "And on little Cathy. And Ahmet and Kemala's daughter, if we can." And on Gloria and unreliable Ted, he wanted to add.

"Are we sure we can keep them safe?" Christine asked.

"We can surefire try," Anthi growled, falling back on her hoard of Virginia words.

"Can we get Cathy now?" Gloria wondered out loud. "And Ted?" Almost an afterthought, it seemed.

"That's where I'm heading," Milt assured her.

Day Five

Afternoon

It took twenty-five minutes through noon traffic to cover the distance back to Rennes-les-Bains. Whereas Couiza was busy, les-Bains seemed almost deserted when Milt drove along the road through the center. Even the media vans looked empty. He could hear voices, rattled dishes, and the dialogue of soaps from the windows open over the street. After he parked near their hotel, the four of them walked up to the institute where Gloria worked. The building appeared abandoned, as though the day was a national holiday.

Gloria opened the hall door to her waiting room, but no one greeted them.

"Aimee!" she shouted.

When there was no response, she headed for her therapy room. "I'll check on Ted," she said as she turned to reassure them.

Anthi, Christine, and Milt stared at one another, their faces stiff with foreboding.

Gloria pushed open her door, hesitated for a moment, then turned to them with lowered head and fallen shoulders. "Where—?"

Christine put her arm around Gloria's shoulders, and Milt rushed past them to check the room where they had left her daughter and partner. It was empty now. Fear danced in his brain that Shanti had dispatched some of the faithful ahead, probably Gerhardt, to pick up Cathy and her father. It was an image he refused to share with poor Gloria. *She has her own terror*, he told himself. *I can't make it worse.*

When he turned back, Anthi had joined Christine's support of the stunned mother. They helped her over to the massage table to sit on its edge.

"The room's the way I left it," Gloria was mumbling. "Why—Why didn't he do something to stop them?"

"He was still out of it," Anthi reassured.

"Why didn't—Aimee?" Gloria cried.

For that, the others provided no answer.

"We do know where Shanti's going to be, don't we?" Christine said. "Shouldn't we head there?"

"What for?" Anthi asked.

"To make sure—nothing happens to little Cathy," Milt volunteered.

"What?" Gloria muttered. "What happen?" Apparently the full horror had not penetrated her shocked attachment to Cathy. "If she's with Aimee—"

"We've forgotten Aimee's old ties to Shanti, haven't we?" Milt said as cautiously as possible. He had no desire to crush her further.

"And there's—Ted," Gloria stumbled on. "He must be with Cathy too."

Milt hated to say what he felt obligated to add. "It's hard to know which side Ted comes down on, isn't it, Gloria? He could turn either way."

"Cathy is his child as much as mine," Gloria said through bursts of tears. "He loves her!"

"And Shanti is his mate. Has been since Santa Barbara, hasn't he?"

Gloria just stared at him, disbelief in her face. Unable to form words herself, she turned to Anthi and Christine for help.

The best Christine could offer came as a question: "Where was it Shanti told you to go?"

In the absence of a reply from Gloria, Anthi jumped in. "Limoux. He said, 'Limoux tonight.' The next town north of Couiza."

"We have to find Ted and—Cathy before then," Milt said, his voice cracking with urgency. "Where would he take her, Gloria?"

Again bewilderment flooded the young woman's face.

"Would they—maybe—go back to the camper?"

When Gloria nodded weakly, Anthi said, "Then we have to start there."

"Can you walk, Gloria?" Christine asked as she raised the weakened woman's arm to guide her toward the door.

"I'll go for the car," Milt volunteered. "You three wait here."

"I'm coming with you, Dad," Anthi said.

In less than ten minutes, the Citroen was crossing the small bridge over the Salz that accessed the shaded area back of the camping grounds. With the Norwegian family's van missing, Milt and Anthi had no problem spotting Ted and Gloria's camper, the only vehicle there at the moment.

"The door's open," Anthi said at the same instant he noticed the sliding panel.

"Not good," he replied.

They left the Citroen on the gravel road and circled on foot to approach the camper from the rear, where brown and yellow plaid curtains were drawn over the wide windows. Dreading the worst, Milt slid along the van until he stood at the edge of the side panel. Then, wishing he were a cop with a pistol, he abruptly thrust his head and shoulders into the half-lit interior. What he saw made him exhale abruptly.

Sprawled on the lowered vinyl bed lay the lifeless shape he recognized as Ted, his red mane a halo spilled chaotically toward the door. Only the labored stentorian breaths reassured Milt that Cathy's dad was more alive than he looked. Milt stepped up into the cramped space but was forced by the ceiling to remain bent over. Anthi appeared behind him at the door.

"Ted, Ted! You need to wake up, dude," he barked as he shook both limp shoulders.

"Gloria needs you," Anthi shouted.

Only after Anthi doused him with cold water from the large thermos under the camper did the young man begin to revive, very slowly. With short breaths to avoid the rank smells surrounding Ted, they continued raining urgent commands and entreaties on his groggy head. "What happened?" "Wake up, you dunce!" "Where's Cathy?" "What did you do with her?" "Do you know?" "Why did Aimee disappear?"

"Where's your daughter, you hairy bastard?" Milt growled, his nerves screaming for a response.

Anthi laid her hand on his shoulder. "He's still out of it, dad. Calm down. Shouting won't do your cardiovascular any good."

The name-calling seemed to sober Ted more than their questions.

"I come—I came to," he stuttered, "Cathy—wasn't—wasn't there."

He seemed to fall back into his exhaustion—until Milt shook him with more anger than before. "Where was Aimee, you freak?"

Restored for a moment, Ted mumbled, "Gone—Aimee—gone too."

"What did you do, Ted?" Milt rattled him again before he could escape into his trance.

"I—tried finding—them." He seemed better able to snag his words and string them together. "I came—back here—somehow. I must have—fallen. My knees—my hands—hurt." He raised the latter to show his palms, bloodied where gravel and splinters had entered his flesh.

"You came back, Ted. Then what?" Anthi pleaded.

"I fell—on the bed. I don't remember—after that."

"Where would you have looked?" Milt was desperate now.

"Aimee's—first."

"Then?" Anthi needed to know.

"Not sure—maybe—I don't know—maybe Limoux."

As their informant once more threatened to pass out, Milt grabbed him up. "You can't sleep now, hash-head. You've got to show us."

"Don't!" he shouted when Anthi applied more cold water. "Don't do that. I'll help get him going."

With support under each arm, Ted was very nearly able to walk the fifty meters or so to the Citroen, where they dumped him into the small back seat so Anthi could keep an eye of him from the front passenger side. Even though the back had no door through which he could take flight, they wanted to make sure he didn't doze off again. She allowed him to sprawl, but each time his eyes began to close Milt saw her give his knee a quick, strong pop with the rear ends of her fingers.

"Owww!" he howled as his eyes sprang open. "Why'd'u do that?"

"Where does Aimee live?" Milt snarled.

"Look—you guys—I want to find Cathy as—as much as you do. If anything—more. She's my daughter—after all." He seemed to be sobering fast now.

"And do what with her?" Anthi demanded. She was thinking, Milt was sure, about the ritual with which Shanti had concluded the morning meditation.

"What you mean?" the younger man asked. "What do—people usually do with— their children?"

"Not certain I know any longer," Milt muttered more to himself than the other two.

"Aimee lives—at the bridge—the one beside the Hostellerie. Okay?"

Milt did not reply but suspected this must be the house on the bridge that he could see from his hotel balcony. He turned his little auto in the direction of the town's back road along the river. Within minutes they were parked on the gravel track back of the two-story dwelling that looked much like a Virginia townhouse except that bright yellow plaster covered the exterior and every window and balcony bore green shutters or green flower boxes overflowing with lavender, purple, blue, and a few red blossoms. They reminded him of his mother's prized petunias lining the front walk when he was growing up.

He asked Anthi to watch Ted while he searched for Aimee. He assumed she would remember his face from his visits to the massage studio.

Although the front door stood cracked open an inch, he knocked. He waited for a response, but when none came, he pushed the door wider and peered into the first room.

Because Aimee kept her home neatly ordered, the three half-empty water glasses staining her glass-top coffee table told him what he needed to know, that she had abandoned the house in a rush, probably because someone—Gerhardt?—who'd joined Cathy (one glass was much smaller than the other two) and her in their drinks had made it necessary. He'd seen Gerhardt at the meditation, hadn't he? Likely Aimee had found a way to send Shanti or him the news that she had Cathy with her now, and one of them found a way to slip out of the auditorium and beat Milt's friends back to the village.

"Aimee. Aimee!" he called up the stairs of the townhouse, certain there would be no answer.

He knew, as he closed the door behind him, they had no time to waste.

"Gone," he told Anthi as soon as he opened the Citroen's door.

"Where?" she exploded back at him.

"See," Ted groaned. "There's no way of stopping him. Everything is scheduled."

"I don't know," her father said. "Maybe to Limoux. We have to pick up Christine and Gloria." He turned his head to address the prisoner in back. "Shut up, you whiner. She's your daughter!"

"But Shanti's bigger'n I am—stronger than all of us," Ted wailed. "He's got the plan—the grand cause, larger'n all our little plans. He's doing good, real, real fucking good. And the Force, the whole fucking universe, is with him."

"You worthless fatalist—I said shut your fucking mouth."

"None of us're going to keep him from it, man. None of us."

Anthi struck his leg, harder this time. "Where in Limoux, crybaby?" she demanded. "Where will they go?"

Again he yelped. "You don't have to do that, bitch!"

"Where?"

"I don't know. Not before dark. After—maybe there are places. It's all scheduled, I tell you."

Before she could ask what places, they were double-parked by one of the giant media vans outside Gloria's studio, and Milt suggested she go in for the others. Even before the three women returned, it dawned on Milt there would be a problem. No way would five adults fit into his little car, and not one of them, he understood, would be willing to stay behind.

Believing there was only one solution, he turned his glare on Ted and asked, "Where are the keys to your camper, Ted?"

"My what?" the captive protested.

"Don't act dumb with me, Curly Locks." He raised his hand, ready to deliver another of Anthi's blows. "Who has the damn keys?"

"Ask Gloria," Ted mumbled, shrinking from the threat of the hand.

"And if not—" Milt cocked his hand and made a fist.

"We keep a spare under the driver's seat."

"That's better," Milt said and opened the passenger door for the approaching ladies. Gloria, he saw, might still be in shock, but her face seemed set with rock-hard purpose.

"Gloria," he said, "you'll have to let Ted sit on your lap—just until we can get your van. It'll work better if you two fit yourselves in up here beside me where there's more legroom." Ted fortunately was no larger than she was and likely a bit less solid.

Christine obviously didn't like getting bumped from her accustomed place, but the alternatives would not do, and the ride was a short one. To avoid the newspeople and gendarmes in the main square, he twisted the Citroen through a U-turn and retraced his route on the auxiliary road back to the campground's parking area.

Once there, Gloria pulled her keys from her pocket and insisted Milt drive the van. It resembled the camper he'd taken in the seventies from Germany across Europe and back. Gloria claimed the passenger seat in order to direct him, and Anthi pushed Ted into the rear. When she told him to squeeze in on the bench-bed between Christine and herself, Milt looked back in time to see Christine wrinkle her nose, and he knew she was reacting to Ted's rank sweat and sour booze.

As he pulled away, he released the clutch abruptly, and the large vehicle ground to a pounding halt, sending those in back to the edge of their bench. "Just testing," he said as sternly as he could. "Seatbelts on, everybody?"

He heard the three behind him scrambling about, and he worked clutch and accelerator together to send the van lurching forward.

"Dad, we're not Keystone Kops," Anthi shouted. "We have serious business to take care of."

"Don't worry, girl. I'll get you there." Then, before she could kid him again, he turned to his navigator. "Is there another road to Couiza, Gloria?"

Her eyes dead on the unprotected bridge they were about to cross, Gloria answered, "I've heard about one but don't know how good it is. It's a roundabout way. Why?"

"There's probably a mob of cops and morbid voyeurs around le *Fauteuil du diable*. What you think?"

"They let us through before. I say we try it," Gloria said.

"And let's hope they don't take this for the Norwegians' van," he said as he pointed them north.

Traffic through the congestion at the murder scene did not move as smoothly as in the morning, but the gendarmes apparently knew the missing van was larger and carried a Norwegian plate. When they saw Milt's US passport and the ownership papers in Gloria's name, they sent the five Americans on their way down through the thick forests, granite walls, and cultivated plots that ran along the Salz River and the Aude to Couiza and on to Limoux.

As they approached the city limits of Couiza, Christine called from the back. "I don't know about you guys, but I'm getting hungry. I think we'd better stop for lunch somewhere. We can't do much sleuthing on empty stomachs."

Milt checked his watch. It was nearly 4:00 p.m. For the first time he realized he was hungry. Because their panicky search began when it did, Christine had not had a moment for breakfast. Christine was not noted for her practicality or her appetite. If she was hungry, then it was clearly time for food. They must not permit the fury of pursuit to drag them out of their bodies completely. Their quest for Cathy required food if they were to continue it.

"There's probably not much open now," Anthi said.

"We'll find a restaurant," Milt countered.

As late as it was, all the restaurants in the town had rolled in their signs, and the best Milt could turn up on short notice in the unfamiliar town was a bar that provided drinks and simple sandwiches.

As the four of them read the newspapers scattered about the smoky room populated by a handful of scruffy guys, he and Christine split a baton with *jambon*, *tomate*, and *fromage* washed down by a Diet Coke. The sandwich seemed to ground them again.

It was fortunate, Milt thought, that someone apparently had censored the papers by excluding the hard news but leaving the sports and business sections plus the local social pages. This way Gloria would not run across lurid photos and reports of Una's death before their journey continued.

Once out of Couiza, Milt steered the clumsy camper along the Aude north through forests, occasional fields of yellow-topped rape, and scattered villages. The air smelled of recent rain on plowed earth. Sporadic bursts of wind off the river swerved the van the way sudden breezes shudder the sails of small boats. Each time, the threat of losing control caught him unawares, and he had to wrestle with the steering. Fortunately few vehicles were coming toward them.

As they entered the outskirts of a town where small fields separated houses from modest factories, Milt feared they could be nearing a moment of crisis since he no longer knew where they were heading.

"Must be Limoux, Gloria," he began. "Did Shanti say where?"

As Milt dreaded, rather than answer she turned to face the rear bench. "Ted, Ted. Where did you guys hang here?"

Milt still wasn't sure they could trust Ted, but he was their only source now.

The way the younger man cleared his throat and the look in his eyes when Milt glanced at him in the rearview mirror meant that Gloria's question had startled him awake.

They were rolling slowly along the black streets lined by huge trees with peeling grey trunks supporting low green and grey leaves shaped like crushed stars.

Anthi spoke up, "Tell us, runt. It's your daughter." She was shaking him again. This time, very firmly.

"I—how would I know?" he slurred.

"You've been here with him, Ted," Gloria prompted from in front, anger mounting in her voice.

"Look for his SUV," Ted answered. "It's black"

"What make?" Anthi demanded.

"I don't know. Porsche—Alfa Romeo—some brand we don't see back home. Big—and black. Even the windows."

They cruised the main road through Limoux, up and down, noting the Bureau of National Tourism, the old hotel on the right, scattered restaurants. Lots of cars in the municipal parking area, lots of SUVs, but none as large and black as the one Ted described. The town appeared to end at a traffic circle just after the last of the one- and two-story commercial buildings. Milt used the roundabout to reverse directions.

"So, what now?" Anthi demanded of the fellow beside her.

"Yeah, Ted, tell us," Gloria added.

"I don't know," he protested.

"Remember!" Milt ordered. "It's little Cathy, and we've got to find her."

"Okay, okay," Ted grumbled. "There's this church—"

"What church?" Anthi prompted.

"One Shanti visited sometimes with us tagging along. I don't know the name."

"We just passed a church back on the right," Milt said, his hope renewed.

"No," Ted said. "It's out of town. The other way." Without looking back, he threw his arm over his shoulder and pointed behind.

Milt saw his arm and U-turned the van in the main street, eliciting ferocious honks from in front and behind but no sound of crushed metal. He raised both hands, shrugged his shoulder at an approaching driver, and sped toward the north end of Limoux.

"Where?" he called to the rear seat.

"At the big circle, seems we took a right and headed uphill, best I remember," Ted said.

Milt obeyed their reluctant guide, who now appeared remarkably coherent.

"Cross over the bridge—that's right. Now, if my memory is good, take this right—right here! Good. And follow this road until you see a sign for— That's it, that sign!"

Milt saw the marker for a church. He didn't have time to catch the name before he was turning up a hill toward a wooded area in which a large grey mass of stone stood. In his rearview he could see fields of rape and grain, but the paved drive kept ascending in a grand curve toward the stone structure, which appeared dark and sealed.

On their right they glimpsed an enormous fountain before they cleared the last thicket of trees and arrived at massive and ancient dark double doors with deep gashes in their wooden face as though from age or an axe. The doorman or custodian, a short man with a big belly and strands of dark hair, sat in a worn chair with a ladder back and oily rope seat propped back against the stones to which the left half of the door was affixed. The stare he gave the van and them challenged their right to arrive in his domain this late in the afternoon. Milt felt it wiser to let the van roll back a dozen yards and park against the church wall out of the man's vision. Up close, the stone of the building looked more brown than grey but was covered with afternoon shadows.

Gloria was out first and pulled back the sliding door for the three in the rear.

"Remember," Anthi cautioned, "this is still a functioning church. I know we are worked up, but we have to respect its religious nature and keep our voices down."

"I don't see Shanti's SUV," Milton said.

"It could be in back," Ted answered nervously, as though his veracity had been attacked. "Or down by those old stables over there." He pointed to his right through the woods to a reddish structure maybe a hundred feet long.

"Are there buildings in back?" Milt asked as he led them toward the main entrance.

"One—" Ted said, apparently reluctant to answer. "A small one."

"Where would they keep Cathy?" Gloria asked, her face twisted by urgency.

"I—I just don't know," Ted admitted.

"We'll start in the main building," Anthi volunteered.

"If that guy in the chair will let us enter." Although Milt knew their arrival irritated the man, he headed toward the main door and gave its heavy timbers a shove. It didn't move.

"The sanctuaire—it close five thirty," the burly guardian grumbled as he rose and staggered, a gigantic key hanging from one hand, over to where the intruders waited.

"We still have twenty minutes," Anthi replied.

That her French was good seemed to vanquish the man's air of superiority. He inserted the key, gave it a turn that required his full body, and pushed the ancient door open. He stood back and, with a mocking swing of his arm, motioned them into the vestibule.

Not in twenty years had Milt stepped into a church this barren. Shadows ruled the interior. Grayness was everywhere. The smell of mildew mixed with candles and incense seeped from the stones. Medallions and a scattering of large paintings dotted the walls, but all were dark with age and neglect. A couple of dozen dingy wooden chairs stood in the nave. The chancel impressed Milt with its shabby grandiosity, so incongruous given the paltry group of chairs.

Without warning, an oversized light clicked on in the small chapel to the left of the altar, the only chapel in the church. The illumination was obviously meant to call attention to the figure housed in a raised glass display about three feet tall. While Ted slumped in one of the rear chairs, Gloria sat, still stunned, a couple of chairs away, and the other two mulled about studying the paintings and small stone items on the walls, Milt stepped up into the chapel to examine what the glass protected.

What he found so astounded him that for the moment he forgot his companions and their grave mission. Clothed in an A-shaped tent of white brocaded silk and a veil of transparent white silk into which white flowers were woven, stood a remarkable female statue above whose coffee-brown face and dark hair a large golden crown rested. Raised in the wall back of her head, a great sunburst of rays and flowers curved around her. A circle of stones, each large as Milt's thumb, stood out from the collar of her dress, the most prominent a red one set between a blue and another that was green. He could not believe they were real ruby, jasper, and emerald but suspected he could be wrong.

In front of her she held a small boy, whose garment seemed even more ornate than hers in that the brocade pictured stars and flowers of gold thread from which giant pearls protruded. On his small head he wore another gold crown, one from whose band four golden arches rose to meet at an apex upon which a small cross, seemingly of ivory, stood. Milt wanted to call this headdress a "miter" but realized his knowledge of liturgical dress was shaky. Besides, his instinct for offbeat religions told him that someone had crafted these crowns to encompass secular as well as sacred powers.

Without his noticing, Anthi had joined him in the raised chapel and stood there as awed as he was. She was the one person with whom he could share his heterodox sense of what the woman represented, since she knew the novel they'd written together better than anyone.

"You know who this is, don't you?" he asked.

She nodded thoughtfully, and the two of them began stitching together the great web of meanings she symbolized. The pair, they agreed, represented no ordinary Madonna and child. It showed in her serene face, free of the terrible split between the sky and the earth, and in her extraordinary complexion. Her color did not derive from pale clouds but from the olive hue of earth, bark, and countless fruits and nuts. She had to be the dark Madonna he had pursued for decades and had evoked in a later chapter of their novel five years ago.

The figure had struck Anthi as the most sublime representation of the dark woman she had ever seen, both in the humanness of her tint and the utter ease of her expression. In the novel he had thought of her as Magdalena from Rennes-le-Chateau, and he traced her back to her source in Leakey's Lucy at Olduvai and to Lucy's ancestors. Back then, however, neither of them knew the story of Magdalena's dark daughter Sarah, whom Anthi stumbled across in her visits to the Camargue. Now that they did, he called the woman before him Sarah and guessed the child she held must represent the pre-Carolingian rulers of ur-France, kings said to carry in their age, like little Charles Plantard in this, the "divine" blood of Magdalena's spouse, a man growing numbers took to have been Jesus from Nazareth. As Magdalena's daughter, Sarah was, they felt, the living Grail of her generation and a vital symbol for all ages in which she was not ignored.

"She's the antidote," Anthi said, "to the poison Shanti, Shanti spreads."

He knew she meant the split that every dualist since Plato, including Cathar Gnostics, would lodge in the human psyche, the division between the body and the spirit, the flesh and the soul, the secular and sacred that had brought even large-spirited Gloria to Rennes-les-Bains and left her so close to offering her own daughter up to Shanti's toxic vision.

All this they sensed in her before Anthi spotted a clear plastic box with a printout that she read and passed to him.

"Here's the local scoop," she said, and he found himself reading her story, a tale confirming her earthiness, her repeated suppression, and her eternal return. The French seemed so simple, the story so familiar to him, that he flew through it, stumbling only once or twice.

A laborer was working his field located in this ancient freehold. Suddenly his oxen pulled up the plowshares and refused to go on. Surprised and irritated, the workman decided that his animals seemed afraid to advance further. Astonished, he looked in front of them. Without knowing why, he decided to dig the soil just ahead of the animals. Imagine his surprise when he discovered, emerging from the earth, a statue of the Virgin sculpted from a dark wood that was nearly black. Very pious, he carried the statue into his humble dwelling, thinking he saw in this discovery the action of the grace of God himself.

In the morning, he was struck into stupefaction! The statue had disappeared. He went back to the place where he found it and saw that the statue had "returned" to the earth where he had discovered it. Seeing here a divine act, he informed his clergyman, who, certain of the miracle, decided to raise a church in this place consecrated to God and the Virgin. Thus it was that this church was founded.

Milt knew the story he was reading did not explicitly account for her most salient characteristic, the color of her skin. For him as for others in past centuries, the dark Madonna had taken on ever deeper meanings, ones he hesitated even now to share with this daughter. In his reflections, she was more of the earth than the blue sky, more of the red flesh than the bodiless spirit, more in the realm of the feminine than the blue Madonna, who belonged to the father's sky. The dark Madonna always seemed more completely human in her sexual being than the divine mother who for centuries had caused humans to long for the inhuman sky—for the transcendent state realized in death.

The figure before him represented the same embodiment of spirit in flesh that he had desired to incarnate fully that first morning on Gloria's table, the union of which Gloria seemed the perfect vehicle, though her own vision had been tainted by Shanti. Was it too late to explain this to her, or Christine, or even Anthi? He didn't want to hear one of them accuse him of macho fantasies and of delivering another lecture. It was time instead for him to show them the union that the statue embodied by acting out the love he felt for them all and to do so by protecting the little Cathy he hardly knew.

As the final epiphany woke him from his mental fugue, he remembered the other three they'd brought with them. When he glanced back their way, they still looked lost in consternation and uncertainty about what to do now. "Come on," he called to them across the gloomy hollowness. "Shanti's not here. Cathy's not either. Let's go." The reverie before the Black Madonna had restored his hope, or at least his energy.

The three women joined him in the vestibule, but they had to send Anthi back for Ted. He seemed so reluctant to leave that Milt suspected he was counting on remaining behind so he could wait for Shanti to show.

When Anthi returned, steering Ted by the scruff of his neck, the five of them stepped out into the light of approaching evening. The church guardian leaped up to hold the door for them and seemed to wait for their reaction. They heard thunder off in the west from where lead-like clouds came rolling in.

"Remarkable!" Milt said, to appease the doorman without hinting at what he in truth had felt inside.

"You must return later tonight," the corpulent man said, addressing Anthi.

"Why so?" she asked.

"For a special celebration," the man said. "In the old stable, after eight."

"The stable?" Milt quizzed, jumping on the man's suggestion.

"It is now our hall of exhibitions," their informant said. "The young holy man will conduct a special—ceremony."

"Guru Shanti, Shanti?" Gloria asked, seeming to ascend from thickening despair.

"Correct, Madame," the doorman replied, to Anthi rather than to Gloria.

"Maybe we will," Milt said, as he herded the others before him.

Ted seemed especially disturbed by the keeper's invitation.

"Quick!" Milt ordered. "We need to get in the van."

"What was that all about?" Christine demanded once they were inside and the doors were closed.

Without facing her, Milt answered, "I didn't think it was smart to let that fellow know our special interest in Shanti's celebration. Just a group of tourists, that's all we are. Ted, here, seemed on the verge of saying too much."

"Me?" Ted chimed in, the quiver of fake innocence in his voice. "Why would I do that?"

"I don't know, Ted," Milt said. "You tell us." He didn't expect a reply and got none. "In the meantime we'll ride around the grounds. Like tourists."

He turned the key, pulled the shift into reverse, and backed out to take the dirt road to the right, the north side, of the church. When they had gone the length of the building, the path divided, the right branch passing by a grove of substantial trees before arriving after two hundred meters at a large house constructed of stones similar to those of the church. Milt chose the narrower path to the left, which led toward a smaller structure made of ordinary brick.

"Is this the building you mentioned, Ted?" Milt asked, command in his voice.

In the rearview, he caught Ted's quick nod, but no words followed.

"What's in there, Ted?" Anthi asked.

"Don't know," he mumbled.

"Could she be in there?" Gloria demanded.

"No, woman," he said more firmly. "Not that I know."

Milt left the path and drove round the yard of the building until he had circled it. Beyond the shrubs and trees to the west, he could hear the roar, and catch scattered glimpses, of the clear Aude as it rolled over stones heading for its outlet he didn't know where. Beyond the river he again spotted thick, low clouds moving rapidly their way.

"It's going to storm," he said. "We'll need a dry place to wait it out."

Day Five

Night

Back in Limoux, at the south edge of the town, they located a restaurant, Le Jardin Gentil, that met the tough standards Christine and Anthi set for healthy food. Gloria and Milt went along with them while Ted seemed to accept his disenfranchised status.

From inside, staring out the large front window, they could hear the rush of the wind, the thunder, and the clatter of rain and hail on the front awning. Flashes of lightning eclipsed the glow of all the exterior illumination. Midway through the uncharacteristically bland French meal (despite clouds of thyme and oregano in the air), Gloria whispered something to Anthi, and the two of them left the table.

Rather than head toward the ladies' room as Milt expected, they stopped at a table where two men in uniform, presumably gendarmes, the police arm of the military, were enjoying their meal. Quickly, Milt was up and standing by their side so that he could hear what Gloria instructed Anthi to tell the officers.

In polished French that made her father proud, Anthi asked them to pardon the interruption of their meal but her friend was deeply troubled because her little daughter was missing, and she knew what the newspapers were saying about children in the region. The talkative officer expressed his concern and agreed that the deaths were terrible. He asked when Anthi's friend had last seen her daughter. Anthi explained that her friend had left the girl with her business partner, who then disappeared. The officer consulted his silent colleague, an older man with a trimmed black mustache, who said a few words in a whisper. The talkative policeman turned to face Gloria as he told Anthi not to worry, that the authorities were looking into the deaths of all children and that Gloria's partner had no doubt had an unexpected emergency come up or thought of something she needed from a shop in Carcassonne. She and Gloria's little one would certainly be back in Rennes-les-Bains when Gloria and her friend returned there.

Anthi sputtered out the first uncertain words of a protest, but the two officials had returned to their food and chitchat. Anthi and Gloria could go no further without accusing Shanti, Shanti, and so far their evidence against him depended on the stoned tale Ted had told them. Anthi, Milt knew, could guess as well as he could what the bon vivant gendarmes would say about that.

"I *had* to do it," Gloria explained in a tremulous voice as soon as the three of them returned to their own table. As she spoke, her eyes moved from Ted, whose face showed his anger, to Milt.

"I'm glad you did," Milt said. "I wish they had listened."

Ted shook his head. "We go to the cops and make Shanti angry, he could hurt Cathy."

"You think he's not planning to, no matter what we do?" Anthi scolded, incredulity in her frown.

"Okay, okay," Christine said, trying to calm the two. "We've got to focus on what's going to happen when we go back to the church grounds."

"Yeah," Milt added. "Who goes to Shanti's 'celebration'?"

"Gloria and I can pretend the way we did this morning," Christine answered. "What you think, my friend? Will he suspect you?"

"What about me?" Ted asked before Gloria could answer. "He'll trust me as much as her." Then he added, "More even."

The addition of Ted filled Milt with confusion. He still had no confidence in the younger man's stability but knew that what he was saying was probably true. The question, as Milt saw it, was whether any of them, including Ted himself, could count on Ted to play the role of Shanti's True Believer without becoming the part he was playing. But Cathy was his child. There was no way they could stop him from going in. And Christine would be there to keep an eye on him. Gloria too.

"Okay," Milt said. "Anthi and I will try to find a way in from the rear of the stables. We need to see and hear what happens."

"You have to be careful, Milt," his wife warned. "Your cardiovascular can't tolerate too much heroics."

"I'll remember," he said, but before she could say more, he added, "The rain's let up. It's getting late, and we have a plan. I'll pay—let's get out of here."

This time at the church Milt drove through the cluster of cars and campers, then passed the church itself and took a dirt path to the right that brought the van to a grove of large trees that blocked it from sight of the stables. Since it was almost time for the celebration, Christine, Gloria and Ted slipped from the camper and vanished through the trees. "Good luck!" he called softly after them.

"Don't wish all our luck away, Dad," Anthi said. "You and I may need some finding a way into the building."

"It's a stable, dear. Surely they won't have sealed off all the stalls." He wished he were as confident as his words sounded. "Stables have those doors that split in the middle, don't they, so horses can stick their necks out."

"I'll carry the tools," she said as she reached for the mustard-brown belt, with a holster for a small screwdriver and pliers, which Gloria had dug out of their camping gear. "You've got her flashlight."

As they stepped from the van and Anthi slid the door shut as quietly as possible, he saw through breaks in the trees the nearly full moon in the rain-washed sky illuminating a handful of columns and the single spire buttressing this side of the church. The scent of freshly washed pine flavored the air. The night, Milt felt, was too perfect for deeds like those Shanti had in mind.

"What do you think of Ted, Dad?" Anthi asked as they moved slowly through the shadows.

"I still don't trust him. I know he's confused, but the stakes are too high for him to act torn the way he does."

"Gloria's too good for him," Anthi announced. "I hate to think she'll keep on with him, however all this turns out."

"One thing at a time, young lady. First we find Cathy—there'll be time afterwards to worry about Gloria."

"*If* we find Cathy. Where do you think she is, Dad?"

"Hell if I know. I just hope we can pick up a clue tonight."

They were within a dozen yards of the stable now, but rather than use the open main door, they remained under the trees and circled to the back. With the flashlight Milt could see mismatched stains where stall doors had been sealed up with bricks. Before the new road cut the church off from the plowed fields on the other side of the asphalt, the stalls must have opened on a large sloping pasture where horses could gallop. With the horses gone, only the stall midway the building retained its original wooden door split horizontally in two.

"Let's see what we can do with that one," he said as he approached the door.

She passed the tool belt to him, and he moved the beam over the wood, bringing it to a focus in the middle where the free part of the upper door joined the lower half. There he spotted an ancient slide bolt that attached with downward pressure to the bottom half. He could already hear voices inside the stable growing loud.

"Let's hope when they converted this place they didn't add a bolt on the horse's side," he whispered. He tugged at the slide, but rust held it fast.

"Here—let me use these," she said as she drew the pliers from the holster and quickly took his place by the door.

"Don't let them hear you."

"I won't." With one hand she wrapped the knob on the bolt with part of the leather tool belt so that it cushioned the blow when she tapped with the working end of the pliers. The first tap turned the bolt, and the second raised it from the lower door. "There," she whispered. "What now?"

"My turn," he said and stepped again to the door, which he slowly pulled toward him.

Like the bolt, the hinges were rusty and gave off a series of high-pitched squeals as the old odors of a stable rushed out to engulf them. Fortunately the crowd inside were still milling about, chattering, and the inner half-wall across the stall, he could see, remained in place to baffle the noise he'd created. This wall would also cast enough shadow, he hoped, to hide their surreptitious entry. He reached inside and searched blindly for a way to release the lower half of the door so he would not have to tumble into an unexamined stall headfirst. *Just too old for acrobatics like this*, he told himself.

His hand struck what felt like a simple wooden latch, which he raised without thinking. Once the bottom opened, he quietly closed the window above and, invisible to those inside, crawled into the stall. He motioned for Anthi to follow.

Groping around in the half light, he discovered that the surviving stall was where the church stored a small tiller and other gardening tools as well as large burlap sacks of grains or seeds. Obviously the building remained only partly converted to an exhibition hall. From the dry scent he guessed the bags held grass seed. These leaned against the compartment's inner half-wall in a way that allowed the two intruders to rest their knees on them and stare like comic-book detectives over the upper edge of the divide at the gathering in the main part of the stable. This was a hundred or so feet long, roughly fifty feet wide, and, to Milt's astonishment, it was almost packed by people, their faces lit by large white lamps suspended from the ceiling. Although much of the stable floor remained dark, trampled dirt, the central third had been covered by wood flooring, the fresh varnish of which assaulted his nostrils from the other side of the partition.

The crowd included the faithful up front—Gerhardt, Ahmet, Kemala, the woman in white and her companion—joined now by Gloria, Ted, and Christine plus a hundred other people who seemed to have arranged themselves in couples. Back of his own group, Milt spotted an older man who could be the silent police officer from the restaurant, but he couldn't be certain because the man no longer wore his uniform jacket. An officer's presence, Milt told himself, would explain the gendarmes' feeble interest in Cathy's anguish.

The absence of children struck Milt immediately. He wondered where they were kept. Where Cathy was. The range of the adults' origins seemed clear in the light and dark of individual skins. Shanti, Shanti had used the Internet to spread his message to all inhabited continents, and the hopeful young of the planet had responded, or at least their self-appointed representatives had. Standing now on a small platform near the door midway the far wall and holding a small bullhorn that he did not raise to his mouth, he was calling them to attention. He wore freshly ironed white pants with an eastern jacket that matched, and he had trimmed his large side-whiskers. His eyes burned like Blake's tiger, Milt thought, but when he addressed them, he projected a gentle voice and calming manner.

"Please, please," he seemed to whisper, though his words echoed from each corner of the stable. "Please give me your attention, so we can begin our meditation. Please. We have much to do tonight, if we are to prepare ourselves."

From where Milt knelt, the young man's face fifteen yards away seemed, if anything, more composed than during the morning session. Even so, the mob quickly became an audience facing him, all senses receptive. As he called them to order, he used snatches of English, German, and French, but when he began his instruction he returned to English and stayed with it.

"Thank all of you for coming tonight," he said. "Your presence itself shows that what we are doing is of vital importance to all the corners of the earth that you represent. We must stop the insanity of the political and economic powers running the nations of the earth. Especially the economic forces, the vast corporations, since in most cases they control the political fronts behind which they hide. You are a true parliament of humankind. You are your nations' representatives, and you, working together, can cut through the pretense of nation states and political bodies to compel the holders of wealth to give up the ventures that bring drugs, exploitation, violence, and even wars into our lives. First you must become masters of your own powers, those that reside in the body."

Here Shanti, Shanti paused in his address and allowed his eyes to sweep the hall as though looking each of his followers in the eye. Milt ducked down before the stare reached the stall. He hoped that Anthi had ducked as well and that Shanti had seen neither of them. Her body, he sensed, had moved at the same moment as his.

From his crouched position, Milt for the first time noticed what ran above their heads. A black loft of some sort, maybe a dozen feet wide, seemed to cover all sides of the stable, and, in the shadows along the brick wall behind them, worn wooden steps descended to the stall. Must be where they stored hay, he told himself, when it was a working stable.

"Our goal tonight," Shanti went on as Milt lifted his head again, "is to make your body the servant of your spirit, to increase the spirit's dominion over it so that when each of you approaches the crisis moment you will be able to carry out your mission. For we will have only one more preliminary performance—before each of you will be asked to play your difficult part in our great project. Then the protest of all of you against the web of insanity that rules our lives will be preserved with our cameras, and that film will be replayed whenever and wherever spiritual men and women like yourselves are compelled as we are to embrace the ceremony of sacrifice. To render up their greatest treasure for the higher cause."

This fricking freak! Milt howled inwardly. It's mass murder he's planning! A bloodbath. He intends to video it. And little Cathy's about to become the curtain raiser for his Grand Guignol, a helpless Judy sacrificed before the horrific finale of this crazed Punch.

He bent over the divide to see how his own group had taken the revelation of Shanti's intent. Only Christine looked alarmed as she searched the rear of the building for her husband. *Over here!* he wanted to call to her. Gloria and Ted were still waiting for the leader to continue.

Shanti had paused as though collecting his wits for his next spiel, and this gave Milt time to calm his passions and see the grotesque logic of all that the insane guru was proposing. Born as the shadow of a murdered brother and sacrificed himself to his brother's absence, what revenge would he more naturally but unconsciously invent than the deaths of others in imitation of his famous predecessor, a pageant of beloved but unfortunate firstborns. And then to cover it over by adding the noblest of conscious projects, bringing sanity to the crazed world at large. The pieces, in Milt's mind, seemed to come together. *How can he be stopped?* he asked himself. *It's the piece that's missing.*

There was no time to figure it out, for Shanti had renewed his instruction. "We do not have adequate room tonight for you to relax your limbs by sitting or lying down, as is our usual practice. We must remain standing as we train our limbs to conform to our wills. And that is just as well, since when we arrive at our moment of destiny, we will need feet and arms and hands." He pointed to his own feet, raised his arms, and spread his fingers wide. Milt thought of an inept politician on the TV news back home, one he used to mock. "Relax; let your eyes close lightly and your shoulders drop comfortably down."

As Shanti took his followers through preliminary breath exercises similar to those he'd used in his morning session, Milt followed along, hoping the focus on nose and abdomen would calm his own revved up cardiac system. But his eyes defied his efforts to focus and wandered to the sweep of the loft as it stretched from above his head to the north and south ends of the building and continued its circuit there under the low hipped roof until both halves ended at the main door on the far side near which Shanti's platform stood. To the right of the door black steps similar to those behind his daughter and himself descended to the stable floor. *Just in case we need an escape exit*, he thought.

"Now, my faithful friends, I want you to relax your shoulders further; let your arms hang loose, and make certain you are standing straight with your head balanced on your shoulders. With eyes closed, imagine a silk string that lifts your head from a point above your ears and in the middle of your head." Milt found this hard to do while kneeling atop the sacks. "Let your right arm hang absolutely loose from your shoulder, and I will show you what power your spirit has over your body." Anthi, when he glanced at her, was also having difficulties following the young man's instructions. This, Milt told himself, was a good thing. We mustn't get sucked in by his hypnotic trance.

"Now focus all your attention on the socket where your arm joins your shoulder. With your mind, open that space, let your breath and energy flow into that socket, enlarging the area. Open it wide.

"With your eyes lightly closed, let your inward eye travel down your right arm, lengthening the muscles and tendons there. Let them relax. Let your mind flow into your elbow. Move all your breath and energy into that remarkable joint, opening it up, expanding it as wide as you can."

Try as he might, Milt in his detective posture could not imitate

Shanti's movements. He wanted to understand them and was almost tempted to stand. He caught himself before his limbs took over. He found his wife and the other two in the crowd and noticed that even Christine seemed to obey Shanti's directions as he led them through the same process for all the joints in wrist, palm, and fingers.

Then he said, "Now hold both arms out straight in front of you. You may have to turn to find a space between the people around you, but make sure they are straight out."

To Milt's surprise, when the three he was watching did so, their right hands stretched three, four, five inches farther than their left. Even Christine's did, and he figured she was probably the most skeptical person in the crowd. Gloria and Ted, of course, had no trouble creating five-inch extensions. They were far gone under Shanti's spell.

"Now, we must repeat the process on the left side—so you won't be lopsided." Shanti let a small cackle escape with his joke, and his followers did the same. Milt had to catch himself to keep from laughing, but he heard a snicker from Anthi. Their leader carried them through the same mesmerizing ritual for the left arm and asked them to stretch out their arms to make certain they were equal length again. This brought a collective giggle of relief from the group, after which their leader changed gears.

"We will work on our spines now. We need to stand erect and tall for the acts we will perform in the next day or two." His face grew deadly earnest. "Once more, make certain your shoulders are relaxed and your head is balanced square upon them." In obedience, his audience shuffled their feet and checked their postures. This time Milt sensed that he and Anthi remained the awkward exceptions.

As their guide continued, however, Milt found himself better able to conform to the instructions than before. "It is essential now, my faithful friends, that you visualize your spine as many spools stacked one upon the other so that your vital energy easily flows up and down and to all parts of your body. Think of the spaces between those small hooked cylinders. For the moment focus all your mental force on those gaps between the vertebrae. There are over thirty of them. Start with the spool at the base of your skull. Expand that space with your mind, make it grow so that you stand a hair taller. Focus all your attention now. Can you feel it budge that tenth of an inch?"

Although he asked only for mental energy, many in the crowd were straining physically to grow. It reminded Milt of the way people obeyed at the Oral Roberts tent meeting he had attended. He was only fourteen then and finally found himself against his will lifting his own arm with the rest and shouting out praise.

Here in the renovated stable, one of the most energetic proved to be the woman dressed all in white. She elevated her shoulders, extended her neck, and wiggled her arms and torso wildly. Again something about her features struck him as those of a woman he had seen before his return to France. He still didn't know where.

Christine, along with Gloria and Ted, seemed to blend with the rest of the crowd.

Shanti then divided the spine into its several regions—only *lumbar* rang a bell for Milt—and asked the devoted to give the parts of each area the sort of expansive treatment they had lavished on the first vertebrae. When Shanti reached the sacrum, he commanded them to gather all their extensions and other parts, and experience their new bodies. "Tomorrow night when we assemble on the cliffs with the river below us, you must stand to your full height and lift your arms upward to support your sacred sacrifice."

Milt failed to catch what Shanti said next, for he suddenly realized that at some point Gerhardt must have slipped from the building without his noticing and was now returning with a small child in his arms. For some reason the child was not struggling. Sedation seemed a likely explanation, given the size of the gathering and the meager age of the child. To Milt's instant relief, it was not Cathy. It was a girl dressed all in white, a costume much like the one Shanti himself wore. Her hair was curly and black, her skin a lovely tan.

Ahmet and Kemala's little girl! Milt told himself. In that second he saw Shanti reach within his white tunic and draw a long ritual blade from the waist of his trousers.

Without thinking, Milt whispered a firm command that startled Anthi from her trance, "Go to the van!" He handed her Gloria's keys. "Bring it to that door on the other side as quick as you can."

Then he was up the black steps and onto the dimly lit floor of the loft. Stumbling over forgotten bales of hay and discarded boards, he hurried to his right as quietly as he could, praying none of the boards had nails protruding to pierce the soft soles of his running shoes. Spiderwebs hung thick from the rafters, and the foul dust his shoes stirred up made his breathing difficult. The hip of the roof was so low he could not stand erect, and this posture threw his balance off so that as he moved he was forced to lurch forward and then catch himself.

Midway the north end of the loft, a stack of boards that looked like two-by-fours, three meters long, he guessed, blocked his way. As he scrambled around the stack, his hip knocked two of the planks loose. He managed to catch them just as they struck the floor at his feet.

Shanti's voice, a high-pitched singsong now, must have covered the clatter he was creating, since the guru did not pause: "Your arms are strong enough, your body tall enough. You will have the energy to follow our God-directed plan through to the appointed conclusion," Shanti chanted. "Just as our friends Ahmet and Kemala will raise up their beloved Mustafia, the Chosen One, for us tonight!"

"Oh my God!" Milt exclaimed, almost aloud. *No time left. I got to hurry.*

He rounded the final corner and began his frantic rush along the west side of the loft. *At least I'm on the van side now. Got to warn Christine and Gloria first. She'll have to decide about Ted. I don't trust him.*

This stretch of the loft presented fewer obstacles, and quicker than he expected he found himself half skidding down his exit stairs into the assembled faithful. He pushed his way gingerly through those who stood with eyes closed and arms up and made his way directly to Christine and the other two. "Take Gloria and get out that door!" he whispered as fiercely but not as loudly as he had to Anthi. Imitating the authority in Shanti's trance-inducing voice, he said, "Go directly to the van. Don't ask questions. I'll follow in a sec." He gave her a gentle shove toward the door.

Three more steps and he reached Gerhardt. "I'll take her," he whispered in the same tone. With force softened by firmness he pulled the lovely dark child from the younger man's arms and quickly wove his way toward the exit.

Apparently Gerhardt, in his own trance, had not had time to react because it was Shanti's voice he heard shout, "Stop that blasphemer!"

Milt was already out though the heavy door, shoving it closed with a heel kick into which he poured his weight. Hands still clutching Mustafia close, he managed to pull the thick outer bar down to block the door. But when he turned, expecting to see the van waiting with Anthi behind the wheel, it was not there. Instead, he saw Christine and Gloria, but not Ted, vanishing under the trees.

Then he heard the roar of the van's loud motor and saw it roll toward them from the thicket where they had hidden it. By the time it had stopped and the two women had scrambled in, he stood at its sliding door handing the groggy but frightened child up to a startled Gloria. Immediately he hopped inside and Christine slammed the door shut.

"Hit it!" he ordered Anthi. But she was already gouging grit out of the sandy soil.

For the first time he realized his heart was thumping wildly and likely had been since his shoes first struck the loft's upward stairs.

Day Five

Late

Shanti's followers must not have known about the stall door, for no one in the camper saw a black SUV monster in pursuit as they turned onto the main road and sped back toward Limoux. It was Anthi who roused them from their brief complacency: "What now? Are we kidnappers now?"

"She's such a lovely little girl," Christine sang as she leaned to examine what Gloria still held in her arms.

"Yes," Gloria said. "But—"

"But she's not Cathy," Milt said from the suicide seat to complete the thought Gloria apparently felt helpless to finish. "I know."

"I say we go to the gendarmes," Anthi offered. "Before they come for us!"

"And do what—" Christine asked, "turn ourselves in as kidnappers?"

"Hand this child—does anyone know her name?" Anthi began, and "Mustafia," the other three answered before she could add, "and turn her over to them?"

"What? Say we found her in the street?" Christine wondered out loud. "Claim she's an Algerian street waif?"

"Tell them the truth," Anthi shouted toward the back seat.

"I'll look after her," Gloria sang out, seeming to forget their true mission.

"Your father would be charged with kidnapping, wouldn't he?" Christine pointed out to Anthi.

Milt weighed the options before him, then said, "Not if we tell the total truth. How could they?"

"They could. Believe me—based on what I've seen of how police everywhere think," Christine said. "Pedophile kidnapper would be the first tag that jumped in their heads."

"Even with you there to back me up?" Milt was beginning to feel the right thing to do had become the least possible thing.

"Anthi and I are your family, dear. We have to protect our meal ticket and our good name. That's what the cops would think."

"Well, there's always the good old traditional way," Anthi said. "The drive-by."

"Drive-by?"

"And drop off. But not on the church steps—the cops' steps," Anthi said. "I'll even stay behind to watch—and make sure she doesn't lie there all night."

"They'll spot you," Christine cautioned.

"I'll wait at a café or bar nearby. Someplace like that."

Once back on the main traffic circle, they spotted the sign Anthi wanted, and she turned toward the office of police. It lay down a narrow side street that led almost to the river. They would likely have driven past except for a cluster of olive green cars near its entrance and a wide glass door brightly lit in an old building of stone that appeared brick red in the imperfect night lights.

"I see a café—it looks closed," Milt said.

"Damn!" Anthi mumbled. She had slowed the camper as though searching for a parking place. Milt knew parking in front of the station was not a good idea.

"There's only one step up to the entry," Milt said. "How sedated is Mustafia now?"

"She's not likely to go wandering off," Christine replied before Gloria could gather her thoughts, so engrossed was she in heaping caresses on this less than perfect replacement for her Cathy.

"It can't be long before Ahmet and Kemala show up here to report a kidnapping," Milt said.

"We can count on that, no matter how mystified Shanti had them," Christine said. "And we better be long gone."

Milt was stymied. Every possibility seemed fraught with risk. He sank deep inside himself, mulled over his options, and then said, "Pull over, Anthi. Under that tree."

She found a small space in the shadow created by the one large elm in the block diagonally opposite their target building.

"I hope they don't have outdoor cameras," he said and reached backward to Christine. "Give me the girl, dear."

Before Gloria could tighten her grasp, Christine eased Mustafia from her arms and did as he asked. Instantly he was out the door and moving silently through the lights and shadows toward the glass entry where a bronze plaque read "Sous-Prefecture." With the quickness of a younger man in full health, he propped the bundle of white silk chiffon, dark curls, and tan limbs against the sill where the door would open. They can't miss you, little dear, he whispered. The officers he saw inside were engaged in high-powered conversation, but they would see the child as soon as they turned. Before they could do so, he was heading back to the shadows where the van was backing up to leave.

Christine pushed the already cracked passenger door open, and he climbed inside.

"What if they don't find her?" his wife asked.

"What will happen to her?" Gloria wondered as though still spellbound. "And Cathy?"

Anthi answered for him: "Don't worry, Christine. I've got my cell. We'll wait three minutes, and I'll call. We'll be out of town."

"They'll track your number, dear," her father warned, realizing no one had answered Gloria.

"Then, we'll find a pay phone." She sounded very sure of herself.

Day Six

Morning

After their return from Limoux, Milt had difficulty getting to sleep. He reassured himself that the gendarmes had quickly found Mustafia—but enough doubt lingered to compound his other fears and keep him thrashing arms and legs about.

They had parked the van for the night back at the campground under the oak where it usually stood, but Anthi insisted that Gloria share her room in the hotel. None of them could predict what Ted might do to Gloria if he found his way back to Rennes-les-Bains. Milt realized too that in Mustafia's absence little Cathy almost surely returned to the top of Shanti's list and was certain to be the chief attraction at the next evening's finale by the river. Yet they had made no progress in locating Gloria's dear girl, and he now had no idea where they were hiding her. Cathy's whereabouts remained the most profound of the anxieties that kept him tossing about in bed. He could not imagine that Gloria was finding it easier to block her own worry and sink into vital slumber.

Fortunately Christine and he had sufficient supplies in their room that when morning finally came they would not have to confront the media mob or any of Shanti's faithful who might be ravaging their usual breakfast spot. Taking what comfort he could find in this small reflection, he ultimately fell out of his tumult into a sleep haunted by dreams. It was toward first light that he found himself walking across a familiar farm following tracks cut through the grass and weeds by dogs. Near the right side of the track he spotted a chest-high pile of rubble, dirt mixed with stones both rough and chiseled, plus what must be charnel-house bones.

He shoved the boulders aside to discover a dark opening the size of a human skull.

More of the rubble simply vanishes to reveal the entrance to what must be a small cave. A rank odor rises to meet him. He wonders if it can be one of the long-abandoned gold mines said to have existed centuries ago on these farms. This one he now realizes belongs to his grandmother.

Instantly he is out on a ledge, the upper arc of the spherical hollow in the earth that is the mine. He leans out over the edge and spots yellow splotches scattered below him in the black walls of the cave. They seem too yellow to be gold. False gold maybe.

Now the crust that forms his ledge feels much too thin to support him. *What will happen if I fall in?* he wonders. *Is there another exit somewhere I can walk to?*

He has somehow to get off this thin ledge but finds he can't squirm backwards lengthwise without pressing too much of his weight on the fragile edge. It's too risky—he can't rush it.

He has to find a way to flip around and crawl forward off his flimsy support. But he can't get the traction he needs. Can he crabwalk his way off sideways? If he falls in, will anyone find him down there? His panic wakes him, his sweating body chilled through.

It was while the four of them ate their limited breakfast on the balcony over the river that Milt, still shaken by his dream and what it said about their horrible quandary, brought up the worry on everyone's mind: the safety of Cathy.

"When I lose my keys," Anthi offered, "I always go to the last place I remember placing them and start from there."

"That would be Gloria's office," Christine said. "Are there any hidden rooms there, Gloria?"

"What?" Gloria said, looking suddenly at Christine. She had

not spoken to Milt or his wife, so stunned was she from events the night before.

"Any out-of-the-way rooms in your studio?" Christine repeated.

"No," Gloria said and retreated into solitude.

"Aimee's house appears empty this morning, the way we left it yesterday," Milt said. He could see the small, neat two-story thirty yards or so up the river from them. "No signs of life there."

"One thing I remember from last night," Anthi said, "was how quickly Gerhardt was able to get his hands on little Mustafia and bring her in to Shanti."

"What are you suggesting?" He suspected where she might be heading.

"That there might be some place on the church grounds, or nearby, that he hides the kids," Anthi explained.

"It's not in the church, that's for sure," Christine said.

"There are other buildings around it," Anthi insisted.

"Mustafia could have been stashed in the SUV," Christine reminded them.

"We can't get our hands on Shanti's truck," Milt said. "But we may be able—"

"—to explore the grounds," Anthi said to speed his thought.

He turned his attention to their quiet friend. "I think you'll be safer, Gloria, if you come with us."

Cathy's mother looked up at him with absolute confusion of grief and fear in her eyes.

Determined as they were, they had no real idea where to start as, after their hour's drive, they let the camper glide past the main door of the church and slip again into the cover of the trees. Rather than stop in the first grove where they'd parked the evening before, Milt let it roll on back to a thicket behind the church. From here they could see the smaller building he had circled the day before, then promptly forgotten, and a second structure attached to the rear of the church itself. This one was made of large brown bricks and was almost as wide as the sanctuary but not half its height.

"Any of you know what purpose that place serves?" He nodded toward the addition.

"It might be the rectory," Christine suggested. She didn't remember much about the church, also Roman, of her childhood, but her guess could be right.

"Or an entrance to the crypt," Anthi added, with a macabre glee left over, he guessed, from an abbreviated Goth period in her adolescence.

"Think it's worth a look?" Milt asked.

The two talkative women consented. As they exited the van, the third followed them without being asked.

With no one in sight, they nonetheless approached the smaller building with caution, fearing the caretaker might any second appear from within. When they reached the far end and the only door, they found it locked.

Milt ran his fingers along the top of the frame but found no key. Anthi searched along the frame on the hinged side of the door. "Voila!" she whispered. But when she tried the key in the rusty lock, it wouldn't move.

"Let me try," Christine said. She rotated it the opposite direction "See what a little expertise can do."

"At what?" Anthi teased. "Breaking and entering?"

"Among other things," Christine replied.

Milt realized they were only trying to dissolve the tension all of them felt but asked for quiet as he pushed the door ajar. Although the shutters were closed, there was enough light to see this was not the rectory. It seemed safe to open the door wider, far enough to make out tools on the concrete floor—shovels, a pickax, a wheelbarrow, several buckets. "I think you are right, Anthi. It's the crypt entry—maybe."

The four of them rushed in, and he closed the door after them, leaving them in the dim, musty heat of the room—but not before Milt spotted a shelve with a row of yellow battery lanterns. These he hurried to before his visual memory of their location could fade. He seized one, found the switch and sent a large beam into the room. "Eureka," Anthi whispered. With his free hand he distributed a light to each of the others. "Love these square ones," he said with enthusiasm. "Hold on to it—you may need it where we're going." He was thinking of the door his beam had revealed in the back wall of the room, one that likely led into, or under, the alcove of the Dark Sarah he'd studied assiduously the previous afternoon. Without hesitation he headed for the door.

As with the first, it was locked, but Christine found a key and opened it with the same flourish as before. Instantly, they stood startled by the abyss of blackness waiting before them. Only when Gloria, alert now, cast her beam into the chasm, could they see that steep, narrow steps, carved from rock, circled down into darkness.

"Let's go, gang," Anthi called to the others as she began the descent, her light bouncing off the opposite wall of the vertical tunnel they must use.

After a dozen or so slippery steps, they exited in a much wider, horizontal tunnel carved originally in the soft stone of the region by underground streams, he guessed, but squared up by generations of human labor, men searching for something, perhaps for artifacts of Dark Sarah. This, he realized, was the subterranean world that had kept her safe for centuries. This was her earth. And the Black Madonna's, he told himself.

Though the air down here was a few degrees cooler, it was also rank and heavy.

They moved their cones of light around the ominous space,

revealing passageways to right, left, and straight ahead. The one to the left, he figured, must lead to the crypt, since it would take them back under the church. The whole area down here resembled the catacombs and Mithraic abattoir beneath San Clemente in Rome. The image crossed his brain of a Roman soldier just returned from the Orient lying on his back under a black bull, whose belly he slashes with his stained sword until he is bathed clean in the blood of the sacred bull. The vision fills Milt with a gross fascination. He can't wash the association out of his head.

"Let's try this one," Anthi called as she sent her beam into the tunnel to their right.

As their feet knocked up the bone-like dust of the floor and their beams bounced from the dull walls, he wondered where his daughter was leading them. And the abattoir continued to bother him.

After a couple of dozen cautious paces, their battery of lights fell on wooden steps that led up to a short tunnel through the rock and, above that, to a trapdoor. From further down the tunnel, he heard the faint rumble of water over rocks and guessed it must lead to the river. He placed his free hand on the wall. It was damp. The river seemed to pull a barely detectable breeze through the tunnel.

"This has to be the house set back from the church," Christine whispered.

"Cathy could—could be up there," Gloria choked, wild with hope.

"If she is, we better keep quiet," Anthi warned. "Wait while I give it a try."

While the others lit her way, she inched up the flimsy planks to the door, against which she pressed softly. It budged, and she pushed it open enough to scan part of the space above. The heat rushed down on them. Even when the hinges protested, they heard no scuffle of feet or disruption of furniture over their heads. She gave a more determined thrust, and they held their breaths and dropped their beams as the trapdoor rose in the air. Still no reaction above, and they exhaled more easily as Anthi's head disappeared into the unseen.

"Nothing," she mumbled and descended to them again.

"Let me see," her father said as he took her place on the steps. When he had the door, he shoved it back completely and moved his head into the unknown space, which he surveyed quickly in all directions. It reeked of fertilizers. In the dimness he could make out gardening tools, a dusty-looking cot, and a desk. "Storage—maybe a monk's cell once," he explained as he closed the trap over his head and rejoined his three companions.

"What's that I hear?" Gloria wanted to know as she pointed ahead of them.

"Must lead to the river," he said. "We won't go there until tonight."

He didn't believe Gloria needed to see the setting Shanti had chosen for his twisted ritual until it was absolutely necessary. Along with this thought, the image of the altar from the Bugarach infanticide rushed like the heat through him. Then the abattoir again.

"Let's take that other tunnel," his daughter suggested. "The one that must lead downhill—maybe toward the old fountain we saw as we drove up to the church."

No one objected. They retraced their way uphill through the tunnel to the juncture where they'd descended from ground level. Here they chose the neglected passage that led right, at ninety degrees from the one already explored. Now the descent became more rapid, and similar, Milt felt, to entering the pyramids and tombs in Egypt. It was also narrower and lower than the first they had taken, forcing Milt and Anthi to lean far forward, doubly tasking his breath and energy. He was sweating now. The walls were weedy and dotted with severed roots. The distance to the fountain had to be three times that to the house behind the church. The earth underfoot felt more moist and slippery, the air danker than before, but less musty than moist.

His shirt stuck to his back and arms. Even the walls were damp. Water must still run through here, he thought, when it rains. They haven't squared the ceiling here or smoothed the walls as carefully.

The descent seemed to have no end. Anthi and Christine were grunting now and complaining. Gloria's blouse had wet splotches across the back and down to her waist, but she seemed absorbed in her desire to discover Cathy. The way she managed to keep going kept surprising him. He intended that her hope last until her child was with them again.

Suddenly Christine's beam struck steps carved in the rock ahead on their left. Again they led upward. Driven by a sudden need to stand erect and stretch his back, Milt moved forward and crawled hand and foot up the steps. Although his change of posture partially relieved his back, it wasn't the extension of muscles he needed. The distance up turned out to be triple that leading to the house with gardening tools.

When he neared the top, it wasn't a trapdoor that covered the exit but a rusted grate roughly the width of his shoulders. He was staring up into an immense granite bowl that he guessed belonged to the ancient fountain. In the center stood a pedestal bearing a smaller bowl. Three doves dotted the lip of this second bowl.

As though his body mimicked the need of water itself to flow, he pressed arms and shoulders against the grate, shoved it up into the larger bowl, and climbed until he was erect. The doves scattered. It was like bursting free of the dark earth into pure air and new life.

There was no one in sight, but behind the pedestal crouched a large white cat, its eyes alert for the birds. It did not stir at the sight of the man who stood there and stretched, then ducked back to lower the grate into place.

"What'd you see?" Gloria demanded as soon as his feet were visible from below.

"It's just the fountain—and a cat. Nobody's there."

Anthi reentered the area where they stood—clearly returning from farther along the passage. "I think I found something," she said and shone her beam in the direction from which she had just come.

As the others without speaking followed her, Milt feared she might be leading them to the discovery he dreaded most.

The tunnel gradually climbed now and widened, the footing grew more solid, the air less moist but no fresher. Five paces ahead of them, Anthi's beam landed on an opening cut in the left wall. It was four feet square and about two feet above the floor of the tunnel. In his mind it was the abattoir again.

As they drew closer, she sent her shaft of light through the opening, exposing a side chamber that resembled a room cut into the rock and the dry gray clay here. Anthi climbed through the aperture, and first Gloria, then Christine and Milt, followed.

The first two in were lighting up every corner with their flashlights. They saw two cots with crumpled sheets thrown back and a rustic table with three metal plates painted white. Scattered on the table and plates lay bread ends, a largely eaten round of yellow cheese, two or three apple cores, and skins from several oranges. A tin of advanced formula for toddlers and a half-empty small milk bottle stood at the end of the table not covered by plates and scraps. This must be where they keep the kids, Milt thought, but he hesitated to share his guess with Gloria.

Then the light in Gloria's hand picked up a small flash of color that drew her instantly to one end of the smaller cot. "She was here!" she cried. "This is the bracelet I made her." Her eyes burning in the flash of the lights, she held up five plastic beads of varied colors with an elastic string running through them.

"They haven't been gone long," Anthi said, poking a finger into the orange peels. "Maybe only twenty minutes or so."

"I wonder if they heard us coming," Christine added.

"They must have," Anthi said. "They left in a hurry."

"No wonder they produced Ahmet's child so quickly," Milt thought aloud. "There must be a tunnel to the stable."

"We know she is alive," Gloria exclaimed. "This is the formula I use when I'm too busy to breastfeed. Ted is with her. Thank God."

Milt wasn't certain Ted's presence was something they should be altogether thankful for. Not if he'd rejoined Shanti's twisted cult and was ready to sacrifice Cathy at tonight's ritual.

On one of the beds a familiar book jacket caught his eye, and his blood pooled in his limbs. It was *Deepest France*—the original hardback from five years ago. It showed silhouettes of a small boy, a woman, and a crow printed in black against a scarlet background. Someone was reading it—and not for the first time, judging from the worn look of jacket and pages. Must belong to Shanti, he told himself as fear and a tinge of guilt shot through his veins.

His blood flowing strong, he focused on a single detail, the edge of a photograph, he thought, marking a page more than halfway through the novel. He seized the volume and flipped it open to the picture.

A woman stared back at him; it was a face he recognized and one he had seen many times—at Shanti's meditation in the stable last night and in Rennes-le-Chateau earlier the same day. And dressed all in white sitting in front of his hotel his first day back.

And—and when? Twenty years—twenty years ago in all the newspapers of France. It had to be. The woman all in white had to be Christine Plantard, little Charles's mother, mother of all France. But aged those twenty years—her face slighty puffy now; the neck larger and looser; the brown eyes, her son's eyes, dimmer; the rich brown hair without its luster. Hidden within the face of a woman ravaged by middle age and the misfortune of her fame, Christine Plantard lay buried. But still alive. If disembodied Gnostics are ever fully alive, he amended. No one knows better than I what she's capable of.

"We have got to find Cathy!" he howled inwardly, just loud enough to freeze the others with his terror.

Day Six

Afternoon

Milt's desperate resolve did nothing to diminish their confusion about the place Shanti, Aimee, Ted and the others were hiding Gloria's daughter now that Shanti and his gang had scrambled out of their lair under the church property. They apparently had come very close to finding little Cathy, but her captors could have dragged her anywhere in the tunnels. The four of them continued exploring the branches in each direction. North, south, east, west they had turned—heading at least a hundred meters in each of the cardinal directions. As far as they knew, an entrance—or *exit*—might exist for every branch for those familiar with the network.

"These could go on forever," Anthi exclaimed as her exasperation kept escalating.

"They create a web. Endless connections," Christine said. "Like something I'd knit in a nightmare."

"Wherever any underground river ever flowed," Milt said, thinking, *For all I know, they even connect with that hollow-earth system at the Bugarach peak. And the cave where she killed her first son falls within the same network.* He remembered the stark scene he created in his novel: the other flashing beams, the dark cords, the jabs with the two knives. The images sent frissons up his back into his scalp.

"I read somewhere they honeycomb the whole of France," Anthi volunteered.

Before they sank into total exhaustion, Christine led them back toward the steps beneath the crypt's entry house from which they had descended. But when they reentered the open area where all the corridors joined, their beams lit up a rumpled figure at the foot of the stairs, a man blocking their way, a rake with long prongs held tight across his chest.

"Damn!" they exploded, seemingly in a single voice as Milt flashed his light up to the face. He recognized the doorman who'd admitted them to the church on their first visit. Here he seemed much larger—an abattoir monster.

"Pourquoi?" the man demanded and, waving the rake menacingly, launched into a string of angry words Milt did not understand. In his free hand he held a large flashlight that he now lit and turned on them.

"He says this is private church property," Anthi translated. "He wants to know why we are here. We could get in real trouble. What do I tell him?"

"I don't know," her father mumbled as he tried to invent a sensible story. "Tell him we tried to visit the crypt and got lost."

She blinked twice then did as he said. As their paunchy impediment swung his eyes-threatening rake again, Milt grabbed her shoulder to pull her back.

"Tell him we need to use the steps to get to our van so we can leave. And be careful."

She tried again. When she was finished, she faced her father. "I don't think he's buying it."

"Try again. We didn't disturb anything, tell him."

Anthi rattled off her French once again, after which the caretaker turned his beam on all of them and examined them head to foot the way a policeman would study a suspect in a dark alleyway. Milt's hope crashed into the tunnel's floor.

To his surprise, after the flashlight examination their obstacle stepped aside and motioned with his tool to Christine and Gloria for them to move ahead to the stairs, then to Anthi. As they disappeared one by one, Milt feared for a moment that he would be left alone with this guardian of tunnels whose words he barely understood.

After another examination with the light, the shabby minotaur signaled him to follow his women. The grotesque figure remained tight on Milt's tail as he went by, the prongs almost grazing his legs as he mounted the first step. He felt it wise not to look back and risk showing his fear.

In this way they crawled quickly back up into the dusty room and hurled themselves out into fresh air. Only now did they realize that the monster had not followed them. Maybe he was gone instead to discover if they had removed anything from the side chamber. Did he even know Shanti's band had used it?

They filled their lungs and expelled the darkness and mildew.

Taking no time to celebrate their good luck, they scrambled to the camper to rest and drink the water Gloria offered from her large thermos.

"Have we run out of workable clues?" Milt asked as he and Gloria leaned over the beige backs of the front seats to face Christine and Anthi.

"I can't think of any," Christine groaned.

A moment of silence passed before Anthi said, "Me either."

"We've got to come up with something," Milt said, urging them to rethink their options. He couldn't shake the abattoir, not the way it had a hold on him.

Memory traces of the abattoir, now that he was out of the church underground, led him to his earlier descents into caves, tunnels, prehistory—the mammoth-painted chambers at nearby Lombrives, where the last Cathars perished at the hands of the Church; the black, always plunging burrow of the half-million-year-old man of Petralona outside Thessaloniki, its tunnels far longer precursors of the low, narrow entries to Giza pyramids. How had humans, even near-humans, lived in this blackness? Like animals, it had to be. But without the high-minded animalism that created the cruelty whose remnants they had discovered up above Bugarach. Now that he thought of it again, Anthi could be right; the mountain's fissures could open to a worldwide network of such caverns, all connected.

And the Hollow Earth legend is real after all, he concluded with a stab of self-mockery.

Even so, he still recalled his own passage into the modern madness as he was led one cold spring morning down into an unbelievably vast salt mine somewhere in the west of France; he didn't remember which village. Local residents within living memory had sheltered there from fire and explosions out of the sky. Worse again than animals, he thought, their bombardment. But sheltered safely, it turned out, like that Madonna safe in the earth. We're retreating to it again, are we—our underground half-life. Could be it's always waiting within us. In Shanti anyway. And all we need are his high-minded junk promises to open the downward door—the way San Clemente above opens to the abattoir. Such high-mindedness might explain a great deal of insanity, mightn't it?

Gloria raised her head, her eyes bright again, and then said, "Shanti mentioned something was going to happen tonight on the cliffs by the river." For some reason, her words broke his bitter reverie and forced relief up through his body.

"You're right," he said quickly. So much had happened in the tunnels, so many trains of association followed, that he had failed to connect the details of Shanti's prediction directly to their desperate search. "Where on the river?"

"From what I recall of his words," Anthi helped, "the cliffs stretch down from the stable and the church to the river."

Christine squeezed Anthi's knee in a familial clasp and turned a beaming face her way. "Good for you, Anthi. We heard the river in the tunnel this morning. It would be an easy run from their cave or the gardeners' house."

Considering the fall and rise of the terrain, Milt figured the river must be no more than a few hundred yards from where the van now stood, but brush and scattered trees blocked its sound and their vision of the rushing waters.

"Shouldn't we head down there?" Gloria asked.

"Get the lay of the land while there's daylight," Anthi urged.

"I don't think so," Milt said. "If Shanti's bunch spots us, it'll freak them. And this is the best lead we've got. We don't want them to pick a new location, do we?"

"We have to do something," Gloria insisted. "I do. I can't just sit like this until tonight."

They could do little until night, they found out, that would lead directly to Cathy's whereabouts. It was Christine, however, who came up with a way to put the intolerable afternoon to good use.

"I think we should find out what became of Mustafia," she said.

"And get arrested for kidnappers?" Anthi cautioned.

"There's a way to avoid that," Christine said.

"I don't see how," Milt objected, knowing he was the one most vulnerable to arrest for Mustafia's kidnapping.

"I could go to the police as a friend of Kemala," Gloria said, obviously eager to stay busy.

"And no one in the Rennes has anything on me," Christine pointed out. "Or even knows who I am."

"But they may know your last name," Milt warned, "the way they would Anthi's."

"I'll use my maiden name," she countered. "It's still on my passport."

Milt's concern forced him to hesitate, but he decided Gloria and Christine felt a deep need to learn Mustafia's fate. He started the motor for the ten-minute drive into Limoux.

The streets around the gendarmerie were far more animated now than the night before. A small market had sprung up a block nearer the river, and the vans of farmers, fishermen, butchers, and impatient shoppers jammed the parking areas throughout this sector of the town. Milt drove around until he found a curb he could ram the tires up on, the way many other drivers had done. Anthi and he, he said, should stay with the camper in case a policeman took exception to his parking.

"You guys need to keep cool in the station, Christine," he cautioned once Gloria was out of the van.

"I know. We're just here as concerned individuals." She was whispering.

"If the cops are looking for witnesses, you don't know what was going on. It was a meditation session, and you are worried about a child who was jerked away."

"Got it, hon." She was eager to get going.

"If they ask how you knew where Mustafa was dropped off," Anthi instructed, "say you saw it on the news that she turned up here. You don't know any of the people involved, especially the fellow who took the girl."

"Of course not," Christine said.

"And help her," he nodded toward where Gloria waited. "Help her contain her emotions."

"Yes, dear." With that, Christine pulled the sliding door shut after her.

Milt and Anthi spent the next half hour staring at one another in the van, paging through Gloria's books and magazines, squirming uncomfortably. When they did speak, it was to express their anxiety about what might be happening in the station.

"Can Christine pull it off?" Anthi asked.

"She can. If Gloria doesn't lose it."

"She's been on edge for days."

"She needs to get the anxiety out of her system," Milt said. "At least until we can do something to solve it."

"Can Christine contain her?"

"If anyone can."

"What you think makes Shanti do these things?" Anthi asked.

"I have a suspicion. What d'*you* figure?"

"Sibling inferiority," she said. "Like me and Nick—but a million times worse."

"That plus—"

"Yeah?"

"A confusion of ends and means. That a lovely end justifies any means. The eternal disease—of idealists."

Anthi looked at him, astonishment in her face. "You think he actually believes his own crap."

"It's possible," he muttered, acting as though he was starting to doubt his take on Shanti. "You must've become more skeptical than I am, young woman."

"I know who taught me, Pops," she said, a note of irony in her voice.

When the two women returned, he could tell immediately that things hadn't gone well. Christine's face showed her irritation. Gloria seemed angry about something, perhaps at Christine, or the gendarmes.

"So they didn't arrest either of you," Anthi kidded with relief.

"Not quite," Christine said, no smile on her face.

"How did it go?" Milt asked and tried to match his wife's mood.

"Mustafia's safe," Christine reassured them. "Her parents came for her last night. They told the cops they would leave the area."

"Good to hear," Anthi said with a nervous bubble of laughter.

"Yeah," Christine said. "Apparently our 'kidnapping' shook both of them up. And gave them time to give Shanti's promises serious thought."

"What about you, young woman?" he said reaching to help Gloria up into the van, realizing as he did so that he regularly used the same designation with Anthi.

"I am relieved to hear Mustafia is back with Kemala," Gloria replied with great energy. "But they should find Cathy, I told them. They should stop all this killing."

Milt looked to Christine for her response to Gloria's outburst. When she just shook her head, he turned back to Gloria. "What did they say?"

"I can't understand their French." She bent her head as though ashamed. "You have to ask Christine."

"Or their English," Christine explained. "Who knows what they made of all Gloria said."

"She didn't mention anything about Dad, I hope, or the way Mustafia got to their station door," Anthi said.

"They won't connect us to that," Christine answered. "Not unless they followed us out of the station."

"Did they?" Anthi needed to know.

"No sign of it," Christine reassured.

Milt didn't feel the same certainty. All at once the fishermen, farmers, jam makers, and shoppers swarming around them took a new identity. Even the little fellow with the snap-brim cap and mustache reading his paper and sipping his coffee outside the café between them and the station appeared to keep one eye on their van. It was like living in Greece again during the Junta years when every American was kept under surveillance.

"We need to get out of here," he growled as he flipped the key to restart the engine.

Day Six

Night

Their afternoon wait became an agony of desperate wills and delayed expectations. The four of them shared the common goal, to free little Cathy and all the other children, but they knew they must wait until at least eight that evening before they could act. Their plans for ways to spend the empty, frantic hours until then kept wavering. Should they scout the river cliffs? Should they search the sites of the earlier infanticides for clues? Should they attempt to kill the nervous hours reading and listening to music? The first seemed unwise, the second a waste of time, and the third lot inadequate. By default, reading, though a futile evasion, won out.

Between Limoux and Couiza, a hundred feet from the road, they found a shady grove of trees with large leaves and white trunks protected on one side by the river. Milt parked the van. He and his expanded family pulled down the old magazines and newspapers stored in the cabinet over the bench bed and pretended to catch up on French fashions, rock music, and deteriorating international politics.

Pretense proved even more impossible for Gloria than the others. She slipped silently from her camper and began to wander the river bank, but she never, Milt was careful to note, entirely left sight of the van. Apparently she was both distressed and afraid. When he got out to stretch his legs, he could hear her muttering to herself. From the fragments he was able to pick up, she seemed to be blaming herself for losing Cathy. He caught the names of Shanti, Ted, and Aimee recurring in her mea culpa. He wanted to tell her she need not blame herself, since her decisions arose from the deceptions of the others. If he went to her, he knew his fatherly protection would likely give way to the emotions he felt during his first session on her massage table. With her dark bangs fallen across her brow and long hair loose now about her shoulders, she was at least as lovely as she had appeared that morning. The mix of impulses felt too creepy for him to sort out, especially given the extraordinary pressure the two of them—all of them—were under.

Ultimately it was pragmatic Christine who came up with the project that brought them back together: a desperate dinner. Along the road she had spotted a sign for a restaurant specializing in trout from the mountain streams.

They backtracked a few kilometers, parked, and hurried to the small white building that housed the restaurant. But as Anthi and Christine reached the steps down to its wraparound porch, a man in a white jacket appeared and replaced the placard on the easel there with another card announcing that the restaurant was full. Milt saw both women shrug in exaggerated disappointment—one more frustrating and failed effort to dismiss the intolerable worry from mind. The waiter noticed their shrug and quickly requested the number of persons. When Anthi signaled "four," he motioned for all of them to come ahead. He led them down the steps and around the building to a dining terrace with half a dozen tables.

Milt was startled to find himself high on a cliff staring out over the river. The restaurant had been built in a hollow created by the waters swirling around boulders and working apparently on softer soil. The terrace seemed to be floating eerily in air over the river.

Their host steered them to the only free table, a not very large one placed against the inner, walled area of the terrace. Above them, the well-lit dining area inside held six or seven tables squeezed tightly together. "It's better out here," Milt whispered to Christine. Despite his larger worries, he felt they were fortunate to be admitted for the final table.

After they were sitting, it dawned on him how carefully dressed all the other diners were. He feared the shorts, T-shirts, sandals, and tennis shoes his group were wearing weren't appropriate. Seldom did he let these things matter, especially when he was traveling. But in this crowd he suspected his clothes would seem an offense to French taste. All the men wore Izod or Polo brand shirts with an alligator or polo player on them and the deck shoes Milt still associated with Virginia Beach shag dancers from the fifties. The women had on sexy sundresses with large flower prints on them and halter tops that tied back of the neck, a style copied from the American fifties too, or maybe the forties; he wasn't sure. All of them looked so much the same that he wondered whether he had wandered into a cult even more rigid than Shanti's and potentially as menacing. Perhaps some twisted Stepford clan. No, he cautioned himself, don't get all nutty now. It has to be they are coming from a shoot for some department store ad.

When the menus arrived and he discovered just how many Euros a kilo of the trout cost, he decided the only cult here might be that of recycled bourgeois fashions. He settled for the fish soup, only an appetizer, while the three women said they would split a kilo of trout. That, he thought, would be enough, and it appeared so when the chef showed them the huge grilled fish. But the chef took it back to the kitchen, and their waiter returned with the morsels he had liberated from the bones. In this new state it seemed a paltry amount for three who hadn't eaten a substantial meal since dinner the previous night.

As he nursed his soup and water (no wine at these prices) through the complete ritual, he pondered his options once they encountered Shanti. Certainly Shanti's people would not allow him to repeat his disruption the night before. The bodyguards would not let him near their leader or any of the children. He would have to count on Gloria or Christine, and Gloria seemed increasingly unpredictable.

The impossibilities continued to baffle him, but he refused to scare his friends with his dread.

Now the rich bisque of butter, pepper, and fish pieces was churning in his gut. Fortunately it did not take his group long to consume their morsels and their salads, and it was with great relief that he paid the bill and escaped from the crowd that, as the meal wore on, seemed to grow more sinister because progressively more focused on the intrusive foreigners.

"Jezuus," he muttered, as they climbed back from the hollow to the parking area, "was that the *Night of the Living Dead* or not!"

"The Stepford wives and their consorts," Christine offered, confirming his own suspicion. "Even Shanti would get freaked by those zombies."

"They're just being French," Anthi explained. "They feel sorry for Americans since Iraq. Genuine sorrow, not their habitual overcompensating superiority."

"Some improvement," Christine mocked.

Gloria remained silent in her own world, the world of dread to which he knew they must now return.

Day Six

The Ledge

With the camper tucked safely in the familiar stand of elms and the dark creeping in on them, they tramped around the church grounds toward the downward sloping hundred meters of low brush that led toward the river. The ill-formed path along which Anthi was leading them ultimately opened on one jagged corner of a cleared field where a grass of some sturdy variety had grown. Here, they spotted an Asian couple coming toward them from a line of trees, the man carrying a small girl maybe five on his back. The woman looked exceptionally tall to Milton for an Asian woman, possibly five feet seven or eight. The man was of roughly equal height, and the girl seemed long and lanky—too old, Milt hoped, for Shanti's purposes. The woman carried herself with an elegant grace, her swirls of raven hair, long enough to reach her waist, flying lightly with each step. She gave Milt the impression that she was in a hurry to leave the river. The man lacked her elegance, perhaps because the weight of the girl pushed his head forward, and he lacked her fine features, especially about his nose, which reminded Milt of a small new potato.

"They not there," the woman cautioned as soon as Milt's group nodded their polite greetings.

"The young guru?" Milt asked.

When the woman nodded, the man said, "She left sign.... ," then corrected himself, "*He* left sign."

The three hurried away along the path Milt's four had worn.

"What was that about?" Christine asked as she halted in her tracks, irritation written across her face.

"We knew it might happen," Milt replied. "After what we did last night, he realizes somebody is onto him."

"You think he has trashed his big event?" Christine asked.

"No way," Anthi said. "Not if his ego is as much at stake as Dad believes."

"We can't let him vanish—he's got Cathy," Gloria blurted with a show of anguish.

"Don't worry, Gloria. He won't just vanish, I promise you," Milt said. Under his breath, he mumbled, "I hope."

They entered the row of trees for ten yards or so, and came out on a granite ledge fifteen feet above the river. It formed a natural floor about twenty-five feet wide and ran along the river for roughly thirty yards. Milt could imagine Shanti controlling his crowd from the boulder near the middle along the trees, but there was no one here; except for the four Americans, the ledge was empty. He couldn't decide whether the isolation brought relief or increased the desperation they all felt.

"I'll get the note," Anthi called as she headed toward a pine to their right, the narrower end of the ledge, where a single sheet of paper had been jammed on the nub of a broken-off limb. Immediately she brought it back to the others. "It doesn't say much."

Gloria grabbed it from her hands, read it quickly, and looked at Milt with disbelief. "It's no help. What does this mean: 'Event moved. Fateful, come to large enclosure in town'?" She handed it to him for an answer.

A quick glance from Milt, then: "More damned enigma. He must mean 'faithful' and—and the courtyard in Carcassonne. Inside the walled city." He remembered the wet, irritating day he and Christine had spent in the rain there.

"We can't waste time," Anthi said and, without pausing to breathe, started back along their way through the woods to where the van was parked.

Day Six

Opposite Direction

Milt had raced the camper half a dozen kilometers toward the medieval fortress before Gloria grabbed his arm. "This is not right," she pronounced with more confidence than he had heard from her since his first morning on her table.

"What?" He faced her.

"They never mentioned Carcassonne," she said. "Never."

"Where?"

"The other enclosure is in Rennes-le-Chateau. The garden with the tower over the cliff."

"Magdalena Tower?" he asked. His memory produced an image of the stone structure and the large flowering bushes in the garden. "Of course." Without thinking, he edged the van onto the right shoulder, checked the side view mirrors and abruptly crossed to the other shoulder while turning 180 degrees.

"It's a natural stage," Anthi said and leaned forward to lay her hand on the back of her father's seat. "He could use the walkway on the tower wall as his platform."

He knew they must hurry, that Shanti would start on the hour but speed his ceremony up tonight, perhaps dispense with most of the hypnotic breathing since only true believers, his "Fateful," would be involved, and they were fully initiated. It would take the present band of apostate intruders a good twenty minutes to reach Couiza and another ten, even at a risky speed, to negotiate the curves up to the chateau and the tower.

Fortunately the sky was clear, the moon nearly full, and the road not heavily traveled. The air had the earthy aroma of a light recent shower. The faithful heading in their new direction, if it was the correct direction, had obviously preceded them, as though someone had gotten early word of the change to them. This possibility did little to calm Milt's racing heart.

Couiza again turned out to be a dead city, few cars moving, even the scattered stoplights flashing yellow in all directions. But when Milt turned onto the zigzag track up, he discovered that Gloria's van was far more difficult to maneuver than either of the small cars he'd used for previous ascents. He already dreaded having to control its bulkiness when he came back down, no matter what the unimaginable circumstances might be. He only hoped they would have Cathy with them. And her mother too.

At the top, every place in the parking lot they're used on his most recent visit was filled. They had no choice. He double-parked the van behind three small cars, and they piled out, grabbing the flashlights Anthi handed them as they went.

Christine and Anthi led the way to the high metal gate into the garden lying between them and the tower where he expected to find Shanti—if they were in time. From beyond the lush shrubs within, he thought he heard voices, Shanti's instructions among them. The gate was locked—presumably by Shanti's guards once the fated faithful were inside. Milt wasn't surprised.

"Come on!" he called. "I know another way. It's longer, but ..." He motioned for them to follow him to their right, along the metal and brick wall surrounding the garden. And to hurry.

The track worn in the gritty clay by thousands of feet meandered around ill-matched buildings of weathered stone and brick for fifty or sixty yards before they arrived at the knee-high rock wall that separated the path from the small churchyard so familiar to Milt from decades before. Without bothering with a rickety low gate, he stepped up on the wall and dropped into the yard. The others followed at once. He turned on his light and illuminated the granite pillar to his left. "Visigoth, I think." He flashed the beam to his right and lit up part of the old cemetery but said nothing.

As he suspected, the door to the church itself was locked, but he leaned his weight against it and some part of the ancient latch within quickly gave. "Add Church B 'n' E to the charges, officer," he cracked and pushed his way into the dark.

To avoid frightening Gloria or Christine, he let his beam linger only a second on the object immediately past the door, the grotesque figure with huge pointed ears of a bat, goat's horns, gigantic nose, eyes like black marbles stuck within larger white ones, an opened-mouth scowl of torture and hunger, skin a ruddy tan over swollen muscles, and the claw-like fingers of a carnivore. Milt had used the face on the paperback cover of *Deepest France*, but he had forgotten that this Asmodeus bore the church's basin of holy water on his back.

To orient himself in a space he hadn't visited in twenty years, Milt flung his beam in turn across the frieze depicting stages of the cross, then over the pews and checkerboard floor of black and white marble, until it found the serene, porcelainlike figure of Maria Magdalena sheltered in her cave under the altar. "There she is," he said. "The church is named for her."

"Dad's favorite," Anthi kidded.

"Sarah's mother," he reminded Christine, "from the other church."

He redirected his light back to the rear of the church and found a spot in the wainscoting behind Asmodeus. "This way." Images from his earlier exploration here with the father of little Charles were coming back to him with every step he took. He headed toward the wall as though he intended to walk through it. Instead, he pressed on a panel in the wood, and it sprang open to reveal a passage leading, if memory served, to steps. He steered them down the spiraling stairs to a basement tunnel. *Underground into memory again*, he whispered to himself, *her safe earth*. After half a dozen careful paces they reached a second spiral of stairs. These he ascended.

They emerged in a room with dull beige walls and two horizontal glass display cases, each the size of a single bed. Around the walls the flashlights revealed posters (were these new?) tracing the history of the region and Magdalena's intimate relationship with Jesus. Only Gloria lingered over any of the pictures, that of Magdalena holding a deeply tanned baby, Sarah herself, against her breast. Milt crossed to the opposite side and turned the latch on the door his light seemed to create there.

Beams preceding them, they entered a *fin de siecle* sitting room with stuffed chairs in dark shades of red and black and portraits from the same era dangling from the walls. He realized the four of them were now passing through the Villa Bethania and remembered one of the portraits was Berenger Sauniere, the priest who established the compound around the old church. His effort now seemed a sort of religious boondoggle dedicated to Magdalena and her legendary descendants.

"Are we lost?" Gloria wailed behind him.

"Dad knows this like the back of his hand," he heard Anthi comfort. He wished she was right.

Without pausing, he pressed through two other rooms, including the kitchen, on his way to the door of the sunporch. Before opening it, he turned and warned, "Turn off your lights right now!"

"Hurry!" Gloria howled but managed somehow to subdue her voice.

Day Six

The Sacrifice

He opened the door and stepped out into a glassed-in rectangular sunporch with stained glass panels that he recalled as purple and green in the daylight. Out beyond them they could see the garden stretching for fifty or sixty yards and illuminated from the far end by the torch lights around the familiar Tour Magdala. *That's the real name*, he told himself. To its right a stone wall rose head high to carry the walkway and stairs that led to the tower. The breeze playing with the torches threw a ghostly riot of shadows and light over this improvised stage.

Milt inched forward from the villa through the shadows with Gloria, Anthi, and Christine following. They moved from bush to large bush—rose, rhododendron, unfamiliar flowering plants, their scents mingled now with the acrid black odor of the torches. Soon the thick protective shadows would give out and leave them exposed. They would be compelled to act. *What's the damn plan?* he asked himself. He still didn't have an answer.

Center stage, between two of the largest torches, stood Shanti, Shanti with the woman in white—his mother, Christine Plantard, Milt was now certain—immediately to his left. At his sides, Gerhardt and three of the faithful formed his guard. A small ornate table, the length of a child, stood before Shanti. It seemed the exact same altar he'd spotted in the filmed aria that he and Christine had interrupted in the movie house their first evening in Rennes-les-Bains. A memory of Christine Plantard working a kitchen blade in the unlit cave where he'd set the sacrifice of little Charles zipped across his brain like the first flicker of a fluorescent light. *Jeez!* he howled inwardly, *her other son.* The clash of images felt far more momentous than he could decipher at the moment.

A crowd roughly half as large as that in the stable last night stood below the stage, nervously milling about. Tonight only the most devoted, he decided. Improvised wooden steps led up from the ground where the audience waited before the stage like fans at a rock concert, half entranced but edgy and impatient for the featured act. A permanent stone stairs ascended from the earth at the far right of the wall. The faithful, it registered on Milt, had arranged themselves once more in couples. From where he stood he couldn't read their faces but knew they must be overwrought, anxious to perform their part in tonight's drama, whatever it was. He identified the mustache-adorned officer from the gendarmes seen in the Limoux restaurant, this time dressed in a white tunic with high collar similar to those Shanti and his mother wore. He appeared to be alone. No wonder the man wouldn't listen to Gloria. I should have guessed.

For the first time, Milt noticed the large lights to both sides of the stage. There must be cameramen somewhere. Shanti wants this horror filmed.

Yes, below the stage on each side, he spotted a large camera protruding from the audience. What a shameless bastard.

Now the officer was holding up what looked like a cell phone. Was he taking pictures too? Twisted as rotten as his guru.

When Milt spied the Asian family, the young girl still rode on her father's shoulders but slumped now against his skull. In that second he realized that tonight each couple had a child with them, and the horror of the mass sacrifice planned this time exploded through him like the heavy corsets packed with C-4 that kept showing up in news photos from the Middle East. That *insane* Middle East, his terror added. And Deepest France, the same!

Instantly, he motioned Gloria, her eyes wild with dread, to the shade of his rhododendron. As he took her hand in his, he searched the mass of the faithful for Cathy and Ted. For good or bad, he didn't see them. As she came closer, he wrapped his arms around her waist and felt the shivers passing through her.

"If you spot Cathy," he whispered directly through her dark hair into her ear, "you will know what to do, won't you?"

She nodded against the base of his neck. He had no idea what conflict was beating against the walls of her brain, but he trusted her maternal knowledge more than his less well-formed instinct. He prayed to the universe he was right to do so.

Pressed tight for support, they waited as Shanti droned on in words Milt felt too agitated to hear. The only phrases he made out sounded like "our purpose" followed by "pure as diamond." He glanced at Anthi and Christine, but they seemed equally uncertain how to act. They were waiting for a signal from him.

From the shadows to the far right of the wall, a figure appeared and moved toward the lighted steps there. It was a man with long red hair.

Milt instantly recognized Ted. He carried a shape in his arms that Milt could not yet distinguish. If it was Ted, the bundle had to be Cathy.

Gloria must have reached the same conclusion. She pulled from his arm and to his astonishment moved along the edge of shadows toward her family.

She joined them just as Ted placed his foot on the first step. With a gentle lift of her chin, she signaled Ted to give her the child. Ted hesitated only a second before, a puzzled half smile on his face, passing Cathy to her mother.

Milt expected her to take the child and vanish—or return to the relative safety of his company. When she did, he wasn't sure what he could do. He feared he had exhausted all his talent for escape the previous night. He replayed that scene in his head, hoping to spot a clue that would help now. The nearest exit, ten yards or so to his left, he knew was locked. To retreat the way they had come, through the villa and the church, seemed too long and complicated, an impossible route. Each of Shanti's faithful likely carried a concealed blade to be employed in the slaughter to come. They would rip Gloria and him to pieces. Probably Cathy too. Were Anthi and Christine far enough away to escape? He hoped.

Again to his surprise, Gloria did not grab Cathy and run. Instead she fell into place at Ted's side and in lockstep began ascending the stairs to the long concourse that led to Shanti and the altar. As one, the crowd released a low sigh of relieved affirmation. *She's flip-flopped again!* he thought in horror. It was as though phases of this ritual long etched upon her nerves were now controlling her, along with the other faithful, from the inside, sapping her will, eroding her better judgment through the force of practiced behavior. She hadn't told him about her own instructions for this sacrifice. Had she blocked it from her mind? Obviously not.

I can't let her do this! She can't! I gotta stop her! Milt howled inwardly. He inched his way rapidly through the eager devotees toward the head-high wooden steps that led directly toward Shanti's improvised altar. He had to slouch as he went in order not to tower above the dedicated couples, who were lifting groggy children into the light. If he timed himself, he would reach the foot of the steps before Gloria and Cathy arrived in the blazing light there above his head. Anthi and Christine, he hoped, would follow him to aid Gloria any way they could. This close in, the stench of the petrol torches seemed to block his air passages, but he fought to keep it from slowing his advance.

The final ranks of the faithful by the wall pressed so tightly together, in apparent eagerness to be among the first to make their Abrahamic offerings, that they checked his progress to the stage almost completely. As a result, Gloria and Ted stood in front of Shanti before Milt could reach the stairs.

His ears ached as Shanti howled over his head to all the crowd: "Our dear Gloria has returned to us! Let us offer our shout of thanks!" The others obeyed and their roar fell like blows on Milt's body as he watched Gloria carefully place motionless Cathy upon the table. The wrong thing, all his insides shrieked back.

The shock of image and shout ran through him like the most deadly assault upon his flesh, the terrible plunge of a 747, a blow releasing in him a sudden jolt of brutal force. Its power enabled him to tear his way through the remaining knot of believers blinded by Shanti's promised peace.

Milt was on the steep wooden stairs now, scrambling for all he was worth, his heart pounding.

As he crossed from the steps to the wall itself, he stumbled against the altar, glimpsed the sleeping face of the child, and then caught himself before he toppled the table with what Gloria had abandoned there. He swerved around the altar and was standing between it and its presiding spirit just as the latter, a now befuddled but angrily determined Shanti, reached inside his white jacket for the ritual blade that had drawn far too much blood. The suddenness of all these acts had taken the guards by such surprise that they froze in place.

In the second Shanti brought the edge down toward Milt's neck, Milt threw both his wrists up in the most desperate of the martial defenses he had learned. He felt his forearm whack Shanti's, solidly, out of reach of the knife. He heard the metal clatter on the stones in the direction of Cathy and Shanti's mother as he opened his eyes wide and bared his teeth like an animal. Pouring all his weight into the blow, he struck out with rage, his fist landing firmly on Shanti's nose. It seemed to crush under the force before Milt closed on his still standing victim, the first two fingers of his fist spread and hooked like those of a bowman, to gouge the phony guru's eyes. Shanti howled out fury and pain.

From the edge of his own sight, Milt caught Gloria as she did what she knew she had to do. She grabbed her darling from the table and handed her to Anthi just as the latter, pursuing her father, reached the top of the wall. Anthi seized the little one and started along the walkway to the stone steps Gloria had ascended.

As Christine moved to block Ted and the guards from following her stepdaughter and Gloria, Milt turned away from Shanti to join the escape—the impossible getaway once the dumbfounded still half-hypnotized crowd sorted through what was happening and rushed toward the stage from all directions.

Milt's movement was a grave error, and he could not reverse himself swiftly enough as he glanced at Shanti's mother squatting to claim the blade. *Is it possible?* he asked no one. Paralyzed now, he watched Christine Plantard take two quick cat steps and, like her youthful self, whip the edge along the right side of her son's throat, releasing the life coursing there.

"You never were half the Plantard your brother was!" Milt heard her cry in words that flamed, as Shanti crumpled to the stones.

Jeezus, she's had practice! was the only thought that streaked through the foreigner's brain before he realized that the fanatics had blocked the four of them, and Cathy now, from all lines of retreat. *They'll crush us,* he thought—*crush us against the wall like roaches.*

And the mob of the faithful would have crushed them all had not gendarmes, for some reason Milt did not understand, at that moment, with sirens howling, lights flashing, and bullhorns blaring, closed on the crowd. They seemed to Milt to charge from every direction like dry leaves in a windstorm. A storm of deliverance he could never have expected.

How will they know what's been happening? he asked in his new terror. *How will they sort good guys from the bad?*

Day Seven

Found

He had inspected the amenities of his Limoux cell before he lay down the night before. By then he was completely worn down from his initial effort to get his story across, through a lousy translator, to the two officers who interrogated him, one of them the same silent policeman with black mustache whose table he'd visited in the local health food restaurant and had glimpsed in two of Shanti's crowds.

They kept going over his account, apparently looking for contradictions they could use to trip him up. They appeared amazed at what he recounted, but it could not have been totally new to them if the silent cop was in fact the man he'd seen with the crowd last evening and in the stable the night he "kidnapped" Mustafia. This was especially true if the gendarmes had been spying on Shanti's people for some time. He couldn't be certain, however, of their sustained surveillance since the silent fellow might now want to imply as much only to cover his own rear as one of the Shanti faithful. During the intolerable questioning it became obvious to Milt that gendarmes had tailed his band and likely followed them to Magdalena garden. How they'd done this so skillfully he couldn't figure out since at no point had he felt their presence, not even when he made his abrupt U-turn on the road to Carcassonne.

As in all his earlier dealings with the French police, he remained absolutely convinced they didn't believe a word he said. Oddly, the inquisitors had shown little interest in the acts of violence he had committed—the kidnapping, the two disruptions of Shanti's ritual, and the brutality of his assault against the guru. Rather, while the mustachioed officer maintained his irritating silence in one corner of the room, itself little more than a broom closet with a small table, three chairs, and a huge one-way window, his assistant, as though operating from an altogether different play book, grilled Milt passionately about what he knew and when.

"So, M'sieur Milton, when did you first suspect this so-called Shantee, Shantee was in fact the unborn brother of petit Charles?"

"Unborn?" Milt thought this a curious way to characterize Shanti.

"Oui—yez. At the temps Charrl was living still, of course."

"I don't recall, sir."

"Thennk, M'sieur," the younger man ordered.

"It must have been—it must have been when I talked with the manager of my hotel."

"And when was that, M'sieur."

"I don't know. Maybe the third or fourth morning we were in Rennes-les-Bains."

"And when did you arrive—exactement?"

Milt rehearsed the relevant details of his return to the Rennes region.

"So that wood 'ave been three or four jour ago? If my math is correct."

"It is very good, M'sieur."

Apparently the assistant was a sucker for flattery, even the false kind, for he seemed to beam, so much so that Milt could hear his superior in the corner grit his teeth and groan.

Nervous, the assistant rushed on to his next area of concern. "When, then, did you first know that the woman in white who was always at Shantee, Shantee's meetings was in fact his mother, Christine Plantard?"

This question pleased Milt because he knew the answer. "Exactement, M'sieur, it was when I saw a photo of her stuck in a book I once wrote about petit Charles and her. I recognized her then, but aged twenty years from when I knew about her before."

Perhaps Milt had smiled ever so faintly because the assistant now rose and attempted to intimidate him by towering above him. He, however, was not a very tall man. "When and where did you see that photograph?" the assistant barked.

"It was when——" Milt began, then stopped. Why reveal their descent into the tunnels under the church if he didn't have to? There was probably another law they had broken: the violation of sacred church property or something like that. "It was in a copy of a book I bought in a local bookstore."

Although the assistant gave no sign he didn't accept his answer or that he knew otherwise, the gendarme's nonresponsiveness had only underscored Milt's sense of being doubted. And this conviction seemed confirmed at 9:00 a.m. when a cop of a lower rank, a tall blond youth with black glasses, came to unlock his cell. He commanded the foreigner to follow him along the corridor to what Milt expected would turn into another rough inquisition. He hoped his friends had said nothing to contradict the story he was trying to tell.

The one thing he would not reveal to the police, he decided, had to be the incredible dream his brain had cooked up during his bone-weary night. In it he was standing in a mighty desert in Egypt, apparently up the Nile near Aswan. Here grave robbers had stumbled upon an extraordinary underground treasure, monuments covered by, or carved to resemble, the roots of a jungle tree, probably an ancient banyan. The roots brought to his mind the walls and towers at Angkor Wat. Except that rather than the towers, here the snaky tendrils concealed carved arches, walls, and blocks of stone. One as huge as a tank appeared to sit within an arch covered with graceful figures from Greek mythology, Theseus with Ariadne and the Minotaur, Perseus and Medusa, and other scenes of slaughter. At the back of this deep arch he saw a tank-like wall of brown stone or clay chiseled with dark, raised-relief moments from Egyptian history and legend, scenes he didn't recognize. One of the Egyptian faces, he now sensed, resembled the dark Madonna who'd stunned him in the Limoux church. Beside her stood a smaller god with a falcon head.

Uncanny, he now thought as he followed the guard, the way dreams worked. What he'd felt in the dream itself was that this desert discovery would become cultural dynamite, destined to ignite a new century renaissance. For that reason he would not tell his inquisitors about it no matter what damage they did to him.

Rather than into the interrogation chamber, his keeper steered him past the hall that led to the room he dreaded. The guard ordered him instead out into a well-lit, tobacco-smelling area. Here a high bar-like desk divided a large public section from another space where bureau officials worked. He recognized that it was into this space he had stared through glass the night he left sleepy Mustafia at their door sill.

Now, in a place occupied on his previous visit by querulous police, his three friends—Anthi, Gloria, Christine—stood in early morning light with Cathy held tightly against Gloria's breasts. He was still focused on them when the guard conducted him to the raised desk, where he handed him a manila envelope containing his belt, watch, and wallet.

Milt thought he heard the young man command him, "En avant! Allez." But before he could comprehend exactly what the words meant, whether to stay or go, the officer with the moustache who had questioned him came from a door to his right and called, "Attendez-vous, Monsieur Walters."

Milt did not move, and the once silent policeman confronted him at the desk while Milt's friends looked on as puzzled as he felt.

"I want to thank you, Monsieur," the officer said in passable English while forcing his stern mustache into a smile.

When Milt mumbled only an astonished "What—" the officer said, "You—your buk has helped us to compreehend much the mind de Madame Plantard."

"You have a damn curious way of showing appreciation," Milt barked before the risk he was taking reached his brain.

"Pleese forgive our inquiry. It was essential—and offeeshal." The officer's embarrassment showed through the gentle smile his face wore. "You lead us to her in her new deguise. She then revert to her true form. We have her now."

"You didn't know she'd come back, passing as a Cathar pilgrim?"

"Not at all. She seem a true dayvotay."

"Maybe she was trying," Milt replied, "but lost control of her son."

"C'est possible," the officer conceded. "But too late now."

"I guess it is." Eager to go, he reached out for the gendarme's hand. Obviously he had been wrong about the man. "If you are really turning me loose now, I need to join my family." As he said this, he wondered if it was only in his mind that Gloria and Cathy had become part of his family. The thought felt curiously invigorating.

"Enjoy France, M'sieur," the officer said and gave the extended hand an earnest shake.

"I always do," Milt said with an ironic grin. "No matter what—"

He turned and hurriedly crossed the room to where Christine, Anthi, Gloria, and Cathy stood in a loose line, waiting to give him welcoming hugs, Christine in front, Gloria and the child at the end.

"Have you eaten?" Christine asked as he swept her to his chest, instantly relieved to be back with his loved company.

The answer was negative, and after time served in the odors of the Limoux cell he had little appetite. Still, within an hour of his release he found himself seated again with his four companions at a metal table on the public square of Rennes-les-Bains.

Anthi had taken charge and for starters had ordered crepes for everyone, excepting only a carefree Cathy, who had enjoyed her brunch on the rear bench while Milt was driving the camper back. When they'd exited the police bureau, the sudden river fog between the stone buildings had been almost as thick as rain, but now the morning sun had burned it away, and light penetrating the canopy of ancient trees brought a calming green tint down on them.

Unlike previous visits to the square, their green metal table belonged this time to the Pizza Restaurant, whose specialty, Anthi explained, was actually crepes, crepes for breakfast, dinner, and dessert. The one the drowsy server plopped on the table before Milt was made of dark flour and bore melted cheese, sliced rounds of tomatoes, crisp dark bacon, and a sunny egg whose yolk had never kissed the skillet. It all smelled as wonderful as a breakfast he and Christine might have cooked together.

Before dipping his fork into the yellow orb, Milt took this rare moment free of the pursuit to enjoy the company around him. His wife, his daughter, Gloria, and the little girl constituted a carefree group now, an amiable handful, he thought. While he paced in his cell, the others had had time to shower and change from their sweat-stained clothing. Now Christine had on her usual knee-length shorts, Anthi the bright flowered halter with the bow behind her neck that she'd worn her first morning, Gloria a lavender sweater-blouse, sleeveless, but scooped just enough at the neck to show off her maternal bounty, Cathy a legless and sleeveless one-piece of blue and white striped seersucker. That their clothes were so familiar endeared them even more to him. These were outward signs that their ordeal lay sealed behind them now, and they had returned to safe routines. He himself was stuck with the open-collared plaid shirt and khaki shorts he'd had on all the previous day, plus battered tennis shoes. To be able to sink back in his chair and savor a second of his quotidian life this way was, he realized, an incomparable gift.

During their drive from Limoux, his gang had brought him up to date on much he'd missed during his night in custody. Appreciating her father's need for stories and his desire to wrap them up when possible, Anthi did most of the talking. She'd occupied the passenger's seat while Christine took turns holding grinning Cathy whenever Gloria needed a break from the anxious tugs at her breast.

"You were worried, I hope, when the cops took me off?" he'd wondered aloud.

"At first, Dad." She looked at him with a teasing grin. "But the officer from Limoux assured us he was just following routine. After all, you had almost gouged a man's eyes out. In front of dozens of witnesses, all of them devoted to your victim."

"That looked bad, did it?" Milt remarked with an odd mix of pride and remorse.

"Where'd you learn a move like that?"

"Later." Brushing the question aside, he moved on to what was important: "How'd you manage to spring me so early? French law doesn't move that quickly."

"Gloria was burning to tell them what you were up to—that you were saving her baby's life. The French, even cops, can go batty over *les enfants*, as you know."

"If I wrote it, it must be true," he said deadpan and paused to wonder whether he believed his own fiction.

"What happened to Madame Plantard?" he finally asked.

"The infamous infanticide?" She looked at him quizzically. "Oh, they've got her cold this time."

Milt had studied the road ahead carefully and said, "She'll find a way. After all, she's still the 'Mother of France' for many. She'll play on their hearts."

"You think?"

"Besides, the man whose throat she'd just sliced was an alleged child murderer."

"Alleged?" His daughter looked shocked. "This from Mr. Fill-in-the-Gaps? Mr. We-Can't-Know-All-We-Need-to-Know-So-We-Must-Imagine?"

"Hypothesis is one thing, young lady. Evidence of murder another. *Deepest France* was our hypothesis."

"But the gendarmes told us you got it right—you helped them."

"I got close to my characters, kept my guesses near to their bones. Besides, they'll buy any story that hangs together and helps them close a case."

Anthi took a few moments to reflect on what Milt would have called his "obviosities," and then said, "One thing you got wrong."

"Only one?" He laughed.

"She didn't kill him."

"Shanti, Shanti?"

"Little Claud, Jean, Julien—whatever his name is."

"She sliced his jugular. I saw it, up close," he insisted, not wanting this menace to be alive any longer.

"The medics stopped the bleeding in time. They arrived with the cops. They had plasma or something with them. He wasn't brain dead."

"So they sewed him back together?" This thought would take a while for him to accept.

Sitting now on the square, he still couldn't grasp all its implications—what it meant for Anthi's future, his own, years to come for Shanti's desperate generation. At least Gloria and Cathy were out of it—he hoped.

Their server, a tall blonde woman with exquisite slow grace and a wonderful smile, arrived with a bottle of red wine that she handed to him for approval before she opened. It was from a Corbieres estate—he knew it would be dark, earthy, good. As strong as granite. He nodded satisfaction.

As before, there was music in the square. But it was not the pop trance rhythms of their first night in town when the little ones went whirling about blindly. This time he heard the bright crisp vocal of a woman chanting in clear tones, "We lay our hearts wide open," before continuing with something about living "mysterious days."

"There's a title in that song," he whispered to his daughter.

"You think so?" she asked, a delighted grin dancing across her lips as she considered his idea.

"You write the story this time, young woman."

Anthi nodded above her glass and took her first sip, then said, "With help, of course."

The server, who had lingered to be certain the wine pleased them all, turned to address Anthi and everyone at the table in a mix of tongues. "*Votre canard au poivre* will appear very soon. *Bon appetit, M'sieur, Mesdames.*"

"Duck with pepper sauce! You choose well, mon enfant," he said to his daughter and shared his widest grin. He could already savor the aroma of the deep red meat and the sting of the various peppers.

"Still your favorite, it appears."

"Absolutely."

While Cathy chirped away and all the adults stuck their noses into the glasses to test the fighting aromas of the mountain berries and earth, he turned to Gloria with his most difficult question, one he had postponed. "What about Ted, dear woman?"

She dropped her head and disappeared deep in an emotion he could not imagine. Then she looked up bravely and said, "They have him in jail. And Gerhardt."

"Are you okay?" He leaned across the table to take her fingers from where they wrapped around the wine glass. From both sides, Christine and Anthi laid caring hands on her arms.

"He was never much good for me. He gave me Cathy; that's about it." She pulled her hand away to hug the child tight in her arms.

"What will you do?" He was tilting forward still.

Gloria looked at Anthi with the glow of gratitude in her face. "Anthi has asked me to drive her back to Paris."

"She will stay with me," Anthi explained, "until she finds work in a studio up there. I hear from reliable sources that she is very good."

"Your daughter promises to help with Cathy for now," Gloria said, still beaming.

"Glad to—" Anthi said.

Milt raised his glass to his lips and muttered an enthusiastic "All good!" as the rich red passed into his mouth. When Gloria, Anthi, and little Cathy started for Paris, Christine and he would, he supposed, follow the Salz to the Aude and the Aude to its conclusion, wherever that might be. After they reached the sea, he wasn't sure where they would go. Perhaps back to Virginia. Maybe on to the city.

Relaxed here with his family around him, he felt partial to stories like this that did not end but spread as his rivers did, forward and backward through time. As long as new stories kept flowing, any sea would seem a tolerable destination.

##